JIGSAW

An Unsentimental Education

A BIOGRAPHICAL NOVEL BY
SYBILLE BEDFORD

ELAND
London

First published by Hamish Hamilton in 1989

First published by Eland Publishing Limited in 2005
This edition published in 2012

Copyright © Sybille Bedford 1989
Afterword copyright © Sybille Bedford 1999

ISBN 978 0 907871 79 8

Cover designed by Robert Dalrymple
Cover image by Luciana Arrighi

Printed in Spain by GraphyCems, Navarra

The way things looked before
later events made them look different.
And this is as much a part of history
as the way things actually were.

Robert Kee

In the end most things in life
– perhaps all things – turn out
to be appropriate

Anthony Powell

Author's Note

The Kislings and the Aldous Huxleys are the Kislings and the Aldous Huxleys and themselves . . .

The Falkenheims, the Nairns, the Desmirails are not Falkenheims, Nairns or Desmirails, and to a large extent themselves . . .

My mother and I are a percentage of ourselves . . .

These, and everyone and everything else, are what they seemed – at various times – to me.

Contents

PART ONE

Antecedent: Germany

A FIRST coherent memory is being wheeled through leafy streets in a pram that felt too small for me (I was well able to walk). I knew it was Copenhagen. I must have been over two years old. Presently I was in some kind of a narrow space and my mother wearing an enormous hat and veil was bending over me for it was she who, quite exceptionally, had wheeled the pram. She spoke to me in the tone of voice in which vows are made. *Please* be good, please keep *quiet*, he hates to have a baby in the hall. *Please just go to sleep*. I did. For the whole blessed afternoon. Elucidation came later, years later, but the actual sequence – the streets, the pram, the narrow space, the urgency in my mother's voice: an appeal to reason and accompliceship, my instant fall into oblivion – is a first-hand memory. The narrow space was the hall of a man's flat. He was a Danish novelist, a bachelor nearer fifty than forty, fastidious, fêted. We – my mother, nanny, I – were staying at an hotel. It was nanny's afternoon off. My mother did not know what to do with me. 'You couldn't be left alone, you were very active. I couldn't trust the chambermaid, she might have told nanny. Nanny wasn't supposed to *know*. *Nobody* was to know. So I popped you into that pram and took you to Peter's. Yes, I took a chance. But you were *angelic*.'

The next flash (days later? a week?) is sand, broad white sand. A beach – it has remained the archetype – we were at Skaagen. Where I wanted to get to was into the water. But between the sand and the water there lay a thick band of small fish, dead wet glistening fish. The whole of me shrivelled with disgust. Nanny, who wore boots and stockings,

9

picked me up and lifted me over the fish. I was in the water – coolness, lightness, dissolving, bliss: this is the sea, I am the sea, here is where I belong. For ever. And then the not-I state fades as dread comes stabbing back: the dead fish, there's the dead fish to cross again, sometime . . . soon . . . almost now.

A third flash. Still Denmark. I am sitting on a high chair at a large table, children around me. The infants' table d'hôte at the hotel. There is a lot of window and it is very light. In front of each plate, in front of my plate, there stands a small china bowl. In it there is cream and in the cream – delight – there floats a whole round yolk of egg, uncooked egg. This egg in cream is to be put into our food. Nannies sit behind us in a circle ready to interfere. I am entirely determined to handle my own egg, to choose whether to stir it into my soup, my spinach or my mashed potatoes and I win.

This is the total of my recollection of Scandinavia, yet what memory selected to retain is indicative perhaps of three future trends: a passion for swimming in the sea (and a controlled aversion to touch live fish), great love of cookery and a tendency to side with lovers.

*   *   *

My father is straining at his watch-chain. He is walking up and down beside the waiting carriage. I am in the back seat with two of the dogs, ready and kicking. (I want to sit on the box with the coachman but *he* won't let me. He is my father. He says it isn't safe.) We are to drive to Freiburg – or Basle – for the day. My mother has not appeared yet. She is late. This is supposed to be terribly bad for the horses. People are being sent in and out of the house. My father is not angry, he is anxious; we are all anxious. This goes on. One dog jumps down, the other follows; they are lifted back. I pray for it to be over. *My mother.* My father pulls his watch again; she doesn't answer him. She is not anxious. This makes it worse. My father now notices that she doesn't carry an umbrella. She looks at the sky. He says, *One always needs an umbrella.* Someone goes into the house for one. He says we won't be able to do what we planned to do – the journey is ruined, the day is ruined. His voice is very unhappy. But convinced. I pray again. Then it is discovered that I have no gloves (I left them behind on purpose). That child . . . they say. More minutes. My father acts out despair. When we *are* off, the relief is great. Of the ensuing journey: the day at Freiburg, or Basle, I have no recollection.

The locality of that scene was a southern corner of Germany, what was then, in 1914, the Grand-Duchy of Baden. The house was walking minutes from the French border, a longish carriage ride from the Swiss. When the war began that summer (I was three) my father, who was too old for war and against it, said that we must all take refuge with his parents-in-law in Berlin. My mother poohpoohed his fears and we stayed put till next spring. She, too, was against war, and talked about it. My father did not. They were matter-of-course internationalists, both of them – they had that much in common. He had been brought up to regard Prussia as a barbarous menace and united Germany a new nonsense. He never changed his ideas. Besides he loved France, where he had spent a large part of his life, and whenever he had the faintest chance of being understood, he spoke French. His was the catastrophic view of events – the war was a dangerous folly bringing ruin to all concerned and best not to be thought about. To my mother it was a matter of people – men and women, she said – what they were capable of doing, doing to one another. She used words like maiming and killing. Most of our servants came from the village and talk about our attitudes seeped out. We went on speaking French and English. One day a stone was flung over the park wall when nanny and my half-sister and I were playing. It hit me on the forehead, just a gash but there was a lot of blood and I howled. I still have the scar, a small one, under an eyebrow. It was nothing, yet the memory worked on. In a novel I wrote decades later, there is a German episode which I called the Felden scandal where a stone is thrown at the child narrator by the mob.

In 1915 our house was shut for the duration and we travelled across the length of Germany to Berlin. It is my first memory of a train journey. I had been told that I might see 'the wounded'. Long grey iron trains, the compartments jammed with people all the way, long

long waits in grey steel-vaulted stations, soldiers on the platforms, in the corridors, looking in through windows, soldiers being helped into the compartment – soldiers on crutches, soldiers with head bandages, soldiers with great casts about their chests – it was impossible not to see them; that memory too has not ceased working on.

My father's parents-in-law who took us in were not my mother's parents but those of his first wife who had died young. It had not occurred to them not to go on treating him as their son-in-law. They were rich, capable of affection, and preposterously limited in their outlook. My father, who was rather nearer to them in age than he was to his second wife, my mother, had been and still was extremely good-looking, *le beau Max* they had called him in his day in the Parisian half-world, and one of his laments was the loss of youth. He could not stand clever women. (My mother had been too beautiful for him to notice that she was one and when he did notice it was too late.) The Berlin in-laws were the heads of a Jewish family, Edwardian Jewish, called Merz in that novel. There I described their characters and customs and those of their relatives and hangers-on. (True to life? I think so, give and take a novelist's margins.) I described their house in Voss Strasse, its back gave on to the Imperial Chancellery in Wilhelm-strasse and the whole block was destroyed in the Second World War. It was a large, dark house, over-upholstered and over-heated; the inhabitants never stopped eating. Some were exceedingly kind, some were critical of our presence. I was a guest on an upper floor leading my own life: I could read by then. I was the only child in the house (my half-sister, their real grandchild, was halfway grown-up). Dinners were family dinners and their number happened to be fourteen: when-ever someone fell out I was summoned to eat downstairs to prevent their being thirteen at table. I was caressed, made the target of sarcastic remarks by uncles and cousins; for the rest they saw to my plate and forgot that I might be alive. I was put either next to Grandmama Merz or at the end of the table; everyone spoke freely in his or her own way and so I imbibed quite a deal of German-Jewish family life, if of a particular kind. (Rather like a child in an I. Compton-Burnett novel, a well-treated child though, and goodness the *milieu* was different! Ivy herself once said to me when I had asked for a ginger nut instead of a ginger biscuit, 'I take it that you were not *entirely* brought up in England?' She said it in her astringent tone, she often made me feel my outlandish place, *she* had no use for 'abroad', indeed it is a thought that in this respect she was quite as insular as Grandmama Merz.)

Christmas. Celebrated on the 24th, on Christmas Eve, at night. In the white and gold ballroom, the one room in Voss Strasse that was not darkest mahogany. For the rest of the year it was shut up, had been so since the two daughters died, decades ago of TB, my father's first wife and her sister, young women in their twenties, one following the other. Now the chandelier is unshrouded, there is a tree, up to the ceiling, ablaze with *electric* candles. (This, both my father and mother said, was vulgar.) Along the walls are long trestle tables with damask cloths to the floor, and on table after table there are presents, not wrapped but displayed like things in shop-windows. Every member of the household has his own length of table and in the middle of each place there is a plate heaped with home-made cakes, marzipan animals, bright apples, gilt nuts. The servants – the butler who rules us all, cook, the maids, Marie and Ida, who have grown old in the house – and some of the cousins also receive money; and the money too is not wrapped, but stands among the stockings and the cigars in small stacks of gold that outshine the walnuts. When I see Christmas Eve, it is always that first minute when we stand and admire in silence. (I don't remember any singing, no one in Voss Strasse was able to carry a tune.) Only my father was not given the plate of sweetmeats, he had a small basket in which nested some coal, only the coal was truffles. I still have their scent in my nostrils.

I met no children, except for one thin, stiff boy who was already a cadet, the son of an army widow who came to read the newspaper to Grandpapa Merz after his nap. This boy – I only remember his surname, von Moser – was brought to tea during his holidays; how he endured these visits, to a girl, at least five years his junior, I do not know. I had a rocking-horse and a toy railway and a toy stable (Merz presents) and we played politely enough. He died in 1918, we heard, of under-nourishment and the Spanish flu.

There was also a charming young man – not in uniform – who used to come to see me upstairs. For a time he was my half-sister's fiancé, the one my mother approved of. (He vanished.) To me he talked. One day his eye fell on a piece of gruyère cheese I had saved from my tray and which was melting in a little pan over the radiator. What's that revolting mess, he said or words to that effect. It's an experiment, I say. 'What for?' 'Eat it.' 'You *are* a pig.' 'Don't care.' 'If you grow up like this nobody will want to marry you.' 'In that case,' I say, 'I shall marry a pig.'

Of what went on outside our hothouse, I had no idea; of Berlin I knew and saw little. Except for one treat I cherished. Sightseeing I called it. It was not being taken for walks in the Tiergarten, the rather dismal public park, or so it seemed to me, remembered only as being cold and dank. The paths were straight with rails round the grass; there was no question of my picking up someone to play with. I think that was a Merz veto upheld by my father – since their daughters' death they were afraid of infection (when they travelled, which was rare, they took their own bed-linen into the wagons-lits).

Occasionally however I managed to get myself taken to that great avenue nearby, the Sieges Allee, built by Kaiser Bill, with its giant marble-works of Prussian history like an over life-size Madame Tussaud's. I've been told since that the sculptures of Victory Avenue, Dolls' Avenue, the Berliners dubbed it, were a pile of monstrous pomposities, the apex of the Wilhelminian era's taste. (It too was destroyed in the Second World War.) I loved it. I would stand before each Margrave of Brandenburg or King of Prussia upon his pedestal and study his countenance and dates and that of his spouse and counsellors – the monarchs were modelled, in white marble, from toe to crest; the courtiers were mere busts. Here then was history in the round, history visible, as well as in nice order, for the statues began at one end of the avenue with remotest Brandenburg and culminated with Kaiser Wilhelm I. Sometimes I was intrigued by an appearance, sometimes by a name; my favourites were an epicene youth leaning upon his shield, Heinrich the Child, and a mysterious personage covered in chain-mail, Waldemar the Bear.

*

Autumn 1918. The war is as good as over. My mother is taking us back to Baden. My father says it is no time to travel. Another train journey. After a time the train goes no further. '*They*'ve taken off the loco- motive.' We are at an hotel, it is evening, there are no rooms to be had, we are in a lounge full of people on an upper floor looking over the square where shouting sailors and soldiers are marching with banners. The shutters are pulled down, we are moved away from windows, some of us crouch on the floor. There is a great noise below and some shooting. Some say it's machine guns, I hear words like Mutiny, Revolution. My mother says it was inevitable and probably deserved, and as for ourselves one ought to be fatalistic. After that nothing more: I may have fallen asleep. An hotel lounge overlooking a square, gun fire and the sound of crowds – later I was told that I had seen the beginning of the German November Revolution.

*   *   *

My father is straining at his watch-chain. It isn't because it is bad for the horses, we have no horses any more, we are poor now. It is still a full-sized carriage, high but light, the shafts have been altered and it is pulled now by two donkeys, one grey, one black, Fanny and Flora. They look small; my father, like the carriage, is too tall for them, still beautifully dressed in his greatcoat, gloved and hatted, long whip in hand. Flora had belonged to a market gardener but Fanny, who had come from a circus and been with us for years, does not take to the new demands; all in all they'd both as soon wait as work. Nor is it my mother who makes us late, she has left us some time ago. So has nanny. It must be 1919. We are back in Baden, at our place, in the village of Feldkirch. An old name – meaning a church in a field. The church, rustic Romanesque, is still there, our house is a *Schloss*, a small château, inside there are flights of rooms filled with my father's collection of furniture and objets d'art, the ceilings are high and to me all seems vast. Before the war, in my mother's time, there was a good deal of life: my sister was with us, and her French governess and there was my mother's maid and a cook and the maids from the village, the butler, also French, the coachman and the stable boy, the gardener and a raffish Italian who ran the electric plant. Now we are only three. My father, Lina, a slight, sinewy elderly woman from the village, and myself. Lina is kind and patient and she does everything. She loves my father, strange as this seems to me; I don't mean in love, I mean sheer, good-hearted devotion. She cleans, she cooks, she airs (we do a lot of airing because of the collection), she does the washing, chops the firewood and carries it upstairs, lights the stoves and the range, looks after the fowls and what is left of our kitchen-garden (the nettles have got the rest) and, helped by me, mucks out the donkeys' stable. We are only three humans but we still have animals: two dogs, a cat, some sheep, always a pig, chickens and geese and a vile-tempered turkey-cock. Only the pre-war cow, the ornamental ducks and the peacock have gone the way of the horses. With the animals my father, who has ceased to ask man or woman into the house, is on trusting terms. The sheep come when he calls them – wild birds come too – the pig rubs his snout against his immaculate trousers, the geese do not hiss and the turkey-cock does not attack him. As for the donkeys, only he could have turned Fanny and Flora into a carriage pair. He loves them, they love him. He also loved me, I know now, but – this is the unhappy part – he could not show his affection, only his anxieties, his fretting, his prohibitions – Don't ride, don't climb, don't run fast: *You will fall*. And I with some curious callousness, with the arrogance of a lively, ignorant, if intelligent child, felt impatience with him and contempt. He also created fear; perhaps because he was not reachable by any give and take of talk, perhaps because of the aura of solitariness about him. Today we might call it alienation. My father in those last years of his life must have been a deeply unhappy man.

When I wrote that novel – *A Legacy* – some thirty years after, I tried to unravel something about his character and his story. To say that Jules, the Julius von Felden of the novel, was my father would be as misleading as to say that he was not. Jules is like my father and unlike; to what degree of either I do not know. My intention was to draw a character in fiction; I used facts and memories when they served and discarded them when they did not. For instance, I never actually knew my father's own father and mother – my grandparents – they having died a long way back in time, and I knew nothing interpretable about them as my father's talk was about events and objects seen from outside, not about people, not about what made them tick. So I invented Jules' father in the novel, the old Baron, out of whole cloth (he who got stuck in the eighteenth century as his son did in the nineteenth); the only fact I know about the actual old Baron, my grandfather, is that he was a High Court judge, which makes me inclined to think that *he* at least could tell a hawk from a handsaw.

Jules in the novel is a man by no means originally devoid of feeling, whose contact with reality is snapped by events at one or two points in his life. He protects himself by limiting his grasp. A man who has lost his nerve. A man also seen in the context of a particular time and the changes in that time. Now my father, too, was a man who had lost his nerve; I can only guess as to when or how. (*He* used to harp on his three concussions – as a young man he used to ride in steeplechases.) Like Jules he was born in the eighteen-fifties; for the purposes of the novel, which I wanted to bring to an end at the verge of the 1914 War, I had to make chronological changes – both Jules and Grandpapa Merz die some five years before they actually died and therefore Francesca, the narrator, had to be born five or six years earlier than I. In the novel Jules' first turning point comes when at the age of twenty he fails to prevent his younger brother's being sent back to one of the notorious cadet schools. The brother *is* sent back and consequently becomes insane. Half a century later he is accidentally shot by an army officer, a public scandal ensues which among other things destroys Jules' self-built world. Was there a victim brother? Was there a Felden scandal? No, and yes. When I wrote that story I thought that I had done with it for ever. Are the facts I am now trying to recall much more reliable than the fiction? My sources are the same – *hearsay*: elders overheard, Voss Strasse gossip, stories my father told me when we were living alone together after the war at Feldkirch, he in his sixties, I a child of eight . . . of nine . . .

He had been brought up in a house like Feldkirch, like Feldkirch before we were alone. There had been brothers, country pursuits, they had been happy. One boy was sent to a cadet school, could not bear it and made a dramatic escape, walking by night, hiding by day, making immense detours to escape re-capture. He reached home half-starved, half-crazed. They fed him up, then sent him back. He tried to kill himself by swallowing a boxful of matches. They sent him back all the same. He did not go mad, he was not put away. In fact he became a cavalry officer, commander of his regiment and in due course he married. How far was he maimed? Too late to say. Eccentric he must have been. Animals were his interest and he had a great way with them. Wild animals. He kept wolves and used to give them jewelled collars for Christmas, or so my father told me without turning a hair. Sapphires (were they really?) for the wolves, *not* for the wife; my father's tone indicated that this was a mistake. The wife was a beautiful young woman with a great appeal to men. My father's brother was stationed in a small garrison town called Allenstein at the confines of East Prussia, and she is supposed to have slept with half the regiment, commissioned and non-commissioned. One Christmas night (1908 or '09) a captain came to dinner; afterwards he pretended to leave and instead hid in the drive. When the house was in darkness he crept back. He had put thick socks over his shoes and he had a revolver in his pocket. My father's brother called out, Who's there? and turned on a light. *He* stood in that light and the captain shot at him and killed him. In prison he wrote a confession saying that he had been madly in love with the colonel's wife, Antonia was her name, and that she had made him do it. She had given him the woollen socks, her husband's socks, and a key. The captain hanged himself in his cell before the trial. Antonia was arrested and tried for murder; she was sentenced to death. A psychiatric expert managed to get her certified and she was not executed – which according to German law would have been by the axe – but confined instead in a mental institution. From that she was released, by the psychiatrist's efforts, within weeks. They went to Italy and got married. The Allenstein murder was a national sensation – the goings-on in one of the Kaiser's regiments, the murder of the colonel by a brother officer and his own wife, Christmas night, the socks, the wolves, the suicide in prison, the beauty of the woman and her getting off scot-free. Some people got extremely angry. Behind the audible sabre-rattling there was a good deal of feeling against the top-heavy military establishment and what it cost; the Allenstein affair provided grist to many mills and was turned into a political scandal by factions of the press, the parliamentary opposition and the public. Maximilian Harden, a hard-hitting radical journalist of the day, wrote a searing leader under the heading of our family name; we – what we were supposed to be and stand for – became a target. (My father was just bewildered and appalled.) The scandal was remarkable for the variety of ill-natured emotions it aroused; it even excited more anti-semitism, my father's first marriage to a deceased Jewish heiress was dragged in and the poor Merzes with it. At the time of the murder my mother was engaged to my father but beginning to have second thoughts. In outline their engagement came about much like that of Jules and Caroline Trafford – he, being susceptible to beauty and vitality, fell in love with her and was single-minded in pursuit; she, caught up in this pursuit, became affectionately amused by him and his archaisms, was tempted by the offered leap into entire change; through this, she believed, she might survive the heartbreak and stalemate of a previous attachment that had come to an end. (The man was long married and too honourable to abandon a wife older than himself, my mother concurring in that decision.) She was about to doubt the wisdom of her engagement when my father's brother was shot and she found it no longer permissible to back out. They were married in 1910. Some people found it amusing to ask when being introduced to her, 'The murderess?' whose name of course she bore now. Eventually she took my father away and they lived in Spain for a time. My impending birth put an end to that. They went back and bought Feldkirch. I owe my existence to the Allenstein affair.

*   *   *

I am trying to climb over a wall. It is the wall that encloses the garden and park land. It is high but there are a few footholds. I fail the first time, the second. I am seen, it's the village postman. What am I up to? Oh exercising, training my muscles . . . Glib lies: it was training all right, training to get over that wall, over that wall and out.

In the long run, the not so long run, my mother had been right – it could not last, it did not last; so now my father and I were living alone at Feldkirch, he was divorcing her. This I was not supposed to know. We did not speak of her. During the early weeks of the new life I was beset by a heavy feeling that seemed to come from inside myself and I could do nothing about. It was there every morning. If a small child can suffer depression, it may well have been this. I could not eat much at table and as this upset my father it did not help the unease between us. I would run round the park three times before meals but found that it made no difference. Now let no one think that I was missing my mother. I was interested – and influenced – by my mother's general opinions, but dreaded being alone with her. She could be ironical and often impatient; she did not suffer little fools gladly. That I was her own made not a scrap of difference. When I was slow she called me slow, when I was quick she called me a parrot. Compassionate in her principles, she was high-handed even harsh in her daily dealings. Between her and my father there had come much open ill feeling – scenes, verbally violent, and these had shaken me. So in my early years (our rapport came later) I was afraid of my mother, more afraid of her, and in a different way, than I was of my father. He too had taken against her, now that she was gone; it came out not in what he said – he said little – but in what he did not say. He, who had once done everything to get her for himself: this puzzled me, how could people change so? Feelings I thought were for ever.

The one person I loved outright then was my half-sister, my sister. They shook their heads over her because she was fond of dancing and flirting and clothes, and got into debt as a girl (in spite of a large Merz allowance); suddenly she had dropped all her young men and insisted, still under age and all, on marrying a man in his late forties. She was warm, generous, pleasure-loving; oddly enough she had taken to me like a mother when I was born (she must have been all of twelve); *she* made no scenes, though she would see that I behaved – with her I felt no constraint.

When the sadness had gone on for some time, a plan came and I felt the better for it at once. I would escape. (Like my father's poor brother.) I would run away to my sister. She was living in Wiesbaden then, a spa where her new husband was deputy mayor. Money I had, having hung on to a large tip one of my mother's admirers had given me in Voss Strasse days; I did not know how far it would go, I had been told that it might stretch to a bicycle. The main problem (*I* foresaw) was to get out of our place. The gates were locked, the downstairs windows were barred, all was heavily locked up at night, front door and side doors and windows and back door, no Yales or Chubbs, great grinding Gothic keys and heavy bars and bolts. The kitchen door had the most modern lock and it was oiled: some secret daytime practice and I learnt to turn it noiselessly. The right time to escape would be just before first light. It was spring and first light very early and this proved a new difficulty: I did not wake up in time. I tried not to go to sleep at all, but when I remained sitting up I expected icy hands to touch me through the bars of the brass bedstead (the house, we all believed, was haunted), and when I lay down I dropped off. Dawn after dawn was wasted. Then one morning I did wake up. I put on a cotton frock and, shoes in hand, crept downstairs. The stairs were stone and did not creak. The dogs did not stir, the kitchen lock turned smoothly (I left it *un*locked behind me, one of the things that appalled my father), I climbed over the wall. I then proceeded to walk, not run, at a good pace. I passed a man who knew us on his way to the fields and called out, *Off for an early stroll* (that too was held against me). I carried a purse and a book, a book about Red Indians, and nothing else. I'd taken no food, not even a crust (something seldom repeated in subsequent journeys). When after an hour or so I got to the railway station I went straight in and asked for a single ticket, half-fare, fourth class to Frankfurt. There really was a fourth class in those days. The half-fare, drawing attention to my age, was not the best of moves. I said Frankfurt instead of Wiesbaden partly because I did not know how my money would hold out, partly to cover my tracks. I was given the ticket and some change and no questions asked. I went out on the platform to wait for a train in the right direction. I first took a local to Freiburg then changed to another slow train to Karlsruhe. Only the slow ones had fourth class, and the German name for these trains which stopped everywhere was *Bummelzug*. At Karlsruhe I changed again. I don't remember my route after that, only that there were more changes. I read my book; I felt no hunger, and I felt quite calm; this was probably my one and only journey without angst. I was resolved to get there – one step after another, and behaved and therefore probably looked as if travelling as an unaccompanied child were the most natural thing in the world. Of course fellow passengers and conductors were trying to ply me with questions and offers of sandwiches and sweets. I warded them off by saying that I was on my way to visit relatives (my luggage following) and plunging back into my book. The sandwiches I refused. To the pursuit that might be – that *was* – going on, I gave little intelligent thought.

My absence had in fact been noticed early and by mid-morning the police were after me. I had been reported by the man who had seen me on his way to work and by the ticket clerk at the first station. Why I was not caught I do not understand, perhaps it had something to do with my taking so many *Bummelzugs* and sometimes the wrong one (we later heard that I had avoided detection at Karlsruhe by minutes), in any case I must have been incredibly lucky. When I got to Frankfurt I took a big chance, I remained in the train instead of going out to get another ticket. I was afraid that I didn't have enough money. Wiesbaden then was occupied by the French. This I had heard but not that to enter the French sector you had to have a pass and that there was a control of passengers' papers on the trains. In fact no one came. We pulled into Wiesbaden; it was mid-afternoon; at the barrier I handed in my ticket face down. No hand was clapped on my shoulder. I asked my way through the town and after a longish walk rang the bell at my brother-in-law's house. I had not met him before. In my plan I had never gone further than the point of arrival. I found my sister away from home and the house in uproar. There had been telegrams about me. My new brother-in-law, a middle-aged man with a bald head, was at a loss to account for my presence; nor did I, now that the moment had come, find anything to explain. He started to question me. I'd felt lonely, I said, I wanted to see my sister. To this I stuck. It seemed hours again before they got hold of her – she was playing in some tennis tournament – and brought her home and I was able to fling myself into her arms.

They were puzzled, they were kind, they did not try too hard to understand; I was not punished. My sister tried to bring some of the enormity of my conduct home to me – my poor father: the many forms of anguish I had caused him. I closed my mind. My future was not discussed, or so it seemed, perhaps I was closing my mind to that too. At any rate I was not shipped back at once, day after day slipped by and still there I was.

And where was I? Once more admitted willy-nilly into an adult world. Wiesbaden town and spa must have been pretty unique in the Germany of that post-war period: it was flourishing. There was work, there was food in the shops. Life and money was kept flowing by the occupying French and more fantastically by white Russian émigrés, grandee refugees at their first stage with jewels to sell still in their baggage before they turned to Paris and to driving taxis. My sister's husband, whose mother had been English, was on excellent terms with the occupying forces and said to be discreetly plotting for a separation of the Rhineland. (For this he paid dearly twenty years on: the Nazis executed him.) He was a man with much musical knowledge and a flair for the theatre: *les spectacles*. As deputy mayor his functions included the administration of the state opera, the ballet and the fireworks. At home he kept open house to three categories of guests, and to these only, senior French officials, Russian émigrés, singers and musicians. Every evening they came. His hospitality and connoisseur-ship . . . my sister's youth, vitality and chic . . . (That marriage did not last either.) Although a bedtime was supposed to exist for me, I saw a good deal of it all, and it seems to have been my lot to have known only the more uncharacteristic enclaves of German life. I was dazzled. The singers sang, the musicians played. For the first time I heard Brahms and Schubert and 'Voi che sapete'; I also heard Stravinsky. (All Voss Strasse and my father had produced between them was Caruso on the gramophone.) A young Hungarian tried to give me piano lessons, a huge old gentleman, a cousin of the late Czarina, gave me ices at the pâtisserie. I was allowed to go to the opera, one night I saw the fireworks. I was taken to the races where someone kindly explained to me the workings of the tote, and let loose about the tennis club all morning. I managed to get work – ecstasy! – as ball girl on the courts.

Treats, long days of treats. Because, it became clear, I was to be sent back. I had only to stay *resolute*, I told myself (like the Red Indians), then it could not happen. They could not drag me back against my will. What was necessary was to tell my sister. If you don't send me back, I was going to say, if you let me stay with you, I'll give up all the rest, the opera, the social life, the tennis: you can send me to a strict day school. That part I had pat but I had no words for the rest – the *Why* not to send me back. My sister was hard to get hold of on her own, she slept late in the morning and after that everybody streamed into her room with the breakfast tray; every day I promised myself to talk to her on the next. When the bad morning came, it was still unsaid. All I could do was go limp and howl. They did drag me down the drive . . . they did take me back. That journey was accompanied.

*   *   *

We are at table at Feldkirch, we are having dinner upstairs in the room we now use in the winter, that used to be called the morning-room. My father sits at the head, he is carving, Lina sits on his right, the dogs are beside us, expectant. What he is carving is a smoked leg of mutton – thin curly slices like raw ham. It is his invention, made from our sheep, killed and cured at home (we don't have money to buy ham at the grocer's), in our way, in his way, we live off the land. My father serves Lina first, though a good deal is whisked to the dogs, I come next. The smoked gigot is very good, even Lina admits. (The rest of the village look askance. South German farmers raise sheep only for wool, they do not touch the flesh of mutton or lamb.) We also have a hot dish, some potato or flour mess of Lina's making, *Pflutten, Knöpfli, Spätzli* – her cooking is atrocious though my father politely directs her. He is a perfect cook, of simple things too (he must have been well ahead of his time); he had taught himself in his youth, watched the French and Italian chefs of the Eighties and Nineties, sat in their scalding commodious kitchens, made friends, drank iced champagne with them, straight swigs from the bottle (imperial pints: easier on the wrist), later simplifying, refining the dishes he had watched. Now alas he can no longer grill or fry, or cook anything over a range at all, ours burns wood and the fumes bring on his asthma. So he cooks by remote control or over a spirit lamp in his dressing-room – exquisite egg dishes, goose liver in foaming butter . . . I, too, am coming on nicely, he has taught me not to overcook vegetables.

In front of each of us stands a large clear glass with a stem, my father lifts the decanter by his hand and pours precisely – each glass is one third full. Lina is about to add water to hers and mine, my father stops her, Water in Bordeaux, *quelle horreur!* I sniff mine, take a mouthful slowly, twirling the wine in the glass, as he has told me to do. He is serious about this as he is about anything involving ritual and skills, but he is not fussy or anxious. Enjoy your wine, he says, and I do. At midday we drink cider – cider made in an old wooden press from apples grown in the orchard; we drink claret at night. We don't have to worry, he says, we have a decent amount left in the bins. He has taught me to pronounce the names on the labels and to look at the pictures of the châteaux, he has been to them, has met the owners. What shall we drink tomorrow? I am sent to fetch up the bottle. I am proud of the job, but when it's late in the day it fills me with terror – two flights down from the morning-room, across the large dark hall filled with crucifixes and statues, down another flight into the cellar; in one hand I hold a candle, in the other I shall have a bottle (*bring it up gently*); I shall have no free hand to cross myself if the ghost appears. He is a bishop, Wessenberg was his name, and he is said to have done a foul deed in this very hall. Lina has taught me an incantation to use if, Heaven forbid, I should see him, a German jingle, *All good ghosts praise God the Lord*, yet crossing oneself is of the essence. When I'm home and safe upstairs in the lighted room with the right wine and the candle has not blown out, my father often gives me a piece of ginger-bread or a few coins. Danger-money. For he professes to believe – believes? – in old Wessenberg as he off-handedly calls the ghost and claims to have found him occupying the chairs he is said to favour in the library and the Renaissance room, chairs I give a wide berth to, the dogs won't go near them, I've seen their hackles rise. Well, once the wine is safely up, it is stood somewhere to settle – that room's too warm, keep it well away from that stove! – and next day I am allowed to cut the seal and, unless the wine is very old, draw the cork, wipe the neck inside and out. The decanting is done by my father, my hands are not strong enough yet to do it properly.

And what do we talk about over our wine, at table and later when we sit by the lighted stove, a beautiful stove made of sixteenth-century tiles? Lina does not say much. She has confided in me that eating with my father scared her desperately at first (*he* said it was the right thing to do in these new times, revolutionary times), now she is getting used to it. Her ambition is to end her days as housekeeper to a priest. My father makes conversation as though Lina and I were real ladies. He tells us stories. About his youth; about Paris; about Monte Carlo and ways of breaking the bank. 'And did you?' 'Oh no! But one *can*. Systems . . . one needs capital . . . ' He tells us about the pair of chimpanzees he kept as a young man first on Corsica then at his villa at Grasse where they used to rush out in the morning to feast on the neighbours' peach-trees. When he married, the Merzes made him give up his monkeys, dirty apes, unhygienic, 'though, you see, they were actually very *soignés*'. He tells us about the time he spent with a group of Mesmerists in a castle in central France which belonged to a Polish count, a queer fellow, who claimed that he could raise the dead.

If my father was not good at showing affection, neither did he show hurt or reproach. When I came back after running away, Lina had scolded, kissed and wept; my father let it pass. To me a curious thing happened; the sadness was gone, vanished; I settled down at once. I missed my sister (I did that for many years after wherever I was), the interlude at her house became paradise lost, a dream. Some time again, I promised myself, there would be piano lessons and tennis; meanwhile I was resigned, better than that: without quite realising it, I was content. My attitude to my father had not changed, I was contemptuous about his prohibitions and fears – I was sure I knew better – his minute protection of me made me rebellious, not grateful, and there was an element of mutual evasiveness in our intercourse. Yet detached as I was from him, I lived in his stories (I played with bits of wood which were the horses he had had as a boy and young man), I looked forward to our evenings – the claret helping? – and was open to the skills he taught me.

When I say that my father did not reproach me, I mean that he never spoke of my having deserted and exposed him (my mother for one, inevitably hearing of the escapade, treated it as a huge joke in her letters); he did scold me about having left the house unlocked, a prey to thieves and marauders. What with the changes brought by the end of the war and the setting up of the Weimar Republic, he saw himself surrounded by an almost entirely hostile environment. Monarchy with its concomitants of courts and protocol was if dull – at some early point in his life he had done his stint as ADC – of the natural order of things: it was *safe*. My mother's defection did not help; nor did our poverty, our being ruined he called it. He felt himself betrayed by her, by his parents-in-law, by the times, by social forces he could neither understand nor name. And by me, God help me. (Are all young children unregenerate creatures? Incapable of moral responses? responses of the heart? Can these be awakened? Mine were not. I was unregenerate and self-absorbed.) What about that poverty of ours? Was it real? Or was it self-protection? Was it relative? I think it must have been all three, and at any rate very bitter for a man in his sixties who had been brought up not exactly to money but to the sweetness of life. (In a moderate, very civilised way: not for him the Merz opulence; his taste was too good, his fastidiousness too great, in their house he held himself aloof like a prisoner of honour at the victor's banquet.) The little money he had inherited he went through early, afterwards the money came from his wives. When the first one died, the Merzes made him an allowance which continued after he married my mother. Now, my mother was gone and Grandpapa Merz was dead. He had died in his nineties at Voss Strasse before the end of the war – I was there: *a death in the house*. The Merzes had been believed to be very rich but the old man had long ceased to look after his affairs and when he was gone there was barely enough left for Grandmama to carry on in that huge house: my father, like many other of their pensioners, was left out in the cold. He still had Feldkirch (bought by my mother) and his collection of objects, to these he was enslaved, the house was a necessary setting to contain them. Were they beautiful? What he was after, ever since he began as a young man to stalk the sales-rooms, were craftsmanship, rarity, decorative quality, not art. He had bought few paintings, and he spurned anything much after 1600. Here too he indulged a gloomy, even macabre trend. Gothic carvings, altar vessels, mediaeval chests, rows of pewter mugs, fifteenth-century bronzes, Renaissance chairs, fragments of tapestries – we lived inside a museum, one that nobody came to see. (If he were here today, could he have borne to turn public?)

How *did* we exist? Well, by barter up to a point; and here my father, being country-bred, developed some ingenuity. For we had no land to live off, only park and lawn, and courtyards and drives where the nettles stood waist high. He had some grass ploughed up (a man and horse came to do that) and put it under potatoes and poppies. The poppies were to make cooking oil, poppy-seed oil – Lina and I had to crack and shell the pods, and my poor father deploring it all, sadly talked of olives. What was left of the lawn was used by sheep and geese. Our cooking and heating was done with wood from the park, and there was enough left to trade in for the donkeys' feed and the fowls', and flour for our bread. We had nearly three hundred apple-trees, good strains and known to be so, both eating and cider; these too were traded: for milk, for cream (we churned our butter), for honey and man-hours. Every few months a butcher's assistant came out from the market town to kill a sheep or a pig. We had poultry, we had eggs, we grew vegetables, and grapes on a south wall. From these in October my father made a small quantity of fine white wine. So much for our table. My father's wardrobe – suits, greatcoats, shirts, boots – was inexhaustible; mine was not replenished. For every day I wore a kind of overall, trousers and apron in one, or my Red Indian outfit, a relic of Merz bounty not yet too badly outgrown. To mass I wore one of my old dresses and over them, as they became shorter and shorter, one of my father's jackets, Lina having adjusted the sleeves and little else. We took in one paper, a local one, chiefly for the agricultural ads; *that* must have been paid for in cash. So must some other items – salt, soap, candles, matches; and being on main electricity by now, my father's mind was much exercised by future bills. The thing that cost most, he told us, was switching on, as the current had to flow in from so far. So we kept lights burning in the morning-room and in my father's suite and went about the rest of the house candle in hand. (I tried to save candles by melting and remoulding the ends but found no way of managing the wick.) I quite enjoyed playing the Robinson Crusoe game, yet in my unfeeling way I was irritated by my father's groans about money. Again, I knew so much better – he'd only have to sell some of the stuff, a few pieces from the collection, and we'd be all right again. Poor man, I fear that this is precisely what he must have done, secretly, agonisingly, in minimal instalments. He would never allow a dealer to come near the place (some prowled), but there were days when carrying a Gladstone bag and looking aloof he drove to the station in the donkey carriage and took the train to Freiburg or Basle. He'd come back in the evening inscrutable, bearing presents for Lina and me. I am sure now that this was the way the electric bills were met and Lina's wages got paid.

My own life was full. I opened up the chicken coops and shut them again at dusk, I fed the geese and made the dogs' dinner (it was served by my father), I fanned the smoke-house fire, turned the joints of pork in their barrel of brine, drew our daily cider. There was no more slow time to dread. There was weeding to be done and watering, and vegetables to be picked and windfalls to be gathered and kindling to be made, and I now could muck out the donkeys' stable on my own. Then there were seasonal tasks, apple picking and storing (on the parquet floor of my mother's drawing-room now empty of its light gracious furniture), the brief vintage, the gathering and stacking of wood, the autumnal raking of leaves ... The leaves were my responsibility (they were needed for the donkeys' bedding as we could not afford to buy straw); spreading and drying and turning, then piling them into the cart and driving them to the barn, Flora between the shafts (Fanny being too tricky). I also had private pursuits. Teaching the dogs arithmetic – having heard of Calculating Horses – trying to make them tap out numbers with their paws, by persuasion and rewards; that was an entire failure. Trick bicycling, on an old machine: I was seldom allowed out on the road so I taught myself stunts in the yard – I could kneel on the saddle going downhill and I could ride backward in tight circles (*not* within sight of my father). And tennis. Solo tennis by the hour with the pre-war balls and the ill-strung racket against the wash-house wall, keeping the score and dreaming of Wimbledon. (Oh, the things I had heard of.)

A new worry came to beset my father. *He* had my custody but my mother still meddled (his word); she wanted me to be educated, so apparently did the law. In the now distant past nanny had taught me my pot-hooks, reading I had more or less picked up on my own, figures I liked to play with; at Voss Strasse I had quite enjoyed the bi-weekly visits of a rather decrepit tutor . . . At Feldkirch we forgot all about it. When my mother nudged our memory, she suggested a governess; my father beside himself with vexation decided to send me to the village school.

The school house was a recent building implanted by some distant authority – a classroom on the ground-floor and some lavatories above, a flat for the schoolmaster and his family – and it smelled of cement, linoleum and piss. Here I was brought one day in the middle of term. The children, about thirty of them, sat on benches, each with a slate before them, girls on one side, separated by an aisle, boys on the other. They were placed according to their age, six-year-olds in the front row, eleven-year-olds in the back. The schoolmaster, a youngish man in a town suit, came in and everybody stood up and broke into a chant, *Grüt'zi Gott Herr Lehrer.* He stepped in front and began to do something quite fascinating – making each row learn a different thing at the same time. The six-year-olds were told to practise their letters – how their slates squeaked – the next lot were set sums, the row behind was learning a poem and the back row was given a map. We nine-year-olds, a girl and I and three boys across the aisle, were made to read aloud in turns. Then there was dictation for some and learning by heart for others; later there was singing and reciting the catechism by all. It was noisy but not really confusing, and I soon got the hang of it. The teaching was done in real German (with a strong southern accent) and the children too repeated their lessons in *Hochdeutsch*, which came out quite stilted, but when they talked, even to the master, they dropped back into patois. Each row formed what they called a school-year; mine had a set of textbooks marked Fourth: a *Fiebel* for reading, a *Rechenbuch* for arithmetic, stories from the Holy Bible; the content of the books, the curriculum (a standard curriculum!) was the same word for word through the whole of Baden and had to be learned day by day, week by week by every child of nine throughout the land.

The girls were meek and most were hopeless at their lessons, the boys were lazy and noisy. The chief punishment was *Tatzen*, pawsers, a beating on the hand with a short swishy stick. If you were late more than once or couldn't do your daily lot you were given two *Tatzen*, for something worse four, for something really bad six. Six was rare. Sometimes the schoolmaster would just hurl a boy over the desk and beat him on his behind. The boy usually yelled (stoicism was not prized). *Tatzen* and spankings would be given then and there in front of the school, the innocents sitting still and cowed with an undercurrent of nastier feelings: *Schadenfreude*, an unholy excitement.

School-hours were not long, the children being expected, as I did, to give a hand at home. One o'clock till four in the afternoon for us in the lower school, seven to eleven in the morning for the twelve- to fifteen-year-olds. So were the holidays regulated by the needs of the fields and seasons – hay holidays, harvest holidays, potato and wood-making holidays. Nor do I remember much homework. When the threshing machine was due or someone was repairing a barn, the school children were given the day off – we'd sit on ladders, forming a chain, handing up tiles.

Like my sister's house, school opened another world for me. Again I discovered the pleasures of social life. First there were the children, though they treated me with curiosity and restraint at first (their parents and the schoolmaster called me by the preposterous name of Baroness Billi – Billi was what my family always called me, a corruption of the last syllables of my first name), I tried to make friends with the zest of a puppy. Where are they now my ephemeral companions of Feldkirch (for my schooldays were numbered)? Where and what are they likely to have been doing in 1933? in 1939? in 1945? Josephina, my coeval, a silent sallow girl with black hair severely pulled back? Clara, another slow child, Katherina who never washed (nor did I when I could help it) and whom I could seduce into mischief, the five Martin girls, each one year older and two inches taller than the next and otherwise exactly alike? The girls were a tame lot on the whole, their idea of play was promenading arms linked down the village street of a Sunday afternoon, bawling sad songs. I soon turned to the boys, forming a gang with three older ones, Alphons, Robert and Anton, as we shared tastes; my Meccano, playing trains, getting on a farm horse when no one was looking.

I was interested in their home life and pleased when my new friends took me to their houses after school. There I was hospitably received by their elders. The meal in progress would be the four o'clock *Z'fiere neh'* in Baden patois which is a language unto itself. The fare was the same in house after house; cold raw bacon, bread and cider. The bacon was cut thick, right off a side in the larder, as thick as a beef steak. The bread was home-baked in big round loaves weighing about five pounds, whitish, not snow-white, good bread not unlike the French *pain de campagne* though harder and closer in texture; and at its best when about eight days old. The cider was spoken of as wine, and not up to ours, as many stretched it by adding water and a powdered stuff, a kind of must, that came out of a cardboard box. Nobody in the village, except the priest and the mayor, drank grape wine, and they rarely drank beer.

It was a small village, one long curved street, unpaved, a few lanes, some two hundred and fifty inhabitants in less than fifty dwellings. They had about four surnames between them, Rinderle, Faller, Martin and Hauser. Everybody farmed (except the priest and the schoolmaster) and nearly everybody farmed their own land. Some had only an acre or two, some had thirty or forty; some were said to be in debt to the mortgage bank, some were quite prosperous; a few did something on the side such as keeping the smithy, the post office (with the one and only telephone which went dead at seven p.m.), the village shop and the inn. All lived much in the same way. The houses varied in size, all were stone and most of them had two storeys. A few were shiningly clean with polished cook-stoves and floors, a dustless quiescent parlour, a main bedroom with a store-bought suite, double bed, wardrobe, framed wedding photograph on the chest of drawers, often a photograph too of a son fallen (so recently) in the war. Some were less speckless, some were sluttish. At the back was the yard with the dung heap and the pump and trough (only the schoolhouse, the presbytery and the château had water laid on), then the stables and barns, and these also were tell-tale. The mayor's were a joy to behold, the stables airy with the straw high and clean, the harness-room sparkling, the milk churns scoured and the apple loft smelling sweet. There was an enclosed vineyard. The mayor, like a few other big farmers, had four horses, most had only one and you often saw a horse and an ox teamed up before a load. Oxen did much of the work, and one man who was also the cobbler had to do the ploughing with his only cow.

When I say that the whole village lived much in the same way, I am thinking of their work, their food, their religion and their leisure. For breakfast everyone had milky coffee made of roasted barley and chicory essence, bread and plum jam. No butter; butter and eggs were for selling. Later on the men in the fields had a bacon and cider break. The midday meal was between eleven and twelve and much like Lina's cooking, starch with an occasional over-boiled cabbage or carrot. The cooking fat was lard. A salad meant a potato salad. Meat, unless some great chore was going on, was for feast days and Sundays. Then it would be roast pork or boiled beef or fowl or a superfluous cockerel. Large four-o'clocks every day, supper at nightfall a bowl of coffee and bread. The clothes interested me less but I can see them still. By today's standards they were dreadful. Shapeless skirts, high-necked blouses, ill-made dresses of cotton and serge. No one over thirty wore any colour other than black and brown. There were no jerseys or cardigans then for women; 'jumpers' had come in, they did not reach us. A girl displayed clothes twice in her lifetime, at her first communion and her wedding, both of course in white. The men made do with dingy work clothes (no trim-cut jeans) and a stiff Sunday suit. Children from May to October went barefoot. Reading? Among adults I saw no print ever, except for the local paper and the mail-order catalogues.

Politics? Well, the men had their council, the *Gemeinderat*, which met in a room at the inn; as for national politics, in spite of the war and recent revolution, feelings did not run high (there was talk though and fear of inflation). During the first post-war general elections in 1919, no candidate for the Reichstag came to address the electorate of Feldkirch. Yet vote they did and it was pretty well known which way. Lina was able to put us into the picture family by family. In spite of my father's predictions, who saw only potential Jacobins, the village went solidly either for the Democratic or the Centre or some agricultural splinter party, all representing the Catholic interest. Nobody voted for the Nationalist and Conservative parties or groups of the extreme right, possibly because they were seen as associated with North Germany and Protestantism. One man only voted Social Democrat, and was labelled *Sozi*: *he* was known as a reckless drunk who had gambled away his land. No votes were cast for the Communists and Spartacists.

Feldkirch had no resident doctor or nurse, no poor-house, no charity, there was no women's institute, no club, no band, no playing-fields, no games of any kind. Some of the women grew a few flowers in front, otherwise there was little gardening except for the pot. There were mouth organs about and a few concertinas, the schoolhouse had a harmonium; no one, including ourselves, owned a piano; nor do I remember anyone with a hobby, there was no stamp-collecting, no chess. What did they do with themselves? There was no radio then, let alone television, no accessible cinema; only two or three people had ever seen a film. Between being stupefied by ceaseless machine-produced distractions and no stimuli at all, there is a world. What *did* they do with themselves? The men could go to the inn to drink and play cards, Gasthaus zum Kreuz, a slovenly stuffy place that smelled of wet boots and schnapps (I penetrated once or twice to fetch lemonade); they could bang away at hares and a few birds (it was flat country with little woodland); they could treat themselves to outings when they had a mare to be served or a calf to sell (a lame cryer with a bell would limp up the street announcing cattle markets and fairs). Young married women and the younger old maids would promenade the Sunday lanes, arm in arm, like schoolgirls, singing away about love, early death and the soldier who failed to return. (Those German songs made me want to howl like a dog, and the tunes were a far cry from Schubert and Brahms.) Young men too promenaded in crocodiles of a Sunday afternoon – they must have been idle hands indeed – passing but not mingling with the girls. Segregation was rigid, one might have been in Latin America or Turkey. Single boys did walk out with single girls (of course!) but it had to be in secret or as fiancés. The secret never lasted – tittle-tattling about one's neighbours *was* a main recreation, and woe to those found out – engagements, unless a pregnancy intervened, were apt to be long.

One solace was the great guzzlings, serious enough at vintage and Easter, whoppers at a christening, first communion or wedding. A pig would be killed, geese roasted, barrels of choucroute rolled out. Relations and helpers would be asked to the spread and as everyone had some kinship with everyone the company would be large. Those who could have no place were sent a *Metzgerplatte*, a great dish high with blood-pudding, spare ribs, hot ham, *Kuttlie* (tripe) and a glutinous meat-pulp of a sausage called *Schwartenmagen*.

There *was* one focal point, one common source of drama, fulfilment, pleasure, and that was the Church and her offices. Feldkirch, man and boy, was Catholic. (It knew one Jew, *the* Jew – not resident – who periodically turned up to buy rabbit furs; Protestants, heretics, *Ketzer*, were purely bogy figures; the nearest they had ever got to one was my mother who had only changed to the true faith when about to marry my father.) In the church there was music, an organ played by the schoolmaster; whoever could sing, sang in the choir; one young man served as verger, others rang the bells, the angelus bell at morning, noon and sunset, the bells for mass, the jerky hysterical fire bells and the slow single bell when someone had died. The small high one for a woman, the deeper one for a man. You listened and said your *ave*, or got ready for church or ran for help or wondered who it might be. Women looked after the altar linen, swept the church – and a beautiful small church it was, pure-arched, whitewashed, plain – it was the virgins' job (virgins of any age) to bring flowers and branches, to polish the censer and candlesticks. The mayor and my father in turn provided the wine for mass; the boys I played with served as acolytes. Rosary and missal were treasured private possessions.

Early mass, daily mass, a low one with a single altar-boy in a penumbra of candles and no music, was poorly attended by pious old women and first communicants. The great occasions were the annual processions at Corpus Christi; and the Patron-Saint's Day that wound round the church and down the lanes and round the park and château stopping under the windows of the bedridden with banners in the wind and canopies under which swayed the statues of the Madonna and Saint Johannes; everyone who could wore white and the virgins were entitled to a blue ribbon. For the run of the year the event was high mass on Sunday with not a pew in the nave unfilled. Here, too, there was strict segregation by sex and age: girls and women to one side of the aisle, boys and men to the other. If you were to be born and die at Feldkirch you would have made your first appearance in church in the front of the children's row and moved backward as you grew up, sat in turn with the young girls, the newly married girls, the married women, the older women, until you were really old and had to sit in the back row. The same if you were born a boy. The château party had their own stall in the choir beside the altar, and we did not come in by the porch but through the presbytery garden and the sacristy. Lina came with us so far then took her place in the hierarchy. I remained alone with my father who, unlike the rest of us, did not kneel but sat in a stooping position that was to be taken for kneeling. I would have liked to have been in the ranks with the schoolchildren, but enjoyed our seats for being so close to the altar. On ordinary Sundays there were two acolytes and the vestments were green; they were violet during Lent, black on Good Friday, red and gold on High Sundays. At Easter they were pure white and gold, and there would be incense and six altar-boys. I watched their every genuflection, knew when they must ring their hand bells, swing the censer, carry the Book from the Epistle to the Gospel side. (I had a secret ambition to do likewise and was laying my plans.)

After mass everyone hung about the church porch; my father would go out through the sacristy and talk to the priest as he disrobed, we would then walk him home through his garden. When I say the priest I mean two men. One was Father Kaplan who had been in the parish since long before the war; emaciated, frail, old, with a noble ascetic face and transparent skin, he was a strange man to be found among us. He lived with an entire disregard for his own comfort and health, and he always said mass slowly with fervour and dignity. His sermons were severe. The village were not at ease and many were afraid of him, yet they were proud to have him. My father deferred to Father Kaplan and spoke of him with affection; to me he was the idea of what a priest was supposed to look like and be. I lived in dread of the day when I should be old enough to make my first confession to him. Now I feel that if by some not impossible chance one had ever been in his prayers that would be a good thing to have had. By the end of 1919 he left us and retired to an old priests' home. His successor, Father Huber, could not have been more different. Spherical, rubicund, a hearty laugh and a voice chuckling away in patois. He gabbled through mass, but when an altar-boy slacked or snickered he turned and slapped his face. He shocked me to the core on the way out of the sacristy by telling my father that he was looking forward to a pork cutlet the size of a lavatory seat (he did not say lavatory, he used a village word). *His* sermons too were severe.

The most popular offices were Vespers and the nightly Rosary during May because in these we could take part. The responses – *Et cum spiritu tuo, Orate pro nobis, Dona nobis pacem* – would not be mumbled by the altar-boys or chanted by the choir but babbled in unison by the flock. If you were good at it and bold, you would be singled out to lead the prayers from a prie-dieu in front of the nave. There you intoned the *Pater* and the *Ave* or, best of all, recited the petitions of a litany in the vernacular. This exalted role was often filled by a young farmer's wife who had acquired her much admired diction while in service at some country house. I aspired to be her rival. I went about boasting that I would be able to recite a whole litany without once opening my missal. It was taken up. One evening in May I found myself kneeling in conspicuous isolation, missal shut beside me, chanting in the right blend of *Hochdeutsch* and patois line after line punctuated by the thunderous response behind me.

'*Du Engel des Herrn:*
'*Bet f'r oonsh!* (Patois for *Bete für uns.*)
'*Du heilige Jungfrau:*
'*Bet f'r oonsh!*
'*Du elfenbeinerner Turm.*
'*Bet f'r oonsh!*
'*Du Rose Davids:*
'*Bet f'r oonsh!*
'*Du Lamm Gottes:*
'*Erbarme dich oonsher!*'

It lasted for the best part of five minutes and it was intoxicating.

Pride before a fall. The assumptions of my social life were rather less secure than I could have surmised and two disasters soon befell me. My father, who never went out except to mass, was not unalarmed by my involvement with the village which he put down to the evils attending my having to go to school. He was not aware of quite how many hours I spent out of bounds as Lina, sensibly, covered up for me. He did not mind the information I brought home about crops and calvings but was upset by my accepting hospitality. His manners overcame his dread of anyone getting a glimpse of his collection and it was decided that I must invite my friends. I, uncertain of the acceptability of my home, asked if we might have bacon. Bacon was not expected, Lina said, she would provide cake and lemonade. So I asked my three chums, Alphons, Robert and Anton, to drop in after school. Lina turned red in the face, burst into tears and appealed to my father in a hysterical voice, Please, *Herr Baron*, don't let her. Then it all came out. The village was talking! Parents were displeased! I had been causing scandal! Now I was about to commit the last solecism –

for a girl to play with boys was simply not done. My father and I were stunned, indignant, embarrassed. She ought to have warned us, Lina said, spoken earlier but she knew that Billi had meant no harm. Harm? I felt bewildered, miserable, betrayed – I had believed myself welcome, liked . . . What had I done? What was I supposed to have done? Lina implied something unmentionable here, some threshold of adult abyss. Then my father gave it his own twist – these were times to lie low: I was wild, I was reckless, *I invited danger*. Decisions were made and unmade – I must stop going to the village, stop going to church, I must stop going to school. We had days of this; then it cooled down. I continued at school, village outings were rationed (the gilt was off that gingerbread anyhow), a gaggle of girls was asked in to play. They came, good God, in their Sunday best and did not enjoy my toys (I kept no dolls); as we strolled in the park my boy chums appeared on the wall and jeered. I could neither explain nor apologise; I survived.

Perhaps I should say a word about our position, real and imaginary, in the neighbourhood. (As far as I can piece it together.) That rural corner of Baden, the Breisach, was full of small villages like ours and many of these had their Schloss, their manor house, inhabited by families we knew but had ceased to see. At Munzingen there was Count Kaagenegg, Baron Neveux at Bingen, the Gleichensteins at Krotzingen, the Landenbergs . . . Most of them farmed, Kaagenegg produced a renowned wine. Before the war they all lived, and were expected to live, in a certain style, providing custom and employment for their villagers, and an element of show with their horses (no one sported a motor car), their house colours and coronets scattered in the German fashion over the silver and the saddle cloths. Now they too felt the pinch, though none I gathered were retrenching in quite our way. Some were slightly eccentric, Neveux never spoke anything but patois and the old Baroness had actually been in prison for watering the milk. Gleichenstein having died, his widow was facing struggles, Landenberg was dabbling in splinter politics, only the Kaageneggs were still wholly rich and grand. From this world my father had made his voluntary withdrawal. He still drank a glass of wine with a farmer after trading in apples or wood, and now and again of a morning he called on the mayor's wife who had been, he told me, a most handsome woman. Every six months or so he asked the priest to dinner and, after days of grumbling and groaning and responsible preparation, gave him a remarkable one. His manner was not conscious, he was gravely polite, trying to look after people regardless of their age or standing; my mother said that whenever he had been absorbed and oblivious of his many dreads, as in courtship or in stalking an objet d'art, he would become happy and animated and could show much charm. So in spite of his aloofness and his own misgivings he was personally much liked by Feldkirch. They did *not* like our new shabbiness, it deprived them of something and they couldn't understand it – the Schloss after all was still there – they were embarrassed by the donkey carriage and my clothes, while to him it was the wise response to an age of revolution. The donkeys were the sand to my father's ostrich head. He was wrong. They had no wish to send us to the guillotine; they missed our liveried servants.

Towards the end of my second Feldkirch winter, when I was getting on for ten, the priest reminded my father that I had not yet made my first communion. So along with some little girls of seven I was put under instruction which took place at the presbytery twice a week. We were now required to go to early mass daily and to lead an exemplary life. The opportunity had come, I thought, for my campaign to serve at mass. When I was word-perfect at the Latin responses, I began with Lina who hugged me and said that it had never been done before. I went over her head and reeled off *Qui glorificat juventutem meam* to my father. To my surprise he was impressed. He didn't see why I shouldn't. Father Huber said it was irregular but didn't see why I mightn't serve singly at low mass. I would have preferred a wider stage but was too pleased to mind. I was given the manual and practised at home, handling a censer (we had so many), genuflecting as I staggered under the weight of a large folio, in lieu of mass book, in my arms. I knew exactly how it should be done. I had watched those altar louts gape and yawn and scratch their heads and all but pick their noses, they missed cues and made mistakes, whereas *I* would do it with precision, quiet dignity and poise. I got as far as wearing a surplice and practising at the real altar one afternoon. Then the blow fell. Father Huber, having presumably got cold feet, asked the Bishop and the Bishop had said No.

My father said how times had changed, if any child of *his* father's had wished to serve at mass the parish priest would not have gone footling about asking for permission. Times have changed again. Would I have been allowed to play altar-boy in the nineteen-eighties?

That fiasco, coming as it did during preparation for my first communion, left me more free to indulge in the doubting mood that led to what I called losing my faith. And, pray, what had been my faith? That of a Roman Catholic savage. Rather less enlightened, if anything, as my missionaries had been peasant women. They inserted into my mind a farrago of hell fire, niceties of ritual and mortal sin; they told me horror stories about the nun who broke her vows and the boy who swallowed a morsel of breakfast before taking communion. I heard little about the mercy of God and man's potential virtue. I heard about sin and the consequences of sin – eternal damnation. I was able to grasp a logical if frightening system; something about its cut-and-driedness, its absolutism, even appealed to me. I *liked* order. (Though order permits less choices.) It was clear what one must not do. The Ten Commandments, the Seven Capital Sins, the Five Commandments of the Church. It was the latter which loomed large. The general Commandments were rather outside a child's range – murder, idolatry, taking another man's wife; while lying and stealing, we were told, were venial not mortal sins. The Capital Sins were too abstract, only the Church Commandments were workaday enough. Two of them, the obligation to attend mass on Sundays and to abstain from meat on Fridays had worried me already at Voss Strasse in Berlin at a time of whole if private faith. As it never occurred to anyone in that Judaic-Agnostic household to take me to any form of worship and as I was plainly not yet of an age to go anywhere on my own, omitting mass could not be so very bad: the responsibility was not mine. But the

Friday meat! Here I should have stood up and refused in public, but I was not of the stuff of martyrs and confessors. So I hid the contents of the delicate chicken sandwich that was sent up to me for my elevenses and spirited the cutlet off my tray; the difficulty in the town-bound house without dog or cats was ultimate disposal. I had to retrieve the meat next day from its hiding places and swallow it myself. Now back at Feldkirch I had more serious reasons for feeling at odds with my religion: I was told that divorced people go to hell. My father and mother were divorced now, so much was at last acknowledged. Did they know about the consequences of their action? Whenever I could not turn my thoughts away from it, I went into a rebellious panic. Such rules, I told myself, were too bad to be believed.

Father Huber began the communicants' instruction by telling us – in such an off-hand way – that we were about to enter an important stage of our lives and ought to practise mortification of the flesh. (That always had an embarrassing ring to me.) How many lumps do you take in your morning coffee? he asked each little girl in turn with a view of getting her to cut down sugar. Each whispered that she was allowed half a lump on weekdays. As we drank tea at home (gift parcels from my sister) sugarless by choice, I felt a twinge of awkwardness and obliged by admitting to a thinly sugared coffee bowl. My father would have approved of this, seeing it as a prudent subterfuge – 'Don't show the difference in your tastes and habits.' (Poor man, I have never known anyone more transparent.) I had offered the falsehood because of not wanting to belittle somebody else's treats, and because of my desperate play-acting to belong. (I went as far in that line as telling schoolmates that the man who came to plough up our lawn was my godfather.) I have long since given up the desire to conform but still prefer untruths to ruffled feelings; those miserable half-lumps of sugar prompted my first social lie.

Unfortunately they started Father Huber's 'spiritual preparation' on a false and trivial note. He took us through the catechism and communion service line by line and that was that. I left the presbytery disillusioned. What had I hoped for? Inspired words, questions answered, fears allayed? A great change in myself? I began to answer my own questions. Surely the Church could not be true because it was unfair. *Unfair.* (Not a Feldkirch term.) *Unfair* that babies had to stay in limbo forever just because no one had managed to sprinkle water on them in time? Unfair that there should be only one safe church when it was chance whether you were born into a wrong one and could never go to paradise? Unfair that if you fell off a horse and died without having had a second's time to repent your sins you were damned for ever? And why should one person be sent to hell for the same sins when another might get off with an indulgence for going to Rome or saying a set of prayers (I did not realise that this was not exactly an original protest). Well: God being omnipotent and just would never allow anything like that. By the same token He was omnipresent which means everywhere, so why were we told that we must worship Him inside a church? Yes, they were all wrong. I convinced myself quite easily and derived a sense of superiority and freedom from my reasoning. Only once during instruction was my imagination fired, that was when we read about the quality of repentance. There was repentance through fear, and repentance through love, love of God that was, abhorrence of our wickedness. But this too was imparted by rote. All might have been different had there still been Father Kaplan instead of Father Huber. When the time came, I made my first communion in a state of smug rebellion.

My second social disaster was triggered off by Lina. 'Give me that comb.' 'I can manage all right.' 'Give me that comb!' I let go, it was past concealment, the teeth of the comb were teeming with live lice. *What shall we do?* Wash my hair in petrol. *He* will smell it. Papa must not know. But Lina was horrified – what if *he* should catch them? I saw: *that* was unthinkable; I gave in. So my father was told the facts of life (I had suspected them): some of my schoolfellows had lice, not all, not many . . . My hair was tooth-combed by the hour, washed in petrol, day after day, before we got rid of them, nits and all. This I submitted to, but now my father put his foot down. It was the end of my schooldays.

*

Hoping to remain unbadgered by the German equivalent of the Education Act, my father decided to tutor me himself. He went to Freiburg and bought a set of schoolbooks; they were secondary school-books and so quite a jump. There were four of these, a geography book, a history book, a German grammar and a French grammar. My father's method was simple, every weekday I was to learn, on my own, one paragraph from each book. By learning he understood by heart; he expected me to be word-perfect. So I memorised French irregular verbs, German declensions, lengths of rivers, the date of Hannibal's crossing of the Alps. It bored me and I got into the habit of putting off the daily stint until the last hour, having some pretty narrow shaves. Once I had to fall back on reciting yesterday's lesson and to my horror got away with it. This left me feeling mean and guilty but also rather cynical about the whole process. It had to be kept up though as the alternative was the threat of a resident governess who, my father said, would ruin our lives. What he failed to take in was the unequal distribution of my daily task: the paragraph I was to learn might run from anything like six lines to a page and a half.

It must have been during that period that my father initiated our nightly sessions of roulette. He produced an authentic wheel from some locked recess and set it up. He acted bank and croupier, Lina and I were the punters, and we soon caught on. Candles, wine glasses, stacks of counters on the table, my father strict in the observance of the disciplines of Monte Carlo. *Faites vos jeux . . . Rien ne va plus!* The wheel spinning and the hush while the tiny ball jumped – *le Seize, Rouge, Impair et Passe*. We played for real money, Lina's wages, my pocket money, and learnt to be careful. (Once I thought I was clever and backed a single chance with the minimum, doubling my stake when I lost; when I tried to do so for the fifth coup running I had a sharp and sufficient shock.) When losses became serious my father would make them up for us, but next morning, in daylight, not acknowledging what his left hand was doing. At night again we were a gambling club, dicing with thoughts of ruin while my father kept up a commentary of anecdotes about young men he'd seen cry *Banco*, lose all and shoot themselves at dawn. For the rest of that time at Feldkirch

I played much solitary tennis.

*   *   *

It was autumn again, some disturbance was in the air. There were letters: something was on my father's mind. I was not told until practically the last hour. One evening as we were sitting in his room side by side, he struggling for breath – as he so often did and I so used to it – he brought it out. Your mother . . . The lawyers . . . You *see* . . . Here were the facts: my father had custody while my mother had access, she was supposed to have me for a couple of months a year. Nearly three years were up now; so far she had not claimed me, or my father had managed to keep her off (something of both I believe). Now the lawyers said that she wanted me, there was little he could do, she wanted me to spend the next half year with her in Italy – I was to start for Florence the day after tomorrow, somebody was going to meet me at Freiburg and take me there. Before I knew what I felt I burst into loud tears. *No*, I cried and for the first time clung to him. My father said – I am not certain whether he said it or whether I only heard it with some inner ear, he raised his hands in some defeated gesture – too late. I cried more bitterly and had the grace to say – to this man who had watched over me, who had done so much for me, to whom I had never shown a loving heart – I want to stay with you. Again he made that gesture: 'But Billi – you ran away from me.'

Two days later I was put on a train. A few months after my father went down with appendicitis. He was operated on in Freiburg, his asthma became bad, he could not breathe lying on a hospital bed; within a few days he died. I knew that he had been much afraid of death.

PART TWO

Fugitives: Italy

THE FUTURE as outlined to me at such short notice had been a home near Florence and a stepfather. It became clear though at the end of the journey that neither of these was to be just yet. My mother's arrangements (as I had to learn) were often impulsive and reversible. The train crossed the Alps over the Brenner Pass and on its slow descent I had the first sight on a September morning of a southern sky and light, and took to it with the alert joy of a creature born in and emerging from the north. We got off, alas, alas, short some three hundred miles of Florence at Cortina d'Ampezzo, the resort. The name might be impeccably Italian, the place was not. The Austrian Trentino was turned Italian only by the Treaty of Versailles, we therefore found ourselves in political, not ethnographic, Italy. Here we were to wait for my mamma at an hotel. 'We' means the last in a chain of travel minders (lawyer's clerks? all forgotten), a girl from Berlin less than twice my age whom my mother had met at another hotel and roped in to meet me at a border. Her name, she said, was Doris. My mother turned up the next day and seemed a little puzzled as to why she had sent for me. Perhaps, she said, it *was* a little premature. Yes, yes, I'm going to marry O – you were told about that? – and live in Florence happily ever after. Though perhaps not quite next week. What she would like to have, she said, was second thoughts.

O was a painter of some reputation, and they were to be married at a consulate. Doris described him as an *interesting* man: mature, travelled – all desirable qualities in our eyes. A word here about Doris because we were to meet her again, in other years, at other stages. She turned out in fact to have been the epitome of a lost generation, the young who came of age in the Weimar Republic. Doris had only lately chosen that anglicised version of her name (Dorle), it occurs to me that there must have been even before Christopher Isherwood and his kind became enraptured by Berlin, a corresponding Anglo (and even more so Americo) mania among bright young Germans, a two-way traffic of sexo-romantic fascination.

Doris then. Of 'good family', North German, though not Prussian; a minor title, civil service tradition; with two or three men of letters, also minor (an uncle, great-uncles), urbane, cultivated, and she intelligentsia by descent and association rather than in her own right. Her mother had died early of TB, and Doris was brought up by a loving and unworldly grandmother, her father too being dead, killed in the 1914 War, and there was very little money (that little to be obliterated quite soon by the monster wave of inflation up into billions crashing over Germany). At our first meeting point the grandmother had already turned her Berlin flat into a pension de famille, the kind where the inmates are friends and most of the friends are artists and actors out of work. Doris despite her extreme youth had been trying to hold down a job or two, typing for a literary agency, some modelling; she hoped to get into films. That summer she had come out to Italy as secretary to an American script writer; that had gone wrong but as she still had a bit of money left she stayed on, my mother erratically befriending her. Doris's face was sallow, large-eyed, her figure thin, flat-chested, spidery beyond the modish requirement of the time. Her talk was of parties, of avant-garde films and young men who were going to be poets and painters. To me she was a new species and a buffer between me and my new-found parent.

Telegrams from O intruded. My mother made no move; she did not tell us much, there was nothing, she said, to explain; she laughed at herself, making a game of it, perhaps a waiting game. (We thought.) Doris fell in easily with the suspended future, I fretted; I could not bear the waiting – never did, never will – and there was the disappointment of not being taken into real Italy. Then one evening Artur Schnabel was playing at a soirée in some villa and my mother, who was as unmusical as one can be, was asked to go. She always seemed to know people everywhere. Doris and I amused ourselves with a night walk among the vineyards gorging ourselves with stolen grapes (while we were both older in many ways than our respective ages, we were probably also considerably younger in others). Next afternoon a young man called at our hotel. Goodness, my mother said, Doctor Caligari, I presume! That's what comes from sitting out a Beethoven sonata. You had better see him, he's a much more suitable age for *you*. So we were left to receive the man my mother insisted on calling Doctor Caligari in the hotel salon. In came a young man of great good looks who did not show the slightest interest in Doris let alone me; my mother eventually appeared, we slipped away and he must have succeeded in taking her out to dinner.

Although so very young and handsome there was nothing sleek or facile about that caller; had one encountered him at another period one might have seen him in a cinquecento piazza standing by the scaffold, never at the thé-dansant. Style, an inbred sadness, a light façade of badinage and pliancy – in a few years and for long after, my mother told us, he would have come into a resemblance with Titian's Man with the Glove.

A week later my mother said that she was going away for a few days. To Florence? *Not* to Florence. And I would be all right, wouldn't I, here with Doris? Of course. No more questions; my mother left. Next day Doris had a telegram about a film test. No, we said, she could not miss *that*. You will be all right here, won't you? Of course. In a way I was. I had a room of my own, my mother had left books, living in an hotel was a fascinating experience. The food, to my thinking, was delicious (mayonnaise on something or other every day), the staff were exceedingly kind. Adult fellow guests tried to ask questions; these I evaded, just as I declined offers of joining them for meals. I ate at a table for one, attended by sweet waiters who brought the dishes for me to look at and gave me second and third helpings of anything I liked. I went for walks, looked into shop windows. I *was* all right; and yet . . . Time did not exactly fly and there was an undercurrent of anxiety, not admitted into articulate thought – Will she come back? Will anyone ever come back for me? At one point I bought myself an Italian grammar; learning by heart and reciting it back, I discovered, was a nice resource.

A telegram came (it was always that: the telephone had not really entered people's lives), it said, *staying till Sunday do you mind.* It was marked *Venice.* She did come back, alone, looking beautiful (but then she always did that). You have been to *Venice?* I said, was it heaven? It was. She showed me snapshots of herself lying in a gondola. Who held the camera? I asked and she looked at me and she laughed. Doctor Caligari? I said (it came to me out of nowhere at that moment to my own surprise). My mother laughed again and seemed quite pleased with me. 'Do stop calling him by that silly name.' And I laughed too and said that I knew it was only the name of a film, and after that and for ever it was as if some ice had been broken between us.

*   *   *

That was the beginning of a time of confusion, sudden journeys, new places, waiting – where did we go and in what order? and who went and who came? How long did he or we stay? Memories overlap, go blank. Alessandro, as we now called Titian's Man with the Glove, had fallen in love with my mother. Intensely so. She, at that first stage, took it lightly. She was amused, flattered, elated. She had never before been interested in a man who was not a contemporary and preferably an elder, and who (with the exception of my father whose cover of eccentricity had misled her) was not at least an equal in what for want of a better term one might call a certain sophistication of speech and mind. Alessandro's mind, she told me, was no more formed than mine. Anyway it was folly: he was far too young. A gap of over, *well* over, fifteen years in cold fact; up to her to stop it here and now. Well, perhaps not *just* now.

Alessandro turned up again at Cortina. My mother sent him packing. Already at some cost to herself? Then relented; then sent him off again. Meanwhile there was the still open question of her marriage to O. *That* would be one way out, she said, but she would not take it, she owed that much to O. He would not take no by post for an answer and pressed for a meeting. She said that she owed him that as well. She asked him to Cortina, he refused; she would not go to Florence. So we moved on to Merano, another resort, a sheltered resort basking in late autumn sunshine. I rather think that Alessandro followed and had to be sent off again. At last O came. For the first time I met an authentic artist. (Snob, my mother called me.) He took trouble to talk to me, I found this handsome; he talked well and seemed to know a good deal about many things; he reminded me of my sister's husband who had let me listen to Stravinsky. (How I longed for us to settle down!) To my mother he also made himself pleasant company. All he asked of her was not to make a final decision now: he would give the other thing six months, he would give it a year, he would wait for her verdict then. She told him that six *weeks* would be too long, if it was to be stopped it had to be stopped now. He must have said, Well then, do. To me she said (in front of me, rather than to me; most of the things she told about herself came out that way), Never marry to run away from something. Once was enough, never again. If I give up Alessandro now I might as well give up the world!

How old was she then? thirty-eight? thirty-nine? (I knew that she'd had me late.) O left, still his unruffled self, making it clear that he did not regard himself as out of her life. Alessandro arrived with such despair over O's visit that my mother went off with him for a week. I was on my own again. The hotel wasn't nearly as nice but there happened to be a Swedish brother and sister staying there, older than I and very wild: they seemed to be able to do anything. They egged each other on, climbing, racing, trespassing, staying up shiveringly late. I became intoxicated by their company, and was hard put to keep up, pretending that I, too, had always lived dangerously. To hold my own I initiated rigging up a begging bowl plastered with a symbol much like a Red Cross bearing the legend 'Soccorso d'Inverno', Winter Relief. We put on our most neat and despised clothes and actually went about the public gardens of Merano collecting for this bogus charity. We made nice money and were levitating with the sense of our wickedness and peril.

My mother came back alone and we moved into a pensione (there seems to have been a small cloud of money trouble looming), pending, she said, a suitable nunnery that would take in both of us. There followed a rather listless time. Shall I send you to school? Should I keep you with me? Either will entail complications. Oh, I've burnt my boats so! Perhaps not all my boats. Will you bear with me a little longer?

*   *   *

It had become winter, my mother spoke of going South. (At last!) She also spoke of the problems besetting Alessandro's future – he wanted to be an architect but had to interrupt his studies, he was one of a large family, his mother the widow of an academic, and Italy facing hard times. One brother was trying to farm, several still at school, another about to marry money . . . You know how tight knit those families are, or rather you don't, but I am beginning to. And how would I fit in? After more delays (my mother's own movements were curbed by a couple of bogeymen, her trustees – always heard of, never met), we set off for Naples. At Verona we were joined on the train by Alessandro. It was the first time we had been travelling à trois and when we got to the hotel and I heard him ask for two rooms only my heart sank: so I was to have a room of my own no longer. When this turned out not to be the case I was as surprised as I was relieved; for all my standing by as it were when men and women fell in love, I was entirely ignorant and incurious.

I can still see, smell, hear what was offered that first night at Naples: the Bay, Vesuvio, dinner on the waterfront – *frittura, melanzane, mozzarella* – the beggars, the songs; the tourist banalities of the Italian South were piercingly new to me; this, I told myself, is where I want to be: I was swept off my feet. (I had also had a round amount of wine.) Next day we went on to Sorrento where we stayed at a cold, clean, whitewashed pensione while my mother was looking for a house. There seemed to be some difficulty and it certainly had to do with money. I was never quite clear about my mother's finances except that hers, too, were going downhill. From having been well-off she appeared to have reached a point where she had to be very careful (this was not in her nature). She had never owned any money, she had the use of money (in trust long before I was born and to come to me ultimately; in point of fact it never did: when the time came it had evaporated, but that is another story). The present stringencies – they increased over the years and, unlike my father, she tried to ignore them – may have had something to do with all those boats she said she had burnt and there was also the fact that she had been allowed to use a chunk of capital to buy the Feldkirch estate for my father at the time of their marriage, and had simply let him keep it after the divorce. Generosity? Fatalism? A sense of having done for good with that part of her life? Possibly all of these.

It was during our stay at the Pensione Emilio that the news came of my father's sudden death. My mother was much affected. She, who had been so full of ridicule, who had been dining out on my lessons and my wardrobe and the tales of rural life . . . She talked about him, torrents of talk: about the old times, the good times, when he was in pursuit, a winged pursuit, in Paris, not much longer ago, she said, think of it! than a dozen years. I listened, trying to blend what I was told with what I had known. Death, the disappearance of a being who had lived, I shut out from thought and feeling. What I did express to myself was that now I would never go back, would not have to go back, *did not want to go back*. That part of my life, that country, was over.

My mother captivated by her looks alone, yet what drew most men and women into her orbit at first meeting was her talk. She was an extraordinary talker, a storyteller who could make the truth with all its ambiguities come whole: the moment, the connections, the perspectives. It was also never relentless, quite interruptible, full of self-mockery, and it was often very very funny. I saw that Alessandro loved to listen to it as much as I did – *that* was our education. We saw that acts had predictable ends and yet not, that there were always more than two sides to anything, and that what you did yesterday would be relevant to things to come. We were avid to learn, both he and I. The talk often began at breakfast, she in her bed, we sitting on it, and the hours went and little would get done. She paid no regard to my age or his feelings. With nonchalant openness she told about that great 'previous attachment', the man she had loved so much and had to leave, and how she had chosen my father – affected too by the magnetic field of his pursuit of her – as a retreat into a different world, and how wonderfully unconventional my father's (he guessed about it all) attitude had been. (New light for me.) Unconventional too, one might say, was Alessandro's attitude: he accepted these resurrections of her past; to him they were ingredients of her legend.

*   *   *

Something went wrong. Alessandro had to go North to see his family. Look after her, he said to me, try to cheer her up; I'll be back soon. How soon? I would have liked to ask. He added on his own: As soon as I *can*.

I was grateful to him for his trust, but I was unable to divert her. She hardly spoke; our meals had become silent. One winter afternoon we went for a walk along the beach. Her steps, she was walking ahead, were uncertain, she had slender ankles and was wearing the wrong shoes, she was not looking where she put her feet. Watching that walk I was gripped by an unaccustomed feeling: pity. My mother was not the kind of person one felt sorry for; she always seemed to be holding an advantage point. She sat down on a rock. I stood in front of her. How *can* he come back, she said, they want him at home, they need him at home – I can see how *they* see it: a foreigner, a divorcée and of course the proverbial woman old enough to be his mother; a dubious Catholic as well. They won't *let* him come back and *he*'s not strong enough.

He *will* come back, I said. He told me so.

And how can it last? He's too young. He'll always be too young. We met at the wrong time. Come to think of it, there could never have been a right time, given the dates of our births. *That* is the inevitable factor. I'm a fool but not such a fool as not to know that we are headed for great unhappiness . . .

'Billi – can you understand that one can miss one human being, *one* presence . . . in the whole of the universe . . . to the point of . . . well, extinction of all else? One day *you* will know too.'

'Yes,' I said.

I was able then to love my mother. I wished her well. I saw that there might be things in store for which there was no help and no answer. For the first time I felt the sting of compassion; I never forgot that afternoon by a grey Mediterranean.

*   *   *

He did not come back. He sent for her instead. She had to leave me by myself again: it could not have been a trickier moment. As my father was dead, a German court was appointing a legal guardian; they would not accept my mother nor anyone she proposed, they required some-body resident in Germany. I said I would have my sister's husband, the deputy mayor. Are you sure, my mother said, your sister is such a bad picker? I like him, I said. He's on our side. I don't think *anyone* is going to be on our side, she said. But all right, let's have him, and meanwhile we'd better lie doggo for a bit – don't open any buff envelopes with great German seals while I'm away.

She stayed away for what seemed a long time. I was beset with the heavy feeling of afternoons, the sense of standing still, of belonging nowhere. It was warm in daytime, out on the terrazzo, on the sunny side of the street, indoors it was cold. I had not known that the South could be so cold. The pensione was empty; the owners, the hard-working owners, the Emilios, were kind to the *bambina*. Oh they were more than that. I was living with the open-armed emotions of Italian working people: their goodness, simplicity, affection reminded me of my father's Lina, but in that village Lina had been a rare bird; here, lovingness splashed like the quick water from the fountains, and the current of shared humanity flowed through the most trivial of daily exchanges. All the same I did not weep in Signora Emilio's arms, nice though it would have been, because of her criticism – unspoken – of my mother. Chivalry forbade. I still had an old racket and found a wall against which I could play tennis solitaire. The ball kept going over garden fences which meant ringing doorbells and apologies; one man got furious and that put a damper on the game. When O was with us at Merano he had bought me something I had much coveted in the shops, a pair of those Tyrolese shorts made of beautifully soft chamois leather, complete with embroidered braces and white linen shirts. To boost my morale I put on these shorts and a nice clean shirt for *la cena* in the evening. I was soon aware that this was frowned upon – girls at Sorrento were no better off than girls at Feldkirch, in an obscure way I was causing scandal again. I hardened myself: I no longer took pleasure in my shorts but I went on wearing them. When at last they returned – this time they returned together, mummy and Alessandro – I was taken to Pompeii for a treat.

*   *   *

Life became settled unsettled. We went to Capri for a time (where someone gave me lessons), then back to the mainland, then over to Sicily, to Palermo, Taormina, Syracuse.

'Are we on the run, mummy?'

'You might call it that.'

'Are you . . . Will you . . . ?'

'No, darling, we're not going to get married. He wants to, I will not. I'm sure I'm right. *Carpe diem*. And don't look so many questions.'

She and Alessandro must have had troubles. I was one of them. (Fancy taking the child with them, *they* were saying; *they* seemed to be looming everywhere.) The buff envelopes were slow to catch up with the postes restantes, but they came. My sister's husband had been accepted as my legal guardian. Then my sister left him, like that, out of the blue, running away with a young good-for-nothing (was there any stability in our family life?) and my brother-in-law, ex-brother-in-law, backed out. I became the ward of a court and the court wanted to know where I was. It was my mother now who was badgered about educating me. On principle she was all for it, being well educated herself, at home as it happened; she believed in tutors though at present this was awkward – local lights were engaged when they could be found but did not amount to much. Alessandro tried to teach me algebra which he knew but was not very good at making clear; besides, my mother, for whom time did not exist, would interrupt.

Another source of awkwardness was my father's will, an impossible will as the courts conceded in the fullness of time. He had left the château and contents to my half-sister and myself provided that the estate was never sold and the collection preserved *in perpetuum*. There was no money for upkeep, to keep the place in repair, the objects dusted and warmed, the taxes paid (there were horrendous arrears). My sister decided to contest the will but could not do so without my consent: I was a minor, my mother's address (by then) was poste restante Agrigento, my official guardian a court. The court prevaricated; meanwhile money was required, considerable sums, and there was *no* money (just a bundle of old banknotes in my father's safe made worthless by inflation). To raise something on the estate required my consent and there we began again. My mother's trustees, expressing dismay and distaste by post, offered to maintain me temporarily if a suitable establishment were found. The German court expressed itself in similar terms. It was not put soothingly and the prospect frightened me. (The court sat in a market town in Baden, the sight of its postmark made me feel sick for many years to come.) At the time my mother just kept our heads in the sand.

'Darling,' (my mother one morning) 'I don't think I can spend the rest of my life at Agrigento, besides it's not as warm – you've noticed? – as it's cracked up to be. Alessandro and I are thinking of going to North Africa, we think we'd like to try Tunisia.'

'Africa!' I said. 'Another continent!'

'You *have* taken to travel . . . Perhaps not quite the moment. You see, we can't have you on the run as well.'

'Yes . . . ?'

'So duck, I think you had better go to England.'

'To an *establishment*?'

'If that's what you call a school.'

'What school, mummy?'

'Ah, there you have me. How can I choose a school from Sicily? Can you see the Italian post coping with all those prospectuses? So I thought I'd better send you to some friends and they'll find one for you. I've written to Susan and Jack – you can't just ask anyone to do that kind of thing for you, but they're very easy-going. They have dozens of children so it shouldn't be difficult. The trustees will pay your fare and the fees. They're both painters; you admire artists, I've noticed. I didn't like to ask any of my stuffier friends . . . Anyway you'll find Susan and Jack charming.'

'Where do they live in England?'

'How precise you're being. Actually they move about a good deal. I wrote to Susan's people's address.'

'Mummy, when am I going?'

'As soon as I hear from them.'

PART THREE

In Transit: England–Italy

A LESSANDRO took me to the Italian mainland by ferry and train, an escort from some agency was to pick me up at the French border, Susan, Mrs Robbins, to meet me at Victoria Station. The middle stage, Naples to Ventimiglia, I was to travel on my own, connections looked up, ticket in hand. Before parting I asked Alessandro, having mustered courage for this along the way, How long will you and mummy be in Africa? He said he did not know, he did not know at all. You do like travel? I said. You see, he said, I've had so little before. What I remember of my own journey is that it was long, bedragglingly long. France did not register, maybe I slept through France. When it came to the Channel steamer I was drugged with tiredness but waked a little to the new smells. I endured the crossing. Dover and the sight of a waiting train – a small-looking train – and other new smells, soot, unfamiliar tobacco. In London it was evening once more – the third? – and Mrs Robbins met me, we were lolling in a wide taxi cab, startled by enormous red buses and then we were in the lobby of the Green Park Hotel (long since defunct), it was heated and plushy and more like the house in Voss Strasse, Berlin, to breathe in than anywhere I had been for years. Can that really be you? Mrs Robbins now said. She called me by my unabridged first name which no one ever did. 'I got the impression you were *much* older . . . That you were supposed to go to finishing school . . . ?' 'Oh, no,' I said.

She gave me another look and took me upstairs in a lift; to a large room with long windows on street-lamps and trees, and a bathroom with cascades of hot water. I was in bed almost at once, a tray came with biscuits and something milky and warm, and I felt I had reached comfort and safety.

Next day, Susan – I was to call her that, and she was charming, just as my mother had said – took me to the National Gallery and to eat at the Chinese restaurant overlooking Piccadilly Circus. Altogether this was a high moment almost ranking with the night by the Bay of Naples – the hub of an Empire, I said to myself. In the afternoon we took a train to the Midlands.

*   *   *

And that was the beginning of a life that was to me intensely exotic and of course to real English people not exotic at all. On the train Susan did a bit of explaining – I knew from the tone that something was up – we were going to her father and mother's house (only for a little while of course), she and Jack had had to give up their cottage, Jack had started doing frescos, frescos didn't seem to catch on awfully well – actually, you see, we're broke. I did see.

The house was on the edge of the town and quite large, and the household too was large. Granny, maiden aunts, unmarried sisters, a line of female servants: housemaids, parlourmaid, cook, and of course the masters, the old people, Susan's mother and father. There weren't dozens of children, just two girls at home between schools, Marjory and Joan, big girls in their teens, older than I, younger than Doris. You're a foreigner, they said. I don't know, I answered. They lost interest. (Hadn't much to begin with.) Meals were worlds apart from any I'd known, twice as many meals as there were in Italy. They were what they were sixty years ago before quiche, kebab and pasta had become ubiquitous in the land – breakfast off the sideboard (this I found splendid), another big spread at four p.m., main meals a steady rotation; after wishy-washy soup and a bit of fish, beef and mutton, hot joint, cold joint, mince, cutlets, hot joint, cold joint – pickles, bottled sauces, dispirited salads, custards, vegetables that were about par with Feldkirch cookery and puddings that were much better. Drink was water, soda water or barley water. Tea was offered again at bed-time. There were morning prayers and these made me feel odd. Was the family Church of England? Now I think they may well have been something more strict and narrow, then it didn't occur to me that there were niceties in heresy; if I had lapsed from my religion, its teachings still told me to recognise no other. No one asked me questions. This may have been a way to make me feel at home. Jack's mother-in-law had given him the use of the garden-room as a studio (this was regarded as indulgence), and he asked me to sit for him; he needed a child for a large composition. When I wasn't sitting I was encouraged to work the pianola – much more enjoyable – as Jack liked music while he worked. For the rest of the time I seem to have been trotting after Marjory and Joan on their not unpleasant round of following an aunt leaving orders at the grocer's and the green-grocer's, changing library books at Boots, taking turns for fetching grandad from the works in the pony trap. Did it really happen? Did people ever live as they do in an E. F. Benson or an Agatha Christie novel? On Wednesday afternoons we went to the cinema, and, casually, miraculously, there was tennis! Tennis with a live opponent on an actual court. Contrary to my early aspirations I never got any good at it at all.

What did I learn, what did I unlearn from that first piece of England? It was all such a far cry from my mother, from the village school, from the Pensione Emilio. I caught on that people did not shake hands every time they met in the morning or parted for the night, that they kept reading newspapers when they were sitting in a room together; I learned of another kind of cold, in bedrooms that were never heated, in stark bathrooms where there was yellow soap and tooth mugs slopping with disinfectant; of a new kind of warmth when you toasted yourself piecemeal before a fire. I learned that servants were not quite so easily people you threw your arms about and laughed and cried with, and yet they were kind enough – it was all quicksand. Jack and Susan, too, were not consistent, they were different on their own away from the family table. There was a brother who did not live in the house, who helped run the works (tractors, I think, agricultural engines) and from his visits one somehow gathered that Susan and Jack were not all that was expected of them. One day Jack said that he and Susan wanted to speak to me, we had a conference, they called it, sitting the three of us in the makeshift studio.

Your school now . . . Susan had been arranging for a place but it's for older girls, so we would have to start again. We've been thinking about it – you know it won't be easy to find the right kind of school for you; Marjory and Joan didn't get on in any of theirs, they loathed each more than the last. So we have a suggestion to make, it's up to your mother of course, but we wanted to know how you felt about it. Would you like to go on staying with us? doing lessons with a tutor? We'd keep the girls at home too and club together so we could get someone really good to teach you. We're thinking of moving to London – Jack thinks he's got a chance to do posters. You'd be a kind of PG, if you know what that is, it'll come to no more than your school fees. What do you think your mother would say to that?

Oh, *she*'s in favour of private education, I said.

What about yourself now? There *are* advantages about school, you'd be with people of your own age . . . You must think about it.

I did not. I fell for the plan at once. No *establishment*, no new change, the line of least resistance.

I took trouble over the letter to my mother, to be enclosed in Susan's, urging our case. By the time her answer came – a reluctant yes – we were already ensconced in a flat in Hampstead. So the pattern for the rest of my childhood and early adolescence was set. It was a key decision and, as I knew even then, it was my own. Circumstances allowed me to make a choice when I was still incapable of weighing what the choice involved. Life with Susan and Jack – once they had escaped their parents and the starched servants – was cheerful, easy-going; they enjoyed being artists even if they weren't successful ones and were light-hearted over their periodic financial disasters. They were nice people, kindly people, naively bohemian, quite as delighted as I was to find themselves eating out at a Charlotte Street trattoria. They were good to me but had no intention of playing foster parents – I was lodger and stranger, a near equal from another tribe; that I was a child was largely ignored; as long as I looked after myself, that was the unspoken compact, and caused no trouble with my shadowy guardians, I could do as I pleased.

As far as my education went, they were as good as their word. At first. They found me a tutor, a woman with a history degree; I bicycled to her flat twice a day, and loved it. No more parroting by heart – I was taught properly. Jack's posters did not catch on, London was expensive, we were being mildly dunned ... After less than a year we left the Hampstead flat one early morning riding on the furniture van – it felt both an escape and a picnic. For a time we lived on the South Coast; in various places, once in one of those converted old railway carriages by a beach, there I used to read in an upper bunk by a one-candle light. Then when finances got really low, we went back to the parental Midlands; then to a series of country cottages, another stretch in London when Susan had been promised a show. So it went on. For my teachers, as in Italy, we had to rely on local lights; some of them were good, others less good. I did work on my own but it suffered from lack of supervision. People we saw were mostly grown-ups, casual ones at that, Susan and Jack picked up friends and we were often a crowd, but they, too, like the rest of our life were here today and gone tomorrow. When there was money there was drink in the house, gin, red wine: Australian burgundy of deplorable memory and Chianti so-called, a meal out, the pit in a theatre ... Second-hand cars were acquired with optimism, parted from sorrowfully. I had pocket money, and we all borrowed from each other freely. My clothes had become almost as run down as they had been at Feldkirch, my daily costume being a blue serge school tunic handed down from Marjory or Joan. When my father's estate was finally settled – the will broken, the house sold, the contents sold – my sister (did I hear from her? a dozen lines now and then scrawled large over a page of crested paper; she had her own troubles, big troubles, but these scrawls conveyed nothing of them), well my sister did an imaginative thing, she wanted me to have my father's gold cigarette case and against much opposition she wanted me to have it *now*. She was right there: it gave me more pleasure than it could have at any later time. I carried the case filled with sixpence worth of Craven A, flashing it around in solemn hospitality. They would have let me smoke had I wished; I tried it once or twice, didn't like it, was never tempted again. When we got hard up at the end of the month, I handed the gold case to Susan (Jack was not to be told) who would take the bus to the nearest pawn shop. It was honourably redeemed each time.

Yes, they were nice people, kind people, who kept going by being able to laugh at themselves and at what befell them; for all their muddling they had strength, a very English strength: made up of modesty, pluck, acceptance of the surface of things – tolerant qualities, survivors' qualities (which can keep the sky from falling). Humour was Jack and Susan's weapon to dilute the anguish of existence with its infinite possibilities of disaster. A useful weapon, a likeable weapon – not a romantic weapon and not the best for getting at the essence of existence. To me then, growing into my teens, arrogant with intellectual desires, bound on some quest I could not have defined, they were not the people to engage emotions or fire the imagination.

*   *   *

Life was further fragmented by stays in Italy at intervals. The idea had been that I should go there for the holidays but as these were irregular and my mother no more settled than Susan and Jack, I went when asked for. I travelled on my own, trustees sent money and that, by going third class, could be laid out to advantage. I contrived stops between trains, dined in splendour at the Galleria in Milan on real Italian food and wine, put in a little dogged sightseeing in places I'd been told of, quite uncertain yet of my own taste. If it was summer my destination might be some villa on the Mediterranean (oh, the clear water of those uncrowded bays), if winter a chalet in the Dolomites belonging to Alessandro's family where he taught me skiing. He and my mother had got unobtrusively married. *Indissolubly* what's more, she said, do you realise there's no divorce in Italy, neither religious nor civil, benighted country (those were the early years of Mussolini). Alessandro would say nothing. I accepted what I found. Most children have a pinch of fatalism and detachment in their composition, they also totter through a jumble of tough observation and absurd mis-judgements. Each Italian visit felt different; some slow almost invisible shifts had occurred, such as the shifts that slide a series of stills into a moving picture. My mother and Alessandro must have been going through a process of establishing a framework, a common ground in the outside world, and there was ever the question – this *was* discussed – of finding an occupation for him. The rented house, the borrowed lodge or flat, was always made liveable, civilised. This they achieved as a team. My mother had a knack of making any room look charming. Alessandro was good with his hands. First thing my mother would hang up her Klee. (She did have a Paul Klee, a present, I understood, from a previous lover, and she took it wherever she went; once when that love was brand new, she had propped up the Klee in the compartment of her wagon-lit.) Then they would move the furniture around and if it was sombre or ugly they'd paint it over with some pleasant colour (this often caused trouble with the owners). Alessandro could knock together an efficient ice-box from old packing cases, sawdust and tin in a matter of hours, then embellish it and the kitchen cupboard with fragments of pastiche – a couple of Braque cubes, a trace of a Marie Laurencin – he was quick on the visual uptake; anything he had seen once, if only in a book, he'd have the hang of it. My mother seemed pleased by such feats and would show them off in her slightly deprecatory manner, as she would show off, say, my spouting chunks of poetry, implying that we, he and I, were rather clever if hardly original for our age and station at things she could have done with her hands tied behind her back. Her married life had an audience now, friends staying at the house, overflowing into local hotel or pensione. My mother's friends they were and during those early years mostly women. She did have women friends and was loyal and devoted to them, as they were to her: attracted – she was always a centre – by her vitality, the flowing talk that seemed to give a point to everything they did, the laughter. They also grew attached to Alessandro. They had come to judge – *Twenty years younger . . . Much* too handsome . . . And what does he *do*? – they stayed to bask in his company. He liked women and showed it, it was as simple as that; he treated them indiscriminately in a light flirtatious way, all on the surface, quite public. It might have given offence, apparently it did not. Yet there was not the slightest doubt in anyone's mind that his entire devotion was for my mother. Alessandro's serious leanings – so far – had been towards women older than himself; his first affair, when he was little more than a boy, had been with a married lady in her forties whom he was still fond of and occasionally visited. As for other friends, he seemed to have shed them for the present; men bored him and men's talk (though he himself was not in the least an effeminate man). He had not shed his family. They too came and stayed, mingling or not with my mother's friends. They – there was Mama and a gang of young brothers and cousins – seemed to have accepted his marriage with fairly good grace: his father was dead and Alessandro, though not the eldest, was his own man. Mama was a vigorous woman, embarrassingly youthful, with a clear face and a manner that often missed being tactful. She and my mother managed; she jangled her son's nerves, which he visibly controlled. My mother, I guessed, was quietly doing something for the brothers, helping to put one through university, pulling strings for another (she had not burnt *all* her boats). That was a period when the money situation was on some sort of even keel, the trustees too had accepted the marriage and were underwriting my mother's refound respectability. We lived in modest comfort. There was little mention of bills and no utopian attempts to grow our own potatoes, which seemed indicators of high financial stability to me. I, by the way, had an allowance now out of my father's estate which was paid by the courts to whomever I was living with. We had servants. A cook, a maid, an older woman coming on washing day (when the wash was taken to the communal stream or trough); I quickly forgot the early skills acquired as a sub-drudge in the German village and became oblivious of housework. The time I had now, I spent reading. They were nice servants, Italian servants, which was synonymous; it was they who provided an element of continuity. Not that they remained long the same, there was no family factotum to follow our geographical changes – Erminia . . . Fosca . . . Renata . . . Camilla . . . your faces and names are as fused now as the places: were you with us at Positano? on Capri? at Fiesole? What remained constant was what they gave to us, to the house, to themselves, a compound arising from their natures and traditions: hard work, dignity, much laughter; cleanliness to the degree where it becomes an aesthetic element; generosity in their dealings: *gentilezza*. It was reciprocated. Here Alessandro was perfect. Mutual respect, trust, emotions shown at crisis times, without familiarity. Young he might be, he was *il signore*, the master. With me, too, it was good. Good at the stage when I was the *bambina*, the child of the house (they, the servants, treated me as such); and still good later when they felt I should reach the *signorina* stage, still easy, affectionate, though it wasn't a stage – if one translates *signorina* as young lady as I suppose one must – I ever came much to terms with.

It was my mother, sad to say, who did not quite fit into that gentle, balanced circuit. Perhaps it was her way of treating everyone as a conversational equal that misfired with these women of Italian peasant stock – her fluidities against their bedrock – she never shirked giving as good as she did not get, so her egalitarian sharpness was meted out however young you might be or ignorant or dependent. And there was her temper. Quick, violent at its peak, soon over. But shocking because such a breach of the ironic cool: the maids were afraid of her (as I had been, still could be). When china got broken or the stove went wrong, they'd come to Alessandro to act buffer. What was worse: they did not really like her. Curious perhaps as my mother thought of herself as a socialist (on Fabian lines). I lapped it up; Alessandro, who followed her lead in so many ways, poohpoohed it. There was a rankling episode when the three of us and a woman friend found ourselves at an hotel at Bologna while a waiters' strike was taking place. My mother went into the street and marched with the workers and banners. Not a half bottle of *acqua minerale* was to be had at our hotel let alone a crust, and the restaurants and food shops were tight shut. We were cross and very hungry. My mother returned with shining eyes replete with the cause and human fellowship. Didn't you get ravenous? we asked. Oh, the comrades had sustained her with delicious salami, fresh bread, *fiaschi* of wine . . . Did you bring some back? Oh, she said – I forgot.

Our own food was good, simple good. Pasta made at home, clear lean broth distilled from a scrap of beef and a barnyard fowl, vegetables picked out in the market in the morning, lemons and olive oil, in those fragile green phials blown at Murano, always on the table; meat conceived as garnish more than hunk: aromatic fillings in *pomodori* and *melanzane,* slivers of veal done with a light hand; salads of tender leaves. And always the abundance of fruit, Sicilian oranges in winter and baked apples and pears; the apricots, green almonds and cherries of early summer; later peaches, figs, melons, at last the ripe grapes . . . It was wholesome food, genuine food, never played-about-with, show-off food, and its basic assumptions were honesty of materials, a feeling for texture and a nice attention to both plenty and thrift. (Indeed, we always ate up the scrap of beef and the barnyard fowl.)

I enjoyed that food, how not? We all did, having healthy appetites but, like the Italians we lived amongst, took it for granted. Now it would be regarded as pastoral, utopian and luxurious beyond the dreams of cuisine naturelle and the cost of health shops. What struck me then was the democratic pattern of Italian meals – everybody who had anything to eat at all ate (with regional differences) more or less the same. It was a very big more or less of course and I felt that I knew something about that too: about rich and poor, village life and château life, Susan hanging on by means of the pawn shop, and the ways Fosca and Camilla's families scratched a living. I ruminated on what went on around me and derived pleasure from sorting out the contrasts. The proper study of mankind . . . ? Food? I might have done worse. Food is as revealing as money and sex, and is revealed more often. People can't wait to tell you that they mustn't eat cabbage or have a craving for puddings; whereas how frequently do you hear, I've got ten thousand in my deposit account, or I can't bear parting with small change? As for truth about sex . . . Anyway at that point I thought little about that and guessed less. I had a kind of unhurried sense that there was a side to adult life – possibly agreeable – that would disclose itself when the time was right, an odd incuriosity possibly prompted by my mother's casual disclosures and my reading so much beyond my years. It simply *was* beyond my years. (A friend once told me that as a small boy – he was the son of Aldous Huxley and thus not exactly reared in an intellectually deprived environment – he had read through a French two-volume history of Anne of Austria under the unwavering impression that the subject was a female donkey: *Âne d'Autriche*. But then the poor chap, like me, was brought up trilingual.) My interest in how people lived was nourished quite literally by the food I shared with them. Table customs, I had long realised, were divisive. What chasm between the aspic-upon-soufflé of our *haute-juiverie* in-laws in Berlin and the sodden starches and cold bacon of the German village. In England I had experienced the alternatives of the imperturbably ordained meals at the parental Midlands home and the casual scruffiness at Jack and Susan's when fending on their own. We did for ourselves – still unusual in the 1920s for people of the middle-class even when badly off. Susan did the cooking, the rest of us took turns in giving or avoiding to give a hand serving and cleaning up. Nobody could say that Susan cooked well or much (though we were fed generously), sausages and rice pudding were about her mark; the bulk of our daily sustenance was convenience food, hideous term, and certainly not as varied or as pseudo-grand as it has since become. No deep-frozen *coquilles Saint-Jacques*: baked beans we had and bloater paste in little glass jars off the corner grocer's shelf, Jello, jam roll, bread and Marmite for tea, fish and chips for supper, with tinned salmon and pineapple cubes as stand-bys. I devoured it all cheerfully enough; what I missed was wine. I had no idea for a long time, that the very best claret, let alone port, was shipped to and drunk by (a few of) the English; I only knew what I saw and that was that wine with meals was an exception not the rule, which happened to be true then for most people. *How* we have changed all that now that England has entered a golden age of wine! (With quality and variety on offer greater than in any other country in the world.) Let us count our blessings.

In Italy we had wine; everyone drank it naturally, liberally, every day, young wine, local and cheap. Ours was chosen by Alessandro or the cook with the same care, no more, as the vegetables and the fish. It was not discussed at table. My claret evenings with my father were part of the world that was behind. Someone sometimes was offered a small glass of vermouth; brandy was kept on hand, Alessandro might be called upon to seal some masculine deal with grappa, besides these there were no spirits in the house nor was there talk about drink or getting drunk although there must have been the odd bucolic soak. Expressions such as having a drink problem had not entered civilised vocabulary. In America Prohibition was already in full swing; in Italy the excesses of alcohol were not yet a 'socially' expected topic.

Our life then during those Italian years was stable and domestic. Though perhaps not that domestic if seen through other people's eyes. Domestic in spirit, say, rather than tangible fact. We never had the same address for long and we can't have had anything near a usual complement of household goods. We certainly never lived, as the French were to remark about us later on, *dans nos meubles*. Why not? Some cautionary instinct to remain in transit? Reluctance to stake upon a future better left undefined? Was it the times? – less than a decade from one war, more than a decade still from another – I do not know. Our attitudes to possessions were not consistent. Alessandro's material belongings were sparse and neat, he dressed with unmistakable if unflaunted elegance on very little; my mother's were profuse, not often utilitarian, seldom to hand and prone to disrepair. While she thought nothing of our living year in year out in other people's sheets and chairs, she seldom travelled without voluminous and unusual luggage. (Never shall I forget the horror, compounded by missed train connections, of her taking a goldfish bowl in live working order.) Still, in those days people did take trunks on railway journeys; my mother's encumbrances shrink in retrospect when I consider that they must have comprised a very fair share of her entire worldly goods. As for myself I had already gone a fairish cycle of from rags to riches, or rather riches to rags because when I was an infant and dwelt in a nursery – the real thing: day nursery, night nursery, an English nanny – in the ugly opulent house of my father's Berlin connections, the cupboards were choked with objects which could be said to have been mine. Doll's house and stable, toy cook stove, toy grocery shop, toy village, clockwork toys, soldiers, puzzles, picture books, plush animals . . . The body of these treasures had been handed down, a few were lavish new personal offerings; I used the pick of them – with intense enjoyment – the rocking horse, the railway train, the building blocks, the tomahawk, the conjuror's box, the puppet theatre, what grist they made for slow-laid, complex games (I nearly always played alone), what diverse lives they opened. At bedtime while I was being scrubbed or brushed I marshalled plans for next day's work in earnest detail with serene absorption till switched off by sleep. It was heaven. Between the ages of three and a half and seven, as I now realise, I was able to lead a life given almost entirely to pleasure. By the time we returned to our house in Baden at the end of the 1914 War, that Aladdin's cave had vanished. Few toys, if any – assuming that some must have been packed – survived our hazardous and protracted journey across a Germany in collapse and revolution, and although the cupboard when we reached Feldkirch cannot have been bare but stocked with relics of our pre-war vie de château, nothing would ever equal the glamorous profusion of the Merzes' accumulated bounty, and in any case existence soon changed radically. My mother went, nanny not long after; what had once been my playroom was in a now unheatable part of the house too remote and spooky even in summer for me to visit ever again; my interests turned to outdoor and farmyard life. When there was time to play, I made my games with shapes I cut out from cardboard boxes, twigs and sticks and pebbles as well as the worn-out tennis balls. Meanwhile there was my father, chained to *his* possessions. The Collection: how I failed, being too young and know-all, to see any virtue or beauty in it (a catalogue of the sale by auction, turned up recently, shows that some of his things *were* beautiful); how I despised him for his attachment to 'objects', objects which I, conceitedly rational, wanted him to sell off so that we should not have to worry over being able or unable to buy other things. However unfeeling this was, the fact remains that the last years of my father's life were almost entirely circumscribed, and not happily so, by his possessions. To this day I have to be careful not to look down on other people's objects and would not own more than a minimum (a relative term) of them, serviceable ones at that, and would swap most potential acquisitions for the joys and comforts, ephemeral though they may be, of the day's living. In my later youth, personal accumulations other than of a featherweight portable nature were not practicable or envisaged. I had a room of my own, blessedly, wherever I was staying. It was seldom the same room the second time round. If I left as much as a pair of tennis shoes, it would vanish. By the time I was thirteen I had attained to a state of possessionlessness appropriate to a monk.

What did we do about books, then, my mother and I? Well, we always had them. Florentine bookshops, parcels from England, finds off landlords' shelves, the Tauchnitz Edition, those invaluable continental paperbacks of that time when even railway stalls would offer well-printed copies of anything from Dickens and Kipling to Temple Thurston and Conan Doyle. My mother's bed was a-stack with books, notebooks, lists, letters: letters received, letters begun, long letters sometimes finished; the paper pond Alessandro called it, and only she knew how to fish it. *The Criterion*? Gibbon Vol. II? Your brother's tailor's bill? Here: under the tea tray, in that kitten's paw (there were dogs and cats sitting on that pond in lieu of ducks and geese). No, we never lacked books, though the books too got lost, left behind, were replaced.

Perversely the sole items that were treasured, kept, passed from hand to hand, were compromising, not to say dangerous, possessions, not openly come by; I am speaking of copies of the *New Statesman* (eventually they included even certain copies of *The Times*). It was I who was charged with circulating the latest issue – children assumed to be politically innocent in the eyes of the strolling Carabinieri – to the dissident's grocery shop or the suspended professor's villa.

When did this begin? At first it was more an undercurrent, a concern shared by some we knew, a distaste rather than a menace, if never quite out of sight and mind; even in my earliest memories of Italy I cannot detach the country from the ubiquitous images of Fascism. Each time I returned there were more black-shirts in the streets, more marching and strutting, more boasts and lies in the newspapers, more posters on the walls. I saw what was to be seen, my mother interpreted and briefed me. What was being put over (by Musso & Co.) was, she was never in doubt, based on trickery and false values, sanctified aggression, pandered to false pride; it made ignorant youth feel important, gave foolish people spurious hopes – it was dangerous stuff. Alessandro, informed by an old, old patience, was more inclined to shrug it off: it was bad, there was little in politics that was not . . . Hadn't they seen it all before, Invasion, Defeat, Occupation; Attila, Buonaparte, the Austrians . . . They come, they go, we survive, it will pass. Everything does, my mother would say, but *when*? And *meanwhile* . . . ? Oh, Italians have no talent for public life, they may be for it – justice, disinterested administration – but they don't know how to get it: they *accept* corruption. (Crack jokes about it as you do, Alessandro.) When their rulers are too bad, they duck; retreat into personal relations, family relations – there you'll find riches of good behaviour, devotion *and* honour as well as endurance and courage. Out in politics they are opportunists and show-offs, clever when they ought to be straight-forward, rhetorical when they ought to go home and think, and they haven't learned how to compromise without treachery. (She would turn to me, Oh how lucky you are being brought up in England, I'm so glad you are getting a liberal education.) It won't stick, Alessandro said, Musso's dream: playing lions, days without pasta, little boys carrying daggers, it's too silly, we're not cut out for regimentation.

Not individually. But what about the yelling in Piazza Venezia? Crowds are vulnerable to a harangue, to torches and lit-up façades and the prospects of glamour, even sham glamour – and not only Italian crowds, are there many people who have learnt to be consistently human *en masse*?

$$* \qquad * \qquad *$$

As it happened I had just been sent for again so I was there in the summer of 1924 – we had taken a house on the Sorrentine peninsula – when Matteotti, the leader of the opposition as it were, was kidnapped and murdered.[1] We were out at sea in an open fishing boat that August

---

[1] Giacomo Matteotti, if I may briefly recall the events, Secretary General of the Italian Socialist Party, then still legal, attacked the Fascist regime in Parliament on 30th May 1924 (the speech was published in the British Press); on 10th June he was abducted by hired thugs; on 16th August his body was discovered. There was an abortive inquiry. At the time the murder appeared to shake the regime up to a point; as we know, it survived.

day when another boat hove to and men shouted the news that Matteotti was dead – his body had been found in a hole. How shocked we were then and how hopeful. In the ensuing weeks people came to us, buoyed, euphoric, counting straws in the wind – the regime would not be able to weather such outrage, Mussolini was going to fall. Too soon it became clear that it had indeed been a turning point, that the deed, the criminal deed, the big enough deed had paid off (as nine years on, the burning of the Reichstag paid off): Matteotti gone, opposition suppressed, *il Fascismo* acclaimed, getting the upper hand. And so more tales – only they were *not* tales – of official chicanery, neighbours and relatives sacked from university posts or refused renewal of their annual patent to practise as doctors and lawyers because they had failed to become party members or to vote *sì* at the plebiscites, house searches next door (always for papers, books, not drugs nor arms), purges, disappearances, nocturnal arrests became part of our daily experience. It was early and at first hand that I learnt what life can be like when there is no freedom of thought, and rule by decree, not law.

One of Alessandro's brothers went off to live in Ireland with an Englishwoman he had met, another decided to continue his studies in Vienna; Alessandro himself suspended all thought of qualifying as an architect. We trundled along day by day: we swam, we walked, we played games, we listened to my mother; often there were stimulating guests. Cousins, too, strayed in, stayed on, a good-looking lot they were, every boy of them. And at the centre of it all was my mother's marriage. What appeared of it, the surface of it was low-key, curiously ordinary as if they were both resolved to ignore their great disparity of age. (In actual years, he was nearer to me than to her.) His feeling for her showed mainly in a kind of watchfulness: whatever she was doing, whomever she was talking to, he was alert, aware of her in the room, in the next room, tense to be off and by her side even before the summons; yet his actual manner was bantering, light, smoothing out the recurrent crises – she was always late, always losing the essential objects, ticket, key, at the stage that mattered. His humorous, protective ease did not tally with the sombre despair of the very young man, the melancholy aloof young man of our first encounters. Was it being married that changed people so? And what of her? It was she who puzzled me. She seemed . . . well, content, complacent one might say, taking his attendance casually (as she did mine): it was well, it was daylight, settled, *domestic*. Had I dreamt it all? The wind of passion, the heart-piercing isolation, the sense of foreboding in the days when we were fugitives at Agrigento?

And then it would be time for me to go. The summer or the span of winter weeks was over; back to England then by another of my devious little journeys. Did I mind? Yes and no. Sad to leave Italy; looking forward to I didn't know quite what (a notion that some day there might be other fish for me to fry in England?). I felt more free there in my detached existence with Susan and Jack, if not without a twinge of guilt about the misconceptions my mother appeared to accumulate about its nature and which I was wary to dispel.

*   *   *

Thus Italy and England as I grew older, as I grew up, were home base. Strictly speaking I had no home in either: I *lived* there, in those two countries – as I would in later life, intermittently, not definitely – lived, felt at home, at home on a visit. Italy I loved. At the beginning, in childhood, the love was romantic: I was carried away by a warmth of life and by the recognition, yet unformulated, that there among those artefacts and landscapes I stood on the ground of an intense and relevant European civilisation (the conscious taking in of the visual experience came later). My attachment to England was instinctive, a bid for, if not roots, a kind of self-preservation. From early on I had the absolute if shadowy conviction that I would become a writer and nothing else; I held on to the English language as the rope to save me from drifting awash in the fluidities of multilingualism that surrounded me. My German beginnings I discounted, sought to obliterate. In this I succeeded for a number of years until the force of circumstances became too great.

PART FOUR

Anchorage: France

1

BY 1926 THE ANGLO-ITALIAN pattern was disrupted: less than two years after the murder of Matteotti, the Italian base was whisked from under my feet. A summons to join my mother came in an envelope that bore a French stamp with over-printed legend *Sanary-sur-mer-ses-sites-son-climat*. When I had managed to separate place from travel slogan, I went to look for it on a map: Sanary-sur-Mer in small print on the south coast of France between the great ports of Toulon and Marseille.

'One autumn in the late nineteen-twenties for no particular reason at all, as it would seem, we began to live in France.' So I wrote elsewhere. It is true, except that it was spring and in the mid-, not the late nineteen-twenties, and that the decision, my mother's and Alessandro's, to leave Italy was a reasoned and possibly a wise one. Without being substantially active as resistants, their views were evident to all who liked to pry. A *New Statesman* once too often under my pinafore. They were compromised. They neither fled nor were they exiled; they left discreetly. They were able to retain their passports – Europe was entering an epoch where having documents was vital – and became officially described as members of the Italian colony in France. So far so rational. It was the choice of their destination that was fortuitous. They were on a train, it was evening, they had crossed the border: they were out of Italy, bowling along the French coast encumbered with much luggage and their three Japanese spaniels, one of them a bitch and near her time. It was a slow train – they had muffed the better connections – stopping every few minutes. I have forgotten where they were originally bound for, Aix-en-Provence? Saint-Jean-de-Luz? They *had* laid some plans. What happened was that after a few hours my mother got tired, and tired of the train. She said they might as well call it a day and get off at the next stop whatever that might be. This they did. It was late, the station was a shed and dimly lit; there was a little country bus outside and it took them and their belongings to the nearest available hotel on a nocturnal waterfront. The Hôtel de la Tour. (Still standing.) Next morning they were able to take their bearings – a radiant day, a view on a small fishing port – and liked what they saw. Alessandro was for pushing on to where they had meant to go, my mother became reluctant to budge. Did it matter *when* one started a new life? And by now there were Chumi's puppies: a hint from the gods to remain? Poor Alessandro, he must have been used by then to her superstitions and the fatalism that so easily served her tendency – alas inherited by me – to settle for the line of least resistance. Within a week they had moved into a furnished bungalow at Port Issol, one of Sanary's small beaches.

That house, the first of many, was rented by the month, and when some time later I too was catapulted into the Département du Var, I saw my summer there as another transitory episode. I was fifteen. As it turned out I remained there for the best part of the next fourteen years. In this manner France became the nearest thing I'd ever known as home.

*   *   *

What was it like that French Mediterranean coast between Marseille and Toulon, Toulon and Fréjus, in the nineteen-twenties? Le Petit Littoral, the unfashionable part of the Côte d'Azur (*not* the Riviera) with its string of fishing ports and modest resorts – Cassis, La Ciotat, Saint-Cyr, Bandol, Sanary, Le Lavandou, Cavalaire, Saint-Tropez? The sea and sky were clear; living was cheap; there were few motor cars, *there were few people*. During the holiday months, cafés and beaches filled with visitors, families mostly from French southern towns, Nîmes, Marseille, Montélimar. Neither tourists nor rich went to the South of France in summer, and no Frenchman born north of Valence would have dreamt of exposing his womenfolk and children to the heat. Some of this changed soon. In that very 1926 Colette discovered the aestival Midi, the clarity of the mornings, the stillness of the sun-struck monochrome noons, the magic of the scented nights. She bought a summer house at Saint-Tropez, La Treille Muscate; clans of artists and writers followed with their entourages. From then on visitors became more cosmopolitan and varied: flamboyant or monastic of habit, famous or notorious, as the case might be. They were still not noticeably more numerous.

Sanary in 1926, like Cassis, like Bandol, had about half a dozen small hotels, some pensions, a score or two of (unheatable) villas for summer letting – were there a hundred who came for the *quatorze juillet* and August? a hundred and fifty? The permanent *local* population was about two thousand according to the Michelin of the time; it *has* gone up since though not horrendously so, while the transient summer population has swollen to fifty thousand by the 1980s – need one spell it out in terms of housing estates, car parks? In the decades of innocence the inhabitants lived mostly off each other and the export of vegetables, flowers and fine fish. They were *cultivateurs*, fishermen, shopkeepers, a doctor or two, the *notaire*, the *pharmacien*, the postmistresses, the schoolmistress, the retired naval officer sustained by opium and his books, the stray Scandinavian artist. The fishermen caught sardines, langoustes, red mullet, rockfish, loup de mer, their wives mended the nets – in public on the quai, in winter in the sun, in summer seeking shade – their children collected oursins and mussels. Inland the *cultivateurs* tended their greenhouses, olives and vines. The wine, some honest, some not so honest, red vin du Var was for regional consumption. A family of Swiss *vignerons*, called Roethlisberger, produced a reputable white wine along with their good red, a forerunner of the big, complex post-war wines that achieved the *Appellation Bandol*. Mimosa and carnations, some of the olive oil, the best of the fish and the first of the vegetables were shipped at dawn, the fresh pick or catch of them, to Paris, London, Brussels. Shipped, if we chose to get up early, under our eyes. Every morning except Monday there was a *criée*, an auction sale held in the square at first light – a display, straight from orchards and steep fields of apricots, narcissi, green almonds, artichokes in their leaves, young peas, slim haricots verts curled in flat baskets. It was long before the nouveau franc, or the new pence for that matter: in England a dozen of claret were still sold in shillings, here in Provence the bidding was not just in old francs but in *sous*, five centimes (small is cheap). I have *quinzé sous, quinzé sous*, fifteen *sous*, the auctioneer would sing out in that nasal meridional tone, accenting every syllable, a gnarled little man as crooked as they come, *trenté*, I've thirty *sous* . . . *quaranté – à vous la jolie petite dame . . . cinquanté sous – à toi, Jo-Jo*. And Jo-Jo in his *bleu*, his singlet and his espadrilles would sling the crate of artichokes into his Peugeot *camionnette* . . .

That square, the Place de Sanary, was the meeting point, the stage of social and commercial life. Its backcloth was the Mairie fluttering the Tricolor from an absurd little tower like a fattened minaret, flanked by the church, a pharmacy, a bakery, the Café de la Marine, the Café de Lyon, and two *bars tabacs*. The front of the square opened on the palm walk across the road and the small harbour, where fishing craft and sail boats lay at anchor, and on the sea beyond.

The rest of Sanary proper, Sanary-ville, consisted of a network of a few narrow streets, cleft by the sun only at noon, inhabited by families of *commerçants* and their shops, butchers and bakers, *épiceries, laiteries, cordonneries, quincailleries*, a couple of *bonneteries* where one bought thread, beach hats and canvas shoes. The houses were modestly urban, late eighteenth to mid-nineteenth century, with bead curtains over the doorways, here and there a stone arch, shutters on every window. Outer Sanary was pine groves and palms to eastward, small hotels, most of them new, bathing huts spread thinly between a flat road and the *plage* of Six-Fours; to westward there were hills, pine was relieved by ilex; villas with gardens of a sort (incipient suburbia) followed the contours of rock-bound bays, Port Issol, La Cride, La Gorguette – which became Huxley territory – Bandol. Inland all this vanished.

Inland lay the back country, sun-baked, cicada-loud, the ageless country of scrub and terraced hills where the peasants lived in their sparse stone-built *mas*, the archetypal Mediterranean landscape of rock and olive, wild thyme, vineyards, light.

This I had known in Italy; here there was a difference, a dichotomy: the timelessness of land and sea, and the indelible Frenchness of so much else; if the Midi was Arcadia it was also a Department of France. La République, Third, Fourth or Fifth – *'Françaises et Français!'* – is as tough, as rooted, enduring, cohesive and diverse as the more ancient meridional civilisations, and the conjunction of the perennial austere beauty of climate and nature – scouring mistral, the unfudging sun – with the sweetness and sharpness and quickness, the rippling intelligence, the accommodating tolerance of the French manière de vivre gave one a large sense of living rationally, sensuously, *well*, of pleasure on many levels: now and before us and for years to come, as no other place in Europe, no other place in the world, France between the wars made one this present of the illusion of freedom.

As I was to learn. Later; imperfectly, conjecturally (the French and their ways are infinitely complex), at times sharply, with conscious joy. Not yet then; not during that summer, my first time in France.

*   *   *

I had come by way of Paris, a stopover not attempted before. So the first time I put foot in France, after a sleepy queasy transfer from boat to train, was on the pavement outside the Gare du Nord. I did not kiss the ground; I found a bus to take me to the Gare de Lyon. The female conductor was unamiable about my suitcase, which couldn't have been large. Having left it at the cloakroom, I had the day before me (from noon that was until the last night-train South). I still remember how I spent it and still blush. What did Ernest Hemingway, James Joyce, and Gertrude Stein feel on their first day in Paris, France? I cringe, for I felt nothing very much. But then these illustrious expatriates had not stepped off the quick green omnibus at the Place de la Madeleine at the age of fifteen and a half. That was where I started. I was not impressed and wondered if I should have been. Nor did I know what to make of the unfamiliar façades of the Grands Boulevards, the slate-grey straightness, the compound gusts of smells:

81

open *pissoirs* with tin screens like fire-guards being prominent and numerous. I ate a hurried lunch at a prix fixe and trotted off again. My mother had told me to go to the Tuileries, stand in the Place du Carrousel and look at La Concorde and the Arc de Triomphe beyond. This I did, and the nobility of the perspectives, evidence that the theme contrapuntal to French easeful dailiness is La Gloire, left me not entirely unvisited by a sense of grandeur. It was so again in front of the Hôtel des Invalides.

I visited the Louvre, experienced dumb inadequacy with the *Mona Lisa* and found more familiar enjoyment in the quattrocento rooms. On impulse I went to the Cluny, stabbed by the unexpected memory that this had been my father's favourite museum (Paris: a place he loved), and felt spookishly pulled back among exhibits I could recognise as the source of inspiration for his own collection . . . Oh, I did fill my day. I walked down the Boulevard Saint-Michel, no associations flowered. I missed the Luxembourg, missed crossing the Seine over a bridge on foot, I missed Notre-Dame. I took a bus instead back to the Right Bank to look at the Sacré-Coeur; it was still daylight, hours before night-life, and there was something menacing about the quiescent garishness of Montmartre. I wandered about, unnoticed, unmolested. Eventually I had dinner in some small restaurant. The food was unmemorable (curious point, that). All the same, I must have lingered because I did not miss my train by what seemed seconds, propelled by a furious guard and scolded by a corridorful of dis-agreeable people.

Next morning I was met by Alessandro and my mother at the modest railway stop that serves Sanary-cum-Ollioules, a dot of administrative France so inconsiderable in the countryside that it might have been in rural Mexico. Now it was my turn to be conveyed to what would doubtlessly be another transitory summer home by that ramshackle little station bus. (It continued its not unuseful career for many years to come.) For me its juddering inside remains the scene of a most painful moment of my early life. Rattling along in heat and dust and din, my mother opposite on the wooden seat sprang an entirely uncharacteristic question: *Have I changed?* It went home: there was no lightness in her tone, nothing of the self-mockery that had seen us through so many predicaments, *she* required something from *me*. Her beauty had been an intrinsic attribute, hers by nature, unassisted, worn without vanity, casually, carelessly as a well-bred man is supposed to have worn his clothes. Now it seemed not so. I did what her question imposed, and I did it a fraction too late, I looked at her. I saw what unasked I might not have seen: intimations of wear. Oh she was still beautiful – some might have said more so – what was gone? a glow? She was older.

I can still hear the answer I gave – again not quite quickly enough – the forced voice (and *what* showed in my face?), an answer to the effect that for me she was, she would be, always the same. I remember the exact words but cannot bear to write them down in their shameful inadequacy. My mother, so merciless on verbal shoddiness, let them pass.

The house was small and jerry-built, a bungalow without attempts at amenity or charm: it was less than two minutes' walk from beach and sea and that was it. One entered through a verandah into the kitchen, there was the salle à manger and two largish bedrooms with a very large bedstead and a wardrobe in each and little else; the walls were thin and the wallpaper florid and hideous. It was all quite clean. For once my mamma and Alessandro had not left their mark beyond a scattering of books and dog baskets; a bad sign, I thought. In retrospect the main impression of those weeks I spent with them was constraint. I don't know what, if anything, had happened; we were talking less. One thing was an evident shortage of money – a consequence of their move from Italy? – embarrassing small economies of the kind that upset the young. *I* was used to them with the Robbinses but Susan and Jack cracked jokes: my mother had almost stopped doing that, another bad sign. She had asked me how much money I'd brought and taken it off me without a by your leave. It was understood that Alessandro knew nothing of this, it was like the pawning of my cigarette case – Susan doing the deed, Jack not to be told: so the women think up the hanky-panky while the men are supposed to keep their ignorance? Perhaps Alessandro *had* been allowed to grasp some facts about the erratic nature of his wife's financial situation, and he – who was a neat man and a realist at heart for all his floating on the surface of the days – had in his turn been shaken into some cognisance. Both seemed troubled. The house was kept going by a *femme de ménage* who came in the mornings, a dumpy woman, not too well disposed; we thought her a slut. Supper was cooked by Alessandro or my mother, both quite good quick cooks and he a tidy one as well. We had no guests. No friends had been asked to stay that summer. At Sanary we knew no one: we had not mixed with the summer people and to the inhabitants we were just that.

The house had neither mosquito nets nor screens which made for fuss and inconvenience in the night (mosquitoes being a much greater plague in those days before the Allied Armies had done something drastic, or so one is told, with DDT); one had to undress in the dark if one wanted to keep the window open, and before that one either had to spray with a substance called Flytox, as noxious to humans as it was to those elusive buzz-diving pests, or fumigate. We used little brown cones, Zampironi, which we stood up and lit in saucers where they glowed then crumbled into dust filling the room with acrid smoke. My mother, an insomniac, took more and stronger sleeping pills. Veronal was one of the most potent on the market then and one could get it without prescription, two *cachets* at a time. The chemist allowed my mother four. (Good nature? Carelessness? *Not* profit: they were a few pence apiece; I never knew. That chemist played a painful part in our lives later on.) I went for the veronal, I ran most of the errands. The veronal induced heavy, sometimes alarmingly heavy, sleep. Once or twice I came home from the beach at two p.m. and found Alessandro saying, I can't wake her up. This would be when the evening before they had talked of his need to go away, go to Paris, go to a city, to see a man, to see a woman who might buy a picture or want her house doing up.

I spent much time in the sea (and loved it – summers without water: salt water, rock-pools, open bays, calm pellucid depths, breakers and spray, were like prison to me), I swam as one might stroll, a slow quiet drifting towards horizons not counting distance or hours. It was then that I did my dreaming, shaped what I had seen and thought into sentences, cadences, meaning (so I hoped) – *words* at great speed were running . . . I was writing in my head. It was intoxicating and elusive. When I sat down before that sheet of paper, it was gone. I never wrote in my youth. I was not one of those novelists who filled notebooks lying on the hearthrug when they were tots. For me that struggle (it is that) long postponed, came later.

On Port Issol, our small beach, one could hire a basic kind of canoe, both flimsy and clumsy but a pleasant means of getting out far and swift. One afternoon as I was about to launch this contraption, I bumped into a child who was splashing in the shallows, a fair lanky girl, with straight short hair, of about twelve or more, nice-looking in a boyish way. I wasn't much adept at social intercourse with people of or near my age, but here we were in the sea. I offered her a ride. She got herself into the thing all right and we struck off, I doing the paddling. The sea was glassy flat, the girl very slight, the going was not too heavy, land began to recede. Annette (names, too, come easily in the freedom of the sea) was smiling; or was the smile a little fixed? The way she crouched and clung might make one think that she was putting on a brave act. What about? True the canoe was badly balanced and none too buoyant, it did capsize quite frequently; what of it? One would right it again and after a refreshing dip clamber again aboard. I was about to impart these cheering facts when Annette emitted a weak sound, *Maman.* I looked round and saw a form, still recognisable as female, on the shore, frantically hopping to and fro signalling like a tic-tac man. Annette, still contained, hung her pretty head, '*Je ne sais pas nager* – I 'ave not learn to swim.' Heavens . . . Gingerly I turned us round, tiptoeing, as it were, with the paddle, got her safely back into her depth and on to land, only to run into a human storm. The first encounter with *la bourgeoisie française à sa proie attachée!* Madame Panigon – *Maman* – knitting dropped, arms raised *au ciel*, vast in wintry clothes, was furious and let me have it. My own mother had appeared – we were only a stone's throw from that beach which had become a stage dominated by a gorgon in full spate. Her voice vibrated:

Madame! Votre fille est dangereuse . . . Cette gamine, she called me, I had tried to drown her child . . . I had done it on purpose. Another figure hovered, another daughter, about my age, *not* in bathing-dress, clucking and moaning, weakly striving for peace; and so did my mother, employing her social graces. It was not a quick process. (Madame Panigon's tirade, my mother later said, had not been lacking in a certain grammatical elegance . . . Imagine an English or Italian mother's syntax in a similar situation.) I apologised for the anxiety I had caused, *not* on purpose, I had not known the facts while there leapt into my head: Now I *do* – frogs can't swim. (Where had that come from? Oh, the multiple sources of chauvinism!) Eventually we all became good friends, after a fashion.

The only other break in our social isolation that summer came when we heard that one of my mother's friends of other times was staying at the Hôtel des Bains at Bandol with a young and glossy mistress (I had seen her). It was Ernst Toller, the playwright and poet. He was a communist then and in exile (Paris, not yet Hollywood and New York where he eventually killed himself), having lately served a two-year prison sentence in Germany (pre-concentration-camp Germany) for his part in some subversive action, and had published a poem written in his cell (like Oscar Wilde, I thought). I was awed – had it been unbearable? Would it show? I was also agog to meet a writer. He came to supper at our bungalow one night (without the mistress, without Alessandro, too, as it turned out, he was spending a few days in Marseille trying to see that man about a job). Home before dusk, still in damp espadrilles and bathing-shorts, I found a youngish man – not yet thirty? – sun-browned, healthy-looking, handsome, sitting on the verandah with my mother. I had offered to do the cooking, and they presently joined me in the kitchen. I remember that he seemed a nice man, an animated talker, even jolly in a gentle way, and he made a nice evening of it, against odds. I do not remember what we, what *they* were talking about, what a poor cheap thing it is, one's memory: Toller, that doomed and talented man, much loved by his friends, and all that I am able to tell about him at first-hand is his niceness about my own foolish predicament. Which was that we got nothing to eat; or rather: little, very late. I was trying to make us a dish of gratin dauphinois, once taught me by my father: finely sliced potatoes cooked in light cream with a touch of garlic and black pepper. The potatoes must be well washed and dried, and arranged in a neat pattern in their dish, and it looked promising enough as it went into the oven. Our kitchen stove burned wood; firewood in the South of France is either pine which makes a quick flambée then dies, or olive, often green, which is slow to ignite then dies and smokes. Need I say more? I still have the strip cartoon Toller drew afterwards for my mother. It shows a series of an anxious figure – me – bending in a cloud of smoke over a tepid stove under a clock (drawn not quite round) displaying the advancing hours. 'Not *quite* ready . . . ', say the balloons from out of my mouth. Under the last image, showing midnight, he wrote, 'But it was delicious all the same.' (Not true: it was shrivelled and still not *quite* ready.)

There are some actual words of Toller's that I can recall – probably because my mother used to repeat them – lamentably they are a remark about myself. He had asked, That your book? (It was *Les Faux-Monnayeurs.*) Then to my mother, Funny kind of girl you've got here, comes in from making sand-castles then reads André Gide.

To my surprise if rather against my will, Madame Panigon began to treat me as an inseparable companion of her brood (this was some-thing to be met often among the French: a great verbal roughing up at the beginning followed by showers of charm and goodwill; one might nearly get thrown out for expecting a table then end up dinner with brandy on the house), I was being drawn into the family bosom. We met mostly at the market or a café (oh not the beach) where my mother often joined us. Madame Panigon was full of bourgeois wisdom, common sense and gossip, and she was far from reticent; my mother found her excellent value. She was the wife of a *notaire* at Montélimar (she revealed, seated, hands never idle, in the Café de la Marine) who was still detained by *les affaires* – she'd left the cook with him, *naturellement*, you know: *men* – but was soon to join his family at Sanary where they annually spent the summer holidays. Conscious, like Mrs Bennett, that in due course she had daughters to marry, she diligently tried instilling strict and cynical *sagesse* into *jeunesse*; her dicta about *l'amour* really shocked my mother being herself – it struck me – a headlong romantic who loved deeply, unwisely and for ever each time it occurred. Madame Panigon however, was increasingly treating her as a crony. I did not mind consorting with her brood. I liked Annette who had some pluck; Cécile, the dumpy sister who looked like the future replica of her mama, I found rather tame and wet (I was quite wrong); if Annette was like a colt, Cécile was like a pretty heifer. There was also an uppish elder brother, Frédéric, a clever fiend, quite well set up, who had his own fish to fry. Most of the year those three were being crammed with Racine, Corneille and Molière at their *lycées*; en vacances they were allowed some dissipation. Many nights I found myself, chaperoned by Madame Tricoteuse, dancing javas, foxtrots and the quick waltz to a concertina with Cécile and Annette. We were looked on as children and rarely asked to stand up with a youth or man (Frédéric too was undisguisedly not interested in the least). We drank tisanes, lemonade or a *bock*, the small measure of light beer. I enjoyed the dancing and did not care with whom.

So that first summer was not all bad and it went fast. Hardly into September, my mother and Alessandro began brooding over moves to make; the first step being to part with me. One day I was taken to Toulon, not to Sanary-cum-Ollioules, to Toulon from where the fast trains went, not in the bus but in Monsieur Panigon's Renault car. My mother saw me off. Give my love to Jack and Susan, she said as the train was about to pull out, And what did you tell me they were actually doing now? Inspired, I asked, 'Mummy, *did* you meet Susan and Jack on a beach?' She did not have the grace to blush, she had the grace to giggle. 'Well – more or less . . . '

2

I was back quite soon. At Christmas in fact, a rarity, we kept moveable feasts. I found them in a villa with a wide view on the sea, in an easy mood. Each day there were hours of warmth around noon, real warmth, we ate our luncheons out of doors on the terrace in shirt-sleeves. I had brought a book for my mother, by a new English writer she had not heard of, expecting he would astonish and please. She read him in one go.

Much had happened to me in the last short three months. I would sum it up as friends, new writing, law courts. The friends I made by chance, the first friends of my own, elders and betters they were, had to be, it was too late to form a bond with contemporaries. I walked into a second-hand bookshop off Bond Street one afternoon, when I couldn't find what I wanted I left my name with an assistant, it was my father's name and she said, I used to know someone married into that family quite well – she mentioned the house in Berlin – are you the granddaughter? I said, no these were connections of a first marriage, the one she was talking about I knew only by hearsay. She remained interested – well and what was I doing . . . ? By myself and all that? I told her that I was living with friends in Hampstead and was educating myself. She asked me to tea the next week.

For one thing I had made a mistake going into that bookshop as they sold only first editions and rare books, nor would I have left my name with the unremarkable middle-aged woman if the beautiful tall young man who might have come out of a Greek poem (Bob Gathorne-Hardy in his youth) had not been engaged with a customer. This is by the way or not so by the way when one reflects on how chance operates. I nearly did not get there, to tea with Rosie Falken-heim. The address was somewhere near Baker Street, there was a fog, I got off the bus too soon, her number seemed not to exist, I turned yet another corner, tried basements, passers-by were strangers and hurried on . . . I felt at the edge of a panic. This still besets me in situations such as these. Impervious to own reasoning, I lose my nerve feeling that I shall never reach my destination but remain lost on some alien road or platform without ever seeing a known face again. I did not throw myself into Miss Falkenheim's arms but must have transmitted a glow of the storm-tossed wanderer's grateful relief when at last I entered her well lit bed-sitter. A tea tray stood at the ready (bespeaking thoughtful preparations); conversation began, easy as skating. It might have been a stiff one-off visit had I not been unstrung and open in my post-panic deliverance. My hostess treated me as though I were a guest and equal, heady stuff. I felt I had plenty to say. Rosie Falkenheim was a woman with a long, sallow, vaguely simian face, some hard crinkly hair, small brown eyes that were humorous rather than sad, and a not very good figure. Clothes hung badly. If you stretched the definition you might just have called her a *jolie laide.* What was not immediately apparent was that she liked, and had a way with, men. She must have been in her upper thirties then; I came to be one of the very few people who knew her story, which was an unusual one. Presently all one could assume was that she had not started life in a bed-sitter in Marylebone. There was fruit and Gentleman's Relish as well as cake for tea. Before I went, Miss Falkenheim proposed to take me to her sister's sometime soon, her sister who was married to the bookman who had recently opened the shop I had strayed into. If Mrs Robbins will allow you . . . ? I forebore to say that Mrs Robbins did not expect to be asked. I left with a book I had been lent under my arm. A rare book? A new book – the kind she read herself. It was *Antic Hay.*

Mrs Nairn – Toni – and her husband lived in a minute flat above the garage in a mews behind one of the Nash Terraces in Regent's Park. A patron, an American book collector, absentee tenant of the front house, had let them have it for an indefinite time. Toni was very pretty in a fragile way – an exquisite small head and pouting profile in the style of Queen Nefertiti (as she *had* been told); there was however a generic likeness to her elder sister (which grew over the years). Toni's figure, too, was imperfectly put together. They talked, drawing me into their private jokes, Rosie's gently dry, Toni's of unexpected ruthlessness. They got on to music: opera: Toni had 'a voice', a teacher whose method she did not approve of and some hope (forlorn, if I read her sister's neutrality). I was probed just a little – most tactfully, but I recognised the undertow: And *where* does your mother come into this? The subject though that was pursued most ardently on that afternoon was poison. Administered by murderers, murderesses preferably. Contemporary cases, nineteenth-century cases, Toni had them at her finger-tips. Toni, not Rosie; Rosie looked aloofly amused. Was Toni interested in other forms of homicide as well? (It sounded out of a phrase-book.) She was. Less so, but she was. Then *I* had to ask. Had she heard of our family murder – my father's brother done in by his wife – a mere shooting? Indeed. Moreover, she and the convicted woman bore the same first name, Antonia. Your aunt Toni, she said. All of this in the quietest of tones among the teacups, rather grand teacups (got out this once).

Presently a heavy tread on the flimsy steep stairs, Mr Nairn coming home from work: a big, slow-moving, handsome man who filled the tiny room. He gave his wife an affectionate pat, nodded to his sister-in-law, shook hands with me. A good face – brown hair, grey eyes, strong teeth – with a calm and humorous expression; I liked him at once.

Room was made for him at the table, the cream-puffs cleared away, a meal of a kind, not quite fish and chips but of that nature, was placed before her husband by Toni with, I thought I discerned, faint distaste. The sisters lit cigarettes. Jamie Nairn spoke little; when he did it was in a deliberate, unhurried voice, a baritone voice (he sang in a choir), dropping some clear declarative sentences into our minds. 'That man came back and paid four guineas for the Meredith.' 'Bob thinks the Browning is a fake.' The sisters, who sometimes helped out in the shop, knew how to take this up; I listened. In the course of this and other, soon becoming frequent, visits I picked up a number of things about the Nairns without being able to sort them out as yet into a coherent whole.

It was evident, for one, that Rosie and Toni had been bred to the customs of another country: urban Germany and unmistakably Berlin. There was still a whiff about them of the intellectually alert, materially indulgent Jewish upper bourgeoisie of that city as they scampered after a bus – they would not walk – to take them two hundred yards up Baker Street. While Toni's transplantation to a London mews was explained by her having got married to a taciturn Scot for her sins (her words), Rosie's must have been due to choice. She was not a premature refugee; this was 1926, if Hitler was already ranting in the wings, he was ridiculed and discounted by the few who had heard of him, not feared. Had Rosie come to England then to hold her sister's hand? Permanently? (She had applied for British nationality.) The sisters did live in each other's pocket, mutually solicitous about sleep and feet and health – Did you get your rest today, dear? – yet also often snapping. Rosie seemed to thrive in England, loving it, loving London, everything English, while Toni was apt to be dismissive. Both showed concern for Jamie's bookshop – founded on a little capital lent by friends. Jamie Nairn, I realised (not through him: he was a modest as well as a silent man) was already regarded as an authority on nineteenth-century manuscripts and modern first editions. He still was, and looked, a young man, in his early thirties, say, his wife probably older by a couple of years. He, too, lent books to me.

I was asked to the Nairns' about twice a week now, tea extending into supper; Saturday afternoons spent keeping Jamie company in the garage as he tinkered with their Morris-Cowley with me being only too pleased to help. (Toni thought I was mad getting oil on my hands when I didn't need to, and made us wash in the kitchen.) With Rosie I had tea only, or a matinée at the Old Vic; Rosie in the evenings was not available. Had I ever been to a Court of Law? she asked me one day, I might find it of interest. So I went to the Strand – she seemed well-informed as to how and when – sat in the public gallery and got hooked from the first May-it-please-your-Lordship. It was a libel case, involving the leader of a well-known band; I don't remember names, or who heard the case, only that the standard of advocacy must have been high. I went again and again (with help from Rosie over the case list), more readily than to a play or film. Everything captivated: the voices, the casuistries of the arguments, the rigidities and drama of that formalised man's world. It was fascinating to watch the chase for the elusive truth, the attempts at getting justice done; watching the wheels of that clockwork being driven on was both food for thought and supreme entertainment.

I only went to civil cases heard before the High Court – libel, disputed wills, divorce; my days in Magistrates' Courts, the Old Bailey, in European and American Courts came much later. At sixteen, not in my wildest dreams – and I had dreams – would I have seen myself reporting a murder or a great political trial. Now that I have, I rather regret that I did not sign those – oh, highly serious – efforts Bill the Lizard.

I owe much of that to Rosie Nairn (she eventually had to take her brother-in-law's name). Meanwhile I had read *Antic Hay* and got hold of everything else by Aldous Huxley, *Crome Yellow*, *Limbo*, the early essays; they seemed to bring to me everything I would then have liked to know and think. That, too, I owe to the Nairns. I never quite knew why they befriended me, a stranger, a girl twenty years their junior. When I had known them long enough to ask – towards the end of their lives – they couldn't remember. Their taking me in may have had something to do with the curious isolation in which the two women – not Jamie – seemed to live then. Rosie had no visible friends; Jamie never brought his men friends home to the mews. Anyway, befriend me they did, and so began what became a pattern in my life: friendships, attachments to a group, a couple, a family not my own, friendships that lasted through the changing stages. That autumn in London was a kind of turning point. I had not been unhappy before; now I was consciously, buoyantly happy, looking forward to something new, something good every day.

*   *   *

I did not mind the Christmas stay – which it was supposed to be – at Sanary with my mother and stepfather. I rather enjoyed it. It is nice to go away when one has something to come back to. After the New Year came a development in my mother's sporadic plans to find employment for Alessandro as a middleman's middleman in the art world. She still had connections with the circle of O, the painter, the man she had jilted. Now someone had come forward offering to show Alessandro the ropes. It meant Paris, Amsterdam, weeks, possibly months . . . Should she go with him? There was the expense, a single man more lightly slips by. Delicacy of feelings was also involved – perhaps it *was* better for Alessandro to go as his own man? And there were the dogs, the puppies were gone, but there were still three Japanese spaniels. All in all, she had better stay put . . . Here at Sanary, in the sun. I like it here . . . There is much to explore. She turned to me, Will you explore with me? Will you stay on? Will you keep me company? She said it most charmingly; I said that I would.

3

Though an improvement that next villa too left much to be desired. It was new, clean, spacious: a salon, four bedrooms, and everything in it and about it hideous. Mercifully it was sparsely furnished. Brass bedsteads, *armoires à glace*, hard chairs, a large buffet stacked with patterned *services de table* which we did not use; we ate off the kitchen plates. There was nothing we could do about the floor tiles – a mustard and violet design – and very cold on the feet. The villa stood at the end of the road that winds along the hill above the bay, the last in a row, empty and shuttered now against winter. It was exceedingly draughty, with rattling doors and numerous badly fitting French windows; we were attacked by cold blasts whenever the mistral blew which it did often, leaving beautiful clear blue-swept skies and a sense of exhilaration. Out in the open that was: the house was unheatable in any contemporary sense, but then we were used to being cold indoors in southern winters. One retreated. Thick sweaters, bed for my mother during the chillier hours. We didn't use the salon at all, and the salle à manger rarely; we made camp in our bedrooms keeping a couple of sturdy little wood-stoves going as well as a minute electric fire. A *femme de ménage* – a nicer one – came early, bearing provisions, lighting the kitchen-stove, knocking at my door as she took the tray with café au lait and two bowls into my mother's room.

Our day began. In the long mornings it was concentrated plunges into *la lecture*. In France backwaters have bookshops; if Sanary did not run to a full-sized *librairie*, it had some well stocked shelves in an artists' supply shop by name Au Grand Tube, run by a charming non-local couple. Here we found what is surely the ultimate in paperbacks: classics of French fiction at one franc twenty-five – three pence. New French books, then as now, did not come out in hardback – how I liked those light white volumes, beautifully produced by the NRF or Bernard Grasset, with their plain covers elegantly lettered like the labels of a first grand cru. That threepenny library was something quite else. Decades before Penguins, and also unlike the present French *livres de poche*, those books didn't even look like books: they were flat, the shape of large notebooks, the paper was cheap and the print was smudgy – what matter, they were treasures; carrying an armful up our hill, I felt rich. I must have read (with earnest marginal notes) and my mother re-read half of Balzac, most of Maupassant, some Zola, Alfred de Vigny, Chateaubriand, George Sand, the Goncourts . . . All essential in their so various ways, my mother told me firmly, if I were to begin to understand something about the country I was in. Flaubert and, prematurely no doubt, Constant's *Adolphe* I had absorbed earlier, at my mother's knee as it were, and however little of their substance I had been capable of extracting, it was a foundation. Stendhal, too, had no part in our reconnaissance at that stage; Stendhal, a sincere and early passion, I felt to be both Italianate and a great writer *hors nation*. By noon we had shut our books, ready to stroll down, baskets over arm, into Sanary. Our bitch, Chumi, went with us. The few errands done, we would seek a sheltered table on the terrace of Chez Schwob, one of the *bars tabacs*. Schwob was a large and erudite Alsatian, married to a large and placidly competent black woman who nursed an out-sized baby while he spouted Heine and Descartes as they sold cigarettes and stamps and poured bright drinks from behind the zinc. Theirs was a steady clientèle of fishermen, masons, sailors, interspersed in the morning by artists, foreigners, French from other parts, and some of the larger-minded notables. In the evenings all these latter went to the more expensive Café de la Marine next door, the day resort of local professionals and *retraités*. The Café de Lyon and the other *tabac* must have been strictly other ranks, in all the years we never saw anyone we knew set foot in them.

So there we sat Chez Schwob, my mother and I, sun-warmed, looking at the sea and tossing boats, drinking a modest apéritif, saluted, addressed, often joined – chairs pulled out, shopping net or newspaper put down – by a miscellany of men and women. My mother, too, had struck up some acquaintances during the autumn months (by way of Madame Panigon, who else?).

We walked up the hill again for our lunch, having been preceded by
la Mère Dédée who cooked it. She'd find the key under the geranium
pot as was the custom of the country. She ran a fish stall, not among
the market hoi polloi but smack in front of La Marine; she shut up at
twelve: my mother had persuaded her to devote l'heure du déjeuner to
us. My mother was being appreciated, I had noted, by the French of
various kinds; that speed of mind which could bewilder or antagonise
the English and Italians was taken in their stride. La Mère Dédée (for
Désirée) was Dédée *tout court* then, the adjunct eventually came not
because of maturity or offspring but because the fish stall having
prospered and expanded she became patronne of a restaurant that at
one point found itself, if unstarred, in the *Guide Michelin*. She was a
proper Provençale and knew how to deal with aubergines, tomatoes,
crustaceans, olive oil and garlic. What we ate – spicy fish stews,
vegetable messes – was local, authentic and delicious. My mother
made coffee for all three, pure black droplets from a miniature
espresso machine, one of the first made, given to Alessandro by a
Milanese friend. Afterwards no sleep for the virtuous: we went back
to our books. I into my bedroom rigged as a study, card-table for desk
by the window; my mother reading and scribbling in her bed, warmed
by such dogs as chose to stay in.

Animals in my family lived beside rather than dependent on us
(though Chumi, self-contained and calm, did not always conceal her
devotion to Alessandro). Her young, males, were a tough lot quite
unlike their over-bred mama; there was, as in all her litters – *her*
choice, *our* casual ways – a good deal of mongrel in them. They roamed
the hillside as they pleased (cars were few); perhaps dogs used to grow
and thrive more easily, I can't remember ever taking them to a vet or
their having shots for this and that; fleas and ticks were all we had to
worry about.

Early evening: early dark. I would walk down again with napkin,
bowl and torch to fetch our dinner. From the same cook-shop the
Cyril Connollys used to get theirs a few years on. I am still moved by
his passage about this simple act in *The Unquiet Grave*, and tempted
to quote from it once again.

... On dark evenings I used to bicycle in to fetch our dinner, past the harbour with its bobbing launches and the bright cafés with their signs banging; at the local restaurant there would be one or two 'plats à emporter', to which I would add some wine, sausage and gruyère cheese ... then I would bowl back heavy-laden with the mistral behind me, a lemur buttoned up inside my jacket with his head sticking out ... We ate with our fingers beside the fire ...

I did not carry a graceful lemur, I might have one of Chumi's pups following me on a string, nor did I use a bicycle as our hill was steep (the Connollys, Cyril and Jean, lived on the flat side of Sanary), the wind though, the smells, the sense of moving through the hibernal Mediterranean night bound for home, companionship, a fire, were the same.

We too ate the dinner I brought back in happy domesticity. My mother, for all her apparent volatility, had a talent for contentment. I have met few women who made so little demand on distractions or entertainment: she made her own with whatever was at hand. If she had lived a life of frequent changes, it was imposed on her by circumstances and perhaps too often by the conflagrations of her feelings, never by a wish for change. I believe that she would have liked permanence; whenever things were good she wanted to stay still ('then the gods won't mind you'); she did *not* like, nor was she skilled, to face or shape the future. When there was no immediate menace, she ignored it. *Carpe diem.*

We did not eat our take-away dinner with our fingers, at least I did not. My mother insisted on eating hers off a tray by the one-bar electric fire; *I* on eating upright at a table properly laid – length of bread, bottle of wine. She had tried to laugh me out of what she called my clubmanly dinners, I said that not bothering to sit up to eat was an appalling feminine habit; we agreed to disagree. To talk – and talk we did – we had to pitch our voices like people addressing each other across a restaurant. Before the end we unnoticingly relented, my mother approaching the table the better to peel an orange, I pacing the floor apple in hand.

That agreeable routine was varied as we got drawn into Sanary winter night-life. Some of my mother's new acquaintances met for a game of cards at the Café de la Marine on Tuesdays and Thursdays, and we were asked to join them. First step was putting dinner forward, these assignations being for a quarter to nine. The *upheaval*, my mother said, like dining out before a dance. To save me another walk down and up the hill, we did our own cooking. She made the soup, potatoes and leeks or potatoes and *cresson*, the ubiquitous good soup of the evening of the urban and suburban French (the peasant's main-dish soup was something else). I made the *oeufs-sur-le-plat* in a couple of small round buttered dishes gently till the whites were set pure and creamy with the yolks still perfect, as my father had taught me when I wasn't tall enough to reach the spirit-lamp (now it was *more* tricky on the charcoal-stove but attention – also taught by him – would do it). These were not the fried eggs of the English hotel breakfast: hardened, browned and frizzy at the edges, spluttered fat congealing into tepid grease. Our bi-weekly menu was always the same: small courses in the pattern of the French en famille at night (who ate more, much more, than we did at noon). After our eggs, we had a slice of ham with a green salad lightly dressed, and to end with a coeur-crème with apricot jam.

The ham was rosy white, the unsmoked kind called jambon de Paris, and it came from a tip-top small grocery shop run without frills other than the quality of their wares by a family from the Basque country who had started commercial life selling cheeses off a barrow. Monsieur Benech, a meagre little man, inevitably stroked his female customers' arms or worse as he brushed past them to weigh out an hectogram of the best butter; one tried to get served by the wife – who pretended that the goings-on were naught – or the amplitudinous aunt; the little boy who did deliveries was the son. Today, Monsieur Benech is no more, the son is middle-aged (and utterly correct), there is *his* wife and other vigorous aunts who help in the shop which still flourishes, a little enlarged – not much – with a few more grandes marques champagnes in stock, English teas, a little *beluga molossol*; butter is sold in packages now but the ham is still exquisite and there is what anyone who ever stood waiting his turn at chez Benech saw before him: their centre piece, the enormous wheel of gruyére cheese, so succulent, so freshly cut – it seemed to go from one minute to the next – that it was compulsive not to leave without a chunk. When Cyril – he does spring to mind in the context – bullied his American in-laws, the Davises, Annie and Bill, into buying him a whole gruyére cheese in Switzerland just after the war *and* transporting it across Europe on the back seat of their car, I'm sure it was the memory of Benech's wheel that prompted him.

*   *   *

The game we played on those winter evenings was that national game *belote*, an unserious subspecies of bridge played seriously. Many a headline had we seen telling of revolver shots fired at a partner who had failed to do the right thing by a trump.

SANGLANT ÉPISODE DANS UN CAFÉ DE BANLIEUE:
OUVRIER MENUISIER TIRE DEUX BALLES SUR SON COPAIN

We did not play *belote* seriously. It was my mother who made that impossible. Curious that someone who set so much store by mental processes could be so off-hand with figures be they presented by clocks, calendars or the bank. She did not count up her hand. They forgave her. Anyway, *belote* in those days was very much a man's game; when 'the ladies' did partake, the men became jocularly chivalrous (neither sex taking offence); the stakes at La Marine were low and the occasion social rather than competitive. The company was heterogeneous though I remember it chiefly as an aggregate: men and women, adult, settled in their lives, formally mannered, fluent and shapely of speech, dis-posed to please (and to be so themselves); their common ground for me was their Frenchness. There must have been, there were, many social and indeed political shades, demarcations blurred and not blurred, not to say chasms. (The French need not speak of class, they just say milieu. '*Cela ne se fait pas*, this is not done, *parmi les gens de notre milieu.*' As clean-cut as that.) One indicator was who asked whom to their house and who met whom only at the café. This was far from all-revealing as at that time entertaining at home was still more or less reserved for family and connections, and not only in the stricter circles. Whatever individually they were, these inhabitants of my first French world, they were not the dukes and Madame de Sévignés of Nancy Mitford's golden vision – there are almost as many ways of falling in love with France as there are of falling in love – my life among the French began with a lawyer from Lyon practising at the Toulon courts, and his buoyant wife, cronies of the Panigons and much birds of a feather; a cousin of theirs, a widow (impermanently, one foresaw) on long visit; the man who owned the second-best small hotel, whose wife stayed at home; the couple, she an ex-schoolmistress, he a Sunday photographer, who ran – over-generously: most of their customers stood in debt to them – the artists' supply shop, M. and Mme Grand Tube as everybody called them – he was indeed enormous. There were also the local house agent and another very large man who lived in a Saracen watch tower he had converted – with great good taste – sailed his own boat, was a friend of the painter Derain and said to smoke opium. Both the latter were bachelors, *des garçons*, a fact that caused some routine banter, the implication being that they were free and lucky to pick and leave their women without trouble. Talk was bright and concrete, rapid gives and takes; subjects: the things that were happening in their and *other* people's lives – who were having or had or would soon be having an affair; who was definitely not and who was most probably not his father's son and whether or not he knew; land: a piece of, reputedly for sale; prices in the shops; wills, deathbed marriages, the *curé*. *He* was always a butt (we never met the poor man who scurried across the main square like a pantry mouse); the native Midi and those who had chosen to settle there, though Catholic to a man, were not *bien-pensants*, some might put their faith in God, none did in the clergy. And so another gratifying source of scurrilous anecdote was at hand.

Everybody believed in the *Guide Michelin*. Here conversation went crescendo: where one ate and what one ate and the way it was cooked and where one might eat next Sunday; poetry welled up in every heart – *Vaut le détour* . . . *Vaut le voyage* . . . One hour twenty-five from door to door, I swear to you, and not a minute more.

That was when we turned to cars. All the world loved a car in that decade, those who had one and those who didn't, even my mother who, mercifully, never learnt to drive. (*I* counted the years before I'd be allowed to.) It was the golden, the romantic age of motoring; cars had ceased to be delicate untrustworthy individuals requiring a mechanic or at least a chauffeur and long hours of waiting by a dusty roadside, were becoming cheap enough to be owned or hoped to be owned by those of moderate means, while the roads were still empty to go fast in: one stopped at will in front of any shop, any house, in the uncluttered streets. One might go anywhere, at one's own time, see undreamt of sites conquered before only on foot or mule. There was the sense of a brave new personal freedom.

We not only shared the pleasures of our friends' Citroëns and Renaults, we were actually being asked – by some – to their houses, to a game of boules, that other lackadaisical-to-impassioned game, in the garden of an afternoon or to déjeuner on Sunday, elaborate and delicious. My mother told me that this could only be permissible by their standards because of our ambivalent position: a married woman on her own (they had had glimpses only so far of Alessandro and were probably saying among themselves that he was young enough to be *my* son, but were too polite to ask questions to our faces), and I – though they called me Mademoiselle, which I disliked, followed by Alessandro's surname – could be regarded as a child, so did not count. We were foreigners, birds of passage, dark horses – spies conceivably – in fact so much outsiders to be admittable *ex gratia*. And how very kind they were to us. We were given the name of the right plumber, the reliable seamstress, shops at Toulon – *les bonnes adresses*. The women left, without intrusive lingering, small presents: the first mimosa, a pot of confiture, lemons in a nest of their own leaves, the recipe for the poulet à la crème we said we had enjoyed.

Such were the pointillist touches that made up existence in that Mediterranean province of France. Pleasure in good living was inherited, instinctive; rarely gross, never snobbish. They liked what they said they liked.

The café put down its shutters at about half past ten, there was no calling of time, no grabbing a last round. We may have sounded sybaritic, talking gastronomy in serious, and in honest, terms, our actual consumption on those *belote* evenings had been modest to abstemious. Infusions of verbena or lime, perhaps a rum toddy or some coffee laced with a teaspoonful of brandy, a couple of halves of light beer. The winner was supposed to pay, though after a token struggle this would always be a man. We got into our overcoats and mufflers, shook hands all round (much less kissing than there is now), said *au revoir* and *à demain* and started walking our different ways into the night. (One walked: people did not take out their beloved cars lightly, the self-starter had only recently come in and was used parsimoniously.)

Nobody else lived up our hill, one didn't even think about being safe, so my mother and I set off by ourselves, taking the longer, winding way not the steep shortcut up from the harbour. The air would be cold and clear, the sky light enough not to use our torches. When we came out from under a thin cover of pines, we stopped to look at the stars. Very happily, though vague about the constellations (Alessandro would have set us right). It was a good cold out here in the open; once inside our horrible villa it was just very very chilly. My mother went straight to bed, I sat at the foot, wrapped in a blanket. There was much to chew over. It was still far from midnight. And beyond . . . It was the time of lucidity, clarifications.

At first she – we – made a few jokes, reminded each other of this and that, then we got down to questions to which I hoped for answers and she begged other questions. How to *connect* (not in a strictly E. M. Forster sense) the recorded past with our fragments of the present, trace sequence from what we had been reading in the mornings to the lives and voices of the day?

The burden of her quest – as I thought I understood it – was that the world, the human world, we were inevitably, inescapably placed to exist in, was shaped – apart from natural forces which were largely hostile – by men and women who in turn were shaped by what others of their kind had done and thought before them. To make sense of it one had to try to find out what people, individually and in society, were like and likely to do, and why.

'The French now . . . ' (She had lived among them before, at the tangent of disparate circles in Paris, at home on her visits.) 'It strikes one how they've brought back that glow on life, though the war – the two last wars – are in their flesh and bone; there's still a sense of national bereavement. They are stoics: soft and tough at the same time. When one thinks that most of it – the killing and the dying, the countrysides laid waste – happened, on *their* home ground . . . They've well earned their joie de vivre now!'

How should we see our friends at La Marine? As Mauriac and Julien Green were seeing them *and* as plausible descendants of Balzacian great-grandparents? *And* heirs of the Grand Siècle? Where did they begin? Where does it ever begin? The Gauls? Charlemagne? Jeanne d'Arc?

'*She* left her mark – on that bone-sceptical people, still half ready for a Second Coming.' Had I looked at that slim equestrian statue on the Place des Pyramides? A more graceful warrior myth surely than the Valhalla vision of the Heldentodt? The French never had to dream up such Germanic props to their superiority: every postman's little boy at the *lycée* knew that as civilisation went France was the cat's whiskers.

Yes – that hyper-civilisation, the glory of art and letters, Versailles . . . At the same time war after war – wilful wars – brutishness, oppression, injustice, *la misère*; and then the great flings into convulsive turbulence: the Terror, Napoleon, the nineteenth-century see-saw when everything went back and burst out again or went sideways – Restorations, Empires, the Commune . . . 1870, 1914, dates branded into every European's consciousness whether he or she was born at the time or not . . . 'And in the intervals of murdering each other, they listened to Lully and Rameau and painted bread and fruit as Chardin did, and the "*Grande Jatte*" and the "*Déjeuner sur l'herbe*", made delicate objects and cultivated that flow of sanity and balance in daily life . . . Able to wound, able to heal.'

How did one connect those spurts of *à la lanterne*, of heroism, endurance, the reeling between the excesses of revolution and bureaucracy, the intellectual rigour and the rhetorical platitudes, the elegance, the arrogance, the exquisite domestic sensuality, the *petit train-train de la vie* and all the niceness and avarice that went with it? Not leaving out the horrors of French bourgeois life – 'They *are* horrors and I'm sure they still go on . . . They are a perplexing people!'

But then civilisation was always a mixed bag. National character? How far did it exist? Once you looked closely, up came the paradoxes. 'Try to pin down the English . . . Try to think of the Germans without parti pris . . . As for the Chinese, you and I can't even begin to think about the Chinese.'

And yet to relate, to interpret, to extrapolate, she would go on, was necessary. To what end? Perhaps it was incumbent on one, on every one of us to take part – oh *indirectly* – in making the world a more tolerable place. 'Besides the human mind craves cohesion, patterns . . . Order. It longs for it all to hang together.'

'I think *I* do,' I said. 'Is that wrong?'

She thought there never had been a civilisation without a deliberately created order as an underpinning; what mattered was the nature of the pattern and how far it would be open to doubt, second thoughts, eventual change . . . 'All's well as long as no one thinks they've got the whole pattern, and that theirs and theirs alone is the right one. No great final answers! Trouble starts when the prophet comes along, the revolutionary, the very clever man, the inspired general . . . '

'Would we have been better off then without great men?'

'Very possibly. If we wanted to live happy. But that, I dare say, is a relatively recent aspiration. Nor does it always have to be a *great* man; look at our plump ranter across the border. When conditions are too bad for too many – and how seldom were they not – there is fertile ground for the likes of Musso. For a herd creed, a cruel idiots' creed. And when the herd wakes up and the orgy's over, the damage has been done. People have died or had their lives spoilt.'

'The Greeks . . . ' I said. 'Didn't they . . . didn't they find a good pattern?'

'Still a part of *our* underpinning. Yes: one likes looking back to the classical world . . . the great spell of the Mediterranean light . . . But mind *they* didn't believe in the greatest good for the greatest number –

think of a slave's life and up to a point a woman's – one's lot depended on having been born in the right place and sex.'

Is pessimism then the only realistic attitude? I asked, and remembered I had read *Candide*.

There have been some pretty rum patterns, she said, and some downright diabolical ones. Blood sacrifices, judicial torture, trench warfare, the infinitely varied ways of men doing harm to men. Quetzal-coatl, free-born Athenians, Roman chauvinism, *all* chauvinism, Holy Islam, Holy Inquisition, Cromwell's armies, Napoleon's armies, nationalism, imperialism – patterns clashing with other patterns. 'Each providing rationalisations for your right, and rather pleasant, duty to do the equivalent of putting members of the other tribe into your pot and cook them.'

'Mummy,' I said, 'are we talking about history or human nature?'

'Both. They do hang together.'

'What would have happened . . . how would it be if some of the big clashes hadn't happened? The French Revolution? Russia? If the changes had come as they did in England . . . ?'

'Not entirely bloodless either – looking at the whole process. But, oh yes, better, no doubt better: a lesser sum of individual loss. I shall always believe in seeing it that way. As to whether anything that happened might not have happened? By a bit of give at one point, a bit of luck? Who can tell? What was inevitable? What was touch and go? One spends much time speculating about just that in one's own life; when it comes to collectives, whether we call them nations or masses or movements, there are so many factors in play at every stage – too many for any single hand, *if* there were one, to guide or manipulate – and so much chance as well.'

'If Lenin hadn't been put on that sealed train?'

'Quite. But there's also the weight of what has gone on before, not forgiven, not forgotten, the chain of reaction to reaction, revenge on revenge on revenge, the avalanche momentum. One can start almost anything; it would appear that nothing can ever be turned back.'

Then there would come the point in the evening's talk, in all our evening talks, when she would throw up her hands, dismissing what she'd been saying. One thing *had* changed, would remain changed: war. Collective attitude to war. There could not be, there *must* not be another war in Europe.

Something *can* be learned if the lesson was hard enough. Up till now every war had led to the next war, a bigger, more catastrophic war; the horror of 1914–18 was on such a scale that the Western world at least is coming to pity and reason.

One day when the histories are written and re-written there'll still be the Kaiser and the Habsburgs and German militarism and French bellicosity, naval rivalry and the fortuitous train of events at Sarajevo, but it may also be seen that there was another, perhaps ultimately decisive, element: people. That war could be launched into because men and women light-mindedly – often unselfishly, I give you, sacrificingly – believed that war was permissible, controllable, some-times *right*; so war – one more attempt at resolving conflicts by killings and destruction – became possible because nearly everyone believed that it *was* possible.

She sat up straight. 'They no longer do. Something has seeped into European consciousness. *You and I shall see no war between France and Germany in our lifetime.* That means peace for England and all the rest.' On another tone she added, 'A wish; of course it's a wish.' Then, 'It goes beyond that – I believe, I almost believe, it's true.'

I took it in.

And what of Alessandro? *He* was no letter-writer, meaning that he wrote regularly enough but briefly, giving his news (moderately good) without describing it or taking up her points. She scribbled to him as often as not but these loose sheaves were seldom finished and randomly posted. The ball, she firmly said, needs returning. 'Unless one is one of those unfortunate women, you know, Mademoiselle de Lespinasse . . . ' She liked good concrete masculine stuff from her correspondent, life, wit, refreshment (a volume of Byron's Letters was often by her hand); not sentiments, 'Well, a small percentage of sentiment. Anyway, talking is easier (alas) and one needs a public. *You*'re serving quite nicely.'

I grinned.

What came from him was reassuring. Contacts had proved hopeful, steps been taken. There were prospects, even results; the small working capital had materialised. He now owns a sixteenth of a Vlaminck, my mother told me, and he thinks he can get a share in a Juan Gris. 'The art *market*! Well named. And he's such an amateur.'

I think, I said slowly (I had a slight stammer and never quite knew whether it was involuntary or put on), 'that he is . . . a very capable man . . . inventive.'

'Improvising. He's flexible. He can't make a career of this – or anything else. We *are* amateurs. I suppose we won't change. It's the way things turned out.'

I was pleased by her insouciance over the Vlaminck; all these weeks, there had been none of the constraint I had felt last summer, the fear of some drastic change impending; I would not break her mood. Perhaps undercurrents, situations, were seldom as one read them?

Eventually she left it to me to keep up mutual reassurance. I managed regular short letters – concrete, I hoped, if nothing more – saying how well she was doing. From him came picture postcards of Dutch landscapes nicely chosen, saying such things as, I know you're looking after her, you would have enjoyed that huge lobster on spiced rice I had today, sending love, A.

Did she miss him? (*I* had not forgotten Sorrento.) In a complacent way, I think she did. Absence, if reasonably short, can be a very charming thing, she told me once. One noon we were standing in Benech's queue waiting our turn. That shop was always full. She sent me off – I know you hate waiting – so I'd had a nip into the bookshop. When I got back she was still standing, holding her basket. I've just been telling myself, she said, that I am a happily married woman. It is rather odd. (She meant what had long been clear between us that she had not been *happy* with my father and not been *married* to the others.) 'I have a husband . . . and daughter,' her tone sustained astonishment. 'It feels rather nice queueing to get dinner for one's family . . . well not for my husband at this minute – but I shall. A *very* nice feeling.'

*

Sanary had a cinematographic theatre, if one can call it that, converted from a garage, and it showed a film on Sunday nights. The seating was hierarchical: below was crammed with local youths, stamping, whistling, cracking *cacahuètes*, holding their girls, filling the air with stinging fumes of *caporal bleu*; the ramshackle balcony, up the uncertain stairs, was sparsely occupied by families of middle-aged tradesmen and notables none of whom we knew or were likely to want to know us. Our café friends looked down on this establishment preferring to drive to Toulon for more recent offerings. My mother and I went. We rather enjoyed the routine of another weekly outing. The screen was bad, the piano lively; the films cannot have been very new but they were good. Movies: black and white, silent. American mostly, as far as I remember, Charlie Chaplin, Douglas Fairbanks, Buster Keaton, Harold Lloyd.

One night there walked into that cinema hall a couple of strangers. They were slim like cats' shadows, matched in size, quietly, gracefully moving side by side. They bore themselves well; we could see their profiles – sharply cut, fastidious, austere, like profiles in the portraits of a Piero or Pisano. They wore berets, and their clothes, elegant beyond daylight reality, were versions of French workmen's dress. Stylish and aloof, they seemed apparitions stepped from the vanguard of some coming world.

Can they be the stuck-up snobs from Paris? My mother whispered to me. The stuck-up snobs from Paris, unknown to all, glimpsed by a few, gliding by in a high long old car so unlike their own beloved new boxes, were the subjects of much adverse speculation at the Café de la Marine. Little, in fact nothing, was known about them to our friends – which was indeed the very thing held against them – except that they had rented a villa – oh no better or no larger than another – on the westward bay. They were an incestuous couple, twins, well at least brother and sister, and if not you could be sure that they were not married – to each other that was: adultery certainly came into it; that's why they had to leave Paris – undoubtedly their native habitat – going South for their health, consumptives, very likely. It was noted that they had not made the slightest attempt to meet anyone; had one ever seen them enter a café? They hadn't as much as acknowledged anyone else's existence.

It must be *them*, my mother said. To me they were the most beautiful pair of human beings I had ever seen.

From then on they, like us, came every Sunday night.

At one point in spring Alessandro returned. He came announced by telegram and carried a briefcase, looking pleased with it and himself. In due course he and I embraced; he touched my shoulder, You *have* looked after her. It was like changing guard.

The three of us spent some pleasant days, my ticket was getting booked, I looked forward to resuming . . . resuming what? I had no words, only felt ready for the life ahead.

My last night but one was a Sunday night, film night. Alessandro decided not to go, he'd been to a good many cinematographic theatres during the winter, he would try to get to grips with some *commercial* papers (he had also brought a typewriter, a neat light portable, which he and I had been practising, racing each other). My mother and I went to see one more Charlot or was it Harold Lloyd? As we were about to leave, the pair of strangers passed us in the aisle. He gave my mother a slight bow; she sketched a smile.

4

Victoria station in early afternoon. Grey; not very crowded; somewhat dishevelled though nothing to what it is now. Hot. Very hot. It was a day in April and one of those untimely heat waves had struck London. If people hadn't actually taken their shirts off, they looked as if they'd like to. Not for relief, for celebration.

Urban railway stations, for those not inured by daily use, are places of angst and trauma. For me they had been so early (the sight of wounded German soldiers helped into the trains in 1915, my mother's leaving me behind on platforms); on the present occasion I had come out of France replete and adventurous enough to keep it all at bay. I stepped on to the relatively sizzling pavements outside and took a bus, top of a bus not the tube, to Belsize Park.

Susan and Jack were as friendly and unconcerned as ever. Marmite flowed. Better than that: special food was fetched, drink too.

The let-down came the day after. What next? A structure was called for. Up to me again. Another pile of books in my bedroom to be gnawed through (my mother had recommended a go at the Victorians), talked over perhaps with bookish friends in the evenings? Now there I was faced with an awkwardness: would I ever see them again? Rosie, Toni and Jamie. The Nairns had been much in my mind during the months in France, daily I'd revved up to tell them what I was living, recounting stories while they were happening, repeating my mother's ideas; in fact I had been pouring out letters to the Nairns in my mind. In colder fact I had not sent them a single postcard. Over and over I had put off the quick word due for the long letter, the letter longer and longer as time went on with preliminary excuses. Four months! (Rosie, I recalled, had seen me off.) *How could I?* It seemed so easy now to have acted otherwise. A horrible cloud of guilt bore down.

Neither the Nairns nor Rosie were on the telephone. Turn up at the shop? A back-door approach: Jamie very likely hadn't taken much notice of my dereliction. In the end I wrote to Rosie. A postcard. I am back – may I come and see you?

We are often, and correctly, told now that anything posted in those days dropped on to the receiver's doormat in a matter of hours. I had Rosie's answer the same day: come to tea tomorrow.

It was better and worse than expected. She was friendly, seemed pleased to see me, she let me explain about the letters in the mind. She became serious – We didn't even know you'd arrived – bringing home what she saw as the enormity of my conduct. She didn't mind for herself, she said. But you have hurt my sister. Toni is easily hurt.

I took it in; much ashamed.

You are not a heartless girl, Rosie said.

No, I said.

Don't do it again. Don't ever do it again to her. (But I did. To her, to others. Is it part of the writer's flaw, wanting to get across so much and shrinking, so painfully, from the execution?)

*

Hurdle two, meeting Toni surprised me. Toni was lively – no reproaches, no mention – a table laid. Then at one point she looked straight in the air and said in a level tone, I've forgiven you. I never do.

I stared at her. Ashamed though I was, this was giving the whole thing too much weight. There she sat with that flower-petal Nefertiti face. 'I never forgive.' And when I managed to say, Why? 'I don't forgive people who do wrong by *me*.'

I felt chilled. Also a twinge flattered – did she like me so well then? or rather was *I* so likeable as to be made the exception?

In no time it all settled down. I settled down. Things resumed much as they had been in the autumn, in a groove now, taken for granted. I slept at Belsize Park, had breakfast with Susan and Jack, did my books; set off, walking a stretch, catching a bus, eating my lunch perhaps on the steps of the National Gallery having attended – what I thought of as – an excellent lecture on the Quattrocento or the Flemish. Round the corner were the attractions of the Charing Cross Road, Soho offering another kind of browsing among the 3/6*d.*, 2/6*d.*, even 1/6*d.*, French and Italian menus; in the Strand barristers crossed the road in their wigs – the streets of London in busy midday, were pleasant places to be in for the young and curious. Then it was time to meet Rosie, tea at her bed-sitter in Marylebone: talking time. There would be books on her table, just come out, highbrow books as one spoke of them then unselfconsciously. She took *The Times*, for the reviews, the theatre critics, the law reports. Politics, except in most general terms, were seldom referred to. (Though, like my mother, she often spoke of the beastliness of the 1914 War.) Toni would come in . . . after reluctant household shopping or her singing lesson . . . Rosie was still rarely available in the evening (except at weekends) so I often walked across Regent's Park for supper with the Nairns.

Their mews sitting-room was, as I said before, small. It contained essentials, a piano, a bookcase, the folding table at which we ate, some chairs – it was *very* small: not unfittingly so for Toni but Jamie filled it like Alice the White Rabbit's house. That incongruity of scale was paralleled when he tried out his bits of German on Toni, who had taught him a working vocabulary. (He used to go to Germany for auctions.) What she had actually made him learn were the diminutive forms of concrete nouns, *das Büchlein, das Tischlein* instead of *das Buch, der Tisch* and so forth. So when that big and markedly unloquacious man called the gas fire in good faith *das Öfchen* (so much harder to pronounce than *Ofen*) the effect was weird. It must have puzzled many a serious Teutonic book collector. Rosie, I noticed, ignored it altogether, responding to him always in good English.

Mostly however – not in baby German – Jamie quietly, sparingly, talked shop. Rare editions, how discovered, whom to offer to . . . prices . . . Toni giving clear-minded attention. He could come out with an anecdote, something Shelley had done or De Quincey had said, he told it as if it had happened the other day and he'd heard of it that morning. Toni talked music, which meant opera. She had a collection of early records of famous sopranos and tenors but did not like to play them in front of us. When Jamie fetched the gramophone, hand-cranked of course, kept in their bedroom under one of the single beds, he would put on a symphony or an oratorio. I sat on the floor, trying to listen, mind wandering.

When it was time to leave, they'd say, 'See you tomorrow, it's Saturday, if the weather holds (were we in June by then?) we might drive to Kew in the afternoon.' I went back on foot; it was a walk, though not *such* a walk, up Albany Street, Regent's Park Road, Primrose Hill, Belsize Park – bushes were scented, streets well lit, one met policemen on their beat; the odd drunk too. Did no one try to pick me up? In London, an hour or less from midnight? If so, he must have been easily brushed off – I don't remember. The Nairns were under the impression that I was going home by tube or bus.

I hoped that I *deserved* it all. In the mornings I wrote essays (on Macaulay who fascinated, on Thackeray who distinctly bored), tortured pieces, overflowing with quotations, leaden with words, were dragged out of myself by the sweat of my brow. Then: thunderbolt. The Robbinses. They said they had something to tell, or rather to talk over with me. Susan and Jack and I gathered in the high-ceilinged dining-room that served as studio. It made me think of the last time,

of the 'conference' we had had in their parents' house when I was a
child – how many years ago? – and decided to throw in my lot with
theirs rather than be sent away to a school . . . Now, it was they who
were required to make up their minds.

The facts were: well, Jack was getting on . . . Painting . . . The
galleries . . . Perhaps he'd been seen around a bit too long . . . It didn't
get any easier to live hand to mouth, hang on to promise . . . Oh, it
had been fun. Belsize Park: they'd managed to stay put a good deal
longer already than they could afford . . . Something cheaper in the
country . . . ? losing contacts . . . there didn't seem to be many cottages
any more to be lent to one . . . And now there was this offer. A JOB.

Art master at a school. In New Zealand. (Or was it Australia? both
were remote to me.) A decent salary. Very decent, Jack said. A three-
year contract; extendable. Passage paid. A house of their own in the
school compound.

Can you *see* us live in a school? What a laugh. Can you see *Susan*? I
thought they already could see themselves – respectability at a certain
point may look adventurous.

Their people were pleased, even though it was the other side of the
world. And it wasn't that Jack would have to give up being a painter –
holidays were long. It would be *warm*, Susan said, sun the year round,
like living in the South again, and I guessed that she was harking back
to a Mediterranean beach of some past summer, perhaps the very
beach on which she had encountered my mother. 'And what will *you*
do?' they asked (as if reading my mind).

I thought of the moment in Italy, at Cortina when the telegram had
come for Doris offering a screen test and I had said You must go, and
had stayed on by myself at the hotel. (That hadn't been so bad. Or had
it?) Now my reaction was dread – What will happen to *me*? I had the
(elementary) grace not to show this and threw myself into discussing
their pros and cons. The pros had to have it. Their families were
already seeing them with new eyes – to the length of proposing to pay
off their debts. (No more pawning of my cigarette case.) Whatever
rigours and stuffinesses they might meet with in antipodean scholastic
life, they would be sure to draw some amusement from; they'd be

much forgiven and liked. (This turned out to be so: reports trickled through that Susan if she had sometimes scandalised, had charmed.) At the worst, we summed up, they'd be back in three years – Jack wasn't getting on all that much – solvent and, who knows, with a show's worth of canvases ablaze with an exotic vegetation.

They were not to sail until the autumn and I was going to spend the best part of the summer months at Sanary, so I did not assist in the dismantling of Belsize Park, and the question of my future could be treated by all concerned with marked unurgency. In the end, with a minimum of misrepresentations, it all slid into a new, or not so new, arrangement.

When I say all concerned I do not only mean the Robbinses, Alessandro (a benevolent word in edgeways), my mother (who could by no means always be relied upon to act passively), I have to include the powers – seen as dark, and largely *in* the dark, but powers all the same – who technically controlled my destiny until I came of age. I was still a ward of that court in Germany. It had a hydra-headed identity because the communications we were so slow in opening and responding to emanated, above gothically convoluted signatures, from a team of *Oberlandesgerichtsrat*s and *Amtsreferendar*s. We forebore to speculate how far they were in ignorance or at least in doubt about facts that must have appeared both nebulous and irregular to those good men (I did not refer to them with such equanimity at the time), so irregular indeed that whenever they took a collegiate look at what in some far-away cabinet must have been my file, they may have felt it best to let it lie. Sleeping dogs in another country . . . They may have prayed as hard as I did to have done with me. Unfortunately there were still quite some years to go.

I don't remember or never really knew how the new arrangement was put over, or who instigated it and why; what seems odder is that it was made at all. A line of least resistance . . . It suited me. What emerged by late September – towards the end of a pleasant stay en famille in France – was that I was to go on spending the rough equivalent of the school-year in England pursuing – pursuing what? – well, my pursuits, and that I was to live in London under the protection, as Victorian novels put it, of Mr and Mrs Nairn (not met, unlike Jack and Susan, by my mother) which in practice meant a bed-sitter in Upper Gloucester Place found for me by Rosie Falkenheim ten steps from her own door.

Independence was to go the length of my managing the monthly money. (So far it had been sent to the Robbinses who had given me a share: well below a dress allowance but good pocket money.) And there I ran into an embarrassment at the outset. The room Rosie had chosen was a first-floor front for something like 25/6d. or 27/6d. a week with breakfast. I had only just realised how little the total amount of my allowance was (and how little the generous Robbinses had been taking for my keep!). There was a smaller room free to let, the landlady revealed, a top-floor back at 21/6d. When I said I would have that one, Rosie did not understand my choice. I ought to have talked facts but lacked the savoir-faire. She and Toni did not think talking money nice and moreover were convinced somehow that I belonged to a well-off family. I said I preferred to be high up; she said, it was I who'd have to live in it, and I knew that she thought me stingy. There'd be more occasions such as this. At sixteen, independence and friendship with one's elders have their strings attached.

*   *   *

So there I was for a good part of the next three years in my room in Upper Gloucester Place trotting about London, latchkey and all. A not inconsiderable slice of life. They say that if you spend thirty years in one place they go in a flash. If this is so, the speed must be terrifying. In my own life, I found that the fragments it got carved into went fast, much too fast – the year in Portugal, the year in Mexico, five in New York, seven in Rome, three years in Essex, the decades, more than one, in Mediterranean France . . . Time split by places, by events – rushing towards the war, blowing away the post-war years – everything that happened as one got hold of it was over.

Is there remission in childhood? Time can feel long – or slow: not the same. I remember such stretches, yet on the whole even then things seemed to – did – pass, change, as one was settling in. So now in adolescence I felt no impatience for anything to happen to me. (Curiosity about people and the world, readiness for adventure, escapades on a minor scale were side-lines, not committal.) I had an instinct that already things had gone too far for me, I should like to have moved backward if one could (backward to where? unanswerable question). Perhaps like my mother I just preferred to remain in the day.

Her tendency not to take care of the Future overmuch may have come from a sense of the Future being already flawed: she had lived as an adult through a war that had irretrievably damaged civilisation; on the private level she had entered one marriage she could not absolve herself from and another bound to give hostages to fortune. My case was different. If I saw the Future as indefinite and not yet here, I also saw it – world and peace permitting – rosy. One would be happy. I might attain the one thing I ought to be, a writer. This by now seemed to have been accepted, by my mother explicitly, '*If* you have the talent'. (The bugbears at the *Oberlandesgericht* had not heard of it.) A most exalted calling – *A Writer*. (I never referred to it as author in my mind; still don't.) I knew that I could never be a musician or a painter, were I ever to make my catch it could only be in words.

In more frivolous moments I thought of being a barrister as immensely interesting and exciting – and it might have been good training for that ultimate vocation – but my sex at the time was against it, not to mention my educational deficiencies. (At that stage I was convinced that I could learn almost anything including a new language in six months flat.) Meanwhile I occasionally faced the question: How does one become a writer? By writing. But the writing – the little that got done – wasn't going well: not the stuff that becomes transfigured into *A Book*. So I stuck to the only apprenticeship I thought there was (today I might have thought of journalism?): I went on reading. Please God, make me a writer, but not yet.

When I am trying to think of those years in NW1, and I haven't thought of them for a very long time, they seem to have been all of a piece, a uniform round. It can't have been wholly like that. There must have been some process of growing up, at whatever rate; life does widen and not only by visits to the British Museum, the Tate and Winchester Cathedral. Yet the only thing that remains vivid is the physical feel of living in London, young and on very little though sufficient money. The buses – one was always running after, catching or just missing a last bus; the queueing for a play in Shaftesbury Avenue; the Lyons' Corner House afterwards (poached egg on toast); Bovril at a coffee stall very late at night; the elegance of Mayfair streets at lunchtime; how splendid the men, how pretty the girls, how well dressed everyone was, how en fête; the smell of the cheaper Soho restaurants (upholstery, grease, spice, trapped air); my digs.

A strip of a room, a strip of none too appetising carpet, a sash window (rather awful curtain), the whole reasonably clean: a respectably kept bed and breakfast place. I had a gas ring (used to good purpose with a pot and a pan I got at Woolworth's), a basin with hot and cold; breakfast was in bed, brought up on a tray, English breakfast, not very well cooked, plentiful, welcome. It was a far cry from the whitewashed space I associated with living in Italy and Provence, but it could do, and it did. One great boon was the bath – half-landing down – generally vacant, with an abundant supply of steaming hot water (our southern abodes depended on rainfall and cisterns, seldom satisfactorily filled, and capricious wood-burning contraptions to warm the trickle).

Part of the day and the late night walks were my own, a solitariness I needed and enjoyed, the rest I played satellite to the Nairns. And it is they rather than what happened to my younger self who occupy my memory of those years: their daily life, their lives, their story. It got to me piecemeal. I never knew it all, but I got to know a good deal. *The Two Sisters.* That would be the title had it been a play (Jamie's role – though this was not evident to me for some time – was not a principal's). Some of it puzzles me still; I never fathomed Toni. Although she remained a great friend; she died in the nineteen-seventies, the result of an accident brought about by her own obstinacy.

In the late Twenties when I shared so much of their London life, Toni and Jamie must have been married for some years. They had met in Berlin (where the Falkenheims came from). Their father had been a doctor who died early leaving his widow – a somewhat over-cosseted woman – comfortably off. They lived in a large, properly staffed, rented flat in the Kurfürstendamm district. There were no brothers. The male element was an uncle, a bachelor who lived well, doted on Toni (said to have looked enchanting in a fragile way when a young girl). He encouraged her singing, took her to the opera, to the great performances of the time, and to suppers at places like Horcher's and Kempinsky's where he gave her caviar (literally), delicate little ragouts and sips of Château Yquem (again literally). This uncle had less time for Rosie, older, more independent and, as I said before, just scraping home as a *jolie laide*.

The girls grew up in that cultivated, liberal society which flourished in Berlin in the decade before the Kaiser's War: professional men, artists, actors, journalists and musicians, bankers and aristocrats with a large but by no means exclusive element of Jews. Under the Weimar Republic, that society, as we know, became even more liberal, talented and mixed. The Weimar Republic (and a concatenation of the economic ravages of the late war, the Versailles Treaty, Allied expectancy of Reparation Payments) also brought inflation of devastating speed and scale. The mark in their pockets became devalued by a hundred per cent, a thousand, a million, a thousand million . . . Paper money – wages were paid daily more than once – was carried about in laundry baskets; what bought a piano last week and a loaf that morning barely ran to the evening newspaper. People in work or who owned and contrived to hang on to real property were able to scrape along; the rentier class was wiped out. Their comfortable income melted to nothing at all, the Falkenheims were left with little besides the family silver. The uncle was dead, his estate vanished. Frau Falkenheim became more idle and difficult, finding refuge in sleeping pills, complaints and neurasthenia; the girls, young women by then, took jobs. They had not been brought up to work, they had been encouraged as was the wont of females in their milieu to put their feet up after luncheon. They were, however, well educated (and connected). They got *good* jobs: Rosie in an art gallery, Toni in a well-known auction house, a Berlin equivalent of Sotheby's. Both women unexpectedly turned out competent. Toni's lot was not made easier by a morbid conscientiousness combined with the double burden of an invincible shyness that covered up an arrogance she had no real wish to conceal. Rosie liked and got on well with her male colleagues.

They managed to keep on the flat – letting go the staff, taking a lodger or two – and to look after their mother and her increasing demands. And it was at that auction house that Jamie, having come over to bid, met Toni and found her charming.

So far so clear. What would follow followed: proposal, engagement, some day Toni marries, leaves for England; some day at some point the mother dies, Rosie in her turn gives up her job, packs up and goes to join her sister and brother-in-law. And so here they are, the three of them, in London. (Rosie, incidentally, without a visible occupation – she only 'helped out' at Jamie's shop the odd afternoon.)

Now and then remarks came out inconsistent with this sequence: dates or events that would not fit, such as Rosie talking about a play she remembered seeing in the West End: so had I, with the Robbinses, surely many years ago? Gradually it emerged that it must have been Toni on her own who held the job in Berlin, and looked after the increasingly unmanageable mother until she died (an overdose?). When Jamie met Toni and Toni accepted him, Rosie had already gone to live – a year ago, several years ago? – in England.

I should now say something about their daily lives. That Toni was discontented with hers was obvious. She missed, she longed for, she glorified Berlin – the theatre, her friends, the life . . . She was fond of Jamie, very fond, that too was evident. (Their bouts of big-man small-woman exchanges made Rosie look very distant.) She was serious about his work, giving advice (sound), doing the bookkeeping, another unexpected skill; the shop was doing well. All the same they were hard up, though living rent free; Jamie, intent on paying back the capital he'd been lent, insisted on a meagre budget. Toni's singing lessons, by a far from top-class teacher, were their one extravagance.

That capital, by the way, came from Toni's ex-boss, P.G., the founder of the Berlin auction house. He had a high opinion of Jamie's abilities and integrity; the money, I understood, had been lent free of interest as a wedding present for Toni. Hence Jamie's determination to repay it as soon, or sooner than they could.

P.G. was an exacting and a complex man, self-made, courageous (fighting a bone disease), witty, generous, a martinet and, on occasions, a charmer. He had the misfortune (one of his least) to become my pupil. That was in the Thirties when he and his family arrived in England as refugees. (I advertised language lessons in *The Times* agony column, though that particular job came to me by way of the Nairns.) I say misfortune because I cannot spell, at least not well enough to teach. He trusted me. Years later the poor man nearly sacked his American secretary because she didn't spell harassment my way. (Not enough r's *he* believed.) I also coached his son – an exceedingly handsome boy – on God knows what pretences! – and actually helped him, with the assistance of Brian Howard of all people, to get into an Oxford college. I often wish I had achieved as much for myself.

Back to Toni. She took being hard up well enough, though Jamie's Scottish little household sums lacked the panache of the German débâcle. What she minded dreadfully was the housework – even at the worst in Berlin they'd had a *Putzfrau*, a daily, doing for them – it bored and repelled her. The mews was decently kept down to the unloved kitchen: but oh, the gloves for scrubbing and the gloves for dusting, the sighs and the lack of interest in her husband's food – man's food, Englishman's food. Well, she gave him his breakfast and his supper. He had his lunches near the shop – somewhere behind Bond Street or Oxford Street – how nice for him, I thought, with a colleague or a customer, the men he brought back the anecdotes from. The sisters had their main meal at Schmidt's, the German restaurant in Charlotte Street, where they met every day at one o'clock. I had been expected to join them; got out of it, couldn't afford it for one thing though it was fairly inexpensive then and a good place of its kind. A sandwich, an apple or, after I reached eighteen, a couple of sausages at a pub were my range, not *Kalbsfleisch* and chocolate cake.

Suppers at the mews were segregated, a bought pie, baked beans warmed up for Jamie, something cold for the women: dark bread and butter, one of the more refined products of *charcuterie* such as *Teewurst* or liver pâté, an assortment of cream cakes – everything from Schmidt's – followed by chocolates and cigarettes. They never cooked, and I dare say rarely ate, a fresh vegetable. We all drank tea. Jamie smoked a pipe.

Goodness, it sounds dreary. It was not. There was much to make it not so: Jamie's friendliness, the flow of talk – books and their authors, music and musicians, art and its collectors – all coming naturally, pell-mell, not argumentative though each had different bents. Jamie might quote Tennyson, Toni would tell me to read *Buddenbrooks* and (curious choice for her) *Tess of the D'Urbervilles*. Rosie picked up *Decline and Fall* the week it came out. Another first I owe to her: Evelyn Waugh. I posted a copy to my mother next day.

Then there was the gramophone. When Rosie wasn't there; *she* really disliked music. Jamie played his Elgar and his Bach and Handel, Toni chose *Rosenkavalier*. What really sent her, as we would now, not inaptly, put it, were the voices of great singers. Once she got lured into putting on Caruso and a rare recording of Emmy Destinn, a soprano she revered. It sounded ghostly, remote and cracked, with some beauty coming through. For Toni it was an ecstasy she ought to have been allowed to have in private.

They were good, those evenings in the mews at Regent's Park. Not just for me. In spite of the smouldering discontent, Toni was stimulated; in Rosie, whatever she was doing, one was aware of something quietly purring away; Jamie was just *quiet*. Not on the surface only, I feel sure he liked his home life.

Rosie and I did things together: afternoons at the National Portrait Gallery, the Wallace Collection, Dulwich (on top of my own, at one time almost daily, hour at the National Gallery). The plays she chose for us would be anything good between Shakespeare and Coward. – She greatly admired the actor Gerald Du Maurier. – We took train day trips to Canterbury, to Ely . . .

On Sundays, when the weather wasn't too vile, we drove into the country, the four of us in Jamie's Morris-Cowley, Rosie and I stuck in the open dickey with a square of oilcloth rigged above our heads in case of rain. Jamie liked country walks, and so did I. The sisters chose to stay in the car, smoking, nibbling chocolates. These outings, picnic and all, were one of Toni's concessions to being a good wife. (How *little* she liked those Sundays, she later told me.) On the way back, as a reward, Jamie would stop at a tea-shop.

About once a month Toni and Jamie went to his mother's for Sunday dinner. I believe she lived in Surbiton. (Jamie took his mending.) Hardly a word was said about these visits – Toni *was* loyal – yet one gathered that mother and daughter-in-law were poles apart in every respect. I never learned much about Jamie's background or early life – though he and I remained on affectionate, if casual, terms for some fifty years. (As Toni so often said: a taciturn Scot.) I knew vaguely that he had been something of a wanderer, that his father was a lay preacher at some time, that Jamie had not gone to university, that there was no family money. A brother somewhere, I think; no sisters. Mrs Nairn's home, Toni's first in England – after their marriage, she and Jamie lived at his mother's for about a year – was the epitome of an English way of life she shuddered from and feared: cosy-spartan England of parlours, yellow soap in the bath and no warmth in the bedrooms, where dad was served first and had his chair by the fire (a cut or two below my own first English experience with the Robbinses' people). That year in Surbiton, if it was Surbiton, must have been a great trial; the more so as it was utterly unexpected: Jamie the happy suitor in Berlin had given her no indications. If anyone was inept at living down being the foreigner-married-to-the-son it was Toni.

Disassociation from her husband's family goes some way to explain the social isolation in which Toni lived during those years. Why no new friends of her own? deigned not? could not? Lack of opportunity I suppose, compounded by shyness, choosiness and pride; in her disillusion with the English she looked rather too often down her small nose. Then there was Jamie failing to bring home his professional friends (pretty glamorous – by which I meant articulate and bright – from what I absorbed on visits to the shop). A simple instinct to keep his masculine world apart? Brief exceptions were attempted once or twice, not doomed to success – Toni's unadjustable attitudes, her housekeeping, their slender means. (At that period no drink was kept in the house.)

Yes, but Rosie. *She* was not shy; *she* loved the English; her feelings about London were much those of Dr Johnson, yet she too appeared to know nobody besides myself and a woman schoolteacher from Watford who faithfully came to tea once a fortnight on her half-holiday. They'd met on some trip. A nice woman, though hardly, I felt, a congruous friend for Rosie.

5

One morning in mid-March – it was at the end of my first winter in Upper Gloucester Place – a blustery cold morning, I went out early for some reason or other. I seldom did, mornings were for 'study'. Going up the street I saw Rosie Falkenheim walking ten yards in front of me making for her own door. She was wearing what I can only describe as trailing evening dress, not a mere long skirt, unmistakable chiffon swirls under a short day coat. She turned into her house. It must have been about half past nine in the morning. She did not see me.

Barely a week later I went out early again (one of those coincidental things that happen to most of us: one hasn't been near some place for years then returns thrice running). Passing Baker Street tube station I saw Rosie emerging from the entrance, trailing dress, day coat, evening bag. It was about ten o'clock, bright daylight. This time she saw me. And that *I'd* seen her.

Good morning, she said.

Good morning, I said in a tone much less assured.

I'm on my way home, she said, and where are *you* off to? (Was there a twinkle in her bright round simian eyes?)

I told her with as much composure as I could and fled.

Later that day I found a note in the hall suggesting we might have a bite of dinner together in Soho – it was a Saturday – something we had done once or twice before and she knew I liked tremendously. We went. To the small Escargot. There were two restaurants called

L'Escargot in Greek Street, opposite one another, both French in the Soho style. The larger Escargot was quite elegant and expensive; it still flourishes (with what is currently perhaps the best American wine list in London); small brother is no more.

As usual she let me take over. We discussed what we were going to eat. I decided the wine.

I had started on the snails I'd ordered for myself (there is a stage in one's gastronomic evolution when one believes that one likes snails very much), when Rosie said in a decisive tone, 'This has all been rather silly.'

I stopped the movement of my fork.

'You see, it's all because of Toni.'

'Yes,' I said. 'No.'

'Toni doesn't want you to know. She doesn't want anyone to know; she doesn't want Jamie to show that he knows.'

I took some bread and mopped up the little pool of garlic butter in which one of my snails had sat.

'You know,' Rosie said, 'I have a friend.'

'No,' I said. 'Yes?'

'He lives off St James's Park. It's a service flat in a block. He likes me to change in the evening.'

That night, and on other nights, I learned some of the facts that make up their story. The beginnings and the present; some of the future I witnessed myself (from side-lines). I shall tell only the much of it that I heard and the little of it that I saw; I could expand my knowledge by looking up obituaries and old clippings, they would yield more facts, they could not give a complete truth. I prefer to leave it as it is, a fragment of private human behaviour. I shall not name names. The Nairns were not called Nairn, nor were the Falkenheims (any more than the Robbinses were the Robbinses). Why, might one ask, after all those years and in our tell-all age? Chiefly because they are people seen only through my eyes: it would be impertinent and in some cases hurtful to publish my, necessarily one-sided, view of people who though they themselves be dead may still be held in affection and esteem, let alone seen in different lights, by their descendants, friends and colleagues.

As far as Rosie Falkenheim's story is concerned, the reason for 'covering up' is stronger: I only heard two sides of it. Of the motives, commitments, feelings of the third and principal protagonist I know nothing, or next to nothing, at first hand.

In the summers, the summers before the First World War that was, the widowed Mrs Falkenheim took her young daughters to a comfortable resort in Switzerland. There between lake and mountains they spent six weeks or more in a good hotel. Rooms with a view, rooms with balconies . . . Palm-court music, excursions, animated social life among an international clientèle. One year they met a good-looking young barrister from England. Not too young – Toni was eighteen, Rosie in her twenties, he, a generation or so older, somewhere in his thirties – old enough to dazzle with conversation and an experienced charm. He was, one understood, already very successful at the Bar. He was un-English enough (a touch? more than a touch of Irish?) to show that he enjoyed the company of pretty women, and attached himself to Toni who, when things were right, could be quite a flirt. They played tennis, they went out on the lake, they danced in the evenings . . . A summer flirtation and seen as such by their hotel acquaintance: the good-looking barrister from England was Toni Falkenheim's beau.

Next summer came round and who happened to be at Vevey, Pontresina or Gstaad (if I was told, I don't remember which): the barrister from England. Again he slipped into his role as Toni's chief attendant. Did she take it seriously? (They knew he wasn't married.) Rosie, who was never able to ask, thought Toni could not have. He may have turned her head a little, but it was all so evidently a pleasant public pastime with a rather worldly man outside her sphere, not a courtship. She *couldn't* have taken it seriously, her real life was already conditioned by Berlin, her music, the spoiling uncle; her crushes so far were for opera singers. All the same she was flattered, he was so intelligent, so entertaining, so many cuts above the other single men at the hotel. Besides she liked him, she liked him very much; he was, Rosie said, a charmer who had much more to offer than his charm. So Toni had the best of it in the mountain days and evenings . . .

Next summer the Falkenheims left Vevey or Gstaad earlier than had been their habit; the good-looking barrister from England, the

Courts not having risen before August, did not come at all. That summer was 1914.

There is one thing not mentioned in this account of the previous years. After the orchestra had packed up their fiddles and the lights been put out in the chandeliers, and upstairs Toni had taken off her dancing slippers, the barrister from England slid into Rosie's room and spent the night with her. Their rooms were on the same floor, she left her window open, he had become quite good at moving like a shadow along a row of balconies.

They corresponded during the whole of the war by way of neutral Switzerland. To write or receive letters from an enemy alien, as each was now to the other, was a serious offence. Their post-box or go-between must have been safe for they got away with it. The obituary I did not read might tell whether he served in the war or did some important law work, as it would give the date of his taking Silk. All I know is that in the early nineteen-twenties he was made a judge. A judge of the High Court in the King's Bench Division. When it had become reasonably possible again for a German to travel, he arranged for her to come to England. Rosie left Berlin, family and job for good and settled – with her own furniture – in that bed-sitter in Upper Gloucester Place.

Their affair had to be kept entirely private which in his position meant secret. Astonishingly perhaps, it remained so.

*   *   *

It took time to get a few of the questions answered, not least because most of them were unaskable. Yet once Rosie had begun to talk, she talked again.

Quite soon she told me his name. I realised that he was not one of the judges whose cases she used to point out to me. I had never seen him on the Bench. Yet what he said in the morning often got into the lunchtime edition of the evening papers. He was a quotable judge, a witty judge, a talking judge – some said too much so – who did not shun controversy. He was keen on some reforms – on liberal social lines – with which Rosie concurred.

How did Toni take it? (We got round to that too.) When she found out, when you told her – you must have had to tell her when you left Berlin? Or did she know before?

'*She did not know before,*' Rosie said.

'All those years when you never saw him?' (What my mother had gone through in Sorrento – for how long? a week, two weeks?)

'And you could only write letters?'

She said she wasn't sure that she had wanted to talk to anyone. 'And I could not tell Toni.'

'It might have,' I said, 'well . . . prepared her?'

'It would have been the same. Toni has her pride. You must have seen enough to realise that. A terrible pride.'

'She *was* made a bit of a fool of.'

'Well in a way; not really. Jack says she was so very pretty then.' (Jack was what Rosie called the Judge though his first name was not John.) 'He enjoyed flirting with her.' She said this with the utmost equanimity. 'We could have laughed it off together.'

'But Toni didn't.'

'Toni didn't. She went white. I first thought: rage. Now I'm not sure. She left the room. I can't forget what her face looked like. We never talked of it again.'

'*Never?*' I said, thinking of the loquacious ways my mother had trained me in.

'Not in any real sense – she knows I see him. That's unavoidable. But she won't speak of him, she never wants to see him again. She can't bear to hear his name.'

I thought of what Toni had said to me about those unwritten postcards.

'I often think it was shock,' Rosie said, 'that dreadful first reaction. Sheer shock. My leaving her, my leaving Berlin was *terrible* for her.'

I did not say: But you did. We just sat and let it sink in.

'Toni and I are . . . ' she hesitated.

'Devoted . . . ?' I put in.

She hesitated again. 'One might say we were tied one to the other . . . It started when we were children, we had to make a front against our mother. Toni was the pretty one, but it was on her that most of the demands were made – Toni is spoilt *and* vulnerable. What *I* feel about her is anxiety . . . I'm always afraid for her.'

'And she? She is very fond of you?'

'I don't know. As I said, we are tied. She can't bear it when I'm not about. When I first went to live in London, she wrote to me every day.'

'Goodness,' I said. 'Real letters?'

'Not *real* letters,' said Rosie. She added, 'I'm not sure that she likes me. She disapproves of me.'

'Is it . . . is it because of the Judge?'

'That comes into it. One of the worst things is that she's not happy here. It's not right for her here.'

'England?'

'Everything.'

'But Jamie – ?'

'Oh Jamie,' she said.

'You mean she shouldn't have – ?'

'I mean she wouldn't have.'

Married him if it hadn't been for her, Rosie's, going off? Was that what she was saying?

'At the time she met Jamie, Toni was still besotted with that tenor,' she named an internationally known singer well beyond his second youth.

'Did she know *him*?'

'Years ago when our uncle was still alive, she made him introduce her; the three of them had tea together or something. Once, for all I know. He's grossly fat too. And married. It was just nonsense. All Toni wants to do with a man is to worship from afar or flirt.'

'But she got *married*?'

'Oh, Toni flirted with Jamie all right. Trouble is, that's not enough.'

I nodded.

'There *are* things you don't know much about yet, my dear,' she said with a not unkindly look.

I was left to wonder whether what Toni had wanted most had been a good-looking man of her own to carry her off to England.

Now that I had the key, Rosie's routine became revealed. With some exceptions – such as the Judge being on circuit – she went to his flat every evening from Monday to Thursday or Friday. She went by underground from Baker Street to St James's Park, and returned, as I had seen, the same way in the morning. She had his keys, came and went quietly, made sure that the lift was empty, avoided seeing a porter too often. On some evenings, by no means all, they had their dinner à deux in his flat; more often she came later and waited for him to return from dinners with his friends or some function. He had a wide social life. He would be wearing a white tie or a dinner jacket, always the latter when they were dining together alone. Hence – on his request? on his taking for granted? – her matutinal evening dresses. Token evening dresses, one might describe them: she dressed conventionally, but not well. Her figure, one must bear in mind, was badly put together and she bought her clothes ready-made. (She once asked me to accompany her to Swan and Edgar's.)

Weekends the Judge spent out of London. He had connections near Bath, a nephew in Gloucestershire, was asked to country house parties, was a good shot. She went to his court rarely; when he had an interesting or sensational case, his clerk would arrange a seat for her. Otherwise she never saw him outside the St James's flat. They did not go anywhere together, not even to a cinema. He had not introduced her to any of his friends; they, like his relations, were in complete ignorance of her existence. So with the exception of his clerk, the man who served their dinners in the flat and an occasional porter (she left before the housekeeper arrived in the morning) she had not met a single soul he knew.

About her finances she was entirely reticent. She had no job; from Jamie I gathered that no Falkenheim assets had been resurrected in the German post-inflation. She did not appear to have money worries – she didn't appear to worry about anything much, except her sister – although she lived modestly she did not live badly, indeed with much less restraint than Toni and Jamie to whom *she* offered treats; she never hesitated before going to a theatre or on one of her architectural trips; in season, though she stuck to éclairs, she had strawberries for me. One had to assume a regular source of income. An allowance – ? hand-outs – ? a settlement – ? from the Judge? I never knew.

High Court judges' salaries were what seemed to me enormous, and certainly a great deal higher, in real terms, than they are today (just as judges themselves were considered more exalted, indeed sacrosanct, beings). Rosie's Judge was known to have a not insubstantial private income as well.

One could not ask as to the why of the bed-sitter, which by the way was quite charming. A large almost square room with decent ceiling height and two long windows. The bed was a divan, the furniture, not too much of it, light and painted (Bavarian peasant baroque?), light curtains, light wallpaper, comfortable chairs, the whole effect very pleasant, and her washbasin and gas-ring – unlike mine – were invisible behind a curtained recess. *I* would have liked her to have the dignity of her own front door, let alone kitchen and bathroom. (The rent of a small unfurnished flat would not have come to more then.) Perhaps she lived where she did as a ploy for security, a safer hide-out than a flat, say, in St John's Wood; perhaps it was just because the Falkenheims were not domestically inclined.

The new novels, always on her table – the Huxleys, the Waughs, in due course the I. Compton-Burnetts – were sent to her by the Judge. That is he had placed a general order with his booksellers; the ones she liked, she took to him to read.

In May I had a letter – well, more of a note – from Alessandro. The bathing in the sea had begun, not just for the hardy dippers, the real deep swims. Your mother says you would like that, she asked me to tell you why not come soon and make a long summer of it . . .

Earlier he had written that they were moving house. *Not* another villa, a Provençal *mas* – eighteenth-century – quite beautiful and uncomfortable.

Bathing in the sea . . . I had not forgotten. A long summer of it . . . I gave a couple of weeks' notice to my landlady, mine or a similar room up the road could be had in the autumn. Another note came from

Alessandro saying that they would meet my train at Toulon station: she wants you to know that there is a surprise but I'm keeping it a surprise.

Since she'd heard about my leaving for France, Rosie had become thoughtful – I'd told her a good deal about Sanary – and one evening she said she was hatching a plan, a bold plan but perhaps quite simple, would I help her? would I do something for her?

Of course.

She and Jack had never been anywhere together (not since Switzer-land, what – ? fifteen years ago?); he spent his holidays in Somerset, in Scotland, in Ireland, he also used to go to Monte Carlo quite often, 'But not any more,' she said, and I thought I saw an expression on her face I had not seen before, quite fleeting, a spasm of acute anxiety. At once she collected herself, 'What I'm talking about,' she said in her usual slow, rather deep voice, 'is that we couldn't dream of going anywhere in England, or really to the kind of places and hotels abroad that Jack's used to and known at.'

'Sanary?'

'It *might* be possible.'

'You'd be safe there, in some small hotel – nobody'd know you, I mean him.'

The plan struck fire. Jack was all for it, I was told.

'He rather likes taking risks,' Rosie said. He was leaving the arrange-ments to her; she was leaving them to me.

A fortnight starting in summer (after the Courts had risen) – they'd travel separately – she to arrive a day or two before him – separate rooms of course – *adjoining*, if that could be managed.

I said I'd see to it.

Bandol had a *good* hotel, I was expanding, but there would be some English – I'd seen copies of the *Continental Daily Mail* about . . . At Sanary the hotels were more obscure. There was the La Tour, very pretty view, but noisy and full of grubby artists. 'I don't think it would do for Monsieur le Juge.'

She laughed and said Monsieur le Juge was ready to rough it.

I said that he hadn't seen the La Tour. There was the Dol, a very snug French, French hotel: commercial travellers all year, holiday-makers in the summer; I knew the owner, I said, recalling with pleasure our *belote* evenings at La Marine. But they'd look foreign there, 'You'd stick out too much.' Then there's the one with the tennis court, that's larger, it's got an awfully gloomy garden, oleander and pine. Ah, Hôtel de la Plage, quite the best, on the flat side of Sanary but bang on the sea and good food, you wouldn't see a foreign cat, only the odd English spinster doing watercolours. 'You'd be quite anonymous.'

Anonymous?

Rosie saw the snag. So did I.

'I suppose he couldn't travel under a false name? Of course not. This is what you actually do when you arrive,' I was able to explain, 'you don't sign a register, you fill up a *fiche*, they hardly look at it afterwards – not like Italy where they pore over your documents and keep them for hours – if you put in your passport number and *Date d'arrivée*. But yes, there's *Profession* . . . What does it say in his passport?'

'I've never seen his passport,' Rosie said.

'They needn't either. Couldn't he put something like *Docteur en droit*, Doctor of Laws – when I *am* one, I shall always put *Femme de lettres* – *Magistrat* too covers a lot . . . Perhaps it will have to be *Juge*, that isn't so very grand in France, he might be just some *juge d'instruction*. As long as they call him *Monsieur* and don't get on to any *Milord anglais* business.'

Here, I wondered, not for the first time, what he looked like. Rosie had not, or did not show, a photograph.

It was decided that I should reconnoitre when I got to France.

While thus conspiring with Rosie, I saw a good deal of Toni; I also saw a good deal more. Despite the baby German and the loyal support of his work, one perceived that Toni treated and, if indirectly, spoke of Jamie with condescension; that she held herself his superior, that is, more civilised, more sophisticated, in a number of implied ways. *She* was not a man (inferior by definition because of men's gross appetites); *he* was not an artist or musician, not a Berlin Jew but an Anglo-Saxon goy. She felt affinity only with Jews (Italian and Latin-American opera singers being honorary ones). She had been reticent about this until the day I happened to refer, I don't remember à propos of what, to my own Jewish origins. (By blood, not by religion or tradition; my mother had set me such an example of entire disregard of race and nationality that I rarely give it a thought. That was still possible – in some enclaves – in the nineteen-twenties.) Toni's reaction to my casual disclosure had astonished me. 'So you're *not* a goy, thank God!' Then she became suspicious and began to quiz me. I didn't have the right kind of hair, or colouring or anything. I assured her that I was guaranteed quarter Jewish from my mother's side with some more percentage introduced by some illegitimate line. Toni said that it must have been instinct on her part that she first took to me and that my mind at least was not pure goy. I took that as the compliment it was. From then on I was treated with more affection and far less formality.

Among the things she thought fit to talk to me about was the Weimar Republic theatre – early Reinhardt, early Elisabeth Bergner – she led me to reading the James Agate of Berlin, Alfred Kerr – the brilliant and original critic as innovatory in his time as G.B.S. Kerr, notorious for his penchant for very young girls – he married a good many – had once courted Toni. On afternoons when we were alone together in the mews, Toni played the piano for me, often Mozart. Music had had hardly any part in either my father's or my mother's life, and this was something I now needed. She offered to teach me to play – then and in later years – unfortunately it remained hopeless: wrong hands, no ear. But I listened. Once when she was practising the Contessa aria for her teacher, accompanying herself, she allowed me to stay in the room. I was in no way able to assess her voice: the sound to me was lovely and her singing moved me much.

A day or two before I was due to be off, Toni and I were sitting on the lawn in Regent's Park on a couple of those hired chairs (a man would come round from time to time to collect the twopence). It was a fine late afternoon in May. I'd been telling her that I was looking forward to my going to the South of France.

'Like Rosie,' she said. It was a whiplash.

I said nothing. How *had* she got wind of it?

'So Rosie's off to France!'

'Not yet . . . Only perhaps – ' I said weakly.

'And you are encouraging her. *Don't.*'

'How did you – ?'

'Don't be such a fool,' she said, 'Rosie is so transparent.'

I pondered this.

'It's *madness.* The press doesn't like him, he can't afford their getting anything more.'

'*More?*' I said.

'That business two years ago. If he hadn't been so well connected . . . The right strings were pulled.'

'Not – ,' I said, 'not – ?'

'No. Not evidence of another sex scandal,' she said in that crisp voice.

I was shocked. She was not the right person to use such terms.

'If you don't know, if she hasn't told you,' she said, '*I* shan't.'

'Of course,' I said quite cold too now, feeling chivalrous, or perhaps just priggish. 'I don't want to know.'

She ignored me. 'It's disgraceful! Henry is behaving appallingly. She's ruined her life for him.'

Henry was the Judge's actual first name. So she does talk about it, I thought, she does mention him.

'The way he allows her to live . . . '

I had at moments thought on these lines.

'*Disgraceful,*' she repeated.

I said reasonably, 'One does see why they have to lead – different lives . . . If nobody is to find out – '

She interrupted me, 'We know all that – "A man of his position . . . " "No breath of scandal . . . " And so on. Of course he couldn't stay being a judge if it came out that he keeps – *keeps* – a mistress. And serve them right!'

Again I was shocked. 'But it's monstrous – people feeling like that, or the press assuming that they do. It's his . . . it's their business – it's got nothing to do with his being a good judge.' I too was getting vehement.

'I'm not responsible for the British gutter press. Or for British hypocrisy.'

'But they *are* monstrous – one ought to try to change all that.'

She paid no attention. ' . . . that hole-and-corner existence, she should never have put up with it.'

'What could she do?'

'She could leave him. He could marry her. Some men do, you know.'

'Perhaps they don't want to,' I said, 'get married.'

'You can bet *he* doesn't. Henry is the most selfish man on earth.'

I tried to think of Rosie as an English judge's wife. Alessandro swam into my mind – he would be, it struck me, perfectly charming to her but he would like it less to be seen with her in public. Then Alessandro was so very young and handsome, yet the Judge too had been the good-looking young barrister from England.

'Let's face it,' Toni took the thoughts out of my mind as it were, 'Rosie's no oil painting,' she used the expression with a chuckle; again I felt unease. The full ruthlessness struck later. Then, she rode on, 'Fat lot of good it does to one in this country to marry a foreigner! – with no money either – our family is rather presentable in Berlin, *here* they wouldn't know the difference. And Henry would never marry a Jewess.'

'He *can't* be anti-semitic! He would be a horror if he were, and he can't be against Jews if he – well, if he loves one.'

'You know nothing about the social anti-semitism of the English,' Toni said contemptuously, 'in Germany it's the plebs' (she used a horrid-sounding German word, *der Pöbel*) 'who are the anti-semites, here it's the nobs. It's their natural order of things, "Oh, he's of the tribe of Moses," ' she snorted. 'Jamie isn't like that, probably because he didn't go to a public school. Henry would never not conform. Except,' she added, 'in private.'

I said quietly, 'Isn't it possible that they both just don't want to get married? Maybe he's a born bachelor – and so is Rosie.'

She turned on me, 'So young and no moral sense.' A pause. 'I suppose it's not your fault.'

I caught the innuendo – used to catching it – my mother did not have a good press with those who didn't know her.

I said. 'I thought *you* would understand.' It was difficult: the last half-hour had been my first – adult – confrontation.

'I?' she said.

I plunged. 'The way you sang "Porgi Amor".' Into her silence I tried to insert what I now knew I felt. 'I'm sure that Rosie doesn't want any more than what she's got. Even if it has to have its – imperfect sides. I know she is – content.'

'That,' Toni said, 'is even *more* disgraceful.'

6

The surprise announced by Alessandro stood square brown and largish outside Toulon station. Wild joy fought with disappointment. It must not be assumed that my thoughts were all concentrated on Huxley, the League of Nations, food and other people's love affairs; I dreamt a good deal about motor cars. And now there was one, not my own but the very next best to it – a *car*. But – the cars I dreamt of had long bonnets, low seats (preferably only two), above all they were *open* cars. Even Jamie's drab Morris-Cowley had a dickey in which one could experience something of the wind of speed. What was parked between the pavement and the dusty municipal palm-trees was a saloon, God forbid *une conduite intérieure*, a family car with four doors, an irremovable roof and what made it look even less sportif an ungainly luggage rack on top. It was a second-hand Peugeot of, as design went, an unusually clumsy year.

My mother, with imaginative abnegation, made straight for a back seat. In front, next to Alessandro at the wheel, joy got the upper hand. He managed to overcome the serious hill that leads westward out of Toulon in top gear. Alessandro had passed his own test only a few weeks ago but already drove with what I felt as natural aptitude and well. He had also learned to talk car.

From the back, my mother was giving me their news, revealing the reasons for the acquisition of the car. All good. (On each of my arrivals

I sought to read the omens.) She and Alessandro were trying their hand as decorators and antique dealers, a spin-off from his really quite successful incursion into the art dealers' domain. Wives and connections were beginning to toy with converting houses in the South of France, and the same kind of people were getting enthusiastic over Provençal furniture, peasant furniture most of it, though some of the better pieces were quite fine, if one liked that kind of thing and wasn't put off by the fakes in auberge dining-rooms. For the moment genuine stuff was still to be found if one knew where to look, and so she and Alessandro were making trips into the hills of Haute-Provence – beautiful country – knocking at people's doors. Paying decent prices too – these rustics weren't born yesterday – meeting some rum characters and getting on with them. Alessandro did.

So does your mother, Alessandro intervened.

We take turns, she said. So you see, we have to have a car. To get up into those wildernesses and bring back the loot. The Peugeot had a sturdy frame, chests and dressers could be carried, cushioned by a mattress, on its roof over the rutted roads. (I was grateful that they had not bought a van; estate cars did not exist in those days, not in France.) Monsieur Panigon had proved a treasure of knowledge and cunning, guiding Alessandro through the jungle of second-hand car dealers in Marseille.

Then we got to the house and all was pleasure. It lay above Sanary, a mile or less inland, off the Route de Bandol. We drove through a gate, left the car in a small yard – plunged at once into the acerbic scent of the Midi: resin, thyme, hot stone – walked round to the front and there it was: the new house was an old house, ochre-washed, one-storeyed, a simple façade of long windows with the faded-blue wooden shutters of the region, standing on the highest of three terraced levels flanked on each side by a row of cypresses. The front door was reached by a short flight of steps leading on to a platform with a brief balustrade. Inside it was cool, the floors plain polished deep-red tiles, the rooms – not many of them – well-proportioned, the walls whitewashed, the woodwork in light colours – I could see at a glance the hand of Alessandro – doors and uncurtained windows gracefully shaped. The original owners? Rich peasant or bourgeois? Building a century, a century and a half ago? One could only guess.

The furniture was unremarkable, not awfully solid, odd bits and pieces, nothing new or newly bought or really ugly, a long way from Galeries Lafayette dining-room suites. Here too I could see that Alessandro and my mother had done a bit of shifting and refurbishing: they'd made it look both sketchy and liveable. (Another good omen.) There was a decent-sized kitchen with a coal-stove, some charcoal burners and a marble sink with a cold tap. The lavatory was modern and clean and had its own window; the bathroom, presumably carved recently out of some cupboard, was a damp black hole the width of a trench.

The terrace fronting the house was roughly paved with stones held together by thistles and spiky weeds, just level enough to play boules and balance table and chairs for eating out on. The two lower terraces were covered with scrub. There was no pretence of a garden in northern terms. (The realities of water did not allow one so much as to think of grass.) What one saw looking out of the front windows was the austere perspective of a cypress alley with a glimpse at its furthest point of the tiled roofs of Sanary.

I felt happy. For the first time since we left Italy, I was going to live in a house one could love. I said as much.

It *was* good, said my mother, and for a rented furnished house it was a miracle. 'You know, the agents told us it was hard to let. The summer people didn't like it. For a time they stopped showing it. The rent is less than what we paid for that silly villa.'

I looked a question.

'Annual rent,' my mother said. Alessandro added firmly, 'We've taken a year's lease.'

'Renewable?' I said.

'Renewable.'

'You might be interested to hear who our predecessors were,' my mother said. 'Guess who had the house last winter? – by the way, it's called Les Cyprès, inevitably – the "snobs" from Paris! You remember the mysterious couple we used to see at the cinema two years ago?'

I remembered.

'The one our friends at La Marine were so nasty about.'

'So they came back?' I said. There'd been no sign of them last summer.

'And vanished again. Rumour had it that she's a training partner of Suzanne Lenglen's and that he's been brought up with Lacoste and Borotra; they go to Biarritz and do nothing but play tennis all day long. Other rumours say they're in Paris settling their affairs and are coming to live here for ever. Someone's actually seen their building site.'

'Where?' I said.

'I've not the slightest idea.'

*   *   *

The omens held. It was a good summer, my third in the South of France. There were many to come, each definable still: different, individual in atmosphere, focus, events; men and women in foreground. The great constant was the climate, the inflexible summer climate of the Mediterranean coast. It embraced, contained, our existence; the ever-present sun and sea, the scented air, the strident sounds of tree-frog and cicada were the element we moved in. From May to October there was no rain, only night-dew, thus nothing changed: the earth was monochrome, the sea reverberated the sky. Morning after morning we woke to clear light, coolness modulating through the hours into the still, unwavering heat of noon, the small evening breezes, the warm night luminous from sky and phosphorescent sea. How permanent they felt, these even summers, how reassuring – this will go on: we shall go on.

Oh the Mediterranean addiction, how we fall for it! Natives most of all; anywhere north of Avignon, of Pisa, as the case may be, they pine in deprivation, exile; while the rest of us go seldom free again of that call of the South after our first weeks on the Ligurian or Aegean. So did I respond when as a child I had looked out of a train window crossing the Alps; later the Sorrentine peninsula gave substance to the instinctive longing. From then the South meant Italy, and my first summer at Sanary had confused and disappointed me. The Mezzogiorno, Midi (by any other name) was the authentic South, no doubt about that, but it also was most certainly not Italy. I missed what I was used to, I missed what I loved, and though rash and ignorant, I was affected by the absence of the architecture that I had become expectant to see springing from the ground at wayside and obscurest village. Poor Sanary offered two fountains, at the ends of the port, each mounted by a statue (female) of circa 1900, one representing *L'Agriculture*, the other *Le Commerce*. It *was* a come-down.

In short I did not take to Sanary at once; hard to explain by any future light. There had been the unsettling effect of my mother and Alessandro's sudden move to France; the vague unease that year, the sense that all was not well with them – between them? – contributed.

How very different were the months that followed so soon after. But they were a winter – sunny in every sense – a winter all the same. And although we were steeping ourselves as it were in Frenchness – those forays into books during the day, those sorties in the evenings – we might have been *anywhere*, it feels looking back, pursuing an existence of our own – a mother and her daughter, a pair of sisters, a woman and a girl – ensconced happily, very happily, in our wind-blown villa like two explorers in their base camp. Such a time never came again.

The succeeding summer, my second French one (a good part of it spent in London on my last lap with the Robbinses) I see as a fore-runner of the third, the present one, the aestival routine of the South of France: active mornings in market and sea, siesta hours enclosed in shuttered houses, nights of eating, dancing in the open air. At home, indications of stability, the trustees and their warnings quiescent, Alessandro finding acceptance as a go-between by a small coterie of artists and their patrons. Locally, new connections had been formed, earlier ones sloughed off. The days were over when my mother had been subject to the courteous, protective gallantry accorded to a woman on her own (a beautiful woman, slightly enigmatic?), she and Alessandro were now facing Sanary life as a couple; we were seen – with me added – as a family, a household.

All this I found consolidated, in undertones and fact, this year: now, 1928. We lived in a handsome house (if without much *confort moderne*); we had a car; my elders were as near as ever to being gainfully employed, enjoyed their teamwork, which indeed seemed to help keeping us in modest prosperity. It had all become quite bourgeois. I no longer went out with a bowl to fetch our dinner from the *traiteur*, we had a maid from Italy now, living in, who cooked for us and did everything else as well. She would have baked our bread, had we not persuaded her that French bread was eatable (which it was indeed in those days before steam-baking). Emilia (procured by Alessandro's mother), lean, wispy, unmarried, came from a Tuscan village, a hard worker, serious though not unsmiling. She saw being in service as a softer life than working on the land. Like Flaubert's Félicité, she was saving part of her wages for a nephew. (To whom, we believed, she was not individually attached, it was more a matter here of family feeling and honour.) She reminded me of our Lina from the German village who had done so much so selflessly for my father and me. Emilia was less elderly, of less pessimistic outlook, less desiccated and a good deal less devoted to her religion. In some weeks she missed mass altogether. Perhaps she believed herself dispensed while toiling in foreign parts; perhaps she was unable to take the Sanary church – very sparsely attended, we heard (I never set foot in it) – quite seriously; perhaps she prayed at home in the darkish, silent kitchen of Les Cyprès while hand making our pasta. She was contemptuous of the indigenous population – of mixed and largely Italian origin – who considered themselves French, and were so by Emilia who understood but did not approve their patois. Like Lina she had an obstinate adherence to some stiff principles the nature of which was often quite unclear to us. As in Lina, as in Félicité – though not to the heart-breaking degree – there was much goodness there. We became fond of her, and she of us. She was not demonstrative.

To us she brought the blessing of an almost entire liberation from housework. We could ask whom we pleased, when we pleased at the spur of the hour as was much the habit of the circle we now moved in, to come and eat with us without suffering the aftermath of hospitality. When one had been at table long enough, one just got up and moved to another part of the terrace and went on talking.

Among these new companions – too soon to say friends, acquaintance too cold – one did not 'entertain', one happened to eat together, in groups of six or maybe ten, in someone's garden, in the bistros of Toulon or Bandol attracted by some spécialité or view.

I can still still hear it: someone driving up to our house, calling out of a car window, '*On va faire une bouillabaisse ce soir chez Justin . . . Vous venez . . . ?*' and be off.

And chances were that we would join them, meeting at sundown outside Chez Schwob or La Marine, deciding who to go in whose car, then on to eat the bouillabaisse or the loup, the handsome big fish they'd caught that morning, at Justin's restaurant on the port of Toulon. And there or wherever else our evening was spent would be a sense of elation, of being en fête, of sharing the pleasure of that moment. Spirited talk bubbled. The company were neither residents nor tourists, they were members of that new wave of artists and writers who had fallen in love with the South of France and were making it their summer habitat. The dozen or so who chose Sanary were painters and their wives, one or two of them also painters, an art critic, some literary journalists. Give or take a few years either way, they were in their thirties – young enough to be casually in fine health, old enough to have achieved a part of what they had set out to do. Some had come up a hard way. (Including, for most of the men, fighting in the war now ten years past.) They had reached a good stage in their lives, enjoying a measure of recognition, lack of material want. They had earned their dinners at Chez Justin and under the jasmine-scented arbours of their houses. Rented: no one had bought or built yet; many later did. They believed that the good times, now they had come, would last. Meanwhile their lives and work were based in Paris, though few of them were born Parisians.

The centre of their circle was a couple: he a Polish Jew, a tailor's son, who had got himself to Paris as a boy; she born, like Colette with whom she shared many attributes and tastes, in a rural corner of Burgundy (or so I always fondly believed). They were the Kislings, the painter and his wife Renée. Kisling, Kiki, was on the threshold then of his international reputation. (Later he became fashionable, some thought over-fashionable – too many portraits of rich women –

followed by relative eclipse. At the time of writing, 1988, France is preparing to celebrate the centenary of his birth in 1991.) Kiki was a charming looking creature, with something of a slender bear about him, short, with his round head, round amiable flat face and Slavic slanted eyes – very clean and trim in his blue cotton trousers and check shirts with the short sleeves; but I oughtn't really to attempt describing him: there is at least one full-length self-portrait of the artist as a young man. There he stands brush in hand in his pale-washed blues and red-white shirt before his easel. I never saw him wearing anything else, not in winter in his Paris studio, not in New York, in exile from Vichy France during the war we did not yet think of then.

Renée, his wife, was a phenomenon, a force of nature which was capable of tender – as well as ruthless – emotions and of many civilised human skills. Her looks were startling: a blaze of vitality and colour, not readily defined in conventional feminine terms – *belle laide* leaves out the notion of scale and sculpture, *bel monstre* gets nearer to the mark. A head of rock-hewn features supported on a strong neck and powerful bronzed shoulders, large prominent blue eyes, heavy-lidded, thickly lined with kohl and a fat blue, honey-fair hair, straight cut, savagely bleached and streaked by sea water and sun, a fringe covering one side of the wide forehead, a nose like a parrot's beak. Her clothes dazzled with strong plain colours; she dressed simply, a pair of sailor's trousers, barebacked singlets, turquoise or scarlet, sea-shells about her neck, shell and ivory bracelets on her arms. It was superb. And when the monster smiled – proffering, it might be, a slice of melon – it was a smile of serene sweetness and sensuality.

This is how I see her (some photographs I have bear me out). Kisling painted her often, mostly when she was very young and not yet fully herself, sitting for him more as a model than a portrait subject; the paintings, good Kislings, if immediately recognisable, are not terribly like Renée: too stylised perhaps, too slick, prettified. Her laugh was huge; her speaking voice gentle, low, fastidious; her language racy or lyrical in turn. When she was talking of a bird, a plant, a dish, *the sea*, she could use inflections that reminded one of Colette and may indeed have had a similar source, a farmyard and orchard childhood in a literate and cherishing family with whom the passion for nature, cookery and French literature played an everyday and equal part.

Her parents might be labelled bourgeois with a slight military flavour (however antithetical that sounds when applied to Renée); her father, dead, had been a Commandant of the Garde Républicaine. For her too the first move towards *affranchissement* had been to get to Montparnasse, on her own, very young. There, like others she took up with, she painted, earned a little here and there and as a model, shared the exhilarating hand-to-mouth existence and camaraderie of artists and beginners. I imagine her at that stage – farouche, incorruptible, devoid of inhibitions of any kind, giving and devouring pleasure.

When Kiki and Renée first lived together and during the early years of their marriage, they were often miserably poor, destructively poor (one has only to think of Modigliani – whom Kisling took into his own studio, at 3 rue Joseph-Bara, 5e gauche, when he was ill, moneyless, in fact dying), so poor that there could be whole weeks when credit had run out, when there was nothing to eat. Kisling survived, and it was chiefly Renée's strength that pulled them through. She had the loyalty, courage, high spirits and tough *débrouillardise*, and she put her hand to anything. It is said that she once got a job helping out in a circus.

Renée – again like Colette – adored her mother, *Maman*. Nothing – defection to Paris, the shifts and wildness of her life, the sexual notoriety later on – seems ever to have clouded that exquisite filial relationship; Renée was and remained a devoted daughter, looking after her mother's every need in the years of her own prosperity. (When *Maman* died, in reasonably old age, Renée distraught, flung herself on the floor, howling with grief.)

Equally, she was a good mother, bringing up her two little boys with a wild beast's protectiveness and tender care (and some strictness). When we first knew the Kislings, the boys, Jean and Guy, must have been about a small three to five, brown as nuts, agile as monkeys, clever, naughty, tough and not averse to using charm. They spent their summers in the sea and part of their winters in the snow (*not* at

Sanary: they were sent skiing). They bore no resemblance to the studious, pale-faced French child expected to swot indoors, for the *lycée*, the *bachot*, the *grandes écoles: their* childhood was spent in brilliant physical freedom.

A good wife? Depends on how one looks at it. What had doubtless begun as a huge love affair modulated to a married couple who had faced the world together and were now enjoying it in perhaps slightly different ways. Renée, if hardly domesticated in the ordinary sense, *was* a home maker. On large and simple lines; no chi chi – much style. *Unlike* Colette, her talents went into life only (her painting stage did not last), into the arts and skills of living. The Kislings' hospitality has become a legend: for its generosity, the vigour and authenticity of the food, its ambience of healthy sensuality. Renée was not just a very good cook – with her own hallmark, nourished like a good composer's by tradition – she was one of the best of the handful of the very best I've known (and I did seek them out); coevals and youngers were her disciples, her influence on my cookery and eating has lasted to this day. (The best known, and professional, of the heirs must be Richard Olney, who ate at her feet as it were in his young days in France.)

Renée in the kitchen, Renée *à table* . . . there was also Renée in the sea – perhaps that was her greatest passion – she was a tremendous swimmer, diver, sailor, she ran her own fishing boat . . . The sea – *la mer*: salt water, waves – was her natural habitat; perhaps she was what she sometimes looked, a sea monster.

Kisling bathed a little, splashing about with the boys (who swam like fishes), I'm not certain even that he *could* swim. He worked extremely hard; during their halcyon times at Sanary as well as in his Paris studio (the large studio attached to the small flat four flights up). He seemed always pressed to produce enough to fulfil his contracts with the dealers; one felt that he couldn't afford to let up. As soon as done, a painting vanished; there were weeks when there was not a single canvas of his on their walls. At the same time he played hard – the big nights, the long nights out, with *les copains*, with beautiful girls, with wayward girls, at the Montparnasse cafés and *boîtes*, the *bals musettes, faire la bombe* as one called it in those days (not any longer). Bounce, vitality:

drink till dawn, at work by dawn, was one of Kiki's things; another was to make big play with women. The joyous cries of welcome – *Voilà les belles filles* – of appreciation, the bear-hugs, these expressed how much he loved them, how desirable they were to him. It added to the mutual glow, it flattered (as Alessandro's quieter but equally automatic, if abstemious, demonstrations flattered), that was how his circle saw him, how he saw himself, a part of his charm – he *was* lovable – his charisma. Renée when she was present, she often was, smiled her serene wide smile. It was also all a little pat, a little loud, a little public. Whereas Renée . . . We are back at the good wife question.

She had been, she could be, a rock to him; and goodness there was a bond. At the same time, her infidelities were frequent, unconcealed, casual on the whole, often concurrent. If they were not flaunted (their very naturalness prevented that), they were certainly not discreet. Renée did not flirt, Renée did not flatter, when she wanted to go to bed with someone – man or woman (*far more* men than women), friend's husband, student, sailor – she made it clear. Then she did. This was accepted. By their milieu, that is, which shared her attitude, and by Kiki (or so it was presumed). If Renée stood out, it was because her actions, as in everything else, were so instinctive and her appetites were larger.

That permissiveness, partly founded on a love of living here and now, and on an entire absence of religious qualms, was, quite consciously I believe, a moral one. A blow struck against possessiveness (bourgeois), jealousy (ungenerous). You don't own anyone, you don't begrudge pleasure to anyone and if it is your own love or lover, let it be. We are friends. *Les amis*, that was the key notion, *les camarades, les copains*. It had applied in war, now it went for money as well as sex. (Something not so dissimilar had been going on, *mutatis mutandis*, in Bloomsbury. Of that *I* knew nothing as yet.) Nineteen-twenties Montparnasse-South of France attitudes were good-natured: antipodal to the chilling, cruel and ultimately anti-human permissiveness of the eighteenth-century French aristocracy as reflected in *Les Liaisons dangereuses*. There pleasure was a means to subjugation and humiliation, the ends of conquest vainglory, power, revenge. One might give a thought to the fact that Choderlos de Laclos' libertines preceded the French Revolution, while those I am talking about followed the First World War.

Much of what I am trying to piece together about the Kislings and their lives and ways was not clear to me all at once during that summer when I first came into their presence; some came gradually, some in retrospect, all the same I drank in a good deal.

The living en fête in the evenings, their maxims of good behaviour. A principle was summed up for me in one not particularly elegant sentence I heard at table one night, sitting – figuratively – at the low end as children and young persons do in France, unsegregated to nurseries or juvenile resorts, expected to take part by listening and speaking up intelligently as the occasion arises. They are not elevated to pretence adults, they're treated as rational children and young persons. I cannot recall who said it – it may well have been Renée herself – but I can hear the sentence word by word, '*Si on est amis, il n'y a aucune différence si on fait l' amour avec.*' Which, in a non-literal translation, said to me, 'If it's a friend, it'll be all right to make love together.' It made a great impression and I salted it away for future use. I liked the easy sound, the niceness of it, and there was the contrast to what I was afraid had shown in Toni Nairn's outburst about her sister's life. That the Kisling doctrine took no account of *chagrin d'amour* nor the pangs of threatened loss (indeed most of the facts of human nature) escaped me. Well, I did not know much about these (except from books).

Or *did I?* What about my mother? Wasn't it odd that I didn't make a connection. Not having been brought up exactly in, say, bourgeois sexual orthodoxy, did I really need the Kislings' exhilarating liberation? Was there not the memory – somewhat remote – of the afternoon I spent in my infant's pram in the hall of the Danish novelist's bachelor flat? And before that, long before, the 'renunciation', a key point in her life, when she gave up a man she found entirely right for herself, because to leave an ill and older wife would have been vile, and so re-cast her life by accepting my father. Now, all that was history, my mother's history; however much she let one into it, it belonged to her and to another time. A taboo remains. One listens; one believes it happened; one does not believe it has a reality applicable to oneself. My mother's past was my childhood's bedtime tales.

What about *chagrins* – and *acharnements* – *d'amour* I had seen with my own eyes? O, serious, courteous, dignified in retreat; young Alessandro in pursuit with melancholy fire, desperate at times; her dash to Venice from which nothing, not six children in a lost property office let alone one child in a comfortable hotel, could have held her back; her desolation on that winter beach. Those events were part of my reality yet in an idiom that was a far cry from Sanary's sane and easy ways; they were on my mother's scale. They, too, were in the past; now was the present, I wished to believe that it should and could be maintained; like peace.

7

That year I *was* writing to Rosie Falkenheim; or rather she wrote to me and I answered promptly. Of course I had told my mother, that was irresistible, and she showed all the expected interest in the story. It was not treacherous, Rosie must have supposed as much and my mother promised secrecy.

Easy, she said, there was no one here to tell it to.

'Madame Panigon would have sat up at what she'd call *un scandale*, but as she doesn't know the first thing about the English ins and outs – '

God forbid, I said.

The Panigons of all the old Café de la Marine befrienders were the ones we had kept up with most. (Monsieur Panigon had shifted his practice from Montélimar to Toulon, and the family now lived at Sanary in a house they'd bought.) *They* kept up with us. Once they had really met Alessandro they became fascinated by my mother's marriage – the difference in age showed, always had, and my appearing to grow up did not help. They acted impeccably oblivious of such facts at the Sunday luncheons and boules (returned by less regular dinners chez nous) which had become a fixture. What they said behind our backs was a different kettle and easy to imagine; even to my face Monsieur's irony in referring to Alessandro as *votre cher papa* was transparent.

God forbid, I said again. They mustn't even hear that a friend from England is arriving, once Elise's (that was Madame; we were on such terms now) curiosity is aroused . . .

'Don't you worry, my little Hermes,' my mother said, 'your protégés will be safe with me. And I shan't tell even Alessandro – though he's not very good, as we know, at telling stories, you never can be sure about what may slip out from someone to whom it isn't important. You have to have a very strong motive to keep a secret.'

'*You* haven't even met Rosie?'

'My motive is *very* strong: lack of an appreciative audience.' She added, 'And I want to please you – and your friend. It's a wretched situation to be in. You must do all you can.'

And so it was decided that *I* must do the booking. It's all quite simple, she advised me, behave naturally: go there, say you have friends coming from England, these are the dates, these are the names, rooms not too far apart would be all right – the rest is not their business. French hotels are civilised in such matters. 'And whatever you do, don't forget to ask about the prices, *that* would raise suspicions.'

It went as she had said. In due course Rosie arrived, the Judge to follow the next day as arranged (the hotel would send a taxi to meet his express at Toulon). I met her train and settled her in at the La Plage. She appeared confident and calm. We agreed that it would be best to avoid all local contact. No, she wouldn't come to our house, thus she'd not meet my mother; whether I would see her was left undiscussed, we were more formal with each other than we had been in London. I asked after Toni (to whom I *had* sent postcards). Rosie smiled. 'Toni has decided that I've gone on holiday in the South of France by myself.' I smiled too. Whereupon she asked me to stay and have a drink.

A couple of days later a note from her was delivered at our house: Jack would like to meet me and was asking me to lunch with them at their hotel next day.

I was tremendously pleased, flattered by the confidence this seemed to show, intensely curious – how not! – and delighted to be meeting an actual judge.

In the nineteen-sixties I was commissioned by the *Observer* to do a profile of judges and their comparative comportment on the Bench. I spent an interesting month cruising between the Law Courts, the Old Bailey and Assizes, an anonymous, silent watcher from the press box. I could make notes; I had access to *The Times*'s Morgue. Some weeks later I wrote the piece in the quiet of an isolated wing of some friends' large country house in Tuscany. I did eight judges, or was it ten? It was tough work – there was a sharp deadline – and I was entirely absorbed in it. Trays of meals and refreshments were deposited on tiptoe outside my door. At intervals I would pace the landscaped garden and the olive groves with alternating elation and despair. I was a prisoner whose release could only be effected by my own boot-straps. (I did appear at dinner.) I could tell a good deal more about all phases of those days, the house, the atmosphere, the bath towels, what we talked about in the evenings, what we drank before dinner: Bloody Marys and on the last night Veuve Clicquot – the rest, the judges who filled my working hours and my dreams, I have almost entirely forgotten.

Well, some were very good, some were not so; one, quite young, was outstandingly, breathtakingly brilliant, and still regarded so now; one was a good *man*, and kind; another remarkably less so. That remains, and some mannerisms, their faces, their voices, their very names mostly, have receded into a muddled blur.

I could still refresh my memory – clippings of the piece exist. When I met Rosie's Judge I was not able to attend as a mute nameless reporter – *no* notebook – indeed I was not supposed to observe at all: I was there as the guest of a friend of a friend: I was supposed to speak, to behave, to be natural, that is, show no awareness of the subtexts of the situation. If I felt awe that was only proper in someone so junior and unlearned. In the end it turned out that I had come to enjoy myself.

Enjoyment elates the moment but is apt to blunt the memory thereof, particularly if one is given a great deal of burgundy at lunchtime.

The Judge, Jack – she called him that, I called him nothing – was certainly a handsome man, substantial without heaviness, senatorial head, hair going grey, wearing an elegant though conventional light summer suit with a cream silk shirt and a foulard scarf for tie – if memory serves, but does it? Anyway, this is how I see him. He began by thanking me for having found, 'found us' he said, such an agreeable hotel. Was I familiar with English seaside resorts? There was a difference. He was entirely at his ease and he was also unmistakably our host, a good host, reminding me a little of my father looking after Lina and myself at table: we were his womenfolk, he was our protector seeing to it that we were cosseted, treated tenderly. The Judge was very nice to me, with a nuance of amusement and no condescension, though without any pretence that he was other than the man he was and I a young girl. I liked that, I liked him, but then I had come wanting to like. He said he knew a good deal about me, that I was interested in law and fond of wine. Rosie looked gratified at this *prise de contact*. He asked if I liked burgundy. I had the sense to tell the truth, that so far, very little of it had come my way. I had come down in the world in that respect at an early age, hardly a drop of a *cru classé* – and that had always been Bordeaux – after my father's death. Since then I had been drinking *good* local wines, a couple of times I had the chance to taste a Côte de Beaune at the Panigons' house though more often they drank Châteauneuf-du-Pape with their gigot . . . I do believe that I really trotted out all this to the Judge. He *had* put me at my ease. He did the obvious thing, saying we must remedy that, the wine list here wasn't at all bad. He deliberated over two or three splendid names, then chose a Volnay, the year and vineyard of which I have forgotten. Can we manage a bottle, you and I? We can't count much on Rosie. I said he could count on me.

What did we talk about? No legal anecdotes, no quizzing from me in that line. He wanted to hear about Sanary, he talked about the French, about fellow hotel guests, trying to make out where they came from, what they were up to. Though he didn't share Rosie's interest in the modern English novel, he was well read in French nineteenth-century literature. He spoke about their plan to spend a few days in Provence, he wanted to show Rosie Aix and the Pont-du-Gard and the amphi-theatres at Nîmes and Arles . . .

How long should they take, could they hire a car? I had just been to Aix with Alessandro, and loved it already. It hardly mattered what we talked about, it was lively and, at least his part of it, good conversation. A cultivated man, not an intellectual, and whatever he might be like on the Bench, here he was private, charming, witty. A tape would have helped more than the notebook: the actual way he talked I am of course unable to reproduce. So there remains but little to report.

The important thing, what I longed to penetrate, was what went on between this man and this woman – the perennial mystery of what there is between two people – that eluded me. How often does one not wonder what thoughts accompany the talk, what is said – thrice quicker than speech – inside the head, and what goes on beneath those thoughts, at the back of the mind; who has not strained to listen to that composition of the said/thought/felt played inside another human being? All *I* seemed able to do was watch the surface while sounding my own feelings.

There were two people, ill-matched in looks (in circumstances too, but this did not show so much), who appeared to get on extremely well with each other, were attentive to each other, were enjoying a holiday, a good lunch, as though they had no care in the world. A couple, married? lovers? new or long so? the surface remained unbroken. I know what I knew and they knew that I knew but they gave nothing away.

Oh yes, we did polish off the burgundy, the Judge and I, in even shares (point of honour). I thought it tasted sublime; and though I told a few Sanary stories I held my wine quite well. This amused the Judge who said I had a good head.

After coffee he went off to have a siesta, this was meant to let Rosie and me have a few minutes by ourselves. She walked me down the drive. I wanted to tell her how much I had liked him and hoped to do so without being intrusive. I needn't have worried. She was radiant. He loves it here, she said, he's as happy as a sandboy. He's admiring himself for having taken to the simple life. And you know, she said, they'd been given *adjoining* not *communicating* rooms. 'But we have our balconies – he prefers them to the corridor; it reminds him of Switzerland and romantic novels. He tells me it makes him feel young.'

Wasn't that rather *unwise*? I said, there were bound to be people out there in the moonlight at all hours. 'That's taking rather a risk.'

'That's what he likes,' she said. 'He's a gambler.' She didn't look radiant any more. 'With a gambler it *is* wise to provide a minor risk.'

I had lunch with them once again. It was towards the end of the fortnight, after they'd come back from their tour of Provence. They were full of it and Rosie delighted with what she had seen. The atmosphere was much the same, except that by now the Judge and I seemed to have become old friends. They had been bathing that morning on the strip of sand outside the hotel. The Judge had complained before of the lack of pretty girls, but today there'd been two fairly ravishing ones. He and Rosie described them. I surmised that they must be the Panigon girls and realised that they were in fact becoming fairly ravishing girls – Annette no longer a boyish child, Cécile losing her puppy-fat and her face getting quite beautiful in a soulful way. Would they be likely to come again tomorrow? Rosie wanted to know, that's the one thing Jack expects on a beach, he doesn't like just sun and staring at the sea. I said I could introduce them. No, no, Rosie said, that would be going too far; and the Judge laughed and concurred.

He repeated the burgundy dare. This time we had a Nuits-St-Georges, and again I thought it was pretty wonderful. The odds are that it was not quite that, and almost certainly served too warm. It is not a wine I would choose now to drink at noon in a Mediterranean August. Whether the Judge was a burgundy man, whether the wine list was poor in claret, or whether the heavier wine (*those* burgundies were heavy) would be more of a test for me, I never found out.

They left on the same day, travelling by different trains, he straight on to Scotland. My mother had suddenly remembered that perhaps she ought to meet Rosie because of me – doesn't she stand *in loco parentis* or something? Rosie considered staying on for another forty-eight hours, then shrank from the anticlimax. I did not see the Judge again, but was able to take her to the station. In the taxi, she thanked me: it was perfect. He says we must do it again. We'll come back.

'I must tell you something.' She became solemn, which was not her way. 'This is the first time – since all those years ago in Switzerland when he was a young man – that we have ever *not* been alone together. I never see him with anyone, I never hear him talk to anyone, other than a waiter or a jury, I didn't know what he was like in company. Do you know,' she called me by my name, 'that you are the only human being I've seen him sitting at a table with, this is the only time I heard him talk to someone *I* know. You cannot understand what this means to me.'

But I could. It came as a shock. I had not imagined their situation in that light before. I never forgot it afterwards.

*   *   *

My own Sanary summer had another two months to go. Much of them spent in the sea. My mother and Alessandro were in conclave doing up a house for a Dutch woman who wanted an all-year place on our side of the coast. What she'd bought turned out to be the mistral-buffeted villa we had lived in the year before, and *that* needed conversion from scratch. Alessandro had been commissioned, and it was riveting to watch the transformations that were taking place, at that point chiefly in their minds: my mother having ideas and Alessandro thinking up ways of making them practicable. He was extremely clever at that: suggestions turned into sketches and sketches into exact designs like conjuring tricks. He engaged a builder, an *entrepreneur-maçon*, and established a good understanding. The results for the present were all destruction: inside walls broken down, windows and doors knocked out, tarred canvas flapping. They were much on the building site, my mother joining him in the late mornings, or rattling about in the Peugeot hunting for furniture in the Haut-Var. Having working parents felt comfortable; when they were at home we played paper games in the evening, my mother and I with enthusiastic commitment, she quite annoyed when I won, which was rare. Alessandro didn't mind losing. His game was patience which he played at all hours. I still see him, that slim young man with his long beautiful hands, bring out the two small packs of pretty cards and lay them out on the dining-table just cleared or on a small one by my mother's bed while she was talking. He had a good repertory and taught me some of it; I have often found Miss Milligan or Nine-Up a soothing resource.

Alessandro was a thin-nerved fellow who kept himself under control. He abhorred stridency, noise, a quarrel. He was sweet-tempered, never quarrelled himself and knew how to smooth out my mother's flare-ups. He did this affectionately with a mixture of good sense, laughter and teasing. It was in *her* nature to end an outburst by laughing at herself. I received a hint that his equableness did not always come easy when one day I went down with a bad throat, probably caught by staying out on a beach too late in the September evening vapours, and unused to feeling ill was expecting care and attention. Alessandro surprised me by being greatly taken aback. Not *you*, he told me, you've *got* to be all right – looking after one woman is enough. He said it not unkindly, but it came from the heart.

Was looking after my mother *such* a strain, I asked myself. Her unpunctuality, her refusal to face decisions or trouble could be exasperating. There must have been more to it: did Alessandro feel he had taken on a kind of servitude? For my mother without being really selfish or egocentric – she believed in putting ideas and ideals first – behaved as though she owned her entourage, and of course above friends and daughter, one owned one's husband. Having seen something of Toni Nairn's marriage put this in my mind; like my mother Toni was possessive and at the same time condescending to Jamie. Was nothing ever as it should be? I thought. And what should, or rather could it be?

Another remark of Alessandro's puzzled me rather more. We were alone; he looked at me; he said reflectively, 'Has it occurred to you that a man might find it difficult to have a stepdaughter?' He said *a* step-daughter, not *you* for a stepdaughter, and it had not occurred to me.

Was it because of my having been ill the other day? He shrugged impatiently; then gave me a reassuring smile.

If at that time I had been pressed to define our relationship, I might have put it: two brothers, like each other, serving – in different ranks – in the same regiment.

I am saying so much about our family life because it must not be thought that, taken as *I* was by the Kislings and their circle, we were really intimate or spent so very much time with them. Twice a week was about it, fitting into the routine of summer life. We (my mother had known Kiki in Paris) were regarded as friends, tangential friends: outlook and habits were different. (My mother would not have dreamt of joining them when late in the night they proposed carrying it on in a *dancing* or *bal musette*; she had never drunk deep or made *la bombe*, and she'd decline for the three of us.) Both Renée and my mother can be called unconventional women; they were not unconventional in quite the same way. What is more, I believe that they did not really like each other. My mother was amused by Renée and liked to hear and tell stories about her outrages; she did not love her. As I did from the beginning. Renée, on her side, had not much use for my mother, for her she was too 'intellectual', a great fault in the eyes of someone who knew what she chose to know by instinct. Later on she told Maria Huxley – she was much too protective of a filial relationship to tell me – that she had always found my mother too cool, too cerebral, too literary. My mother would sooner talk about a plant than grow it. Incidentally Renée held the same view, in stronger measure, of Aldous, and used to commiserate with Maria, who saw her point. Those two women were growers of plants.

There *was* an intellectual astringency in my mother, she was serious not merely about books but about the world and the people who had to endure it; and this for all her laxities and omissions injected a certain mental discipline – quite absent in Renée's living – into our life, however uprooted. And I felt an allegiance to that.

I had also come to feel that Sanary *was* the true South, and that Sanary and the French were for me. I had fallen for it and for all that it had offered already. Here was my home, here I was going to live (with a necessary foot in London, indefinably acquiring what it would take to become what I should be), and here, the gods willing, I was going to write my books. There was one more thing which set this summer apart from the ones that followed. It was my last as the young person at the low end of the table; I was growing older, I would become a participant.

8

In England also I was presented with a widening of the social scene. It came about in this way: almost parallel with my mother and Alessandro, the Nairns were relatively prospering. Jamie had been offered a partner- and directorship in a distinguished book-dealers' firm bringing with him the goodwill and stock of his own shop. Debt paid off, a salary coming in, Jamie and Toni found themselves securely and nearly comfortably off in a matter of weeks. The first thing Jamie did was to take a cottage in the country to spend their holidays and weekends in, something he had longed to do. On my return from France, Toni and Rosie were already trudging round second-hand shops, warehouses and stores trying to acquire cheaply furniture, curtains, floor-covering and anything else needed. They'd been told to keep to bare essentials; essentials, however bare, tend to be numerous and varied, so for the sisters it was quite a task. Jamie went out on Sundays to do some plastering and painting, and I accompanied him to help. We made an adequate job of it, no more (compared to Alessandro). The cottage was in an Essex village, in decent repair, roomy, dry and rather pretty. It had a garden, well stocked with raspberry and gooseberry bushes, a lawn Jamie looked forward to mowing, and a strip of orchard. There was a scullery where he proposed to keep a small barrel of cider and a small barrel of beer. I had a long look at the cook-stove. It was years before bottled gas. Toni? I said. Jamie looked surprised, then thought she should manage, anyway *he* would be bringing in the coal.

Shortly after Christmas the cottage was more or less ready for habitation and we were able to spend a first weekend. It was mid-winter; indubitably. We did not spend days and nights in extreme discomfort – there were good fireplaces downstairs and small ones with pretty grates in the bedrooms, Jamie did keep us supplied with plenty of wood and coal. The lavatory was indoors, there was a boiler and an airing cupboard, cold water laid on and a supply of paraffin lamps, in a word all the comforts of the English country. It required *some* work, not *hard* work though, and took up much time. Jamie was happy; evidently, if silently; for the Falkenheims already come down from steam-heat to electric fires, it was another matter. If they suffered, they also remained silent. Not ineloquently so – Rosie kept on her fur coat (Berlin relic) during meals urging Toni to do the same. Toni withdrew behind her princess-on-the-pea look. Meals. I decided that we'd reached a point where I must induce Toni to come to terms with some of the basic elements of cookery: this was not the time and place for delicatessen food which anyway was running out. The stove was lit (by me) and going, which included a nicely heating oven, I was able to point out the simplicity and wonder of the baked potato. From where I led on to further steps: chops in the frying-pan, a vegetable – Look, just a little water on the boil. Toni, stiffly, bowed to fate and duty. She could not be gentled further into making soup. There *were* tins. My turn to bow. Jamie, who as I said was happy, did not or preferred not to notice; he was used to his mother doing everything and his wife a little.

Respite was at hand. A literary man, a friend of Jamie's, had a house at Finchingfield the village next to ours. He was A. J. A. Symons, the bibliographer of Yeats, the future author of *The Quest for Corvo*, a founder member of the Wine and Food Society, and married. He asked Jamie over for drinks on the Sunday morning, to bring his wife and friends and stay for lunch to escape the horrors of the first days in the new home.

We went, we stayed, were given a very good lunch indeed, drank claret, played games into the afternoon. The house was Jacobean, filled with objets d'art, sybaritic. It was also filled with guests, well read, amusing, not particularly accommodating men, two or three fast women (or so they appeared to me). Our host was wildly erudite and undisguisably eccentric, his wife chic, slim and ostentatiously made-up. There was another new milieu, one I had wished for and imagined: *English*, the educated, the literate English whose horizons embraced

France, Italy, Greece and beyond. At the end of a short bicycle ride in Essex I had arrived at a side-stream of the English literary world. I had found my first Garsington.

The analogy should not go too far. At Finchingfield the accents were, besides books and talk, on very good wine and games. Heavy bridge (and possibly, I think, house-party affairs) for some of the women, for the rest their version of the war game – a combination of strategic planning and strenuous hide-and-seek to which the convoluted house cross cut with unexpected staircases exactly lent itself – played with bravura, utter devotion and mostly in the dark. It was enormous fun.

It could also be eruptively noisy. One was apt to fall out of broom cupboards or down some backstairs, and there were the whoops of joy of the winning side.

Toni winced at the very idea of these rough and stupid games and would not participate. That at the outset of a social life was a mistake. Rosie must have seen it – she knew a thing or two about accommodating oneself – but was too loyal to her sister to do anything but side with her. So when the light went out, a safe retreat had to be found for the two timid women, a small sitting-room where presumably they sat munching chocolate biscuits, shuddering at the pastimes of the English goys, and reading. (Toni had come armed with Thomas Mann, in German, how else; Rosie snatched up a Siegfried Sassoon of A.J.'s, a sign perhaps of her not undivided allegiance.)

A.J. liked Jamie and Jamie liked A.J. Finchingfield became a fixture. We were asked over for luncheon or dinner or both at least once a weekend, and in the Easter and Whitsun holidays Jamie walked and I bicycled over almost every day. A.J. (always addressed so) was impersonally, informally hospitable, one joined in whatever was going on, food appeared. (One didn't notice any servants or an absence of servants; there must have been some village people who came and went.)

I was tolerated probably because of my enthusiasm (still much the young person at the low end of the table), Toni was accepted as Jamie's wife, and Rosie – when she did come down – as someone in her wake. Toni did not shine at Finchingfield. She rejected what was on offer covering her antagonism by a ruffled aloofness: polite refusals all the way, No Thank Yous ringing out when the Château Palmer went around. It irritated and enraged me because it diminished her – *and* Jamie; Finchingfield did not see what *she* had to offer, what they saw was a namby-pamby outsider who made no effort. In that situation – it had to be seen as one – Jamie's weapon, or just nature, was unawareness.

Jamie was expanding. No money pressures, success in his work, he had his two and a half days a week in the country, pottering in the garden, long walks, a part – a not unlively part – in the pleasurable round of Finchingfield. What Toni had hoped for, but not uttered, was a month on her own staying with friends in Berlin, instead the money had gone into the cottage and a slightly newer Morris-Cowley. What *she* had was two and a half days a week in the country – the cook-stove, the fires, the washing-up, and the social round at Finching-field. For the present she remained quiescent.

Rosie, for her part, was complaining about Jamie, he was letting Toni do far too much, Toni ought to speak to him about it – Jamie was the most selfish man on earth. (Was not that what Toni had said about the Judge?)

All seemed well in that quarter. France had done Jack so much good, Rosie was telling me, he got through the last Law Sittings without getting so restless and bored.

Bored?

It's been terribly frustrating for him these last years, but I believe he's feeling much better now.

I had to ask what she was talking about.

'I thought Toni would have told you about it. She knew.' And then it came out. It was a midweek winter afternoon and we were having tea in her room, she was not going to join him that evening so we had planned to have a bite together at an ABC later on. She was smoking – Turkish – I was not.

'It was dreadful,' she said. 'The worst thing that ever happened. You see, I had his note, he had posted it to me. For three days I didn't know he was alive. There was nothing in the papers – I could do nothing – I didn't dare ask anyone.' She spoke drily and quietly. I sat still. She got to the beginning.

'He *is* a gambler – a real one. So that winter,' she gave the year, 'he was getting more and more depressed and anxious. I knew he had worries but he wouldn't tell me what they were. Then one day he did: he was owing a large sum of money, more, far more, than he could pay.'

An old, old story – could it happen to a judge? For some months he had been losing, and losing again: horses and cards. (He gambled in private houses, never at a club, though abroad he played in casinos at whatever was going, *chemin de fer*, roulette.) He was owing his book-maker, he was owing friends, people who trusted him. But now he thought he could see a way out, there was a race coming up, he had been told of a horse . . . He would scrape together such credit as he still had. Rosie pressed her savings on him, he took them – they weren't much, every hundred counted, he told her, with *that* horse: if it won he'd recoup himself.

It didn't. The week after he told Rosie he was going away for a few days to sort things out in his mind. He left her thinking that he was going to stay with some of his cronies in Gloucestershire. Instead he went to a country hotel and took an overdose. By a miracle he was discovered in time, rushed to a nursing home and eventually revived; another miracle, the whole thing, suicide attempt, gambling debts and all, was kept out of the press, hushed up with the help of col-leagues, connections, friends. Other friends stumped up the money. The whole of it. He was alive, he was free; rumours there had been, yet his career was intact.

They made him give his word never to bet on a horse again, never to touch a card.

'He hasn't, of course. He *can't*. At first he was *so relieved* . . . That awful threat gone. Everything again before him . . . That did not last. Now he misses it most of the time. It is very hard.'

I thought about my father's make-believe roulette we had played at Feldkirch – *had* it been make-believe to him? I thought of his anecdotes about men shooting themselves at dawn in Monte Carlo. So such things really happen, I thought.

'Poor Jack, poor poor Jack,' she said, 'and I . . . I thought I had lost him.'

'Now put on your coat, I believe it's got quite chilly.' I did as told and out we walked into the dankish night and the ABC in Baker Street.

The next thing Jamie did was to buy a dog, to take on his walks. When it arrived it was an upstanding rough-haired terrier puppy called Tommy, a sturdy, steady fellow. Not for long. The Falkenheims, who had never had a live animal in the house, fell for him with injudicious rapture. I had not seen them so demonstrative, so willing to perform hand-maidenish tasks. Never was dog so petted, so walked at all hours, so brushed and combed and dried, so rushed off to the vet; the prettiest basket, the softest cushions, the finest mince, bowls of creamy milk, shares of their own biscuits. They trembled for him when he had to cross the road, meet a strange dog or God forbid attempt to chase a cat. If need arose they would have protected him – heroically in *their* case – from a mouse. Jamie shared their devotion to Tommy but tried to make them exercise constraint. In a matter of weeks the dog had become a timorous, nervous thing.

Not so timorous and girlish though that he would not have enjoyed a go at the war game when the fun began (the Finchingfield dogs got kicked out of the way, only the Pekinese held its sofa place). Toni absolutely forbade Tommy's taking part, the noise would be bad for him. So she and Rosie would crouch in the back-room with the wretched dog, trying to stop his ears.

It made them all look ludicrous. I was irritated and unwise enough to try to get this point of view across to Toni. I was not in her best books at the time; she was displeased about my rushing off to Finching-field at every opportunity, hinting even that it must soon be time for me to go back to France (this reminded me that I was their guest in Essex and that this might cease). After Rosie's stay at Sanary, Toni had tried to turn me into *her* friend first and foremost, something I had to treat with tact, particularly as Rosie, considering herself the lucky one

in the major aspects of her life, was prone to give way to her sister in all
else. Then Toni, smouldering, was confronted with my infatuation
with Finchingfield which I conducted without any tact at all. So when
now I criticised her comportment there, she told me that they were
superficial literati, not artists, spoilt into the bargain, that the men
gossiped like washerwomen (they gossiped) and that anyway the place
was not at all suitable for *me*; she felt like writing to my mother.

What about?

For one thing, they drink far too much.

They do, I said, and I love it. What else?

Immorality, she said in a clipped tone, and would not say further.

Perhaps I was right about their having affairs? I thought. There was
an aura of eroticism at Finchingfield, not all the time, not when the
more austere men held the talk, but when the lights were off and the
game was on there was a whiff.

Unsuitable, she said again.

I shall be eighteen next year, I thought, but did not say.

9

I saw them again! In bright sunlight, less than ten yards from me on
the port in early summer, my first days back at Sanary. It was not the
long high car that had aroused such disapproval among our café
friends, it was a dwarf-size, improbably antiquated three-seater, one
might have said three-wheeler, looking like a cross between a sun-
dulled black beetle and a hip-bath. They stepped out of it with the
utmost grace.

I was standing outside Chez Schwob, where I'd left a vegetable
basket, sheltered to see without being seen. She had been at the wheel,
now she stood up. She wore a short blue linen skirt and a little faded
cotton top, a beret clung to a side of the narrow well-shaped head; in
full day too, the structure of the face, all profile, evoked the paintings
of the Florentine Renaissance; the colouring was matt olive set off by a
brilliant splash of lipstick, the hair cut very short was sleeked and
darkened by the application of a transparent substance then the rage

sold as (Josephine) Baker-Fix. His head was bare, the hair brown and straight, he was in canvas trousers and an open short-sleeved shirt. They wore their rudimentary clothes with incomparable elegance and neatness. At close range, they looked akin rather than alike: his profile was equally clear-cut, smooth-textured, yet, although still youthful – they were both approaching thirty – it was stronger (and became pronouncedly so in middle and old age), some Frenchness had modified the Piero della Francesca look; in him there was much Clouet – and a great distinction; unlike Clouet's sitters he was extremely slender and moved with feather lightness; together they projected a dreamlike amalgam of an historical past with an ultra post-war modernity.

And now they were three: from the back of the hip-bath there arose a young man like a hunk of Greek sculpture from the sea. He was of more solid clay: compact, bronzed, muscled, an unambiguous Mediterranean archetype; and beautiful in the way of the very young. He was in bathing shorts and a narrow singlet that left his torso almost bare. All three wore true Basque espadrilles, close-fitting like ballet-shoes, stiff with dazzling whiteness.

I think I must have run most of the way home to Les Cyprès. Mummy – they're back. Who? She began, and relented.

'I've seen them too . . . the mysterious strangers of the cinema, your Heavenly Twins.'

Who are they? I said.

We did not find out in a day. We did not find out in a year, the years; some of it is taking a lifetime. To begin with, though, we met them. Quite soon.

At first impact, people convey no more than their present face-value; more is revealed as one begins doing things together: pieces of their past – what may have shaped them, what they have lived – become known gradually, a remark here, a statement there, supplied by themselves, by third persons, by gossip, imagination, deduction. Of the sequence, the future: what will become of them, what *they will become*, new friends know nothing.

One thing was true, so much my mother could tell me, they *were* going to settle here, they'd begun building a house in an olive grove a few hundred yards up the road from us. Walls could already be seen beyond the trees. They looked, she said, as if they *were* going to do, God forbid, a Le Corbusier.

One afternoon a few days on, the Peugeot stopped halfway between Sanary and our house. It was not a good car. Alessandro and I had been up the hill encouraging the conversion of his client's villa that was going into its tenth month by then. We got out, Alessandro opened the bonnet, set to fiddling with carburettor feeds and sparking plugs to no effect. A car drew up behind us. It was not the black beetle hip-bath, it was the low, high, clean-lined vintage car, and the man who got out of it was one of what my mother so annoyingly persisted in calling my Heavenly Twins. He approached us, made a slight bow and introduced himself. Of course we failed to catch the name. '*Je crois*,' he said in light pensive tone, '*que nous soyons un peu voisins.*' It struck me as charming shorthand for: We shall be practically neighbours once our house is finished and we've moved in. (There was also the subjunctive.) '*Vous permettez?*' he enquired of Alessandro, and plunged long clean hands into the Peugeot's belly.

Eh bien non, it was not the petrol flow nor the *allumage*, it was, he feared, something – spelt out to Alessandro – that would have to be dealt with at some length. For the moment though, *je peux vous dépanner*. Alessandro proffered tools, he waved them aside, went over to his car and brought back an impressive kit. (Is he a mechanic then? I thought.) Quite soon the Peugeot guttered into faltering life. He took charge: if you're quick it'll take you to the nearest garage – they are robbers but no worse than the other lot, and not bad at the job. He'd follow in case the Peugeot stopped again as well it might. Then he would give us a lift home. Perhaps *la petite* – that was me – would like to come in his car now.

At the garage, he negotiated with the patron (whom he addressed with *tu* not *vous*), we learnt that spare parts were likely to cause trouble; our still nameless rescuer proposed telegraphing to someone in Paris who would put the *pièce* on the next train. All this was executed with calm and rational competence, as though his own time were of small account and helping strangers out the most natural thing in the world.

On our way home, riding high, first relief gave way to a new dismay. The Peugeot, however special its treatment, would be out of action for more than a matter of hours. *Tonight?* Alessandro and I cried simultaneously, looking at each other.

Ah, said our friend, you too are going to see *Topaze*.

We were. Toulon has a municipal theatre of respectable size and attainment. That night a guest company was performing the comedy, now a classic, about administrative goings on in Marseille by Marcel Pagnol (author of *Marius, Fanny, César, Jean de Florette* . . .). How were we going to get to *Topaze*? (Toulon was unreachable, worse, unreturnable from, by public transport in the evening.)

He would have proposed to offer us a lift, he said, as he and his wife were going (*that* put paid to the Heavenly Twins and the incest gossip in one swoop), were it not (more subjunctives) that he had promised to take his mason and family – Marcel Pagnol had huge popular appeal, more than half of Sanary were going. We shall have to think of something. He left us at the gate of Les Cyprès, getting out of the car to shake hands. Something must be arranged, I shall let you know. There is not much time.

Hurry or not, I could not forbear to ask, 'What is the name of your motor car?' 'It was designed by De Dion-Bouton in 1911,' he said. 'The *carrosserie* is by Gallet.' I all but bowed.

An hour later he was back. My wife thinks it might be 'amusing', he uttered the word as if he were slightly distancing himself from it, if we took everyone to Toulon in a private bus. He happened to have a bus. She was arranging to invite the *commerçants* and anyone else who wished to see *Topaze* to go in our bus. He would not come in now, there were things to organise, but we could count on the bus being outside Les Cyprès at a quarter to eight tonight, and he hoped that Madame votre Mère – whom he had not met but had the pleasure of having seen before – would do them the honour . . . he was off.

And so it happened. The bus appeared, a long, narrow, open-roofed thing, painted tarnished green, a crocodile of a bus, far from new – all their vehicles, I was to learn, were idiosyncratic. It was still daylight. He – in overalls – was at the wheel, she had the seat beside him – in a white off-the-shoulders dress – doing the honours. The bus was already half-filled with miscellaneous Sanary figures. We recognised Monsieur and Madame Schwob with a glowingly nubile daughter, the Benechs of the wheel-of-gruyère shop with son and aunt, and surprise – how had she come to consort with those snobs from Paris? – Madame Panigon with her two girls and their brother Frédéric who looked grown-up and not unsmart in a dark suit. No one of the Kisling crowd appeared. The Third Man, the young god seen on the port, was there, making himself useful finding seats for elderly Sanaryans at the further stops.

A genial hilarity had been generated; we sat in the row next to the driver's, and from behind us came the flow and thrust of animated French cross-conversations. The crocodile was on its way. Young male members of the outing began by shouting jocular encouragement which changed to sighs of appreciation as our speed increased. Never have I sat in bus so smoothly and adroitly driven, and so fast.

We alighted in the Place du Théâtre, our host drove off to park and reappeared ten minutes later in the stalls having taken off his overalls.

Topaze, the play, was a tremendous success, we all laughed till we ached, not least of all my mother. Well after one a.m. – French plays even in the provinces do not begin nor finish early – we made our way in several groups on foot up to the boulevard. Word had gone round: *Rendez-vous à la Brasserie de Strasbourg*. It was *the* after-theatre supper place in Toulon, and renowned for its choucroute garnie. There we assembled, happy and hungry, at one long table pulled together for our party running along an entire wall. There was no placement. I noted that our host, who came in late, put himself next to my mama. I, for my sins, found myself next to Frédéric Panigon, Cécile and Annette's elder brother (the boy to whom it didn't occur to dance with us at the Café de la Marine – that was three years ago) who was usually away beavering at his *lycée*. Apparently no longer so, he had entered university reading law at his father's wish, as he was trying to tell me. *He* wanted to be a painter, did I think . . . ? My mind wasn't on it. *Peintre-artiste*, he said. I was trying to watch our maîtres-de-plaisir even though I couldn't catch what they were saying. He was talking quietly to my mother; she, though she sat next to the young god – who kept performing small services such as filling her glass, with nothing more than Evian water I noted – was talking rather insistently across people and table, acting very much, a touch too much, the *animatrice* of the occasion. (I would have liked looking at her in repose, which I imagined most became her face. She was high-pitched when she ought to have been still. Then I scolded myself for such carping.) At any rate, a good time was being had by all.

The ride home, under the open roof, through the cool air and early dawn was an enchantment.

Well, my mother said next morning, well . . . ! It was splendid, I said. *Topaze* was, and extremely well acted, she said, but the whole thing . . . Yes, that was splendid too . . . A shade too much so.

'You enjoyed it?'

'Oh yes. Everybody enjoyed it. Madame Panigon seemed quite won over.'

'So?'

'There was something of a stunt about it, contrived – the bus out of nowhere, the wholesale seduction of the populace . . . Too literary to be true, like a charade out of *Le Bal du Comte d'Orgel* – *gens du monde* coming down from heaven.'

'I've read it.'

'*You would*,' my mother said. 'But did you *understand* it?'

'He was not much more than my age when he wrote *Le Bal*.'

'And died almost at once. He, my dear, was a genius.'

'I haven't . . . ' Alessandro said.

'Heard of Raymond Radiguet,' my mother cut him short, making dishonours even. Then she said very sweetly, 'Believe me, both of you, there was a *Comte d'Orgel* flavour about last night . . . . It must have been all *her* doing. I'm sure she dreamt up the whole thing. He's a quiet man; probably very patient.'

'The *cavaliere servente* business,' Alessandro said.

'Do you mean the young man?'

'He means the young man,' my mother said.

Alessandro, speaking as a man, said, 'But she's got no sex appeal.'

My mother, speaking as a woman, said, 'There's not much of it in him either, I'm referring to her husband. I would qualify that to: not yet. There is something . . . suspended about him. One can't tell why. As if for the present they were both playing a part. They *are* extremely attractive. He'd be a difficult man to know; I think he's got principles, more hardened than you would expect from his age and manner. I'd say there was something unusually disciplined under all that urbanity and . . .'

'Charm?' said I.

'No,' she said, '*Grace*.'

'What did you talk about?'

'*Topaze* of course. We agreed that beside the fun it's a good play. I asked him if the goings-on at the Marseille city council were really as hair-raising. *Pire*, Madame, he said, *Worse*. Councils in France were run by scoundrels, *des escrocs* was his word, petty scoundrels compared to Marseille, there I must think of Chicago. He's awfully down on politics, politicians, *des salauds*, the lot of them; he's rather like the Kislings there though I very much doubt that he has any liking for *les gens de gauche*. What he seems to stand for are clean hands, disillusion, withdrawal. The war has left us all bankrupt, he said, and he did not mean it in the financial sense. One could see him as a monarchist – if restoration weren't such a *cause perdue* in France – he's far too intelligent for that kind of faith.'

'He *is* intelligent?' I asked.

'Very much so,' said my mother. 'One wonders what he'll do with it.'

Their name was Desmirail. Philippe and Oriane Desmirail. Despite their air of kinship – underlined then by their comportment – they were not blood relations. Nor were their origins Parisian; they had been educated, and spent a portion of their adult lives, in Paris. She had been through *lycée*, he through *lycée* and a *grande école*:

Condorcet and Polytechnique. (The latter, the bastion among other disciplines of science, mathematics and high IQs, is not to be confused with any current British polytechnic.) Philippe was the descendant of a family of *grands magistrats* who had served the administration of their country since Louis XIV. Their ancestral home was a fortified Romanesque château in the Ardèche still lived in by his parents at the time I am writing of. His father had been a president of the highest constitutional court of France. He was an avowed agnostic and had been a Dreyfusard at the time when it was hardest to stand up and be counted. His mother was a devout Catholic and iron-clad anti-Dreyfusard. For some years their domestic life, dutifully adhered to, had been under strain. This, however, was some time before Philippe's birth.

Oriane was the daughter of a *grand industriel* from the North. The family had been marginally ennobled under the Third Empire, something that had to be lived down or could be dropped into the conversation according to the company. Her mother was an amiable chatterbox, her father a member of that pinnacle of intellectual distinction, the Institut de France. He had a large and discriminate collection of Impressionist, Post-Impressionist and contemporary painting, a collection begun at about the time when Philippe's mother was a member of the public who had to be restrained from taking the sharp of their umbrellas to Impressionist canvases. Both parents doted on Oriane, who was an only child, and who beside her looks pleased by being bright.

Philippe Desmirail had three elder brothers, all reputed brilliant, virtuous and attached to one another. The long holidays of their childhood and early youth were spent at the château in the Ardèche and on the property of a cherished grandmother near Biarritz. The brothers, one after the other, were killed in the 1914 War. When the third was gone by 1917, Philippe was still one year too young to be called up. He was a delicate adolescent, shattered by his brothers' deaths. He joined up all the same. It was said that his mother, who subsequently never went out of mourning for her sons, told Philippe that it was fit for him to offer himself to his country, it was now his turn. He was not killed, he was not even wounded, he caught pneumonia after some months in the trenches, was gravely ill for a long time and did not fully recover until some years later. Eventually he resumed his education but afterwards declined to embark on any official or orthodox career. Instead he joined the forward-looking Maison d'Editions of Bernard Grasset, a publishing house in which it can be said that interesting things were happening. (It was young Bernard Grasset who in 1913 had brought off the coup, that left so many red faces in the French publishers' and critics' world, of publishing the rejected *Du côté de chez Swann*; rejected through the good offices of André Gide by the NRF which later had to buy back the rights of *A la recherche du temps perdu* at the expense of a very great deal of face and money.) At the time Philippe joined Grasset, some of his own friends such as Jacques de Lacretelle were making their name as writers. He, though not a sedentary man and without any literary ambitions of his own, enjoyed his brief publishing career very much, and never quite severed his connections with Bernard Grasset. Brief, because it was soon found that his health would not stand up to confinement in a city; he was ordered out of Paris and recommended to live in the country, preferably in sea air. A prescription he has adhered to till today. This cannot have been his parents' choice: this excessively gently mannered man had inherited his mother's iron will. It seldom showed. In fact it was imperceptible to most.

At first they went to live alternately and impermanently on the Mediterranean and the Atlantic coasts. *They*, because by the time Philippe left Grasset, he and Oriane were married.

They had known each other for some years. They moved in a milieu of highly educated, upper-class, post-war young, who had lost ideals and aims but retained their manners. (And the scruples which these comprise.) They had turned – privately: they were no socialists or reformers – against patriotism, militarism (that above all), religion, bourgeois values; they still believed in individual good behaviour. They wanted a good time – what else was left? – and sought it in amusements they devised themselves: *fêtes costumées*, motor rallies, dawn sorties into the country to catch a view of a cathedral in a certain light, hoaxes of a sophisticated nature. Unlike Evelyn Waugh's Bright and Young they wouldn't have dreamt of leaving unpaid bills or burning cigarettes on other people's carpets. They drank little. Alcohol – apéritifs, pastis, even wine – was felt as part of a gross national heritage. Abstemious was more elegant. (I am writing here of a small and ephemeral coterie of the Desmirails which they had already left behind by the time they moved from Paris. Some of its spirit lingered.)

Besides such an outlook, Philippe and Oriane shared many tastes. Their three major interests at that time were the new French literature, tennis and motor cars, on Philippe's side to the point of taking them apart and putting them together again in his own way. His friends said that given a pram, a tea-kettle and a clock, he could make them run. Philippe's mind was trained, precise; Oriane's mercurial. To her father's and her teachers' disappointment, she had not wanted to go on to university, no career or employment had been envisaged, thus a quick, sharp, able, and soon restless, mind remained unharnessed to any defined or useful purpose for a good many years; decades in fact. Philippe had shown no great desire to get married to anyone, Oriane had shown a great desire to marry him. Somehow they got engaged. To the distinct approval of their friends and their respective families. Philippe insisted that there should be a year of reflection, Oriane agreed. Granting mutual freedom was part of their modern values. So they went on, he with his publishing, both as ringleaders of their *petite bande*. When the year was up he told her – quite casually and coolly it was believed – that they might as well call it a day. Perhaps he was not made for marriage, perhaps he was not ready for marriage, and so he supposed was she – there was not much point in marriage as an institution if one did not wish to produce, if one felt one ought not to produce, children: children in the world as it was were cannon fodder. Slightly to his surprise, Oriane now turned her back on modern values and became unhappy and upset, using the weapons that are at hand for a woman in her situation. Philippe was a man who would not willingly inflict a hurt; among his many principles was that of honouring one's word (however conditional), he readily gave in. He liked her very very much and they got on extremely well.

Their friends – who were fascinated by that visual illusion of their alikeness – proclaimed that they were made for one another.

In an early period of their marriage they fell among a serious tennis set at Biarritz whose mainstays were three of his boyhood friends. Serious is an understatement. Philippe's chums, the three young players in question, were Borotra, Brugnon and Lacoste. When as youngsters they had started learning tennis together, Philippe, who was a few months older and advanced in chess, began by beating them quite easily at the beginning of the holidays; after a few weeks they had drawn even, by the end of the summer it was hard for him to get a game, he was outclassed; for ever. This did not mean that when they were united again at Biarritz, Philippe did not make an acceptable partner; he might have reached top-class himself had it not been for his lack of physical stamina. At one time he was ranked in the lower half of the *Seconde Série de France*; Borotra & Co. were of course at the top of the *Première Série*.

The real discovery, however, was Oriane Desmirail. They made much of her at Biarritz; the great Suzanne herself, Suzanne Lenglen, played singles with her. She showed big promise, they all thought, and began grooming her for world class. For some strenuous months Oriane's abilities were harnessed to a purpose. Too much so. She had two things going for her, a chess-player's mind and the will to win; it was her physique that was not up to it. Her coaches kept her training eight hours a day for weeks on end. One day she collapsed on court. It was diagnosed a heart attack. She was twenty-four. She recovered quickly, and it was not the end of tennis for her (her ranking eventually was near the top of the *Seconde Série*). But it was – definitely – the end of public tennis (and that settled purpose).

The allure of the Biarritz tennis club had been the main reason for their staying on the Atlantic coast; Philippe, congenitally *frileux*, needed a warmer winter climate; their respective parents were pressing them to settle down; they both loved the austerity of the Provençal landscape and had liked Sanary during previous stays. So now there they were, having acquired their piece of land, watching over their house going up.

The house, architect-built – not by Le Corbusier, as my mother had flung out, nevertheless by one of his French disciples – was a present to Oriane from Oriane's father.

Behind the young Desmirails there was a good deal of money. Solid old money on Philippe's side: land, urban real estate, government stocks and bonds (not so solid); less, and less old, money but large present revenues on Oriane's. As far as the young couple and their prospects were concerned there were snags. At the end of the war Philippe's parents had decided that their surviving son must in no way be advantaged by his brothers' deaths. Dispositions therefore had been made for one quarter only of the estate to come to Philippe, the other three quarters were left to charities. (With, it was said, Philippe's entire concurrence.) His father also felt that it behoved Philippe – now that he was improved in health – to earn his living as best he might. Since he was not trained to be a country doctor or anything in that line, and that to attempt farming in the South of France where tiny parcels of land were held by rooted and tenacious peasants, would have been clear madness, the setting up of a business – some cottage industry? – was seen as a solution. It was a moral question for the Desmirails, not one of commercial success or gain. As soon as Philippe had devised some scheme, his father would provide him with the capital required. Meanwhile and since the beginning of the marriage, Oriane was receiving a large allowance from her father (supplemented by accounts at one or two maisons de haute-couture where most of her simple-looking clothes were made).

And now there was the future house, Oriane's present purpose.

I had been wondering after that theatre night whether we – I – would be meeting the Desmirails again and, given the heterogeneity of the first occasion, on what footing. Some people are brought together by their dogs, with us it was fated to be cars. Alessandro and I were caught on a somnolent hot early afternoon on the quai at Bandol – deserted by the boules players now asleep – by Oriane Desmirail, also not keeping siesta, passing in a Citroën. Alessandro was trying – *trying* – to teach me to reverse on our Peugeot. Now that I was eighteen, he was teaching me to drive. Oriane stopped and watched my efforts which did not improve by observation.

Dear children, she addressed us with what I must call a mocking smile (she was a master of that as I was to find out).

'My dear children, don't you know the first rule about learning to drive a car?'

'This one has a tricky gear . . . '

She ignored me. 'The first rule is never to be taught by a member of one's family. The second, not in one's family's car.' Pause. 'We must do something about this.' She looked at Alessandro. Then, gaily, decisively, 'I'm sure we've got a car for her to learn on – not this great big thing. Now listen to me: passing one's driving test is quite a serious business in the Département du Var.'

We listened.

'Why don't you come to us tomorrow at this sort of time, say three o'clock,' she gave the name and way to the furnished villa in which they were camping. 'We'll get you properly taught and you'll be able to get your *permis* in no time.'

And who is going to teach me, I thought, aghast.

'Not by our family either,' she said as though she'd read me. 'We've got just the right man for you, he's a mechanic and driver, he does donkey-work for us. He'll shout at you too, but in the right way . . . So, *à demain*,' and she was off.

I did not recognise it then for what it was par excellence, a Desmirail gesture. Desmirail gestures were always carried through.

The first day was a débâcle. I arrived. I was wearing a white linen skirt especially washed and ironed by Emilia. The Desmirails were standing on top of their steepish drive debating with the man who did the donkey-work what car I'd better learn on. Philippe thought La Sarah, it was small and light and easy to turn. La Sarah turned out to be the black beetle, Philippe had not made her himself, at least not originally, nor was Sarah a whimsy name but an authentic make of car long defunct, which Philippe said had been underrated – and I guessed discontinued – in the 1890s. It didn't have a self-starter, the cranking handle was a trifle obstinate, so I'd better begin by starting her in her accustomed way. They told me what to do. Loosen the handbrake, give her a good push, be ready to leap in as soon as she begins rolling downhill, shove into second gear, ignition on ...

The donkey-man made a demonstration. It worked.

La Sarah was got back into place, engine switched off again. My turn.

What I had not minded, in my various eagernesses, was that the car had been losing oil. There was a sizeable black pool on the drive. I gave my push, gathered for the leap into the car, put a foot into the oil, slipped, fell and lay floundering on my back in a greasy pool while La Sarah was rolling down the hill. Philippe retrieved her in one bound. To get *me* up took more time. For one thing the three of them were standing about laughing to split their sides. 'She's a clown,' they cried, '*un cloon!*' That's how the French pronounce it. Eventually they pulled me up. I will not go into how I was cleaned and re-clothed – one does not improvise hot water in a rented villa in the summer in the South of France, and although I was young and thin, I was not thin enough to get into anything of Oriane's.

When it was over, they decided that I had better learn on the Citroën, not the big one, Oriane's and the newest in the stable, but on the 4-Chevaux. The 4-HP was a little three-seater with a back like a canoe. It was smaller than the present and sophisticated 2-Chevaux. It had once been painted grey, boasted a strip of running-board, and again there was no self-starter. This was just as well, as, when doing your test then, you were required to be able to start your car by hand.

Well, I learned to drive on that 4-Chevaux Citroën and I still hold it in affection. I was well taught by the donkey-man – a tough little chap by name of Baluzet, with meridional speech and gestures that came straight out of Marcel Pagnol – passed the test, practical and oral, which was quite a stiff one, and got my *permis de conduire*, as Oriane had ordained, in a couple of weeks. I still have it and I still use it – French driving licences are valid for ever – a pink square of cardboard much the worse for wear. The photograph was last changed – at the Préfecture du Var – in 1949.

My mother wrote a thank-you letter to Madame Desmirail.

All the same it was not quite the introduction to Philippe and Oriane that I could have wished. Cloon is who cloon is seen. The Desmirails had a penchant for the comic contretemps; it was their addiction to Chaplin and Buster Keaton that made them turn up at that cinematograph. They are reviving my moment of floundering in motor oil dressed in white linen to this day, it stereotyped some of my subsequent relations with them. I'm not a banana-skin type. I regard myself as fairly handy in many practical domains of living, in the context that is of other friends and places – with the Desmirails I can't escape recess into cloondom as expected. I once fell off the quietest horse ambling quietly on a Sunday morning with Philippe in the heart of the Touraine; there was the incident of the backwards running electric meter on a journey with them in Portugal; quite recently I bumped down a length of their staircase smashing with me a whole tray of breakfast china.

10

In our Sanary corner, the next phase of that summer, 1929, the summer before the Wall Street crash, was uneventful eventful. Everyone was busy being energetic at a leisurely pace. The Desmirails were building, so were we in a modest way on that conversion (with many a piece of excellent advice from Philippe who in the teeth of his Corbusieran architect was designing his own plumbing), the Kislings were laying foundations for a fine large house planned by Renée on an incline above the Bay of Bandol. Philippe revealed his scheme for that future gainful occupation, he was going to start a – much-needed – bus line between Sanary and Toulon. The splendid open-roofed Panhard, *le car du théâtre* in the local mind, was the first of a line of second-hand buses he was setting out to acquire. It also explained Baluzet, the donkey-man. Philippe was looking for a site on which to establish shelter and a workshop for that coming fleet while calmly engaged in disentangling – not fighting – the red-tape involved in obtaining the necessary licences. Oriane found the project amusing and was throwing herself into it.

As she did with their other new concern, the tennis club. For the first time in my memory of Sanary, tennis was to be played. There was one existing court, more derelict than not, and that Philippe and Oriane took over and restored to reasonable efficiency. They wanted to play tennis; this they could have done on the perfectly good courts maintained at Bandol by the Grand Hôtel, but they wanted to help kindle a little enthusiasm for *le sport* which was so lagging among the French. The owners of the court, running a melancholy hotel in a pine-wood *côté de* Six-Fours that was not doing well, were only too pleased by the prospect of life the club might bring. The Desmirails ran it in an informal way – it had no name, no changing-rooms, no subscription fee, no rules, no bar. (Tea or lemonade or an apéritif could be ordered at garden tables nearer the hotel.) One became a member when invited by the Desmirails. Here was a difficulty. That there was no player to stand up to them was inevitable (except for the dazzling apparitions of a star or two in transit from a tournament at Monte Carlo or La Ciotat), what they'd hoped was to train up some of the local young. Working lads did not bite: too busy, too shy. If they were to turn *sportif*, it would not be with this little white ball, tennis was still a bourgeois game in France. So the club had to consist of us, that is Alessandro who was good – and became more so, as one tends to when up against superior players – my mother who was quite good (when she put her mind to it), a colonel, British Army, retired, who had once played for the Davis Cup, the colonel's wife, and myself who was no good at all. The only trainable French roped in were the young Panigons. Frédéric came because he liked trying something his family wasn't doing, Panigon *père* having never played anything but boules; Annette, the coltish one, showed some talent; Cécile, whom the Judge had declared a ravishing young girl, hovered about the baseline in languid feminine fashion, uttering little cries as she missed yet another ball. She was worse than me.

The Desmirails soldiered on – Philippe with exquisite politeness, Oriane with jokes, often sharpish – coaching us as well as they could. Doubles helped. Philippe with the colonel taking on Oriane and Alessandro achieved quite an exciting game to watch. What held me – and even made my mother come to the club more often than she might – was the way the two Desmirails moved about a court.

I have not mentioned their third, the young god, their shadow. It is because he did not shadow them on tennis afternoons, Oriane ordained that he must work at certain hours. He despised games, or so he said (he would have looked ungodlike beside Philippe). He was a painter or trying to become one, and the son of a Parisian family much connected with the arts who were, according to Sanary gossip, not over-pleased with him at present. His name was Louis. Oriane had found him a *cabanon* in the back country, an abandoned goatherd's hut, and rigged it up as a studio and a place to camp in. For a part of each day he was banished there, and from her presence. For the rest of the time he was seen following the Desmirails wherever they went, looking out of the back of their cars, a pace or two behind them when they walked. Sanary was delighted about him and the situation. They called him the *cavaliere servente*, the *cicisbeo*, the *amant en titre*; some said it (the situation) was a *ménage à trois*, others that Philippe was a cuckold, others a complaisant husband, still others that Oriane was an *allumeuse* who kept the poor boy dangling. (These speculations came to us by way of Madame Panigon who was unable to decide which version pleased her most.) What was evident was that Louis, in spite of Alessandro's dictum that she had no sex appeal, was besotted about Oriane and only took his eyes off her to scowl at anyone who dared to do the same. He was a dark-faced young god who would have bitten as soon as barked; Oriane kept him in bounds. What she felt was not known, what she made evident was that he was her property, *public* property at that. (People did pause and stare when these three miraculously handsome people passed.) What happened in private – Louis, twenty? twenty-one? was a consenting adult – one could guess at, no more. Philippe Desmirail's dignity, affability and calm remained impenetrable. There were subjects one could not speak to him about.

Philippe treated Louis, who also regularly dined at their house, with the affectionate camaraderie a man might show for a younger man he liked. On the surface then they were three intimate friends who enjoyed – Louis did not always look unhappy – going about together, the heart of a *petite bande*.

The Kislings did not join in the local gossip at all; there was little to gossip about. If Oriane Desmirail had a lover, well who had not? Nor did Renée come anywhere near to joining the tennis club. Me, to my joy, she sometimes took out fishing in the early morning. A message would have come the night before – the tide was right – I would be down on the port before the break of day, and we, she with Léon the sailor who looked after the boat, or just she and I, would go out on the dawn sea, still, flat and grey, far out beyond the sight of land: fish, then swim off the boat and swim again, and return before high noon. That was magical.

The Kislings and the Desmirails – in different degrees and ways – had sloughed off pre-war values, led original and independent lives. They were on good terms, would join at a café table or a restaurant dinner, yet there remained a mutual lack of warmth. Also of approval. For the Kislings, the Desmirails, whatever their behaviour, remained *gens du monde*; the Desmirails' reservations were less conscious and more disguised as they professed to like and respect artists (some years earlier Kisling had done a portrait of Oriane commissioned by her father). On the individual level the situation was even less favourable. Renée distrusted Oriane (she once told me so), and Philippe for her was just another of those poor cerebral creatures not much use in shipwreck or in bed. Philippe for his part not merely disapproved of Renée's general conduct – her loud laugh, the large and pungent feasts of *aioli* and bouillabaisse, the left-wing sympathies, the undisguised *couchages* which included Léon the sailor – he actually, rare for him, detested her. Even today when she is long dead, he cannot speak well. (She was a sensualist all through; he, as far as the French context allowed, came nearer to a puritan.) It astounds and dismays me that two people of outstanding, if disparate, qualities could see nothing in each other.

A similarly negative alchemy operated between Philippe and my mother. On good surface terms to the end, they did not like each other much. They did not say so; there just was not in either a spark of admiration (she once told me that a man oughtn't to have too many virtues). That lack, too, grieved me. It had taken me a while to see it. I shall never cease to puzzle over that cat's cradle of human sympathies, of attraction, non-attraction, revulsion. As a novelist I ought, at least sometimes, to get it right.

It occurs to me – a little late – that I have not said what my mother looked like. She was beautiful – a beautiful woman – this I have said, more than once, and left the idea afloat in the reader's mind. Perhaps I did not attempt description because to me her image is inconstant and elusive. The face under the enormous hat bent over my pram is not the face of the mischievous parent I was landed on years later at Cortina d'Ampezzo, or the face touched with foreboding on the Sorrentine beach, the face changed – so lightly – in the station bus. The two most present, and very different, versions in my mind's eye are the way she looked during that contented winter she and I shared in France, and a studio photograph by Man Ray taken in the early nineteen-twenties where she is presented as a formal dark beauty, dark hair, dark eyes, with an inward air of serene repose. She must at times have looked like that in life, though the photograph has not caught her vitality, her animation. What it did catch was a glow, the glow on the face of a woman painted by Giorgione.

Later her face became etched with a tragic refinement such as one might see in certain Rembrandt portraits, with lines and features grown more Jewish now than Latin.

I am apt to see men and women in terms of paintings; the likenesses meant to be generic rather than exact. To conclude on a more factual plane about my mother's appearance: she was by no means short without being noticeably tall, her figure was very feminine, with a certain well-carried opulence; her arms and shoulders were rounded, her hair chestnut and her colouring olive (which made her having a blue-eyed, very fair child – pinko-Aryan she called me when in the mood – surprising to her, my father also having been dark); her hands were pretty and a little too small. She did not bother overmuch about what she wore, in fact she could dress quite badly, apt to fling on, buttons the wrong way, something she'd acquired because she'd seen it look good on someone else. It did not matter. She had radiance, she had presence.

Near the end of June we were sought out by a reappearance from what was to me already a remote past. A car drew up outside Les Cyprès, a smart Chrysler roadster. A young woman got out, very thin but quite smart as well. She asked if my mother lived here. I recognised her. She had looked a waif and she still looked a bit of a waif in spite of the Chrysler – sallow and large-eyed and flat-chested. It was Doris von R., the girl from Berlin, my mother had met goodness knows where and who had been supposed to look after me at Cortina d'Ampezzo on my first stay in Italy, and instead vanished lured by a film test. It was only seven years or so ago. She took a bit longer identifying me.

She had always wanted to meet my mother again, she said, and now here she was giving her sweet grandmother a holiday in the South of France. (The grandmother, I remembered, who had brought up this orphaned stray and tried to make ends meet by running a pension in Berlin where all the guests were friends and out of work and seldom paid and got fed all the same.) Doris said she'd left Mammerl at the hotel for a rest after their journey, the Hôtel de la Plage by the sea (I noted: the Judge's hotel, the best, a good sign). At this point Alessandro appeared. Here Doris was quicker off the mark if jumping with surprise. 'Dr Caligari, I presume?'

'Shsh,' I said. 'Not any more. They are *married.*'

'Your mother married *him*?'

'She did.'

'Oh.' Pause. 'How very nice.' Pause. 'He's changed less than you.'

Well: my mother joined us, Emilia was asked to provide tea, before long Doris was telling her life story and presently Alessandro turned the Chrysler for her and the two drove down to fetch the old lady up to our house. When they came back he was at the wheel ('she drives abominably,' he said aside to me). The grandmother, as thin and more frail than Doris, turned out not only sweet but witty and wise. They stayed for dinner, the next day we had dinner with them at their hotel, we took them to beaches and into Toulon, showed them the sights and so it went on for the rest of their stay which was just under a week. During it we learned a good deal about Doris, past, future and present.

She had been a gallant girl when she fetched up in Northern Italy, left stranded by the American script writer to whom she acted secretary. She must have been more or less the age that I was now. She was still gallant. She needed it when she got back to Berlin and the pension and a life of uncertainties and excitement. Inflation, poor health, boring jobs, underpaid, attempts and failures at the stage, talented friends, freedom, ideas and ideals. Love affairs with adorable and impossible young men (her description) – actors, poets, writers – that fizzled out if they did not end in disaster. Flirtations with radical causes. More than one of the impossible young men had been Communists or near-Communists. The only thing for decent people to be now, she told us; Germany was getting disgustingly nationalistic, we could have no idea how horrible the right-wing people were becoming, openly attacking the Weimar Republic, 'They even speak of *war*.' Her friends said the Republic was weak, split between the Democrats, the Centrum, the Social-Democrats, the Communists.

My mother's old left-of-Fabian leanings were stirring, she asked whether they were still talking of Rosa Luxemburg whom she had always admired. 'Oh we do,' Doris said, 'and the officer swine who murdered her.'

Had she, Doris, ever been a Party member?

Not quite. She nearly did at one point ... But now ... Well now that things had so changed for her, now that she was engaged – she didn't think Paul would like it. Paul was her fiancé. Not, she reassured us, that he wasn't on the right side – he had voted Social-Democrat – only he didn't believe in revolution. 'He's much older than most of us, he's in his *thirties*.'

We listened.

He was an architect, the kind that builds department stores and hotels, but we mustn't think he was a philistine, just because he'd got so much money.

We said of course not.

The facts were that he was a serious man, and very much in love with her. They were going to be married. As soon as they could that was. He had to get a divorce first. Oh that was all right – he and his wife were quite in agreement, they were very good friends and she too was going to marry someone else. No one was hurt. It would have been very wrong to break up a marriage – one didn't do *that* – wouldn't we agree?

The three of us said yes.

Weimar had made the German law quite civilised; there didn't have to be guilty parties any more – it could all be done on incompatibility. The law was sensible but it still took long, bureaucracy . . . the courts were slow . . . It'd take a year, perhaps more, before she and Paul could get legally married. Meanwhile he wanted them to be fairly discreet – politeness towards his wife. He had given Doris the car – 'it belongs to me' – and suggested taking her grandmother on this holiday. He had given them so much money. 'You can't imagine how good he's been to Mammerl – he wants her to close down the pension and live with us. He's building a house by a lake in Bavaria. And he's so good to our friends, he's finding them jobs and giving them things, he's changed our lives. I'm very fond of him. But it's strange to be suddenly so rich; I don't know if it's right.'

The evening after they'd left, we talked them over. My mother said how much she had liked Doris – a good girl, a brave girl . . . Oh yes, quite silly at times, and rash – the kind that comes to grief. All looks so well for her now, yet somehow one fears . . .

Did they think she was attractive? I asked.

My mother looked at Alessandro. He reflected. 'She's got more sex appeal than Oriane.'

'For you?'

He laughed. 'You know, I don't really like those skinny women. Besides she's too young.'

My mother laughed too. 'She's about *your* age, I would say.'

'At least two years younger,' he said with contempt.

'I do wish her happiness,' my mother said. 'I hope to God it'll all come off and she'll marry that possible man. I'm afraid he's a bit too steady for her. She may even do something quixotic about having too much money.'

'She drives so badly,' Alessandro said gloomily, 'she's got no idea how to handle a car – not that she's clumsy, or very reckless, just fatalistic and vague. The risks for the poor old lady!'

'The risks,' said my mother, 'for the poor young girl.'

11

A combination of circumstances persuaded my mother to leave Sanary for a few weeks. She was the kind of nomad who prefers not to budge. The senior of her trustees had long been nagging her to agree to a personal encounter – there really were things to be signed, discussed, decided – he was prepared to meet her at any mutually convenient place, somewhere in Switzerland, say. For a time she deferred. (All he wants is to rub it in about my declining fortunes.) This was all too true. Yet as Alessandro was continuing to earn a reasonable living, her apprehensions of being told about her future diminished and she began to think that she might even be able to charm the old devil into a further decimation of her capital. At any rate he would pay (out of her capital) for the journey and stay in Switzerland or wherever. She recalled some resorts on the Lake of Lucerne that were rather pleasant in the height of summer. She had been told she'd been staying far too long at sea level. This gratuitous advice had been tendered by a doctor who entered our house briefly once or twice when Alessandro ran some carpenter's tool through his hand and for my occasional bad throat. The doctor was recommended by a pharmacist, the same who used to supply – and still did – my mother with sleeping pills. I say gratuitous because I was not aware that she'd had a consultation. He must have taken an interest in her as he was being shown out, on the doorstep as it were. He told her she looked run down to him and ought to be thinking of a change of climate.

My mother did not pay much attention to her health, therefore nor did we. She treated it rather like her clothes, careless, if open to suggestions. There *was* her insomnia; we were used to that and she dealt with it – reading late, sleeping late, more often than not with some soporific.

The doctor, the pharmacist had chosen, was a man of depressing appearance. Gaunt as a starving horse, yellow-faced with darkly-ringed, sunken eyes and a few strands of flat black hair, dressed winter and summer in a greasy black suit – in short he looked straight out of a bad horror film. His name was – I cannot help it, that *was* his name – Joyeu, Docteur Joyeu. One can predict the jokes. Behind his back they called him Docteur Lugubre and they were fond of saying that he was not as jolly as he looked.

Because of his advice or not, my mother became charmed by the idea of Swiss mountain lakes. Emilia was due for a month's holiday, this fitted in, so on the first of July they both departed, my mother for a few days with her trustee at Lucerne followed by some weeks of rest-cure further up the shore, Emilia for her native Tuscan village, leaving Alessandro and me alone for the first time under the same roof.

Not for long. Not for long in any twenty-four hours under our own roof. Such was our friends' and neighbours' concern for our state – abandoned by wife, by mother, abandoned by the *cook* – that we were being asked for elevenses at the café, for luncheon, picnics, apéritifs and dinner. *Les garçons*, they called us, the bachelors, and Sanary strove to improve our lot. (They seemed somewhat amused by our position.) Alessandro and I took to the whirl like ducks to water. We gave up any pretence of housekeeping. A *femme de ménage* had been secured for us; she did not turn up regularly, nor did we pay attention to her comings and goings, give any orders or get in provisions. All was well as long as the house looked reasonably clean (not Emilia clean, that was not expected), and if returning at some late hour after an evening with the Kislings at the *bal musette*, we found our beds had not been made, it hardly mattered. On the rare occasion when we had not been asked out for a meal, we took each other to the bistro.

I also gave up any pretence of work (Alessandro, always con-scientious, went on supervising the converting villa). Up till then, summer months and all, I had set aside a few hours each day ploughing through books, writing précis, trying to master miscellaneous grammars. (Someone at Finchingfield had come up with the apparently sound idea that one thing I might be eligible for in spite of my lack of formal education was an interpreter's certificate which could be obtained then from some branch of the Chamber of Commerce by sitting an exam without having attended any preliminary school or course. This seemed tailor-made, and was welcomed by my mother as a means to appease my guardians. So one day I had put my name down at an office in the City, I forget exactly where, was given a leaflet with recommendations and told to present myself for a viva and a written examination in some two years' time. I took it lightly, except for the closer look at grammars.) *Not* so now. No grammar, no books, during those weeks Alessandro and I were on our own.

We swam, we played tennis. Some of it with the elder young Panigons, Frédéric and Cécile, who seemed to be a good deal under foot. Well, their parents gave us some jolly good dinners; whatever fun we made of Madame Panigon, she knew her food – not in the Kislings' Homeric style of hospitality, but in the established mode of French provincial cooking south (not too far south) of Lyon – and Monsieur was the only man we knew who had anything like a cellar. We played *belote*, we played *chasse-coeur*, we played mah-jong. Philippe liked card games, though never played for money; I saw to it that we didn't miss a chance of going to the Desmirails'. Oriane would sit by, sewing.

Even Louis asked Alessandro to come up to his cabin and be shown his paintings. We went. What did you make of them? I asked Alessandro afterwards. He doesn't work enough, Alessandro said.

'Because of Oriane Desmirail?'

'Who else?'

'It isn't *her* fault,' I said.

'Oh *fault*,' said Alessandro, 'things just happen to people.'

It was as if the good days could never end. And what are we doing today? we'd ask each other, happily, when we met in the morning. We still made our own café au lait.

We seemed to be growing younger, as though we were living a second youth; or perhaps Alessandro was growing younger and I was growing up.

As we arrived at the building site one Saturday morning, we found that the villa had reached a stage of near-completion. The masons' work was done. The new doorways and casements were in place though not the actual doors and window panes, the verandah and entrance hall were still roofless, open to the sky. There were no stairs up into the house, so the workmen had laid a gangplank. They had gone the night before leaving everything clean-swept and bare; tools, buckets, concrete cleared away – what we had before us was the shell of a house, empty, bare, a skeleton: a place for children to play in.

It was Alessandro's idea. We must have a party. For all our friends. Here. *Tonight*. And let's dress up. As what? We can pretend we're on a ship – we'll have a boat party. Tell everyone to come as sailors, that'll be simple enough, they won't need real sailors' clothes.

We set to work there and then. We took turns driving around in the Peugeot giving out invitations (*tout Riseholme*, I would have liked to say but could have shared the joke only with my mother; Alessandro did not care for the Lucia books, any more than he did for nonsense verse, he found Edward Lear embarrassing; I also had to suppress the unwelcome thought that there was a touch of Lucia in Oriane). We got in provisions, we collected what was needed, Madame Panigon lent us a large bowl, we took the washtub and every glass we could lay hands on from Les Cyprès, Louis offered to go into Toulon to get Chinese lanterns, we borrowed more glasses, a gramophone and a stack of dance records, Chez Schwob let us have a block of ice.

By sundown Alessandro and I got down to making the cup, our notion of a planters' punch: we poured bottles and bottles of dry white wine from the Co-op at Saint-Cyr into the bowl, and quite a lot of white rum, added a lemon and kilos of peaches (peeled and stoned). We set the bowl into the washtub on the block of ice, and went home to dress up.

Alessandro lent me a pair of his tennis trousers (we had to roll up the legs a bit), striped French sailor jerseys we both already owned, and *voilà tout*. Then he made us up. That he said was important, *that* would make us look disguised. He flattened and darkened my hair, which was very light and flying about, he gave me a deep walnut complexion, black eyebrows and sideburns drawn with charcoal. When I saw myself in the glass, I was entranced: I didn't recognise the boy I saw, I *felt* disguised. I had not worn trousers before (women were just beginning to wear them on the Riviera side of the coast, calling them beach pyjamas; we didn't yet, except for Renée Kisling). Nor had I been to a fancy-dress party, so did not know what it could do to one. It was with surprise and delight that I began our evening.

Which went awfully well. People liked the gangplank and the half-dark empty house, they admired the way we had hung the Chinese lanterns from the rafters and the trees – it felt a bit like being on a ship, say a river boat. They liked our punch. Madame Panigon, otherwise in ordinary dress, wore a French sailor's hat with pompon. We danced on the terrace; we all danced, regardless of age or sex. I felt carried away, ecstatic, outside myself, I was probably quite tipsy but less by wine than by disguise. Everyone was a bit tipsy, not very tipsy, the punch can't have been very strong and one did not drink *very* much: it was a summer-night's romp.

Renée was not there, she'd sent word that the night was ideal for fishing. I was aware that the Desmirails hadn't come but it didn't damp the *élan*. I bounced about re-filling glasses, dancing with every-one, men and women, I even seized Madame Panigon and led her into a foxtrot. She did not seem displeased.

At midnight (as it was later established, we weren't aware of the time) there was a sudden great bang: pistol shots and savage yells – a young pirate swung down from the rafters, knife in mouth, skull flag in hand, leapt lightly to the ground . . . Two more were storming the gangplank . . . Surrender . . . ! Surrender . . . ! Levantine pirates, their stylish captain in wig and kerchief, sea-boots and cloak, scimitar in hand . . . his slim lieutenant bristling with daggers and cutlass in belt . . . they wore half-masks . . . The dancing had stopped, all stood still – for a minute the illusion held – not of a live pirates' attack but of a mêlée with some precisely executed ballet where the principals looked stunning. Then revealed: Louis, Philippe, Oriane.

They had conquered. Gossip and envy were suspended, showing up our slapdash efforts not minded, the Desmirail touch had made something of our party (with *much* ingenuity and trouble): for that night everybody admired, cherished, loved them.

When it was over, it was the break of a clear beautiful morning. Alessandro and I stood among the débris, feeling well, feeling fine, still charged with energy.

Let's leave this mess, he said. We went down to Port Issol and swam, then drove home to Les Cyprès, got what was left of the make-up off our faces and changed into ordinary fresh clothes. It hadn't occurred to either of us to go to bed.

It was Sunday. Need we really go back and face the job? Alessandro said. The *femme de ménage* might be got to see to it tomorrow. Let's go off somewhere. Let's go and spend the day at Saint-Tropez. I said yes at once, the party was still in my bones. So we walked out of the house, put the key under a flowerpot and set off.

First we stopped for some breakfast at Chez Schwob which was already open. Whom did we find there but the three young Panigons eating ham sandwiches with their bowls of coffee; they too were loath to call it a day. We told them where we were off to.

Chic alors, said Frédéric. Saint-Tropez, then as now, was the place to *faire la bombe* where people thought they'd have a wild and with-it time. The Panigons asked if we could take them. Why not, said Alessandro. Let's all go. I was not enthusiastic. Annette was a nice *child*; Frédéric saw himself as a rebel and an original young man; Cécile, though rather sweet, was grindingly genteel. Between them they kept telling us how fortunate we were to live in such an advanced, artistic, stimulating family, what a privilege it was for them to know my mother. At the moment they would have to ask theirs for permission. She'll be in bed, I thought. Anyway, you had better get your bathing-suits, I said.

Up at their house, Monsieur Panigon was still or already about, reading *Le Petit Var*. Frédéric handled the negotiation. He made the idea of a Sunday's outing in the company of an older man, a married man, sound reasonable. (Alessandro, in fact, was somewhat nearer to thirty than twenty.) You're of age, my son, said Monsieur Panigon, do as you like; as for the girls, *non*. Annette is far too young – out of the question. Very well, said Annette, with a little sulk, she hadn't seemed too keen in the first place. '*Papa* . . . !' Cécile turned her great cow's eyes on her father. Frédéric didn't let her go on. Please, he said in manly tones, may I take my sister, I promise to look after her.

He combined sounding respectful and a man of the world. It worked (he must have tried this before, I thought). Very well, my children, said Monsieur Panigon; he called Alessandro last night's amiable host. No need to wake your mother. *Amusez-vous bien.*

So we started. The two men in front, Cécile and I in the back. She began again about how much she admired my mother. *Si fine, si cultivée, quelle intelligence* . . .

'*Tu as de la chance, ta maman te fait lire.*'

My mother made me read? *I* read. *I* wanted to read. Then I had to retract this in my mind – it must have come from her, from my mother, the example, the inspiration, the impulse. I said as nicely as I could to this girl who bored me, '*Yes*, my mother made me read.'

She went on to tell me that things were otherwise in *her* home.

From Sanary to Saint-Tropez was (in pre-autoroute days) an eighty kilometre drive. After Hyères we discussed whether to take the sea route and bathe or go inland and have a *casse-croûte* at the Auberge de la Forêt du Dom. As it was still early we decided to do both. We swam – the Panigons quite passably – then climbed back on to the N98 by the narrow zig-zag above Bormes-les-Mimosas, and at the Auberge they gave us *pissaladino* – hot bread baked with black olives, anchovy, olive oil – and slices of smoked wild boar (a beast said to be rampant in those woods) with a *coup de blanc*.

On the last lap, I drove with Alessandro sitting beside me. You're getting quite good, he said.

'Philippe Desmirail has been putting me through my paces. Double de-clutching . . . He says one should learn to change gear, up *and* down, without using the clutch at all.'

'Don't try it now.'

'Oriane says *he* can drive when he's asleep.'

'Don't try that either.'

'Philippe says I *shall* be quite good after a few years' practice – a good average driver.'

'Not very flattering,' said Alessandro.

'He says I haven't got it in me – getting to the top.'

'What does he say about my driving then?' said Alessandro.

'That you are a natural, you'll be alpha minus.'

Titters of approval from the back of the car.

At Saint-Tropez we found that the yacht belonging to some clients of Alessandro's was in port, the Schroders, Americans who had bought a picture through him and might buy another. The four of us were made welcome on board, finding a number of people of various nationalities on deck below an awning, about to start making cocktails. Mrs Schroder, who kissed Alessandro on both cheeks, was impeccably sunburnt, smoked through a holder, and looked extremely smart. They all looked extremely smart – ages I guessed to be between thirty and forty, and Mr Schroder, who wore a yachting cap, much older. The cocktails were orange-blossoms: gin and orange-juice shaken with crushed ice. They tasted fresh and cool, and we were very thirsty. I sat facing the colour-washed houses of the Saint-Tropez waterfront, with the sea gently moving under the boat, and felt that life was good. This bliss was prolonged as luncheon was very late – I'd never waited so long for a meal before – there was much talking and more orange-blossoms got shaken, when we ate it was well after three o'clock. Lunch was served by a member of the crew, and was long, slow and delicious. The main component was a great deal of lobster. Afterwards everyone retired. Cécile and I were given a small cabin. We still felt well awake and Cécile started prattling.

'*Tu sais, il est beau, Alessandro.*'

The French use beautiful more easily for a man. I supposed I knew what Alessandro looked like, though when one sees somebody every day . . .

'Yes, he is that,' I told her, '*beau.*' (Not like Philippe: different.)

I heard her ask whether my stepfather possessed a heart. Sleep cut me off.

We were aroused with long glasses of iced tea and offers of a shower. Presently the whole party went ashore and met at the Escale for apéritifs. It was near sunset. Euphoria held. Later on we had dinner. Mr Schroder kept ordering wine. Then came brandy. We danced during dinner and afterwards. There was a tangible eroticism over the whole of the Escale, being with the Kislings had taught me to recognise it, feel it. Alessandro danced with all the women in our party, coolly, impartially. He danced with Mrs Schroder, whom he called Betty, he danced with a very good-looking Rumanian woman (who fascinated me), he danced with Cécile.

I too danced the whole time, with men from our party and once or twice with men from other tables; with some – so I thought – I had interesting conversations. Frédéric Panigon asked me a second time, which I found superfluous. He was better looking than he was in the Café de la Marine days, he had filled out a bit, he was a quite well set-up young Frenchman, though all very average, nothing to write home about. I let *his* conversation wash over me. It was again about how he felt wasting his time being a law student, how encouraging it was for him getting to know people like us, it might even persuade his family to let him study art. My guess was that Madame Panigon did not rate us much above gypsies.

By this time I was really quite tight. I did not feel outside myself as I had the night before, just far from daily life, free, carried along, floating. I didn't like, nor was interested in anyone in that crowd – except perhaps the Rumanian woman, but she took no notice of me – nothing mattered much, as long as the fête went on.

When the Escale closed down, it was proposed to move on to a club in the upper town. Is it two o'clock? Alessandro said. It was. Two a.m. in the morning. *Your parents!*, he said to Frédéric who said, '*Bougre,* some Sunday outing.' That was nice and cool. Cécile said, '*Oh mon Dieu,*' and looked terror-stricken. As well she might.

What shall we do? Drive home as quickly as we can, was Alessandro's first decision. Goodbyes all round had to be said and thank-you and kissings on both cheeks and when shall we meet again. That took time.

We were none of us sober now. At last we four went to find the Peugeot. What can we *say*, we asked each other on the way, we *are* in the soup. Drive back as quickly as we can, Alessandro repeated. We'll think up a story en route.

We got into the Peugeot and Alessandro drove off in fine style. The street leading out of Saint-Tropez from the port is a one-way street, cobbled, narrow. Alessandro accelerated, hit a gutter, hit the kerb: there was a jolt, there was a clink, he attempted to drive on, but the car was stuck. The men got out. The right front wheel was dented and the tyre flat. The men swore. Got to change the wheel. They set to. Alessandro swore – the spare was flat, he meant to get it seen to yesterday, Saturday that was the day of our party, and forgot. *What shall we do?*

No garage would be open, let alone willing to mend a tyre at this time of night. Better get some sleep, make an early start, sensible thing, got to find an hotel.

Saint-Tropez in July is always chock-a-block. We tried a few of the smaller hotels in back-streets, the sign on the doors said *Complet*. We saw another modest hotel plunged in darkness but without the forbidding sign. We roused a disagreeable and disgruntled man who looked us over coldly. No luggage. Alessandro pulled out his wallet. Two rooms left, *Messieurs-Dames*, small ones, separate floors – along here, this way . . . He shuffled on in front of us, then behind us, and before we knew where we were Frédéric and I had been pushed into a cubicle filled by a large bed. The man had disappeared, so had the others – up some staircase. Once more, Frédéric said *bougre*. I opened the window and the solid shutter, letting in the cool night air. Frédéric switched off the light, a bulb on the ceiling. We got out of our clothes, we didn't wear many, and into the bed. Frédéric began making love to me. I had expected nothing and anything during the last twenty-four hours. My main thought now was: soon I shall know all about it.

It could be said that I had or I had not had a sexual experience before. I didn't know how to evaluate an incident that took place a year ago. A connection of Alessandro's, a cousin much removed, was staying with us for a few days at Les Cyprès. He was a handsome fellow, older than

Alessandro, tall, with curly brown hair and a noble face, and he was one of the dullest and dumbest men I've ever met. He could outdo mute Englishmen in talking about the weather, which where he came from did not give much scope. He was stupid and obstinate and single-minded to boot, and much teased by family and friends. They called him Tempo-Bello, because his stock phrase was *Oggi fa tempo bello*. Today the weather is fine. It was a pity: with his looks he ought to have spouted Il Tasso.

He asked me to go for a walk with him after mass. He was able to assemble that whole sentence. I told him I never went to mass. Then agreed to meet him afterwards at the church. It was an autumn Sunday shortly before my return to England, and already a bit cool on the beaches. We could walk on La Cride, a promontory where one some-times had picnics, then climb down to the sea for a quick swim off the rocks. I knew every inlet. When I arrived at the Place de Sanary I saw Tempo-Bello lounging outside the church. He had, as was the custom of Italian men of his caste, not joined the congregation but loitered at some paces from the door for the duration of the service. (When they hear the sanctus bell, they approach, stand in the doorway, genuflect, cross themselves, presumably say a prayer. After the elevation of the host, they are free to stroll away.) Tempo-Bello and I drove to La Cride and set out for our walk.

Flung over his shoulder was the white and scarlet cloak to which his family was entitled. It was a stylish thing out of a Carpaccio painting or the bull ring. When we came to a fine-branched ilex, he flung it on the ground. La Cride on a Sunday noon is an isolated place. I thought he wanted to rest and smoke, and sat down beside him. There ensued, at once and in complete silence, what I had read about as heavy petting. I was too surprised to be taken aback and almost at once surprised again by entirely unexpected and delicious sensations. When we stood up again – he did hold out his hand to help me – Tempo-Bello picked up his cloak with a swing and resumed our walk as though absolutely nothing had occurred. He was his smug self and entirely composed. I was not, but concealed this, waiting for a lead from him. None came. No word, no smile, no caress. Up to this I could have taken what had happened as natural and friendly. His silence made it into something appalling. Shameful, furtive, *wrong*. I became wordless myself. We went back. (I did *not* want to bathe with him from the rocks.) When we got to Les Cyprès I was struck by panic. In a few minutes I would be sitting down to lunch with my mother and Alessandro. What if they suspected, what if they guessed? How would I be able not to give something away? Now I felt fear as well as guilt. I was unable to look at Tempo-Bello; if only he would not come in, find some excuse . . . He did come in, leaving his cloak in the hall. The teasing started at once: Did we have a nice walk? I turned to hide my face. 'What did you talk about? What was the subject of conversation?' 'He told me *che fa tempo bello.*' How did I manage to trot out the old joke? How did I manage to sit through the next hour? How did the others not notice my state of acute embarrassment? Embarrassment, *that* was it. That was what remained.

The next day Tempo-Bello again asked me to go for a walk. *Passeggiata?* he said. He'd got it down to one word. Like Walky to a dog. So had I. I turned away with a flat No. The day after he left. In spite of the terror at that Sunday luncheon, I soon got over the incident. It had not, I told myself, invalidated the seductive ethos of the Kislings': *if one is friends, it's all right to make love.* Tempo-Bello was *not* a friend and what we did was not making *love.* So that was that. I told nobody; but that was because I didn't know anyone suitable to tell. It could be seen as a comical story, what with the cloak and the insistence on mass. (Years later I did tell it to someone. To two people in fact. First to Maria Huxley who said, Do tell Aldous, it's the kind of thing he likes to put in his books. I did, and he was much amused, and I did another volte-face – I was rather annoyed: I thought he lacked feeling and did not see all the points.) When my younger self had reflected on the episode, which was seldom, there remained only, as I said, that residue of embarrassment. There was also the faint memory of those delicious sensations.

Frédéric. What *he* would have said to me I shall never know for we both fell fast asleep. One moment I had felt entirely lucid – rather pleased: *Now I do know and it is surprising also not surprising at all.* I remember feeling that. (Young persons do not really need diagrams or instructions from parents or school.) If anyone was surprised it was probably Frédéric when he met no resistance. He was very sure of himself – this was evidently not a new experience for him. I did my best not to let him suspect that it was that for me. It didn't hurt very much, nothing to fuss about; mildly disagreeable all in all. There were *no* delicious sensations. I didn't like Frédéric any the more or any the less, I distinctly wished it were someone other than he, but did not know who. It must have been at this point that I plummeted into sleep.

Next thing was a knock and someone inside the door. It was Alessandro fully dressed with broad daylight shining in from the un-shuttered window. He didn't look at the bed, or more to the point, at Frédéric and me in the bed with the sheet quickly drawn up to our chins. 'It's a quarter to seven,' he said in our direction, 'get ready and get going.' He looked awful. Alessandro could look melancholy and fine-drawn, now he just looked wretched. 'I knocked up a garage, they are mending the tyre now. Meet me there as soon as you can, it's called Excelsior and it's almost next door.'

I was still too much in sleep to take in implications, and so I dare say was Frédéric. We did as we were told. In the corridor on our way down he gave me quite an affectionate peck on the cheek. '*T'es un brave type,*' he said. I was a good sport. He was looking at it as a windfall. Well, so in a way had I.

From the garage we drove off at once. We would stop again at eight o'clock, Alessandro told us, when post offices were open, and send a telegram to your parents, with luck they'll get it within an hour, they must be sick with worry.

Frédéric came to. *Oh, good God,* he said and began looking awful too. All turned now to poor little Cécile always so cowed by her ferocious mama. (I still had visions of Madame on that beach accusing me of drowning Annette.) Cécile astonished us by firmly saying, 'We had a burst tyre, it can happen to anyone, they can't eat us.' She didn't look frightened, she looked serenely composed. Then I was struck by a new thought. So I could see was Frédéric. Had the disgruntled man at the hotel led *them* too into a cubicle with one bed? It was more than likely. Then . . . ? No, that was not thinkable. Frédéric's face said, my sister? My thoughts, my mother?

I could not see – awake now – much sense in a telegram preceding us by little more than an hour when they had expected us back the night before. Alessandro and Frédéric though felt the need of such a buffer. We sent it from Cogolin. I remember what it, after some discussion, said:

Panne d'auto tout bien arriverons de suite

Car breakdown all well arriving soon. We had discussed concluding either with *tendresses* from the Panigons or *amitiés* from Alessandro and me, or with both. In the end we just put our four names. That was Frédéric's idea, in case they thought that *panne* was softening for *accident* and one or more of us were dead.

Getting off the telegram was an achievement, we allowed ourselves to linger at Cogolin for some coffee. Alessandro had a Fernet-Branca at the *zinc* – he had a hangover, poor man. I had not. I felt fine; the party spirit was alive again. I went off to find a *boulangerie* to get croissants; Frédéric went with me. When we got back to the café, Cécile was holding Alessandro's hand, discreetly disentangling it when she saw us approach. Frédéric turned pale. *What shall we do?* he said to me. We sat down at their table, shared out the croissants, pretending we'd seen nothing. Alessandro was having his second Fernet-Branca. Cécile coaxed him – maternally! – to drink some coffee. She looked radiant.

We stopped once more and that was for a brief swim off a small beach east of Hyères. It would make us feel more presentable, we said. After that we went straight on. Alessandro drove, with Cécile in front; Frédéric and I sat in the back. Well out of sight-line of the driving mirror (*that, too, he had done before*), Frédéric put his arms around me tightly – nothing more – and kept them so as we were speeding along, and there they were again, the delicious sensations. Faintly but recognisably. I gave myself to them. (With little connection with Frédéric.) I also did some thinking: This is *not* a love affair. Perhaps it could be said that I'd had an affair with this boy (I put it in the past tense). It is not what I want. He was still holding me and I wanted it to go on: my thoughts were paradoxical, given that situation.

As we got near our destination, the silence in the car was broken. *What shall we say?* was the gist. It was his responsibility, said Alessandro. Fat lot of good, said Frédéric who had become agitated. 'You are both stupid,' said Cécile, 'listen to me,' and again she astonished us. 'We had this flat tyre – they can see the wheel, the one in the boot . . . '

'When did we have this flat tyre?' Frédéric shouted.

'After dinner – too late for the post office – so then we *had* to spend the night at an hotel. That's all.'

'Too late for a garage?'

'*Mais oui. Nous avions dîné un peu tard*. How could we have imposed the dinner hour on Sandro's friends? We'll apologise of course. They'll be furious, they like being furious, Papa too, and because they've been anxious. They may not be so very furious in front of Alessandro.' (Mightn't they? I thought.) 'It'll pass. What can they do to us? In eleven months I shall be twenty-one.'

'We're not talking about eleven months, *ma fille*, we're talking about *now*,' said her brother. Alessandro just groaned.

None of us mentioned the pitfalls in our tale. Each surmised; none asked questions. It was decided that the brother and sister accompanied by Alessandro – naturally, as the outing's host – were to face the music. I was to be dropped off at Les Cyprès, the assumption being that the less there were to be cross-examined the safer. One less to blush.

As we were driving through Sanary, I saw Oriane Desmirail walking through the square. Instantly I asked Alessandro to stop, to let me out, I'd remembered something I had to get. *Do* stop. I said *Bon courage* to Alessandro as they drove on to whatever awaited them. I forgot to say goodbye to Frédéric. I was off like an arrow.

I caught up with Oriane on the port about to get into her car, the small Citroën. Oh, there you are, she said, Philippe and I have been looking for you.

'We've been to Saint-Tropez.'

'Ah. You've been making *la bombe.*'

'We did rather.'

'Deserting your friends. We wanted to help you clear up, and we wanted to ask you to dinner last night.'

'*Oh,*' I said, 'if *only* I had known.'

She raised an eyebrow and took this up. 'If only . . . ?'

'I would have gone to dinner with you.'

'Quite right, instead of gadding about with those boring Panigons.'

'How did you know?' I said.

'Somebody saw them in your car. Everyone knows everything in Sanary.'

Not everything, I thought.

'Saint-Tropez *is* fun, or didn't you have any? Why would you've rather had dinner with us?'

I knew the answer to that. With sudden clarity.

'Diane,' I said.

'Diane who?'

'Diane chasseresse, Diane the Goddess.'

The eyebrow again. 'Yes . . . ?'

'*You,*' I said.

'Astride a 4-CV Citroën? *Malheureuse, vous me rendez ridicule.*'

'Is that a quotation?' I said.

'It is.'

'*You* could never be ridiculous,' I said.

'Whereas *you* might?'

'I wouldn't mind. I'm only a mortal. May I tell you something?'

'Would it amuse me?'

'It well might,' I said with some grimness.

'In that case, do tell me.'

I looked at her. Straight. With complete concentration. Then I uttered the three fatal words.

The three fatal words – they are three in French as well as in English though the pronoun is not in the same place – the words every human creature, one hopes – or despairs – uses once, more than once, too often, in his or her lifetime. Meaning them, thinking to mean them, not meaning them. I meant them. And when one does that, one is transfigured. Knowledge had descended on me in a span of seconds.

The pronoun I had used was *vous*, a shade less trite than the *t'*. How did Oriane take it? If it is the declarer's great moment, it is not always the declaree's. She, poor woman, treated me no better than I deserved, absurd rash young fool. Perhaps a little worse, being Oriane. But then I didn't know what she was like (that was *one* of the things she pointed out to me). What I had known was that mockery was her strong suit.

'You've chosen an odd time of day for making your dramatic announcement,' she said, and bade me look about me – housewives who knew us were scurrying around with heaped market baskets looking for their cars. And it wasn't only the wrong hour, hadn't I made other mistakes?

'Louis and I thought it was Philippe?'

'Oh I do love Philippe,' I said, 'but with you ... with you ... '

'With *me*?'

'It's not the same.'

'Of course it's not the same. *What* is it then?'

'I cannot say it again.'

'The dramatic announcement?'

'It was true,' I said.

'Truth,' she said, 'is such a feeble excuse for so many things. What did you expect from me?'

I tried to think. 'I don't know. Nothing. I really don't know.'

'Oh dear. How inconclusive. Do try and make up your mind.'

And so it went on. She blew hot and she blew cold. Oriane was good at that too. I knew I was being teased. I knew I was making a fool of myself. It changed nothing. Finally she offered me a lift home. I turned the starting handle for her and meekly climbed into the car. At the gate of Les Cyprès, quoting the clinching line of Victor Hugo's poem about the French captain discovering that the wounded soldier whom he is offering his water bottle to on the battlefield is a Prussian officer, '*Allez, buvez quand même*,' she asked me to dinner that evening. 'Bring your handsome stepfather,' she said over her shoulder as she drove off.

I did not go into the house by the front door. I climbed into my room through the window, locked the door and pulled in the shutters. *Le Rouge et le noir* swam into my mind, the most heroically romantic novel I knew – my head, too, was full of French quotations – with Julien Sorel's flash of revelation as he leaves Mathilde de la Môle at dawn: *Il était éperdument amoureux. Eperdument*, I repeated to myself. Lost. Lost in love.

12

For some days, three of the four who had been to Saint-Tropez lived enclosed each in a private universe of troubles and emotions. Pre-occupations and feelings ran parallel. The fourth, apart from relief which is soon forgotten, experienced merely bafflement. I, as one of the insulated three, only perceived or thought about this a little later. Soon enough. I was not able to stay behind a locked door for long.

The first thing that penetrated the armour of my own obsession was that the relationship with Alessandro had changed. Camaraderie had been replaced by complicity. Unavowed, and thus uncertain, complicity. There had been no word spoken. Then Cécile Panigon sought me out – she *had* to talk, she said – and made clear a situation I hoped did not exist.

Incidentally, all had gone miraculously well for her and her brother on their return to the parental roof. Madame Panigon's mind, so readily suspecting adultery, incest, sodomy, rape and worse between any two people in her sight, did not proceed in this way at all when it came to her own offspring. That was the miracle. Fully aware of the season's *situation hôtelière*, it did not occur to her for a second that the girls, Cécile and I, had not shared one of the rooms allotted, while *les garçons* occupied the other. The key figure, Cécile, had looked as if butter wouldn't melt in her mouth, enabling Frédéric and Alessandro to control their nerves. So all went well. Of course they were given a terrific dressing down (I had a full account): they oughtn't to have gone in the first place, they might all have been killed in that car . . . so inconsiderate, so selfish, so ungrateful . . . no one deserved such children

. . . But it was all about bad manners and the dangers of the road.

Yes, but the perils, as I saw, as I was forced to see now, were not over. Cécile had been seeing Alessandro, alone, as often as they could. (As I might have noticed.)

She said, 'I love Alessandro.'

She had no inhibitions about the three fatal words; she made them sound like an incontrovertible mathematical statement. I was silent.

'You can understand me?'

That was a hard one. Perhaps one can only understand oneself. Imperfectly.

'Cécile . . .'

'He is so sensitive, he knows so much, he's so interesting – he must have learnt so much from your dear mama, she's given Sandró *so* much.'

I winced at more than this version of his name (she pronounced it *à la française*). 'Cécile,' I said, 'what *is* to become of this?'

'He doesn't love me,' she said. 'I know he doesn't.' She said it with dignity and courage. 'He is very nice to me . . . *il est si gentil*. But he only loves *votre maman*. I don't mind what he feels as long as I can be with him.'

'Cécile . . .'

'I know that we haven't much time. I call him *mon papillon*, my butterfly who will soon be gone.' I groaned. She looked at me anxiously. She really had enormous eyes. 'You don't think we are doing wrong? *Votre maman a l'esprit si large* . . .'

My large-minded mother – on her own account she had been that. I dared not speculate further. 'What about *your* father and mother?' I said.

'They can't stop me seeing Sandró. They'd lock me up if they knew but I'd get out and run away.' She got down to what she had come to talk to me about, she was asking me to help. 'If you are afraid I'd tell anyone, you're wrong,' I said proudly and coldly. 'This is not *my* business.'

It was not what she had meant, the help she needed was *now*. She had worked it all out. They would only have these few days, it wasn't easy for Sandró and her to get off on their own – he wouldn't like it if it came to a parent crisis – she had to invent opportunities and excuses, such as for instance spending an evening at the cinema in Toulon with *me*.

I laughed. 'And go on my own and brief you on the film afterwards?' Lying for them . . . Well, lying to the Panigons. *Was* it only to the Panigons? 'Yes, I will,' I said, feeling heavy at heart. Whatever I did or failed to do would be treacherous. If I refused at this point it could only cause more trouble, more unhappiness. I said again that I would do what I could. Yet I didn't really want to know too much about the whole thing. I ought to have felt more sympathy for Cécile, for her being so much in love. I did not accept her as *ma semblable, ma soeur*. In fact, I could not bear the thought.

'A pretty kettle of fish,' I said.

'*Pardon?*'

The same day Alessandro spoke to me. He looked careworn.

'Cécile has been to see you? She told me she would.' It was the first time her name had been mentioned between us.

'Poor little thing,' he said, 'poor little thing.'

'Alessandro,' I said, 'how was it possible then?'

'Saint-Tropez. I'd had too much to drink.'

'But . . . why now?'

'You must have heard it from her – she's taking it seriously. Terribly so. What can you do? What can a man do? Tell her I found a woman in my bed, I hardly knew who she was – that's how it happened. Goodness knows I don't want to hurt her, I can't just push her off. You see, it doesn't matter so much to a man, one way or the other . . . She's really rather sweet in her way. I like her. And it will all come to a natural end very soon.'

'She knows that.'

'She's a good, loyal girl.'

'Loyal to you. She *does* admire you.'

'God, yes.'

'Isn't it nice to be admired?' I said. 'I wish someone admired me.'

He laughed. 'We don't get much of that at home, do we?'

It was not what I had meant.

Alessandro turned gloomy again. 'I don't want to get involved with her blasted parents. You think Panigon'd fight a duel?'

'*Père* or *fils?*' I asked, daring to go fishing.

'Oh *père*, of course,' he said, ignoring the bait. 'But I think not. He could make things unpleasant though. With good reason. Funny thing, Cécile is a good liar, you wouldn't think she had it in her.'

'*L'amour*,' I said.

'Oh please. *I* never dreamt this could happen – damn Saint-Tropez – I haven't slept with a woman, or wanted to, since the night I met your mother.'

We said nothing for a moment.

'How . . . how will she take it?'

'I don't know,' he said. 'Perhaps I shouldn't tell her.'

'She must understand such things.'

'You can't be sure with women. They're easily hurt.'

'She's different.'

'She is different,' said Alessandro fondly, 'and not *so* different. *I* must not hurt her. I don't want to hurt anyone.'

'Dear Alessandro,' I said, 'poor *dear* Alessandro.' Then I told him I was going to see the new film at Toulon this evening, on my own. He patted me on the shoulder, but he still looked careworn.

In the end I did not see the new film on my own. I went with the Desmirails. I mentioned it to them, they said good idea, we all went. Philippe, Oriane, Louis, I. I had been going about a good deal with them, mostly *à quatre*. The result of my disclosure on the port that morning, the only result one could say, was that Oriane now regarded me as a piece of her property. Not very valuable property. Well below Louis, I had been attached to her cortège. I, too, could now be seen in the back of cars or walking a step or two apart carrying coat or basket. In the mornings I would hang about the Place waiting for her to appear, rush to her car, open the door before it had stopped, kiss her hand – as Philippe and Louis did on greeting her – snatch at anything portable. Then I'd follow her to Chez Benech, the *crémerie*, the fruit stalls. When my presence bored her – often – she showed it, that was part of her on-and-off technique. When I did something clumsy, she was genuinely cross. One such occasion was when I took a fine ripe melon from her hands and put it on top of some small cream cheeses. In later years such incidents were transformed in anecdotage: the lovelorn page putting the melon on *les fromages à la crème*. At the time I was made to feel the fool I was.

She could also be charming to me, most so when Louis was about, hinting at shared private jokes, ruffling my hair, touching my hand. It did not take much to make Louis jealous, she always knew how to bring him to heel. There was none of that – no irritation, no flirting – when Philippe was present; I was treated (by both of them) with open affection as a well-liked, if somewhat absurd, young friend of the house. They liked to pretend that I was instructed beyond my years and nick-named me *Dix-sept ans: Je sais tout*, the title of a popular review for the young. Sadly aware that far from knowing it all I was even no longer seventeen, I got Philippe to impart to me some of his manifold knowledge: *he* was both wonderfully instructed and instructive. I could make him tell about Paul Valéry and Valéry Larbaud and Marcel whom he'd been brought to see as a boy and if anything took against, to the disgust of Oriane who was *Proustienne* to her fingertips. He would feed my curiosity about book publishing, French political institutions, car engines, map-making and the drafting of timetables. The latter attracted me by the numerate ingenuity it required. Our calculations, if on a small scale, were no idle pursuit: the Desmirail bus line was to come into operation before long. There were to be seven buses to begin with linking Sanary to Toulon by two routes – one taking in Ollioules, the other La Seyne – at exact suitable times for getting people to work in the mornings, returning them at lunchtime and after entertainments past midnight. Working this out – computers had not been invented – was an intricate and enjoyable job with graphs spread all over the floor; Philippe said he was using the principle employed by the French National Railway network. It was important to get the service from La Seyne right as that rather deprived township, situated on the other side of the Bay of Toulon, was mainly inhabited by men who worked in the naval shipyards whose means of getting there were by steam ferry. Philippe hoped to provide alternative public transport by road. La Seyne had something over thirty thousand inhabitants. 'You'll be needing seventy buses soon, Philippe, not seven,' Louis said. 'You'll be a millionaire.'

'Not *Philippe*,' said Oriane, with slightly less scorn than pride.

'Why can't Philippe become a millionaire?' I asked.

'You'll understand all right when you know him a bit better.'

'Oriane,' Philippe said firmly, 'I refuse to believe that one cannot earn money unless one behaves like a crook.'

'Depends what you call a crook. Everybody is entitled to look after their own interests.'

'Anybody who commits or condones a dishonest act is a crook.'

'*You* would call evading one's taxes a dishonest act.'

'It is,' said Philippe.

I should not have liked to contradict that quiet tone.

'You are the one and only Frenchman who thinks so,' Oriane said.

'Then I must be that Frenchman,' said Philippe.

I resolved that, when the time came, I too would not evade my taxes. My immediate problem was, however, not to make sheep's eyes at Oriane in Philippe's presence.

Unrequited love. There is nothing new to be said about it. Whether it befalls one at eighteen, at thirty, at seventy, the pangs are much the same: the delirium, the hopes, the despair, the waiting. At eighteen one may believe oneself to be uniquely stricken, at thirty one may be able to say that no pain is irreversible, at seventy one knows that it is: irreversible.

Requited or not, some things can be said *for* it – the virtuous resolutions, the ecstasy of a presence, a rare soft look, the wholeheartedness, the being *alive*. My feelings were not deterred by the full awareness of my age, sex and station in life (none), but my comportment was. I valued Philippe's good opinion; possibly more than Oriane's. His example was teaching me *tenue*: grace – stoic or hypocritical – under pressure. I don't know how far I succeeded. Whatever Philippe saw, guessed or knew about emotional human relations, he did not wish to know, nor appear to know.

Another thing in favour of besottedness is that it insulates one from much of the rest of the world, it muffles other pangs and dilemmas. Inevitably I had been running into Frédéric Panigon, treating him without self-consciousness as I always had, that is off-hand and reasonably friendly. At first this puzzled him. He wouldn't have liked it any better if I had thrown myself at his head, or heaped reproaches, but may have felt that some kind of recognition or attention was due. This I failed to provide. After one or two refusals, casually given, to go dancing or for a swim with him, he was showing bewilderment, then umbrage. *Vous êtes une drôle de fille*, he told me, an odd girl (we were back to *vous*, thank goodness).

I probably should have had – but *could* not muster – the grace to explain. I would rather have mounted the scaffold than bring Oriane into it. What might have been said was: 'Saint-Tropez was a fortuitous, an opportunistic thing. You used me, I used you to help me through an unobtrusive rite de passage. Are we not quits?' Only an older and a very worldly woman could have said it. Or could she?

I took refuge in telling him we had so little in common.

'You are wrong to equate me with my family.'

I said his family had always been very nice to me, pleaded an engagement and escaped.

Next time I saw him – Sanary was so small – he told me I had time for everyone else but him. There was little to contradict here. 'You are seeing my sister often enough.'

I recognised the acres of thin ice, and forced the feeble reply, 'Oh girls like doing things together.'

He glowered at me. 'You know that Cécile *est bien malheureuse?*'

'Well *I* am not,' I snapped, 'and neither are you. You are not in the least unhappy, don't pretend.'

At this point someone else came up – you also never stayed long tête à tête with anyone at Sanary – so I escaped again.

But I had hurt his amour propre. I would have to reckon with him:

he knew too much. I wished I were in the position to have someone throw him into the Bosphorus. Or the Neva.

If he tried to seek me out at Les Cyprès, I would not have known, Alessandro and I these days still spent little time at home. One place I was safe from Frédéric was at the Desmirails'. They and the Panigons did not entertain each other in their houses, only we foreigners were the wild cards in their social game. As the purported chaperon of Alessandro and Cécile, I had to go into hiding on some evenings; the Kislings lived too much in public, the Desmirails were of course ideal (and not in the know, though I was being pumped by Oriane). They were good to put up with me so often, and at least I provided them with some amusement. One night Philippe and Louis were talking sport and getting on to boxing. Was there such a thing as a straight left, I wanted to know, and what exactly was an upper-cut and how was it done? Philippe and Louis stood up and demonstrated basic movements, I stood nearby to watch them. 'What was this one, how did you hold your elbow, do it again.' I leaned forward to get a closer look, next split second I had crashed to the floor. Later I found myself on a sofa being revived by Oriane with a handkerchief soaked in eau-de-cologne. I had received a true knock-out (and a huge black bruise). They were concerned, they were also writhing with laughter. That misadventure as well has passed into anecdotage (and cloondom).

'*T'as l'air triste, mon coco*,' Renée Kisling said, 'come out in the boat with me.' I would not, it could mean missing Oriane on a marketing morning, she did not come every day. Renée gave me a pat on the shoulder: she made no comment, asked no question, did not insist.

There had been letters from Rosie Falkenheim. She and the Judge rather hoped to come, still hoped to come, did not think they could come, were unable to come to Sanary this summer. The Judge was worried about something and thought he ought not to be leaving England. He would be spending his holidays in the West Country then Scotland as usual. Toni and Jamie were going to be in their cottage in Essex; she, Rosie, was going with them. Toni needed company and support – she still hadn't taken at all to their country life, nor to Finchingfield where Jamie was spending most of his time. Those games were going harder than ever . . . It might be less awkward for Jamie if Toni did not detach herself so obviously from his friends and pursuits, those Finchingfield people were almost openly trying to console him. She had tried to make Toni join in just once in a while but I knew how stubborn Toni was.

I did, and could see them still cowering in that back room with young Tommy, the dog. I was sorry Rosie couldn't have her time at Sanary with the Judge, sorry the Judge had worries, yet it did not really sink in.

We now knew the date of my mother's return. On the eve Alessandro and I had another talk. In the house, by ourselves. It took a long time to get going. Eventually he said, 'It would be best if we forgot everything that's been happening during the last weeks.'

'Other people know.'

'They won't be shouting it from the roof tops. With any luck.'

'Aren't we glad she's coming back?'

'Once she's here,' he said, 'it will all seem like an idiotic prank. Except . . . except for Cécile. She's crying a good deal now though she tries to hide it from me.'

'Oh Alessandro.'

Again he took some time. Then he said, 'What about *you*?'

'What do you mean?' On the immediate defensive.

He made an effort. 'What is going on between you and Oriane?'

'If you are talking about Madame Desmirail, that is entirely between her and me.'

He let this imbecility pass. Very nice of him too.

My make-believe collapsed. 'I'm sorry, that was extremely silly. The answer is nothing, of course. Nothing.'

'You mean,' he smiled, 'Madame Desmirail doesn't . . . ?'

'Oriane doesn't.'

'But you *will* go on seeing her?'

'Running after her, you mean,' on the high horse again. 'Oh yes!'

'You know people are talking.'

'Are they?' I felt flattered.

'I beg you to be *careful*.'

'Why?'

'For your mother's sake.'

Very unhappily, I said, 'You mean . . . you mean she would . . . disapprove of me?'

Again he was slow. 'Her own instincts are so different.'

'She believes in tolerance.'

'She doesn't always go by her theories, she's not as rational as she and you like to think.'

'*What shall I do?*'

'Not take it too seriously, give it time. And again, be *careful*.'

'You mean not tell her?'

'That might be sensible. Though I don't know, she might just tease you.'

'That I'm used to,' I said, 'but it won't change me.'

'You may change yourself – in due course.' (Here I was tempted to tell him about Frédéric, but refrained.) 'Meanwhile I wish you the best of luck with Oriane – though I don't hold with her much myself – or with anyone else you fancy. As long as you are discreet.'

I didn't see it that way: I didn't care what anyone might say. Since we were having this – could one call it family? – talk, I brought up something that had been long on my mind.

'Alessandro,' I said, 'what was wrong that summer, the summer you and she left Italy, our first summer in France?'

'1926,' he said. He had caught on at once. 'A good deal was wrong. For one thing there was no money. She'd been spending far too much – and some on *my* brothers – the trustees were frightening her badly, they wouldn't go into capital again, for the time being they were reducing her allowance to nothing at all. I wasn't able to earn anything then . . . She didn't know what was to become of us.'

I had guessed most of this. 'She's not easily frightened,' I said.

'She's capable of panic. The future looked impossible for us. Well, then she went to Paris. On her own. I didn't quite know what was in her mind, I thought she was trying to get some of her old connections to help find a job for me. I knew she was going to see O.'

'Yes?' I said.

'What she actually did was to tell O that now she might consider marrying him. You must understand that she was in a panic.'

'To the point of leaving *you?*'

'It was an impulse. She couldn't stand the insecurity, and . . . ' he hesitated, 'you know that from the beginning she was afraid I was too young for her . . . that some awful fate was in store for us.'

'Then *she* would bring the awful fate about? I can't believe it.'

He said, 'She was fond of O. *I* couldn't believe it when she was marrying me instead of him.'

'You were running away with her,' I said; 'there was no question of marriage then.'

'You have a long memory,' he said.

'O. was very gentlemanly. *You* insisted. You should have seen yourself in desolation, goodness, you were romantic, you *were* le Prince d'Aquitaine.'

'Who?'

'He of the doomed lute and melancholy's black sun.'

> *Je suis le ténébreux, le veuf, l'inconsolé,*
> *Le Prince d'Aquitaine à la tour abolie.*

'Though I didn't know the poem then.'

'Yes,' Alessandro said, '*we ran away together.*'

'She couldn't have planned to marry O,' I was still reeling, 'you're Italians, you can't divorce even if you wanted to.'

'I don't suppose she was thinking of legal technicalities. She had some vague idea that O might be rescue – he's a generous man, something might be salvaged. Don't ask me how. She doesn't see obstacles when she doesn't want to.'

'Alessandro,' I said, 'what *happened?*'

'That was the bad part. You see, O was living with a young woman, they weren't married, but it had been going on for some time – your mother didn't think that would be much of an obstacle.'

'But it was?'

'O must have told her so. I never knew exactly but it seems he made it clear to her that all was over between them. As for her offer: no thank you. That gave her a shock. Nothing like it had ever happened to her. She felt she had lost her power. She was not in a good state when she came back from Paris.'

'Was that just before I arrived from London?'

'It was.'

'And she told you?'

'Not at once.'

What about yourself, Alessandro? I wanted to cry, how did *you* feel? but could not.

He said, 'I understood her. I should have liked to have been able to warn her.'

There was a pause.

'You said that O behaved like a gentleman that time at Cortina – you must be right, he did an extraordinary thing – a few months after their disastrous meeting in Paris, it was he who got me those art contacts in Amsterdam, who started the whole thing rolling.'

'In a way a happy ending? How did she take it?'

'In her stride.'

'But she didn't go with you.'

'Quite.'

After a while, when I had taken it all in a bit more, I said, 'I see even less now why *I* have to be so discreet, so careful?'

I should have left it alone for there followed what I remember as one of the oddest parental conversations.

'Discreet for her sake,' he said, 'I didn't explain it properly, for her *reputation*'s sake. You know she has this past – she talks about it often enough – so do her friends. They talk of her as someone who rode roughshod, a *grande amoureuse* who had little regard for conventions, there was her life before she married your father . . . Now whatever *you*'ll do, they'll say she's been a bad example – *telle mère, telle fille* – a chip off the old block: it will be blamed on her. They'll say she brought you up badly. I won't have her talked about like that, you *must* see this.'

'Alessandro, you're being absurd.'

'Please be good,' he said, 'or they'll think she's been a bad mother.'

Early in the afternoon of the day my mother was to return, Cécile came again to Les Cyprès. I assumed that she had already said goodbye to Alessandro but did not know where or how. I was in my room, lying on my bed, trying to read, treachery and guilt were already casting their shadows. Emilia was not due back from her holiday till the end of the week, Alessandro and I had done some cleaning and tidying (not that this meant so much to her, it was he and I who minded). We had decided against cooking a home-coming dinner and ordered a special one at a bistro instead – with luck some of the Kisling crowd might be there.

I got up and pulled out the desk chair for Cécile. She preferred to stand. She would always love Alessandro, she told me, her butterfly who would soon be gone, there could be no other man for her. She had no regrets. Nor fears. As soon as she was of age, she would leave home and study to become a painter. 'Sandró knows about *la peinture*, he tells me I have some talent. I was always serious about this, not like Frédéric who only wants to be an artist to annoy papa. And don't worry – from today on I shall not betray myself, nor him, by a look or a word.'

'It will be hard for you,' I said, feeling sad for this girl whose heroics and banalities I shared.

She burst out, 'I have one regret, I would have liked *d'avoir porté son enfant.*'

I was aghast. *Might have borne his child.*

'Cécile, is this possible?'

'I asked Sandró, he said it could – at Saint-Tropez.'

An abyss opened. So young persons did need diagrams and instruction from parents and school.

'That night he was quite drunk, poor Sandró. He would have gone to sleep, I don't think he even remembered who I was. He has no idea that I was aware of it. He thinks it would hurt me . . . It was I who said to myself, *quelle chance!* You see, I was in love with him before, *I* did not allow him to go to sleep.'

I was at a loss for a comment.

'So there might have been *un petit bébé*; but no, it was not to be. It would all have been so different – perhaps your *maman* would have been happy to share Sandró's baby, as she hasn't got one of his of her own. She's too old now, isn't she? Do you think she would have been pleased to have a baby in the house?'

*   *   *

August was an awkward month. Our days were spent in a miasma of unease. My mother had arrived tired after a long railway journey made not less taxing by the contretemps that for her beset such enterprises. She had mislaid – well, perhaps lost – a piece of luggage; the *douanier* at the border though, when she was unable to lay hands on her keys, had waved her on quite charmingly.

No sooner in the car on our way back from the station than she began to complain about the futility of her Swiss stay – it was dull (I might at least have tried to write her some amusing letters about what was going on at Sanary), it was expensive . . . yes the air was good and it was cool but what was the good of that as she was back now stewing in the summer heat? The trustee? Hopeless and tactless. She mimicked him, 'It is just as well that your spouse is providing for you now.' She had persuaded him that her requirements came to more than that, and got round him in the end; say, half round. 'He told me it was my choice, if I decided to go on the way I wished to, there would be nothing left to come to my daughter. That's you, my dear. I told him you were young and strong, and were going to get whatever came out of the sale of your father's bric-à-brac. I hope you agree? Anyway aren't you going to be a distinguished novelist and keep us all in our old age?'

She was not pleased by our dinner arrangements. 'You might have had enough imagination to see that after weeks of Swiss hotel food I'd rather eat at home.' We could have pointed out that *soupe de poisson* and *agneau des alpes* Chez Marius was not like Swiss hotel food, but were too cowed. Chez Marius turned out to be three-quarters empty, we had a table on the terrace to ourselves. 'And what have you two been up to?'

A light question requiring a light answer. The fraction of silence broken by chatter could not have been lost on her.

Inevitably Sanary set up entertainments to celebrate her return: inevitably Sanary told tales – good-natured tales – how bravely Alessandro and I had carried on during her absence. The party we had given on the building site became very glamorous in the telling. 'While I was battling for your future among the stodgy Swiss, you might have waited till I was back.'

'It wasn't planned,' Alessandro said, 'it just happened.'

Indeed, I thought. 'You wouldn't have enjoyed it, you don't like dance music and no conversation.'

'Obviously my highbrow daughter does.'

I understood that her displeasure came from a sense that we were on our guard, that there was something wrong. Alessandro was at his most gentle and affectionate but unable to suppress a touch of sheepishness; I recalled how much as a child I had feared her temper, and was afraid again. We constantly had to lie by omission and simply did not do it well enough. And so it went on.

I survived a dinner party at the Desmirails'. That went off as if there were no thin ice. I could not be otherwise with Philippe, and Oriane was enjoying herself in her way. She praised me to the skies, kept telling my mother what fun she and I had been having, I was such a good companion at marketing and walks, I had such a sense of humour. It made me very unhappy. Also I was not sure whether my mother was not taking it with a pinch of salt.

Alessandro and I survived – barely – a dinner party at the Panigons'. Cécile behaved well, not attempting to exchange a look with Alessandro, nor to snatch a word with him by herself, sustaining the expected level of conversation. I admired her courage and self-possession, but during the long evening felt that Alessandro was unsure whether she would be able to keep it up. One did not have to know him well to perceive how nervous he was (he – not she – pleaded a bad headache).

As the party was moving from the dining-room into the garden for a digestif, Frédéric caught me on my own and tried to kiss me. I rebuffed him.

'Why do you treat me like this?'

'Leave me alone,' I said.

'Is this the way you behave to all the men you tumble into bed with?' he said furiously.

'Don't be such an ass, Frédéric.'

'Bitch!' he said. '*How* I long to tell your mother.'

Here we joined our elders round the garden table. During the next hour I watched Frédéric drink three glasses of *eau-de-vie*.

'I'm sure that idiot sentimental Panigon girl is in love with Alessandro,' my mother said to me, 'did you notice how she avoided looking at him. Was that for *my* benefit? Did he flirt with her?'

'You know what he's like, he flirts with everybody.'

'Everybody isn't stupid enough to think he means it. That girl's a fool.'

'I don't think Cécile is a fool,' I felt obliged to say. 'She's a nice girl really.'

'I dare say. But so *heavy*. She'll look like her mother in no time but she'll never have her quick wit. What a family. I confess to a weakness for Monsieur, he knows his classics, he's good with women and he can be an entertaining raconteur. So unlike that oafish son of his, what's-his-name, I bet he has intentions towards you. I didn't see you respond. You wouldn't have such atrocious taste.'

'I don't like him much,' I said.

'I didn't think for a minute that you could.'

Oriane was getting more bored and irritable with me every day; she was getting bored and irritable altogether. There had been few opportunities to impress or organise: the theatre bus and the pirates' entrance were a long way behind. Philippe (whom she always treated with the greatest courtesy, as he did her), occupied with engaging and training personnel, suggested a tennis tournament: there were a number of decent players, men and girls, among the present guests at the Grand Hôtel at Bandol, they'd be pleased to take part in a small but properly set up tournament at Sanary. Oriane took it up sharp. The court was put in super trim, trophies, an umpire's chair, boxes of new balls procured, a draw worked out, invitations issued for spectators and participants. Oriane sewed arm bands for chief organiser (herself) and linesmen. The date fixed was the first week in September. The main attraction was to be Madame Mathieu, a very high-ranking woman player indeed and a friend who promised an appearance for the final rounds (if this was to be believed).

I was delighted by the whole idea, relieved by the distraction and as serviceable as allowed. Louis was much scolded; he found it hard to give his mind to tennis as he was in serious trouble with his parents who had made producing a stipulated amount of work the condition for his being allowed to continue painting on his own instead of being returned to art school in Paris. He had chosen to paint at Sanary in order to be with Oriane, being with Oriane meant little painting, that was his dilemma. Get a couple of kerosene lamps and paint at night, she advised him, at least it'll make a change from your sun-drenched Provençal landscapes.

When Oriane began talking Wimbledon traditions, my mother said (not to her), 'Poor Emma Bovary had a dreary life, a dull husband, little money, *she* had some excuse . . . Your sorceress Oriane has got too much of everything. I'd like to see her in a job; I wonder what would suit her best, being headmistress of a very grand finishing school or running a maison de haute-couture?' All the same my mother consented to take part in the great event.

The first snag came when Alessandro and Cécile Panigon were drawn to be partners in the mixed doubles. Cécile solved it in her own way: by leaving Sanary.

She waylaid me in the Place one morning as I was waylaying Oriane. She looked controlled and determined and very sad. She was going away for a time, an indefinite time, she would be looking after a great-aunt who lived near Valence who was a bit of an invalid, a difficult woman but really not *bien méchante*.

'But Cécile . . . '

'It was the only way papa and maman would have let me go. They think I am mad, I tell them one should sometimes sacrifice oneself.'

'*Must* you go?'

'I can't stay here. I embarrass Sandró. And,' she added simply, '*je suis trop malheureuse*.'

'How will you be able to bear living near Valence with the really not so nasty aunt?'

She lifted her head. '*I shall know that I am doing it for him.*'

I thought of Rosie Falkenheim and what sustained her.

'I have something to ask of you – will you give him this note?'

She produced it. I froze.

'I can't,' I said.

'*Please.* Just slip it into his pocket. It will be the last time.'

'You must see that I cannot.'

'You are young, like me, don't you understand love?'

'I cannot betray my mother.' That was love too. Not fear. Though fear came into it. Indeed.

'You did so before.'

'By silence.' No decent person in my position would have talked. 'I could not betray Alessandro and you, I had no choice. It was bad enough. What you are asking now is active betrayal.'

She said again, 'Please.'

I shook my head, and felt that life was awful and that no one should be asked to live it.

'If you won't take my note, will you give him a message? Say, "Cécile is going away tomorrow. This afternoon she will be at the place you know, at the hour you know, she has to see you once more."'

Again I refused, feeling like Judas and Peter in one. When at last she left me, she looked sadder than when she arrived. That morning I did not seek out Oriane's car on the port. I slunk home.

Whenever in later life I wait for a lover who might be late, who might not come, I think of Cécile Panigon that afternoon waiting in the place I did not know and did not wish to know of. There is no absolution.

'*T'es un brave coco*,' Renée Kisling said, 'come in the boat with me.' I felt that I was neither good nor brave, but said that I would go. She and I spent some, almost silent, hours far out on the sea and this was healing.

When I got back I heard that the Desmirails were giving a party that night for some of the tennis people. I was not asked. I was wretched again.

Midway through the tournament – which *was* well organised, which *had* a good standard of play – I found myself booked into the last eight without having shot a ball in earnest. I had not wanted to take part at all but Philippe had decreed that original club members however bad should play in at least one event. I was not booked for any doubles, and expected to be quietly out (0–6 0–6) in the first round singles. As it happened two of my opponents had to scratch – we did not have a full complement of players anyway – and there I was. Hardly had I taken in that news when we heard that the girl I was now to face – one of the better players from Bandol – had done something stupid to her ankle and was uncertain whether or not she would be all right next day. Philippe was amused.

'We'll have you playing in the final yet,' he said.

'Don't be stupid,' said Oriane, 'the final is going to be Madame Mathieu against me.'

On that evening, a Thursday, the Bandol contingent was giving a dinner for the Sanary one at their hotel. Afterwards we sat on the terrace over *fines à l'eau* and orangeade. Oriane, whose table I had joined, was in a brilliant mood. On one side of her sat a British Army officer, a captain whom she had made tournament deputy-head, arm band and all. He appeared to be eating out of her hand and bewildered by her at the same time, and did not contribute much to the conversation, which on her part was extremely lively and included me. She was being nice, in the intimate way she chose at times, calling me her dear young friend, alluding to books she and I had read. At one point Frédéric Panigon – still in the men's doubles – appeared from another table. 'Come for a stroll with me,' he said unceremoniously, 'I want to talk to you.'

'Can't you see that she's talking to me?' Oriane said, continuing to do so. For a moment or two Frédéric stood his ground, looking cynically down at me, then desisted and walked away.

'Is something wrong?' said the English captain.

'I think he's been drinking,' said Oriane. 'He's got no manners, though he's not a *mauvais garçon*.'

We broke up early because of the next day's tennis. I had come with my mother and Alessandro, and joined them again in our car. Alessandro had a job manoeuvring it out of the hotel yard alive with people and other cars leaving and turning. As we were getting clear and into the drive, Frédéric ran up to us, jumped on the running-board on Alessandro's side, shouting into the open car window.

'*Vous avez mal gardé votre fille, Madame! Elle court après les femmes* ... D'you hear me? Your daughter is a slut ... She runs after women and she ... '

'That's enough, Frédéric,' Alessandro lifted a hand off the wheel, gave him a rough push and drove on.

How much my mother – or bystanders – had heard I was not sure because though screaming, his voice had been quite thick.

'And what did you think of the food and wine?' my mother asked, when we were on the road, not adding, 'Mrs Lincoln?'; she would have been well capable of it.

Further on, she said, 'Oughtn't we to have given that uncouth young man – I always forget his name – a lift?'

Arrived at Les Cyprès, we bade each other a good night.

Next day, Friday, early, Philippe and Oriane came to see me at the house. Philippe looked as if he had heard a very good joke. Oriane looked tragic. 'Congratulations,' he said, 'we just heard from Miss Beauchamp' (the girl I was to play in the last eight later that morning), 'her ankle is worse: you are in the semi-final.'

'That's impossible,' said Oriane. 'Madame Mathieu, three times French champion – '

'*I* am to play against Madame Mathieu?'

'She must scratch,' said Oriane, 'we can smuggle in someone from the other side of the draw.'

'*That*'s not done,' Philippe said. He gave a wink, '*Not* Wimbledon tradition.'

He was enjoying himself, he was also both kind and efficient. 'Billi will play,' he said, the childhood abbreviation of my name, which my mother generally and he sometimes used, implying a kind of paternal reassurance. 'It is the proper thing to do, and she is brave, and she'll do her best, who can do more? Janette Mathieu is a very nice woman who won't care two hoots, Oriane, that you haven't been able to provide her with a Suzanne – in fact she may be relieved that it is *not* Suzanne.'

Oriane looked as though he had been spitting in church.

And so it happened. Philippe was angelic, umpiring the match himself, arranging it to be played, unannounced, in the luncheon hour, with few spectators about. For me there was no known face other than Alessandro and the ball boys. Madame Mathieu appeared with her clutch of rackets, a small woman, feminine rather than athletic, possibly turned thirty (they didn't reach their peak as early as they do now). It must have been explained to her that I was a beginner who had not arrived at the semi-final by her own efforts; in any case it was clear to her what she was up, or rather not up against from my first return of service. Philippe was right, she was a very nice and a very kind woman. She showed no surprise, dismay or condescension, she carried on for all the world as if she were fighting a plausible opponent. She must have adjusted her play but with no sign of doing so, and she still played magically well, employing her art to draw me into her rhythm; within minutes she had lifted my play. I lost all nervousness, concentrating only on movement and response. She gave me chances to play to the limit and beyond of my ability. It was an intoxicating experience. For once in my life I physically knew good tennis, a sensation of swiftness, heat, engagement, of skimming through air feet above the ground – a suspension of gravity I had known skiing – I wished it would not end. It did soon. A two-setter. Twice I'd got to fifteen, once to thirty – all, and I believe they were honest points, given Madame Mathieu's lowering her game. When we shook hands, she said, *Bien joué*. Alessandro made approving noises; Philippe got down from the chair, kissed me on both cheeks and said, *Bravo, mon enfant*. (Oriane, who was on the premises, had not come to watch.) I thanked

Madame Mathieu – who into the bargain was easy to talk to – it was all due to *her* kindness and great skill.

The other semi-final was played that afternoon and won of course by Oriane with such publicity as Sanary afforded, and on the Saturday took place the main event, the final between her and Madame Mathieu, and an exciting as well as a most elegant match it was. Oriane, too, lifted her game to and beyond the limits of her capacity. We saw the top professional (not professional in today's sense) pitted against the brilliant amateur stretched to the utmost. Madame Mathieu – as had been expected – won; the match went to three sets, and once in the second set Oriane led 4–1. When it was over the loser had an ovation, people crowding round her; Oriane looked pleased with herself and had full reason to be. I queued to say my word, she did not notice me.

The prizes were given at a reception that evening. It was made a formal affair, with the men in dinner-jackets. The La Plage would have been the suitable venue yet something was due to the proprietors of the court, so it was held at the gloomy hotel. Oriane liked a challenge and had devised decorations to transform the restaurant into a pastiche ballroom. Her post was on the platform – decked out with Tricolor and Union Jack – players and public sat at tables arranged in a semi-circle below her. (I was with my mother and Alessandro, and had been prevailed upon to wear a pale blue taffeta semi-evening dress my mother had got for me some time ago at the Galeries Lafayette; her choice of unsuitable clothes was not restricted to her own.) Oriane's deputy, the English captain, called out the names of victors and runners-up, who then walked to the platform, received their trophy – in the men's singles and Madame Mathieu's cases, a small silver cup – a hand-shake and, if female, an accolade from Oriane. When it was her turn, she stepped off the platform, Philippe took her place, the captain called out her name, Philippe bestowed the prize, Oriane received it with grace and there was another ovation. She then resumed her place: it was the turn now of the runners-up of the various semi-finals to be handed their prizes. I had not foreseen this and was as surprised as the rest of the audience (that semi-final had been played in camera as it were, few even knew it had taken place) when my name was called by the captain.

'Mademoiselle who – ?' Oriane said in a ringing tone.

The captain obligingly repeated my name. Oriane still looked blank.

'You *must* go,' Alessandro whispered. I got up and walked forward, heads turning to see what the cat's brought in.

Oriane handed me a silver stamp-box without looking up, omitting to shake hands. As I walked back, a few baffled people attempted applause.

When we got home that evening the storm broke. I have to use this cliché as no other description serves. My mother was in a whirl of passionate fury; I had forgotten what her temper could be. I will not have *my* daughter humiliated and made a fool of in public, that was the theme.

'It was disgraceful . . . Not that you didn't bring it on your own head . . . But how *dare* she . . . ' It was the sound of her voice that made Alessandro and me bow our heads. 'Who does she think she is . . . ? That . . . that second-rate Madame Verdurin – well, and so was Madame Verdurin: second-rate.'

At least my mother had not resisted making a literary joke; checking at once that somewhat lighter note, she thundered on, 'She *is* a monster, I *will not* have my daughter treated in this way. She must be *shown* up.'

It was dumbfounding to see my parent turn into a tiger mother.

Presently she changed the target of her wrath. It was my turn. 'She's got to go,' she said to Alessandro. 'She must leave the house. I don't know what she's been up to, I don't know what's been going on – and I don't want to know. No explanations please. One thing is clear, she's been given too much freedom. Sanary is no place for her.' She addressed me directly. 'You will leave for England at once. Alessandro, you must telegraph to her Nairns, they'll find her a room or something. Tell them she'll be arriving tomorrow. And now I don't want to hear another word.'

We had entered the world of anger and telegrams.

*

224

Next day was Sunday. Very well, so it would have to be done on Monday morning, and I would leave by the afternoon train. 'Meanwhile you are not to see that woman again.' It was a very long day, even with a little packing to do. My mother and Alessandro went out for both luncheon and dinner.

'We shall make excuses; we will also say goodbye for you: you've been recalled to London to resume your studies.'

Before leaving next day, my mother made me a short speech, 'Remember you are a goose and a fool, not a martyr. You are not afflicted by a great love, you are afflicted by a crush. It happens to everyone, though I'd think you are a bit too old for that now. You're not a schoolgirl, and I never treated you like one. You are very immature. After all the trouble I've taken . . . A disappointment. Come back when you are in a more reasonable mood. And don't go about thinking of yourself as a doomed Baudelairean pervert burdened by the love that dare not speak its name. I rather suspect you *have* dared.'

Alessandro took me to the station. There had been no time to get hold of my trustees for travel money, so I was sent third class by the Dieppe–Newhaven crossing, and with very little money left on me. In the car we had been too dejected to speak. On the platform Alessandro said, 'I am very sorry it had to end in this way. It's not your fault. She is under a strain. It will all blow over.' Before he left me, he slipped a banknote into one of my pockets.

PART FIVE

Landslides: Sanary–London–Sanary

1

IT HAS OFTEN been said that nothing is ever as bad or as good as one thinks. For some time, I thought it was very bad, I felt crushed and in exile. My mind and emotions were confused, having lost trust in myself and people I loved. Who was right? Who was not? One major shock was London, the transition from Mediterranean summer to the bed-sitter in grimy Upper Gloucester Place. The excitement, the sense of freedom of the former years had evaporated entirely – how could I ever have been happy living here? – in every fibre I was missing Sanary, my elective home.

I had not felt weighed down by such stony desolation since the time in my early childhood when it compelled me to run away from my father's house. I recalled this now and looked back at my own ruthlessness in horror – *I* had been unhappy, so I was driven to escape not counting the cost: to him, who had loved me. At least I was no longer capable of that; or so I thought. My father . . . The life I led in that country, Germany, which I instinctively turned my back on . . . It was a long time ago. Now there was nowhere to run away to: then I believed I had arrived in an earthly paradise, now I had been returned from one.

The Nairns were good to me, far above my deserts; I told them nothing. The story, so freshly happened, seemed untellable. I should not have known how – with its farcical elements – to put it across. Besides I feared Toni's disapproval, her sour intolerance. (Here I did her an injustice; later, in the predicaments of my adult life, she often gave me the benevolent sympathy she had lacked when dealing with her sister or her husband.) Rosie I should have liked to consult and was held back by the fact that, in spite of the immaturity I stood accused of, I was *her* confidante, a shred of self-esteem I could not afford to give up. All I said was that I had been foolish and been thrown out of the house. Sent away, I put it. They asked no questions.

It was Jamie – a man to whom one did not talk – who brought solace. 'That girl is in trouble,' he said to Toni, and set out to find me some work I could do.

I would have thought it impossible that giving lessons in French conversation and translating booksellers' and auctioneers' catalogues would assuage my feelings, but in a measure they did. The French lessons were fun, the translating, laborious and exacting, needed disciplined concentration. Earning money proved delightful. For the French I was paid 3/6*d.* an hour – for the unqualified 2/6*d.* was the going rate but Jamie's connections were generous and rich – the catalogues came to a very small sum per column; it all added up. (If I saved enough, I might be able to return to France on my own some day. That didn't bear thinking about yet.) One obstacle in my new working life was my atrocious handwriting, due to natural inability or to never having been properly taught. I learned to draw clear figures and wrote words in block letters. A laborious job indeed. It kept me busy.

On weekends the Nairns still took me to their cottage. Visits to Finchingfield were not a source of unmitigated relief, the pastimes and flesh-pots, the atmosphere were too like, and yet not, Sanary. The loss of self-confidence – needed in that milieu – did not help. There were other barriers. I had become aware of the perils of divided loyalties. Toni's antagonism and passive resistance had borne fruit: A.J. and his wife and friends had come to regard her – and her over-loyal sister – as tiresome nuisances, negligible appendages to Jamie whom they frankly tried to compensate for his dull home-life. In theory the sisters had a standing invitation; they only went as often as required to avoid an open breach. Jamie did not go to Finchingfield for every meal, when he missed one he usually went immediately after. When he did this again one Sunday after lunch (out of tins 'prepared' by Toni – I was too depressed to cook) there was an outburst. *I* had heard bigger and better; judged on its own it had substance and volume, variations – *molto agitato, tempestuoso* – on the theme of being a man's kitchen drudge. When she had stumped upstairs for her afternoon rest, Jamie and I crept about, quietly washing up, scrubbing the kitchen floor, laying a careful table for tea. In whispers he asked me to bicycle over to Finchingfield for the loan of some cake or petits fours, and himself stayed at home for the rest of the day.

Jamie was *very* fond of his wife; he was just not, as I must have made clear, a demonstrative or – domestically – a very noticing man. He liked being with her, eating the food she put before him, listening to the gramophone; he also liked his masculine life at his book business and among his bookish Finchingfield friends. What I – and probably he himself – was less aware of was that he had come to feel at ease with the Finchingfield women who paid him much attention without making any apparent demands. It struck me that he used less often the German diminutives taught him by Toni, and that the best stories he brought home from work were saved for his weekend parties.

Toni during those months *was* left a good deal on her own. (Rosie could not be counted on, the Judge was spending more weekends in London.) My company was welcome for which I was grateful in turn; I was bound to join Jamie less and less at Finchingfield. When the weather turned bad in November with fog on the roads and the cottage colder, Toni stayed put in London while Jamie would be given a bed from Saturday to Monday by A.J. Naturally, I could not go with him.

Finchingfield friendships flourished on propinquity, shared days, shared games, shared jokes; there was no real place for the outsider or occasional guest. My contact with them slackened during that autumn – subsequent events cut it off altogether – as it happened it was not renewed in later life. I lost little Garsington and, perhaps, vistas, opportunities . . .

My time in London was tied to the convenience of my pupils, not laggard children for the most part but busy bright young men preparing for service or commerce abroad. I discovered that I enjoyed teaching – modulating my accent from French-French to Anglo-French according to requirements – and found that I had some aptitude for it. Other hours were filled grappling with the catalogues, learning trade terms, converting inches into metric sense and back again. I no longer went to galleries, law courts or museums. For the rest I was back in the old insulated life of afternoons with Rosie and evenings with Toni.

Rosie was well; her equable contented self. Jack's worries, she told me, had receded. He seemed less troubled. She did not know what it had been about. Once he had said, I've been lucky.

'You can't mean – ?'

'Oh no. Not that. He has not been near a bookie or a gaming club. When a man like him gives his word . . . '

I took hers for it.

There had been no communication with Sanary. This was ordinary, letters in my family were a matter of good intentions. Had I any? Ought I to make the first move? What should I, what could I, say? *No explanations please*, was still ringing in my ears. On some days I felt mutinous. And let down: I had seen a side of my mother that I wished did not exist. Most days I was only unhappy. I felt much guilt about Cécile (the whole thing), none whatsoever about Oriane. How I wished though that she had remained my secret. (Ah yes, discretion . . .) Oriane did not bear thinking about. And her, too, I wished to see perfect. Actual absence was not so painful as I felt it ought to be; it was almost a relief. I shrivelled at the thought of how she'd look at me in my present dingy circumstances. My one emotional extravagance was persuading Toni to sing Mozart, a sweet sad indulgence I should not have liked to hear my mother's comments on.

I cannot say that time flew. It passed. Three months had gone when the olive branch arrived. It came in the form of a letter from my mother in her own hand. It had a beginning, a middle and some postscripts. This I learned after I opened it which was not at once. It had come by the second post; when I saw the envelope I began to shake. I bolted out to Rosie's next door. She had just come in.

'What *is* the matter?' she said when she saw me.

I began to stammer, then brought it out, 'I got a letter from my mother.'

'Yes – ?'

I had to explain that it was the first . . . well, the *first* . . . Without a further word Rosie did a sensible and unexpected thing – she behaved like a man – she took me to the pub up the road and ordered me a small whisky and soda. It did wonders.

After that I was able to open the letter, in my room, by myself. It began, 'Dear wayward daughter, why don't you come to us for Christmas?'

You never do, do you? We're not proper Christians . . . This year we're planning to spend the worst of it at Arles so that we can get to that midnight mass at Les Baux, I hear they sacrifice an actual live lamb at the offertory, that ought to be pagan enough . . . and the drive through that Dantesque landscape at night, Alessandro says there will be a moon, should be stupendous. Why don't you join us at Sanary the week before, then come back with us and stay on. Alessandro could have written you about plans, but he tells me that I must write to you myself. He says I behaved badly to you. Perhaps so. One does. You ought to know my beastly temper by now. I still think you are a goose, but a dear goose (sometimes). Anyway much is forgiven and most is forgotten.

She had also forgotten to sign it, the letter went straight on into postscripts.

PS Philippe Desmirail often calls, enquiring tenderly about you. That eccentric saint likes you very much, he really does. We don't see Madame Bovary – if you permit me to call her that – perhaps she is in hiding, maybe Philippe has given her a dressing down. More likely she is plotting some spectacular *crémaillère* for their new house which is supposed to be finished early next year. It's sheer white cubes and terraces in the centre of their olive grove, and I have to admit that it fits rather well into the landscape.

PPS Louis the Satellite has been granted a stay of execution by his parents, he's even been allowed to go skiing with the Desmirails at Christmas. Have I not mentioned that they will be away? Don't bristle: *that* has *not* been part of my plans. They'll be back early in January and you will have plenty of opportunity to see them should you so wish.

PPPS Did you see – or have you become too insular? – that, sadly, the Briand Government fell in October. All the *right*-minded people here gloated. That mindless, sheep-like right–left divide of the French is deplorable and so entrenched, it'll be their undoing. Will it ever come to an end? Now they have Tardieu God help them, not that he will last.

PPPPS I must stop. I hope you're pleased with such a long letter, and I do hope we shall all be civilised when you are here, and that you haven't taken to harbouring resentments. I don't think you will. You have such a gentlemanly nature.

*   *   *

My feelings were mixed. Relief, tears, exasperation, rage, fond laughter. In the end, relief won and fond laughter.

Ma mère est une femme impossible, I said to myself in French, I must try it out on my pupils. I giggled. It was a long time since I had.

*   *   *

Well, and so I was back. No longer exiled. The whole of that stay, as she had wished, was civilised and very very pleasant (with a residue of unease, I think, only in me). All as before between us, or so we tried to make it. Alessandro's converted villa was finished, turned into a liveable house, delivered. Its new owner was pleased enough with it to have got him another commission, a ruin of a *mas* in the back country between Bandol and La Cadière. My mother was to do the furnishing, not this time in rustic Provençal. So the Peugeot had outlived its utility, there was now a brand-new Ford convertible, American-built. It was black, a smart colour then. Alessandro let me drive it. We went to the midnight mass at Les Baux – which was a touch for *les touristes*, and the lamb was led out alive – slept at Arles and walked next morning in the Cloister of St-Trophime, then on the Pont-du-Gard and to Le Nôtre's Garden and the arenas at Nîmes – the three of us happy in places we loved. On the third day we went down into the Rhône delta to Les-Saintes-Maries-de-la-Mer and Aigues-Mortes, and felt subdued by an eerie emptiness of winter. On our way to Sanary we were basking again, eating lunch on the Cours Mirabeau at Aix, sitting outside in the Café Les Deux Garçons in the mid-December sun. At Les Cyprès, Emilia had laid a fire of olive logs, which my mother lit. For kindling there were cypress cuttings, the chimney smoked a little but the smell was delicious.

Social life was in abeyance, the Kislings as well as the Desmirails had gone skiing. Sister Annette, the youngest Panigon, told me when I ran into her on the port, that Frédéric was away doing his *service militaire*. New Year's Eve we spent at home on our own, eating oysters from la *mère* Dédée, followed by *boudin blanc*, drinking Cassis which was then the liveliest, most aromatic dry white wine to be had in Provence. At midnight Emilia joined us, and my mother made us perform superstitious rituals recalled from her diverse origins, ending as the Romans do by breaking some glass. We each made a wish (undisclosed). My mother said, 'May we all live happily ever after.'

On New Year's Day – which in France was *the* day of the Christmas season for eating as well as presents – we were bidden to a large déjeuner the Panigons were giving for their cronies. The long menu was well composed and far less heavy and indigestible than what would have been unavoidably put before us in Britain. We began with a platter of *fruits de mer: palourdes, claires, écrevisses, oursins*, followed by *quenelles de brochet* as light as feathers, then some *din-donneaux*, small young turkeys, roasted unstuffed in butter, served with their own unthickened roasting juices and accompanied only by a creamy chestnut purée and a sharp salad of watercress; some carefully chosen cheeses and a *bombe à glace*. We drank Cassis with the shellfish, Pouilly-Fuissé with the *quenelles*, Bordeaux with the roast birds, burgundy with the cheese, and champagne (sec not brut) with the ice pudding. Brandy, *eaux-de-vie* and liqueurs – how not? – with the coffee. My mother and Monsieur Panigon fenced politics, from opposite viewpoints, with light-handed give and take, never clashing, never conceding. Cécile's continued absence from home was much commented on.

Voyons, leaving her parents even for *les vacances* . . . This sudden devotion to an aunt . . . no, a *great*-aunt . . . ?

'Yes,' said Madame Panigon, expanding, 'we couldn't understand it at first, a daughter of mine turned into a sister of mercy! Now,' (archly) 'we can guess the real reason why Cécile left her comfortable life with us . . . My daughter is a deep one . . . '

We all looked up.

'She is more astute than I'd given her credit for. She's one to look to the future.' Madame Panigon smiled smugly. 'My husband's aunt *est une femme aisée*, there's a pretty fortune. *Une tante à héritage* – Cécile is making the sacrifice of her youth looking after her . . . Need I say more?'

A few days into the New Year, the Desmirails were back. No moves to be worked out, we soon ran into each other on the port. Oriane didn't treat me like a long lost friend, she treated me like a friend who hadn't been lost at all. Another status quo ante: I was restored to my place as a minor possession. *I* tried to hang about her less; *she* was less irritable and provocative, her general tenor playful, affectionate. She still teased; as she had every right to as I was still besotted and it showed. Most times she liked it to show, I knew this now; much as I was inclined to admire, I no longer admired all the way. Feelings were made still more complex by my fondness for Philippe, and for Oriane and Philippe as a couple.

They brought back snapshots from their sports d'hiver: on skis too they looked like cut-outs, elegant shadows; Louis beside them was flesh and blood, handsome flesh and blood.

The Desmirail bus line, La Compagnie des Transports du Littoral was to be formally opened on January 15th. Everything was set up. Seven old buses of the lumbering noisy kind, doors and window-frames rattling, engines and brakes and tyres put into perfect trim, maintenance and repair shop complete with petrol pump and empty lot where the ancient vehicles could spend their resting hours. The timetables, impeccably synchronous, were printed and so were booklets of tickets. Oriane had designed and Louis executed posters announcing the birth of the Company. And there was the staff: Philippe was going to be manager and his own chief mechanic with the donkey-man and two lads under him. He had found, trained and briefed nine drivers who were to act as conductors as well. They were local men, and not to wear uniform except for white and blue caps displaying the letters CTL. Each bus was to have a number and fly a small house flag – sewn by Oriane – from its bonnet.

'Who will bet that she's going to launch them with champagne?' my mother said.

I became fascinated by the economic and organisational details, and sat in on the discussions. The drivers' pay. (Monthly according to French custom, English workmen are scoffed at for not being able to manage their expenditure for more than a week at a time.) Most of them were married men, and Philippe offered a generous living wage which was accepted without comment. The majority of Sanaryans, usually including the mayor, were Communists; on the other hand few if any had truck with a union. Philippe also insisted on paying for substantial accident insurance for his drivers (well above the requirements of the law) and that too was accepted with no more than a shrug – Well and good, and more fool he. So, how to balance overheads with income? How much would passengers think right to pay? How much was needed for them to pay? Should there be a surcharge after 9 p.m.? 12 p.m.? Season tickets for the commuters from La Seyne? Then there was the argument about the secretary's salary – they'd taken on Josée, a local girl, trained *dactylo* and rather pretty, who was to do the letters and bills, receive and count the cash in the drivers' money bags. Now French women, especially young ones in that kind of job were as a rule *not* paid a living wage, the assumption being that either they didn't need it as they were living at home, or if not, that there were always ways for a reasonably attractive girl to make ends meet. Oh nothing as crass as prostitution, just an arrangement with a steady older man who'd naturally come forth with the occasional or regular *cadeau*.

Look here, Philippe, they told him, she doesn't expect it, her father runs a very nice ironmonger's business . . . Don't be absurd, nobody pays more than eight hundred francs . . . Well, *some* go as high as twelve, and *that's* exaggerated . . .

Philippe listened politely, then went and proposed the salary he had had in mind. We were not told how much that was. Josée, unlike the men, showed her pleasure and became devoted to his interests.

On the morning of the great day, friends, notables, everyone connected with the Company including drivers' wives were invited to a *vin d'honneur* on the bus lot. The big Panhard, the handsomest of the string, decked out with blue and white ribbons was launched by Oriane breaking a bottle of champagne over its bonnet (my mother's bet had not been taken on) as it was slowly driven by Philippe himself on to the road and its first trip Sanary–Toulon–Sanary. The other six followed at intervals each with a full complement of festive occupants. The Company had offered free rides for the entire day to every inhabitant of Sanary. It was amazing to find how many people had business to transact that day at Ollioules, La Seyne and Toulon.

Each bus was accompanied by a friend on its first journey, a sort of godfather or mother seated next to the driver. I had been allotted Bus No 6, and was therefore in a position to witness the first dilemma faced by the Desmirail line. As we approached the bus stop – new as paint – at La Seyne, we found a largish crowd waiting to try out the transport that had been widely advertised in *Le Petit Var* and on Louis's posters. When they found that there wasn't even standing room, they became offensive. The free-riding Sanaryans snug inside the bus laughed and jeered. There had been the previous *vin d'honneur*. The frustrated crowd responded, the youths inside asked for nothing better and it looked as if a fine *bagarre* was to erupt. Just before it came to blows, two sensible men first blocked, then pulled shut the entrance door and shouted to the driver to be off. This he did, followed by jeers and threats.

Bus No 7 ran into a similar fate. The prospects of the Compagnie des Transports du Littoral didn't bear too much thinking about.

Next day the donkey-man called at Les Cyprès to leave three neatly shaped strips of pasteboard inscribed with our respective names. They were passes for free travel on the CTL. A covering word from Philippe expressed his hope that these might be of some small service to his friends.

I do not quite know what had made me tell my family on arrival that I would stay for one month only. Some instinct must have come into it that it was time for me to stop being bundled about and exercise my own choice instead (as well as an instinct for some detachment from Oriane?), but then my *choice* was staying at Sanary, not in London which I had ceased to love. I had liked my work there – if giving improvised language lessons can be called work – had liked the sense of independence (and self-importance?) it had given me, and I fancied it my duty not to let my pupils down. No illusion of being indispensable: merely the facts that I had entered an implicit contract to get them to a certain stage, that they or their parents would be inconvenienced having to make a change, that I *was* getting them somewhere (my own love of French playing a part). It was nice having a little more money: not having to depend at the end of the month on the punctuality of the trustees' cheque, buying more books, drinking better wines in Soho with Rosie. So I had told my pupils that I would be back after a month of extended Christmas holidays, then take them on for three months more.

To my mother I said I would be back at Sanary in April, if that was convenient. She took it nicely: I must do what I thought best – by the way, was I working on my interpreter's exam next year? indirectly, I said – she would miss me, I should think of Les Cyprès as my home and could still change my mind about leaving. I was pleased with that, and with myself for a show of independence. Or was it a pig-headed whim?

I sometimes wonder whether my staying on that winter would have made any difference. It is an uneasy thought. Yet I cannot really believe that my presence would have had an influence on events. True, I might have been a companion to Alessandro who did not like doing things on his own – he had just been given a third commission, a villa to convert at Le Lavandou (the Wall Street crash had not much affected affluent Europeans yet) – while my mother was tied to decorating the place above Bandol; but then I can reflect that Alessandro and I had spent time on our own before and look at the results.

Between the bus launch and my own departure, Doris von R. reappeared well announced this time by post. Paul's, her fiancé's, divorce was dragging its slow course with no prospect of their getting married before late summer or the autumn; she, Doris, was recovering from a bout of flu, Paul thought it would be good for her to spend some months in a warm climate rather than hang about in freezing Berlin: he was taking a few days off to bring her South, and would explain everything himself. She was sure that we would like *him* and she hoped we'd like the idea of having her live near us for some time.

They arrived (by train and wagon-lit), she looking as much like a waif, though a cherished waif, as ever. Paul, lover and protector, the architect who wasn't a philistine although he built department stores, turned out to be a tall blond Jew with a charming careworn face, looking older than his age which was the early forties. We booked them into the Hôtel de la Plage which kept one floor open during the dead season. He was able to spend only two days, and did indeed a good deal of explaining, closeted with my mother.

The weather was exceptionally fine – blue, wind-still days – Alessandro, Doris and I spent the late morning hours in one of Sanary's most sheltered winter corners, Schwob's outdoor terrace, absorbing the sun, talking little, glancing through newspapers, looking at the sea, drinking innocent things like grenadine and vermouth-cassis. I was having serious second thoughts about going to London.

Paul meanwhile was telling my mother that Doris's health needed watching, just watching – after all her mother had died of TB at just about her age. There was no question of *that* with Doris, so far she was just delicate, as we could see. She had been seriously undernourished as a child during the war, and poorly fed afterwards in the pension years. Yes, the pension was closed down – after a fashion, Paul explained – Grandmammerl was staying on in the flat to which she was attached, as she was to Berlin, she belonged there and too old to change, that's why he had not dragged her here. Nor was she left rattling on her own in a large empty place, it had been arranged that she kept on one or two of her lodgers, the ones she liked most.

Paying lodgers? my mother asked.

Not *regularly*, perhaps, Paul said with a smile. Nor should young Doris be left on her own, she was no good at looking after herself. Berlin was not the right place for her at present, too many rackety friends, late hours, too many night clubs . . . It was the life she was used to. Poor girl she'd never had much of a chance. All that would be different when he could look after her properly. What she needed now was warmth, some feeding up, no snacks at three a.m., and someone to keep an eye on her.

My mother apparently said she would.

His wife, Paul told her, had offered to take Doris on a cruise or to winter sports. She *was* a very nice woman, she liked Doris, they got on. Civilised. He was a lucky man. However, it wouldn't do – the divorce for one thing if it came out . . . and his wife, here he smiled again, did have other commitments.

In the evening we all tried to decide where Doris had better live. My mother proposed at Les Cyprès with us, it would be nice, she said, to have something young in the house.

Alessandro and I avoided looking at each other, something we often thought wise to do.

Paul thanked her but thought it would be better if Doris stayed entirely independent. Alessandro knew of a small house nearby which it would not be beyond the wit of man to heat adequately. Again Doris let Paul speak for her. She was not domestically inclined he said, hadn't even cooked a breakfast in her life. Besides starving, keeping house would be no fun for her – what she liked, and hadn't had much of – unless you counted the grandmother's pension – was hotel life. And so it was to be: a sunny front room was booked for Doris at the Hôtel de la Plage, she could eat there or with us as she felt like. Having just devoured Emilia's dinner, Paul agreed. He tried to express his admiration of her cookery; as he had no Italian and poor French, my mother relayed the compliments to Emilia. She received them with dignity. *Signor*, she said and gave him a slight smile. (He was a man who exuded kindness and strength.) He went on to say how much Doris looked forward to future enjoyment of Emilia's delicious food. Again my mother translated. Emilia's face closed. A clipped *Sì, Signora*, and not a glance at Doris.

I hoped that this passed unobserved by our guests. Emilia approved and disapproved in a mysterious way.

Some practical questions remained. Paul wanted to leave her with plenty of money – to be able to buy clothes, to go over to Villefranche or Nice where there might be friends. A bank account? She wouldn't be able to manage one. Cash in the hotel safe? She'd manage that even less. He'd better leave it all with my mother – Doris said that would be all right. Paul was about to produce manilla envelopes, my mother had the blessed sense to say, You'd better leave the money and the bills to Alessandro. Doris again concurred.

Then the men discussed how to get Doris's Chrysler roadster to the South of France, as Paul felt she would like to have her car. Some reliable tourist to drive it down? Shipment by train – not easy in those days, with a frontier and all. They hoped to find a way before long.

When Paul left – greatly relieved, he said, to be leaving his dear girl in my mother's hands – he and Doris took a taxi to the station so as to have their goodbyes on their own. We all said how much we had taken to him, and how devoted they were to each other.

On that morning I had a letter from Rosie Falkenheim. Some details about Upper Gloucester Place no doubt – oh dear. I put the letter in my pocket. I opened it after luncheon. Rosie did not express herself particularly well on paper, her letters were understated, brief, one got their gist. When I had read this one, I showed it to my mother. She said two things, *Women, how* they carry on, most of them don't seem to know how to run a marriage. The second, This, dear girl, is a cry for help.

From *me*? I said. How could *I* help?

'You can't. I should have said, a cry for the illusion of help. It often comes to the same. Unburdening oneself . . . A new witness arriving on the scene . . . Perhaps your friend, I mean the obstinate one, may even be waiting for someone to jolt her out of her folly.'

'You haven't met Toni.'

'Real help is usually unlikely,' said my mother.

What had been in Rosie's letter simply was that Toni had forbidden Jamie to go on seeing Finchingfield, or rather she had put an ultimatum: he must choose between her and those people. It wasn't clear what that choice involved, except that Toni would not put foot into the Essex cottage as long as Jamie had not renounced the visits to his friends. The letter ended, 'Now Jamie is digging in his heels, not that I blame him, he is selfish, but you shouldn't make a man look a fool. Unless something stops Toni soon, they are both headed for a great deal of misery.' A postscript said, 'It would be good to have you back, I hope you haven't changed your plans and we can expect you on the twenty-third.'

'What *is* so wrong with Finchingfield?' my mother said, 'It can't be just those games?'

'It is. Her not being good at them . . . *She's* convinced she is superior, *they* take no account of *her* – it's all a matter of hurt intellectual pride,' I said, feeling I'd hit the nail on the head.

Oriane put herself out persuading me to stay. 'You *can't* miss the house-warming, our *crémaillère*.' This was to be on a day in mid-March which happened to be my birthday. In the end she relented, 'We'll give a party for your twenty-firster instead. In two years' time? That's a promise.' (It was one she kept.)

2

But I had not hit the nail on the head. When I arrived in London I found that matters had got worse, much worse. There was no longer an ultimatum; for Jamie no more choice. The question was not Toni putting a foot into Essex but Jamie putting his into their London flat. Toni had asked him to leave.

Rosie was calling her sister a mad woman and her brother-in-law a fool. I had not unpacked yet: *what had been happening?*

'Jamie's been having an affair with Cynthia.'

'Oh.' Cynthia was a Finchingfield habituée, a young woman I rather liked. 'Oh. Why?'

Rosie exploded. 'Why do people have affairs? You should have asked why it hasn't happened earlier: Jamie is an attractive man . . . given Toni's attitude . . . '

'But is it . . . is it serious?' I said.

'I wouldn't have thought so for a minute. Toni does.'

'She knows?'

'She knows.'

'Oh my God.' Then, 'How did she find out?'

'In one of the oldest ways. Basically there are three: the well-meaning friend, finding a letter, confession. The first two may be odious but the third is the most culpable because it's so stupid.'

'You mean Jamie . . . ?'

'Yes. He did.'

'How could he?'

'He was very down-hearted about that ban on Finchingfield. I don't believe that Cynthia thing started before then. It might of course and in that case Toni acted on instinct, but I don't think so. Well, he defied the ultimatum, he thought Toni was being unreasonable, and went on seeing his friends at the weekend. Toni stuck to her not coming to Essex and was icy to him in London. Finchingfield – they are bright people – saw that Jamie had been put into an intolerable position, they sympathised . . . A little feminine sympathy can go a long way . . . It can be consoling – among other things. I'm being a realist: an affair must have been quite a change for him. So now he had one more reason for not giving up Finchingfield. Hung for a sheep . . . '

I tried to take it in.

'So far so bad. Then Jamie must go and have flu. During the week. In London. Bad flu. Toni looks after him, worries, gets the doctor in, does all the right things. Jamie is touched by her nursing – he must have longed for all to be well again between them. They *are* fond of each other – deeply. So he tells her he will cut down on Finchingfield, not all at once, he can't drop A.J., and – you won't believe this – there is someone else, he told her, he can't hurt by an abrupt break, it would be so rude: he's done something he feels awfully sorry about and hopes Toni will understand and forgive, as she doesn't set much store by such things herself.

'And indeed at first my dear sister didn't have an idea what her husband was talking about. So Jamie spelt it out: he'd been having this affair with Cynthia and it doesn't mean anything and he won't do anything like it again but Toni must see that he can't just walk out on Cynthia from one minute to the next.'

'He must have been delirious.'

'He *was* running a temperature. Look at it this way: he was feeling low, he was feeling guilty all round, he was feeling fond . . . Wanted to eat his cake and have it.'

'I always thought Jamie was such an intelligent man.'

'Oh intelligence,' Rosie said.

I girded myself for the crucial point.

'Toni didn't say a word. Nursed him for two more days. When he was fit to get up, she told him to leave.'

'Just like that?'

'Just like that.'

'What did he do?'

'Jamie was shattered. He didn't know what to begin to do, he couldn't believe it. Toni stayed silent. It was morning and as he was dressed, he decided he might as well go out to work. At the door Toni said to him, "You haven't packed. You ought to take at least one suitcase now, the rest can be sent on later." "Well, if you won't have your things tonight it will be your fault." '

Jamie went to his office and somehow got through the day. At teatime he took a bus home. He let himself in with his key. Toni hadn't put up the catch or had the lock changed or anything of that kind. When she heard him, she appeared at the top of the staircase, the dog bounding down, she said, 'I told you you were not to come back.'

She said it in such a way that he pushed the dog in, and left.

'Yes,' Rosie said, 'she hadn't locked him out, he didn't attempt an entrance – it must have been a matter of her will. He came straight here.'

'How long ago was that?'

'The day before yesterday.'

After she had given him some tea, made him lie down, seen him into an hotel, she had gone to her sister.

Toni had been calm, monosyllabic, stonily determined.

'Determined to what?'

'Ruin her own and Jamie's life, I should say.'

And this is how things stood on my arrival. They did not stand still. Next day Jamie received a letter at his office. In reasonable language Toni wrote that it would not be right for her to stay on in the mews flat as it had been lent to Jamie by his American patron, she would therefore leave it as soon as she found a place to live in. It would be helpful if Jamie would give her an indication as to the rent she would be able to afford. She was leaving all future arrangements to him. Perhaps he would also advise her about an inexpensive lawyer; lawyers, she supposed, were indispensable for the divorce. There were unlikely to be any points of disagreement, perhaps they might be able to manage with one only? She had complete confidence that Jamie would be honourable in the necessary financial dealings. She signed herself, Yours, Toni.

'Divorce?' Jamie said to Rosie and me, 'she hasn't mentioned divorce before.'

'She was taking it for granted,' said Rosie.

*   *   *

To me Rosie said she would like to shake her but would try reason again . . . For the third time. Alas she knew her too well.

She came back defeated. Toni would say nothing beyond: He is in the wrong. His fault. He must pay for it. I cannot remain married, I'm divorcing him, I have no choice.

243

'That's cave-woman's talk, Rosie,' I said, 'didn't you argue with her?'

She had. Again and again and again. One could not argue fruitfully with Toni.

Jamie was convinced all might still be well if only they could talk. He would ignore that letter. What he needed was an hour alone with her. Not in the flat – he would not force himself on her there.

Rosie suggested a meeting in her place. Toni turned it down.

Jamie had some new ideas, and asked Rosie and me to meet him for lunch at the National Book League. I would have been interested in the venue, now it hardly registered. Jamie explained that he had not apologised enough – he could see that now – he needed an opportunity to put that right. He would promise Toni not to . . . well, not to . . . to see Cynthia any more. He had not done so since . . . since he had told Toni.

Rosie remarked drily that if this was so an apology in that quarter might be in order too.

Jamie looked if anything more unhappy. *She* – he meant Cynthia but didn't much like to speak her name – was a very independent person; divorced, we knew, didn't we? living on her own. A good job in publishing. She would be horrified . . .

Rosie gave him an ironical look.

He wouldn't drag her into this mess, Jamie persisted.

Silence. There were quite a few silences during that lunch.

What would we think of this? Jamie asked, what would *Toni* think of this? He would get a few weeks' holiday from the firm and take Toni to Berlin. He would be able to afford it if he gave up the Essex cottage, which, he would tell her, he was now ready to do.

Where could he meet her to present these projects?

We concocted that I should suggest lunching at Schmidt's restaurant in Charlotte Street to Toni. Jamie would appear two minutes later. I would vanish, he would have his say. She could hardly evict him from a public place – or could she? – we counted on her shyness.

Jamie asked if it was a good idea if he were to bring the tickets? Ostend ferry, sleepers to Berlin.

'I shouldn't,' said Rosie.

'Flowers?' I suggested.

'This is not a farce,' said Rosie.

It was not. I got to Schmidt's early, feeling horribly nervous. At one o'clock sharp: Toni. She was looking at the menu she knew well – *Schmorbraten? Schnitzel?* – when he loomed over her. I had seen him come in. She looked up, through him, at me. 'Traitor.'

Jamie, hovering, looking very big, said her pet name, a German diminutive chosen by her. Toni addressed the air. 'If he does not leave at once I shall tell the waiter that I am not sharing my table with this gentleman.'

Jamie heard, said her name again, turned to go, I rose to go with him. Toni – with that concentration of will – said, '*You* are lunching with me.'

I had at least the guts to tell her about the Berlin tickets and the rest. Her face did not open. 'And make a nineteen-year-old girl the messenger?' she said.

'He came to tell you himself.'

'Too late.'

That evening Jamie moved to his mother's at Surbiton. He had not begun to think of giving up. He wrote Toni a long letter followed by notes appealing to the emotions. They were returned to sender.

It was unthinkable for Jamie to leave Toni without money. So a weekly cheque began to be sent. And with money Toni was able to act. She went to look for a flat. Compelled by pity, protectiveness and the vague hope of instilling some discouragement, Rosie and I went with her.

*   *   *

Rosie not relinquishing her engagements with the Judge, I spent most evenings at the mews alone with Toni. She was too unhappy to be left on her own. I'd bring some food, small things she liked, she hardly touched them. I got in a bottle of Bristol Cream, she did not touch it;

I brought some wine and I drank that. I was working out how I could approach her. Evenings passed and the openings were in my mind only. You cannot really mean to divorce Jamie? Toni, you must know that Jamie loves you? Toni, will you not forgive him?

I could hear her answers too clearly.

'What were you two talking about last night?' Rosie would ask me. 'Thomas Hardy.'

She pulled me up. 'Someone *must* try – she's too deeply stuck already, she's got to be prised loose.'

'I'm not the right person.'

'Of course not. We'd be hard put to find one. If her uncle were still alive . . . He was a worldly man, she adored him, he might have knocked the nonsense out of her. As it is, we haven't *got* anyone else. In Germany the Courts have an official reconciliation service – I don't know if they have anything like that here. I must ask Jack.'

'Can you see Toni?' I said.

Rosie was distraught but she could still laugh.

'*You* will have to try,' she said, 'you needn't tell me that you are not a worldly uncle . . . You have a mind of your own, and Toni is extremely attached to you.'

'Is she? She's more than that to Jamie and look what good that's done.'

'He has *wronged* her. You haven't.'

'So far.'

'You must give her a shock, show up the enormity of her conduct. Have the courage of your convictions. She's locked herself in – smash through something. Think of poor Jamie – think a little of poor Cynthia who must have been made to feel pretty guilty by now . . . Think of me.'

'*You* haven't done anything.'

'If Toni succeeds in losing Jamie, I shall have to live with her for the rest of our days.'

'I hadn't thought . . . '

'No. There have been rather too many things to think about.'

*

One request Jamie had not complied with was a lawyer. Toni went and found one somewhere in North London, more or less by a plate on the door, and instructed him to start divorce proceedings. From this man – whom Rosie encountered and disliked – she learned that her alimony would most likely amount to one third of her husband's income. Toni who knew Jamie's assets to the shilling – they consisted, besides a small savings account and his car, quite simply of his salary – realised without batting an eyelid that she would not be able to afford to live in the vicinity of Regent's Park. The flat hunt moved from NW1 to NW3. (She must find a place, she said, near somewhere she could walk the dog.)

I had drunk some wine, I had persuaded Toni to drink a thimbleful of the Bristol Cream. She had begun to tell me it reminded her of her uncle's Château Yquem. I was telling myself that I had nothing to lose but a friend. I did not want to lose this friend. What she was doing went against all I believed in, and I hated it; I longed to help. Not only for Jamie's and for Rosie's sake, I could not bear her desperate unhappiness, I too was attached to her. Nor could *she* afford to cast me out as well. Smash through something, Rosie had said. Well . . .

I don't remember how it began; soon we were in the middle.

'What *is* so frightful about what Jamie's done? Do you really believe that two people must or can stay faithful to each other for ever?'

'No,' she said.

Thank goodness, I thought.

'We are not talking about two people, we are talking about Jamie and me.'

'The principle is the same.'

'I have nothing to do with other people's principles.'

'Only with your own?'

'Yes.'

'Where do they come from, your principles? Religion?'

'I am not religious,' Toni said, 'I wasn't brought up to believe in a God.'

'Not in a God of vengeance?'

'We were not orthodox,' she said crisply.

'Ethics then? Right and wrong?' I rushed on before she could cut in. 'I have no religion either but I do believe it is *wrong*, profoundly wrong, to own one's loves . . . to be possessive . . . jealous . . . '

She did cut in: '*I* am not jealous. *Jealous* of that woman, Cynthia, or whatever? I hardly remember her, they're much the same at Finchingfield . . . She is nothing to me.'

My momentum was stopped.

'*Jamie* has done wrong,' she said with finality. 'He must bear the consequences.'

'For heaven's sake! You turn it into *lèse-majesté*. He loves you, you love him . . . '

'I do. I never forgive – he ought to have thought of that.'

'You said that to me once – your never forgiving – I was shocked then.'

She remembered at once. 'But I did. You were very young.'

'And it was a minor offence.'

'Don't be frivolous. You're getting it from Rosie.'

'Sorry,' I said. 'I am most serious – I think it is abominable to throw away your marriage . . . for what? Because a man had made love with a friend?'

She winced.

I went on: 'It's natural. It happens. It need not mean very much. Even my ex-Church regards it as an absolvable sin if you repent.'

'*You* were brought up without morals.'

'I was not,' I said fiercely, 'my mother taught me morals. Not in your narrow sense – I know it's wicked to begrudge pleasure to those we love. Toni, *be generous.*'

'*He* did not think of me. He broke his faith. What you regard so lightly is a betrayal. Perhaps you are too young to know.'

I saw that it could be. A betrayal. Not in their case though. I should have liked to take her hand, put my arms round her in an up-rush of pity. 'Does it hurt *so* much?' I asked.

She was silent.

'It does help if one tries to see the other side,' I said, 'if one can push out resentment. It really does.'

She stayed silent.

I mustered courage. 'May I ask you something? Are you so offended because you yourself feel that going to bed with someone is . . . is not a good thing? that it is something . . . coarse?'

'It is coarse,' she said. 'One should avoid coarse things.'

My turn for silence. When we spoke again, we were arguing in circles, separate circles.

'Think of *yourself* then,' I said, 'will you like living without Jamie . . . a single woman . . . leaving this flat . . . Do you want to undo your life? Can't you see how it will be?'

Toni lifted her small fragile face, 'Of course I know,' she said with unflinching calm. 'It's unfortunate, he is spoiling my life – he should have thought about it before.'

The flat was found. A few steps from Parliament Hill, just the thing for the dog. Jamie was flabbergasted then sentimental about losing Tommy as well. I won't have him cooped up at Surbiton or at Finchingfield, Toni had conveyed. Jamie eventually responded with: Tommy loves us both and Toni would be more alone without him. (At that point I felt that I would like to get married to Jamie.) Toni was not going to be alone. The flat she chose had two bedrooms and a rent she could not quite afford. Rosie had been right. Toni proposed that they should share it.

'*You can't*,' I said. I knew what her independence meant to her.

'I must,' she said. 'I've looked after Toni since we were children.' Now she too was unhappy.

Toni was about to sign the NW3 lease when she thought it might be a good idea if Jamie had a look at it first, and at the flat – plumbing and wiring – he was good at that: a man's job. In her absence. Jamie did.

While discussing this with Rosie, something struck me. Why doesn't she want to go and live in Berlin? One would have thought that's what she'd do – return to her Berlin.

Ah, no. It *had* occurred to Rosie. In fact she'd talked it over with Jack. He agreed that there were two reasons against it: Toni had left

Berlin on the arm of her handsome young Englishman; she would be coming back alone, divorced, years older with her early prettiness nearly gone – she would not be able to bear returning on these terms. The other reason, Rosie was afraid, was herself. Toni would not live anywhere for long without her sister being near her. That curious bond. Whatever its origins, it was an inescapable fact. Jack acknowledged it too.

'And you comply?'

'Within limits.'

'You will live in Parliament Hill,' I said, 'but not in Berlin?'

'My life is here. My life is in England, nothing could make me leave. Quite beside the fact that I never liked Germany.'

I asked her what the Judge was making of it all.

'He didn't think she *would* go to such lengths . . . But then, he says, one never can tell what a woman won't do.'

'He does think she's wicked?'

'*I* think she's wicked and not quite sane. Jack says she's stupid – Jamie will feel he's well out of it, some day – he says it *is* jealousy, of the narcissistic kind. Toni can't bear anyone being preferred to her in whatever capacity. History is repeating itself.'

'She didn't forgive the Judge for you. Now it's Jamie. Though it's different.'

'*Very* different,' said Rosie. 'For one thing, Jamie still prefers Toni. It all started because Toni was being unkind to him.'

'What will become of Jamie?'

'Women will want to console him, eventually he'll allow himself to be consoled. He feels baffled and hurt and terribly sad and he'll miss Toni badly, but his heart isn't broken. Perhaps Cynthia herself will make an honest man of him by and by.'

' "What a woman won't do"?' I asked, 'What would *you* do?'

'In Toni's situation? I'd choose not to know. And if I had to, I'd do anything to keep the man or get him back. No reproaches, no ultimatum, best behaviour, not showing one's feelings.'

'And the feelings?'

'I should mind dreadfully. Do you know I was even scared when

Jack admired those pretty girls on the beach at Sanary. If he really fell
for somebody, I should suffer very much.'

'You would? There are still so many things I cannot imagine – or get
wrong – perhaps I'll never be a real novelist . . . But you haven't told
me if you would forgive him, the man who was unfaithful to you?'

'If I loved the man, of course,' Rosie said.

In no time at all the removal men were at Regent's Park. (Most of the
furniture – Berlin relics – was Toni's, including the piano.) Then it
was Rosie's possessions' turn: her Bavarian peasant baroque arrived
and was distributed at Parliament Hill. The flat there was high-
ceilinged and a good deal larger than the mews. Rosie's new bedroom
was not, and it lacked the pleasing proportions of Upper Gloucester
Place. Now there the two were, the two sisters (with the dog and his
basket). How swiftly lives are uprooted, the trappings of life dis-
mantled. I found it terrifying.

They said it was pointless my staying on by myself miles away in
Upper Gloucester Place. Their neighbourhood was not a bed and
breakfast area; they proposed I'd stay with them – it was March, it
would only be for some weeks. I said yes. They bought a couch, and
so there I was too, sleeping in their sitting-room. It was not very
convenient, and it took longer to get to my pupils in whose houses or
flats I taught. But small matter, it was worse for Rosie who could no
longer get to St James's in the evenings by a direct tube train, she had
to change from the Northern Line; it took nearly twice as long. What
did the Judge say about that? I asked her.

'Nothing. He's not familiar with the London Underground
system.'

Again many evenings were spent by Toni and myself alone in the
new flat. There had been a crisis when Toni told her sister that she
could not possibly come home in bright daylight in evening dress –
what would the neighbours say? 'What they wish.' Rosie had treated
the request with such contempt that Toni knew defeat. She was
mortified but the subject was ignored from then on. The sisters still
lunched together regularly at Schmidt's (reached by Underground

without change); the dog was walked by Toni whatever the weather morning and afternoon; I was out most of the day.

A new trouble arose when Rosie's school teacher friend from Watford was due for her fortnightly tea. Toni said that woman mustn't be told about any divorce.

'And why have I moved up here then?' Rosie too could sound very chilly. 'And where is Jamie supposed to be?'

'You can invent something. Say Jamie is out at work.'

Rosie was able to put a stop to this nonsense as well. It did not diminish our anxieties about Toni and the future.

'One thing I shall have to be firm about,' Rosie told me, 'that's our holidays. Jack says we can go to Sanary again this summer.'

'Splendid.'

'Let's hope I can arrange something for Toni.'

It was not just the atmosphere of the flat that got me down, it was the unreasonableness of people and their capacity to hurt each other – if relatively civilised and well-meaning individuals could do so much violence to their loved ones, what about the vast ignorant mass of humanity labouring under so much greater injustices, grievances, hardships, triggered by ideologies, nationalism, class hatred? Once you can say, and *believe*, We are right – They are wrong, is that not when wars break out? I thought of writing about this – the links between private and mass catastrophe, but lacked the knowledge and skill. Not for the first time I lamented the fact of my not being able to go to university (my fault? whose fault? circumstances?); I would have read history, not literature.

One fine afternoon I was walking with Toni and Tommy on Hampstead Heath, the dog tumbling happily on the grass.

'Jamie must miss him,' I said.

'And he misses Jamie – I wish this divorce wouldn't take so long.' She had learned that it wasn't even on the lists yet.

'What?' I said.

'Once it's absolute, he can come and see Tommy. And me. I hope he will. I'm looking forward to it, *I* am missing him so much.'

'*Toni*,' I said.

'He can't remain my *husband*, there's no reason we can't stay friends.'

April. I'd done my time; done my duty to the pupils as I saw it, equipped them with some subjunctives and a useful amount of slang. Sweet escape.

I told Rosie I should be booking rooms for her and the Judge before long: Hôtel de la Plage. Something to look forward to.

This did not mitigate my feelings about leaving them. All the same, sweet escape.

3

I went by the Newhaven–Dieppe route again, by choice this time. I liked pacing an open deck on a long crossing, breathing the salt air, thinking quick thoughts. I was pleased with the presents in my bag. There had been no new novel by Aldous Huxley since *Point Counter Point* nearly two years ago, so I got an Ivy Compton-Burnett, her second novel *Brothers and Sisters* which had come out last autumn, for my mother, wondering what she would make of it. I was also bringing Earl Grey tea from Jackson's, ginger biscuits, a cardigan for Emilia, Dunhill cigarettes for Alessandro and Dunhill tobacco for Philippe (which it turned out he abhorred, he only smoked *caporal* in his small white clay pipes); I couldn't think of any suitable offering for Oriane, so let it be. On the train I woke as usual at Marseille: soon after, one saw the Mediterranean and the Mediterranean light, later the line ran above the bay of Bandol, close to the sea, not far behind the Kislings' new house.

At Toulon I was met by the donkey-man in the Quatre-Chevaux. *Votre papa* asked me to fetch you, he is occupied (with the two conversions they had now on their hands, no doubt). And how are Monsieur and Madame? I asked, meaning the Desmirails. '*Bién, tout le mondé va bién.*' Oh, this blessed Midi accent, I realised how homesick I had been. And how was the CTL, how were the buses running? Full tilt, everybody using them, no standing room on any run, trouble was that everybody wasn't paying, too many blokes thinking themselves entitled to a free ride. There Monsieur had made a mistake from the beginning – we all knew Monsieur.

At Les Cyprès my mother and Alessandro were both standing and there was an atmosphere in the room that seemed to speak. My mother greeted me with affection, Alessandro was tense and mute; as Emilia came in and we embraced, they stood apart and still, not looking at each other. I became tongue-tied. At last Alessandro said, Perhaps you would like to wash and unpack first. My mother said vaguely, Doesn't she want some lunch? Lunch wouldn't be for another three quarters of an hour, Emilia informed her. I went out with her and did as I was bid. Perhaps I was dreaming; transitions, arrival, make things feel strange.

Later at table they had little to say then would ask about London in spurts. 'Quite a tale to unfold,' I said and there was another silence. When I had given her the Compton-Burnett, my mother fingered it like an unfamiliar object – very nice – and put it down. Now she seemed restless, shoving the food about her plate. What time is it? she asked. Alessandro told her. Oh, she said. Soon she asked again. I remember that luncheon, sitting at that table, in that room, with the minutes ticking away and the silent voices. I am still there at times. Of what we were given to eat I have not the slightest recollection, the first meal back in the South of France with Emilia's house dishes.

They didn't seem to want to bring it to an end, my mother drinking an unusual amount of espresso coffee. 'Will *you* tell her?' Alessandro said.

'I will tell her.' She rose, so did I. 'In about ten minutes,' she said and went out, Alessandro following her.

When I went, she was alone, lying on her bed. 'Sit by me,' she said, 'as we used to, discussing peace and war late at night.' There was animation again in her voice, a degree of eagerness. Her eyes looked different, fixed somehow, and shone – might she have a fever? She spoke.

'Alessandro has fallen in love with Doris.'

. . .

'Poor Alessandro. He didn't mean to. It happened.'

. . .

'It does. *I* should know.'

. . .

'*And* I should have known better – that time with him. Then I knew this was bound to happen . . . Some day . . . These fifteen (let's say) years' gap in age. Later I forgot about it. It was all so daily, so solid . . . Wasn't it?'

. . .

'Now they are home to roost, the fifteen years.'

. . .

'Don't look so stricken. He's not going to leave me. He told me so. It's going to pass. It's just a thing that struck him – *them*. She's madly in love with him.'

. . .

'We shall have to live through it – all of us.'

. . .

'I am doing *my* bit.'

. . .

'No, he didn't tell me. He's wise. Not my own intuition either. I think of her as about your age, I like her, it never entered my head. Curious, I had some suspicion about that Panigon girl last year. How did I find out? My own fault – you know me, I haven't got your scruples, I read other people's letters – curiosity: they're so revealing – the fool girl wrote him a note, I'll spare you the details, the kind of note we all write in the circumstances, My darling, so wonderful being with you this afternoon, I want you to think of me etc. etc. The fool Alessandro left it in his pocket.'

. . .

'No, round-eyes, I did not go through his pockets, the note happened to fall out of his jacket.'

. . .

'What did I do? What did it do to *me* . . . Shock, then raging pain. I made the most appalling scene – if you think you know my temper, you don't, nor did *I* – it shook the house, I howled at him, the things I

255

called him . . . And all the time the fury and the pain. You don't know what it's like when someone who you thought loved one, goes away and does the same things with somebody else. *You* wouldn't know – you didn't get anywhere with your Oriane, poor child. Take it from me, unfulfilled love – not that I've known much of that – is a hundred times less painful than abandonment, replacement . . . '

. . .

On a calmer note, she went on, 'I am not abandoned, I am not replaced. He tells me again and again. (And I ask him again and again, as I know I should not.) He will give her up, he's trying to give her up. Poor little Doris.'

. . .

'No. Even when I am furious, it's only with him. She is a good girl – if feckless – a brave girl, uncomfortably whole-hearted. That doesn't make it easier.'

. . .

'Where is Doris? She left. They're trying absence. Never a good idea. At the moment it's a relief. The situation here was impossible – her down at that hotel, my knowing and not knowing when he was seeing her. Having dinner the three of us here, his seeing her home. He put her on a train to Berlin a few days ago. (He won't let her drive that car across Europe on her own. It's still sitting here.)'

. . .

'Paul. Yes, poor Paul. She's going to tell him. Thinks it's more honourable and all that. I have a feeling he'll be both heart-broken *and* very nice about it.'

. . .

'You think *I'm* being nice about it. Oh my dear! I wish I could be. Consistently. I'd like to be on principle, by temperament I cannot. Not unaided. There is something else I have to tell you.'

. . .

'Bad? I don't quite know. Well; I'm sounding so reasonable – so forgiving as you touchingly put it – on Dutch courage.'

. . .

'I've not taken to the bottle. When it all began – that must have been early February, shortly after you left – when it began for me with the note falling on the floor a week or so later, I was in such despair – even if this blew over it might be just the beginning: you see, age, getting older, is irreversible – I made scenes day and night, especially at night. I couldn't sleep, I wouldn't let *him* sleep; I was like the proverbial wounded animal: uncontrollable. Fortunately a remnant of the intelligence the gods gave me told me that this must not go on, this *was* the way to lose him – Alessandro is not of tough clay – I was destroying him and myself.'

. . .

'Indeed, *you* knew nothing, innocently trotting about London. We seldom know how the other half live. I went to that pharmacist who likes me, I told him, *J'ai du chagrin*, there's some trouble in our *ménage* – I didn't have to say more, the French understand about such things – I need something to calm my nerves. He gave me a bottle of a stuff called Paciflorine, and of course some more veronal. The Paciflorine smells as if it had valerian in it – isn't that what they give to cats to calm them down? – well, it didn't me. It made me drowsy that's all. It didn't touch the fury and the pain.'

. . .

'Yes, it was horrible. You're a kind-hearted girl. I went back to my pharmacist friend who said he couldn't do anything more for me but if I really needed help, I might try le Docteur Joyeu. Remember? He came to this house once. I went to see him, he lives in what looks like a half-empty house – no apparent wife, just a creepy little servant who opens the door – in that pine-wood behind the tennis court. I told him, *Docteur, mon mari me trompe* – pure French farce – my husband is unfaithful, I can't take it and make scenes day and night. He made no comment except saying that he could give me something that might save my marriage. He produced a syringe and asked me to pull up my sleeve, and gave me a hypodermic injection. It took just a few seconds. I was to go home and report next day.'

. . .

'In no time at all I had an extraordinary sense of lightness, I felt like floating in body and even more so in mind – lucid, serene, aloof. I could think about Alessandro and Doris and it seemed small and remote, everything was easy – one would just love everyone and be good and it would be all right. The universe is *All Right*. It's the most wonderful feeling – one is no longer vulnerable or human: all sorrow dissolved, filled with an extraordinary sensation of well-being.'

. . .

'Perhaps that's what the saints mean when they are talking of ecstasy.'

. . .

'No, it does not last.'

. . .

'Next day I went back to Docteur Joyeu. I told him about the effect. He seemed pleased – if that man can ever look pleased – he said I was a very good subject, and did I think that with this treatment I would be able to keep the peace? I could stop a world war, I told him. He gave me another injection, and wrote out a prescription to last a week. One in the morning, one in the late afternoon. Would I be able to do it? Give myself a hypodermic injection? with a needle? Of course not! It's quite easy, he said. I dare say. Nor did I fancy coming to the Villa Joyeu morning, noon and night. Perhaps my husband could do it? He will, I told him, he's very good with his hands. Tell him he must sterilise the syringe. Each time, he said.'

. . .

'So Alessandro gives it to me. You had better learn how to do it, in case Alessandro isn't here. Because I have to have it three times a day now. Sometimes four. But the good doctor is getting stingy with the prescriptions, he tells me I must try to manage not to take the treatment more than three times a day maximum.'

. . .

'Now? That wonderful feeling? No, not like the first times; it's not as intense any longer, and it fades away more quickly. You can feel it leaving . . . '

. . .

'What happens then? when the effect wears off? I become raging and frightened again, and very very nasty to Alessandro. You see, I am two people now. And I don't want to be the other one, I want to be as you find me now. That's why I must go on with the treatment.'

Very gently I said, 'Mummy, what is it . . . this thing that helps . . . this thing Alessandro gives you?'

'Morphine.'

4

If Alessandro (and I) lived from day to day, my mother had to live from hour to hour. During the good ones, distractions were welcome. Friends of hers, the Roy Campbells, proposed to come and stay for a couple of nights. Roy, she explained to Alessandro, was a South African poet of some power and eccentric habits who wrote, she insisted, in English and in Zulu. He and his wife lived in great discomfort at Martigues, the fishing port on the other side of Marseille.

They arrived one morning. Roy handsome in his wild and unkempt way; Mary, strikingly Welsh and gypsy. I shall not go into much description of them: Roy Campbell has written quite enough fiction about himself. His luggage consisted of a marketing bag sagging with a weight of bottles – litre-bottles of red wine 12% proof (it went up to their room). As he came in, I am almost certain that I saw him raise his foot at our bitch Chumi who was about to inspect him. A horrified look from Alessandro prevented the kick (if kick it was meant to be). After this Roy glared at the dog.

In due course the five of us sat down to luncheon. All went well on our part (my mother had been given her treatment earlier), Roy drank a great deal of red wine (ours), there was no lack of conversation. Afterwards he dropped what was for me a bombshell: he casually asked to be taken to make a call on Aldous Huxley. I thought he was raving. (He often was.) He persisted; his old Oxford friend had bought a house at Sanary.

It was a shock because I had been hoping to meet this writer whose work I idolised some day. *Some day – not now*. When I could hold my own, when I had become a writer myself (if ever?). All the same, when Alessandro agreed to take the Campbells on a search for this author he had heard my mother and me talk so much of, I did not stay behind. My mother did ('Writers should be read not seen'). It was a hot early afternoon in spring. I felt like some girls are said to feel when taken to their first dance before they are old enough to wear the clothes they like.

We knew nothing about Huxley, his age, his life, married or not (one presumed not), what he looked like, publishing being more reticent and impersonal in those days.

We set out. Mary Campbell next to Alessandro; Roy, clutching his clinking marketing bag, with me in the dickey. En route a labourer who did not keep siesta, thought he'd heard an English *homme de lettres* was converting a house he had bought on La Gorguette (a promontory between Sanary and Bandol). We found it. The Villa Uley existed. Sanary had not been talking about this; it was typical of Aldous and Maria that wherever they lived they were far less touched by common gossip than most people are. (Because of the dignity and friendliness with which they comported themselves?) Again, I shall describe neither their appearance nor their house – and only a little of that slightly farcical afternoon of our first encounter – I have written enough about Aldous Huxley (*not* fiction). Here I shall bring in him and Maria only in so far as they touched on our daily lives, our story and myself.

What I have to repeat is that Alessandro after five minutes of looking at Aldous, all the six-foot-two of him, sitting on the floor covered with builders' dust sorting books, slid out of the house again, turned the car and sped off to fetch my mother. (Maria who had observed his vanishing – little ever escaped her – surmised that she and Aldous had displeased in some marked way.) Presently my mother appeared. (In her benign and animated incarnation, looking only faintly ravaged.) She and Aldous struck talk at once and did not stop for the rest of the afternoon (we were asked to stay for tea), taking evident pleasure in the discovery of each other. None of Aldous's redoubtable silences, dreaded by his family and friends, that day. My mother instantly took to Maria as well; the rest of us sat back with enjoyable attention. Roy fidgeted a bit, his old Oxford friend proved a less convivial figure than he had imagined, he did not dare to fetch his marketing bag and contents from the car. Not that any of us had much refreshment, my mother had seized the teapot as it reached the table and held on to it firmly while engaged with Aldous. She had forgotten she was not in her own house, in turn forgot to do any pouring out: cups remained empty. This was standard absent-minded behaviour. To us, not so to the Huxleys. Maria did not intervene because she was convinced that my mother had found something dreadful inside the teapot (my mother had lifted the lid and gazed abstractedly inside). Meanwhile, with her free hand, she ate all the bread and butter, remarking how delicious it was and why did we never have such a thing in our house. In fact, she was herself. No undercurrents were apparent (not even to Maria then); I would like to think that during those hours she had forgotten them herself, lulled and seduced by Aldous's effortless intelligence and calm, the beauty of his voice, Maria's *gentilezza*. (One's mood, and behaviour, always lifted to a better plane in the Huxleys' presence as I was to learn quite soon.) My mother looked absorbed, Aldous and Maria, too, showed signs of fascination – Roy Campbell, it would seem, had brought them a rare bird. A friendship began.

Not with me at that point, nor with Alessandro – they took little interest in us (as Maria told me later). Alessandro was like one of those men she did not marry when she lived in Italy as a girl. I was a young person at the end of the table. (Did I mention that I knew Aldous's books almost by heart? I kept awed silence.) About the only thing Maria said to me during that first visit was, Our little boy will be here with us for his summer holidays, it'll be nice for you to meet each other. (When in due course Matthew arrived, he turned out to be nine years old.)

That evening we heard the red Bugatti (the sports model Maria drove with splendid skill and speed to Aldous's delight) snorting briefly outside Les Cyprès: Maria was leaving some tuberoses and a loaf of the delicious brown bread for my mother. A typical gesture: kindness with some teasing thrown in (and a grain of rebuke).

A note on the phenomenon of fashions. Maria had been wearing trousers, white sailor trousers with wide bottoms; my mother followed suit next day, Alessandro was sent into Toulon to buy trousers at the Bazar des Mécaniciens on the port. I didn't lose hours doing the same.

At Les Cyprès we jogged along through May. My mother's twenty-four hours' cycle followed a fairly even keel, if even keel is the right term for heavy late waking over-clouded soon by despondency (Alessandro bore the brunt of that), relieved – after the first injection – by mild euphoria silent or loquacious, followed through luncheon by irritability and strained waiting, relieved again by euphoria and so on through the third injection to the midnight dose of veronal. She struggled to remain kind to Alessandro and objective about their predicament, and most of the time succeeded. Even during the waiting hours – 'It can't be only half past five!' – she was able to make jokes about herself. It was seldom that I could hear – Les Cyprès was a well-built house – a voice raised.

Alessandro and I were waiting on her in a state of suspended hope. If I was helpless, he was doubly so. Bound by his own feelings which I guessed to be between guilt and longing. Did we behave like ostriches? It would look like it. We were learning, but we were learning in the dark. There was no one to ask. We were both quite ignorant about drugs. They were something one read about in adventure stories (Sherlock Holmes, Chinese opium dens) and the gutter press (fashionable young women sniffing cocaine in night clubs). My mother's treatment was medically obtained (we avoided talking much about Docteur Joyeu) and administered by a kind of nurse's routine, a meticulous process, tedious if you had to follow it three times a day (we tried to keep it down to that). The needle and the glass syringe (no disposable ones then) had to be sterilised, that is boiled for some ten minutes in a little saucepan, kept covered, allowed to cool, assembled again. At first Alessandro had done this on the kitchen stove – la Signora's medicine as far as Emilia went – when it continued he became discreet, bought a spirit-lamp, kept the paraphernalia in a locked drawer, carried out the process in their bedroom.

He had two conversions on his hands, Le Lavandou and La Cadière, my mother no longer much helping; both were nearing completion, he *had* to be out of the house some of the time. So, as my mother had suggested, he taught me to give her the treatment, prepare the syringe, open the little ampoule with the miniature file provided, apply the disinfectant, give the actual injection. It is not something one likes doing, I recognised it as unavoidable and minded every time.

We instinctively knew that we must keep people from knowing. For my mother that meant above all the Huxleys. Seeing them did her a great deal of good, she made efforts to keep up a façade, with them she was at her best. (Which meant careful timing.)

Though Aldous kept utterly regular working hours – two or three in the morning, at least two more in the afternoon – he and Maria were quite social. They had people for lunch and often dined out or had people to dinner; when the house became properly habitable (with three guest rooms) they generally had friends (interesting and charming) to stay. Then there were the picnics, the hilarious Huxley picnics, on beach and cliff and wind-swept plateau, nocturnal picnics with Aldous's planter's punch to drink, Maria's eccentric food – she was fastidiously anti-food but fed children and guests – fried rose leaves, fried zucchini and rabbit, quince jelly to eat, games to play. These and music at night – Aldous's Beethoven records listened to in hammocks in the garden under the stars and leaves – were sheer enjoyment, giving in to the moment. (Over, when my mother felt the first twinges of restlessness.)

As I said, we jogged along through May. At the back of our minds there must have been a belief in an eventual solution: the Alessandro-Doris situation would end . . . the need for the treatment cease . . .

Alessandro? Did he have moments of remission on those outings, listening to Artur Schnabel playing the First Piano Concerto? It was precisely at a soirée where the maestro in person had been playing that he and my mother first met. Then they sat out the music. Now he was receiving letters from Berlin through the poste restante. Where he read them, if he destroyed them, I did not know. What came out was that absence, as my mother had foreseen, was not working. Presently, Paul proposed an opposite remedy.

Paul had taken it both badly and well. He was very unhappy, he still wanted to marry Doris. He insisted on going on supporting her grandmother and on Doris accepting his allowance. He tried to take it as a coup de foudre that must be allowed to run its course. He went on seeing Doris, was kind, made no demands. What he suggested was that Alessandro and Doris should go away together for a month or two . . . Travel. Doris intimated that she would be content with this – a stretch of time with Alessandro, limited happiness. Ultimately he only loved my mother, he would never give up his marriage (he had as good as told her). As to Paul, she did not want to think beyond her time with Alessandro. She might remain single, living only in the past . . . (This reminded of Cécile Panigon: *she* was in Paris by now with the blessings of the difficult rich aunt, studying art; single or not, one had not heard.)

Gradually Alessandro enlisted my mother's support for Paul's idea of cure by proximity. He tried to persuade her that this would be the solution – some weeks, a couple of months perhaps, on their own: it should be enough – such things run their course, he wanted to go to bed with Doris, not make a life with her. He thought he knew himself enough, he knew men . . .

Here my mother quoted some lines from the 129th Sonnet.

Alessandro sighed. Could she not simply regard it as a kind of delayed wild oats? He *would* return.

All as before? How can it be?

Different. We can have a long time before us yet, he told her. A good time.

My mother's first reaction was not favourable. What she called her bad incarnation came to the fore. There was a scene; I was called into their room by her; it was the first one I witnessed. Later, unopposably, she asked for the fourth hypodermic.

In the days that followed she became consistently more and more reasonable and sweet. It was truly extraordinary. 'I must let the dear boy have what he wants . . . ' I was elated by admiration, Alessandro by gratitude. And in that spirit the actual plans were made.

My mother became interested – together they weighed up different countries, then decided on Spain. He had never been: my mother knew Spain well, indeed she and my father had lived a year or more in Andalucia – a closed, early nineteenth-century Spain of few foreigners and abominable roads. They had to leave – regretfully – because it was not considered safe for my mother to give birth there. (I was conceived at Cadiz: sherry and the Armada.) It was not a woman's country; she remembered my father's Spanish valet who whatever happened in the house never took her side. That was near Ronda – they had driven up there in a horse carriage, there was no railway, oh the dust in the air, the lack of springs in the carriage, but the nobility, the grandeur of the landscape ... Alessandro ... and Doris, must go to Ronda. Seville? Holy Week – incessantly noisy – there she had fallen for a small boy, very fair and blue-eyed, most unusual in Andalucia, who had danced in the ritual ballet round the altar with much grace; she had lit a candle and made a wish that her baby should look like him.

I didn't come up to expectations, I said. She laughed.

Otherwise Seville was overrated, so was Granada, more essential to see Cordoba, and he *must* go to Madrid. Alessandro had already thought of it: the Prado.

He arranged to meet Doris's Berlin train at Marseille, and go on from there. My mother had wanted her to come to Sanary first and stay with us for a few days. Alessandro prevailed in discouraging this.

They would travel in Doris's Chrysler – what luck it was still here, parked in our yard – he would leave his car for my mother to be mobile. I was to drive her; I said I would. With great care.

To me he talked over money arrangements. He had been paid, or nearly all paid, for the two conversions, so there was a substantial amount in the bank; out of it would have to come outstanding bills to carpenters and masons – 'See to it that she doesn't do anything foolish, she's capable of spending money like water.' They had a joint account. (There was a small branch of the Crédit Lyonnais in the main shopping alley at Sanary which opened twice a week.) Alessandro would have liked to leave most of the money with me, but I was unable to open a bank account – still legally under age. 'Would you like me to keep it in the mattress?' On the whole he thought not. 'She's promised to let you take charge of the cash she draws, just watch out for her writing extra cheques on Tuesdays and Thursdays.'

I thought I ought to know, among other things, how much she had to pay Dr Joyeu on her weekly visit for the renewal of her prescription. Very little, Alessandro said, just what he took to be the going rate for a brief consultation with a country GP. He named a small sum.

The nearer we got to the date of his departure – early July – the more precarious my mother's state became, the fourth injection being routine now. With that her control held; there were no more scenes. No blackmail.

Addresses needed delicate negotiation. They agreed not to corres-pond. (No postcards from the Alhambra.) Alessandro did not reveal an itinerary; he would telegraph *me* as they moved along, where to reach him, reach him in an emergency. He did not have to add *only*; he knew I was resolved to leave him alone.

Nor was there an explicit date for his return, some time in August seemed to be the understanding. Whether that meant beginning or end, no one said.

The first address he left me was c/o American Express, Barcelona.

When he had left, my mother, buoyed by her own magnanimity and courage, was almost in high spirits, and full of plans for our entertainment and occupation. She was going to give dinner parties, go on sightseeing trips – 'We have the car' – she might take up writing again. 'I do have notes for my essay on Stendhal and Flaubert.' It was the first I heard of it.

*   *   *

None of the plans worked.

She insisted on giving me dinner at Le Sourd, so we drove there. Le Sourd, elegant, not large, practising a restrained classical cuisine, was then one of the most expensive restaurants in Toulon. We'd been there before, taken by one of Alessandro's patronesses. My mother ordered – there was no gainsaying – an elaborate and heavy dinner: I must have this and that and so would she . . . It was a Sunday; the place had undoubtedly been bustling at noon, now it was nearly empty with the waiters glum and tired; the French do not dine out much on Sunday night. My mother picked at the first course, some delicacy barely in season; the duck looked huge on her plate and she could not touch it. By the time they wheeled in the paraphernalia for the crêpes Suzette, she told the head-waiter she was taken by a malaise, and me to get her home without delay (she needed the fourth hypodermic). As expeditiously as I could, I paid for the uneaten dinner and drove her back at speed.

When I went to the chemist with the *ordonnance*, the weekly pre-scription, the pharmacist asked me to wait. The shop as usual was full of people. He beckoned me to step behind the counter and come into his cubby-hole.

'*Mademoiselle*,' he said, 'I cannot go on filling these prescriptions – not week after week, not for these amounts . . . Docteur Joyeu exaggerates . . . ' He said it sadly, considerately, also with exasperated firmness.

I was dumbfounded. 'But these are medical prescriptions!'

'For *what*?' he threw at me, 'for what medical purpose?'

'I suppose,' I said, 'to calm the nerves.'

He looked at me with pity and more exasperation.

'You must understand: pharmacists are controlled . . . There are laws . . . ' He talked about narcotics, *stupéfiants* . . . *la drogue* . . . Terrifying words. 'That's what your mother is playing with.'

'She needs it,' I said.

'Yes: *now* she *would* need it.' Again the anger and the pity.

This was panic. 'What are we to do?'

'*Je suis désolé pour vous, et pour Madame votre mère*. Her husband, I understand, is away?'

(And there is not going to be an SOS to American Express, Barcelona, I thought. Anyway, it'd be too late – What would *I* do if I went home now empty-handed?) Again I asked, 'What are we to do?'

He would give it to me this time, he said, not to would be inhumane, *and* dangerous. He would also go on until . . . until other steps could be taken, to honour a prescription every now and again. Meanwhile he advised me to try some other pharmacies.

There was only one other at Sanary, I interrupted.

Oh, he would avoid Sanary altogether. I must go further afield, Toulon, perhaps Hyères . . . And not to the same too often.

Bandol? Bandol was nearer, I said.

'Too near.' He hesitated, hesitated again. 'Docteur Joyeu is reputed to be . . . to be somewhat free . . . '

I caught on that it would be prudent to go to places where Docteur Joyeu was unlikely to be known, and to produce a better reason, if asked, than *nerves*.

'What *is* it prescribed for?'

'Pain.'

'Yes.'

'After accidents, wounding in war, operations.' There were other conditions for which it might be required. 'Now if for instance your mother suffered from attacks of a certain kind of asthma, it would be given to relieve an acute state.'

He did not make it very clear to me, as I think he meant to. 'You are saying it would stop an attack?'

'Definitely. It can be very useful, in some cases necessary.'

'You mean *if* my mother had such attacks . . . ?'

He suggested that she talk it over with her doctor.

So what was I going to say handing in a prescription at Toulon or Hyères?

'You might say that the patient is suffering from heart asthma – this is far from correct but they wouldn't expect anything more precise from a young lay person like yourself.'

I thanked him.

He handed me a week's supply, the flat cardboard box with the two layers of twelve ampoules each inside, and a few extra ones in what looked like a half-packet of cigarettes.

I thanked him again.

'And do try not to let your mother take more than her ration.'

'She's been very good,' I said, 'she's not asked for more than four a day for several weeks.'

He threw up his hands: 'Didn't you know that the dose has been *increased*? Twice . . . Once in April, and again last month.'

Contemptuous of my stupidity, he talked milligrams. 'That's why I can't go on, that's why I had to warn you.'

Finicky man, my mother said. Very well, you must go to Toulon, there are two pharmacies to every street.

When I repeated what I had been told about attacks she thought she really ought to see Joyeu about them. 'I'm afraid he's not a really first-rate diagnostician.' She must have done something of the kind because shortly after she began to talk quite seriously about her dreadful heart condition.

The threatened dinner parties did not take place, in fact we saw little of our friends. In certain moods my mother began to fight shy of them, in others she would hare off on impromptu calls. That had become one of my worries, her sudden vanishing on her own. I'd come home from market or the sea, and she was gone without Emilia having seen her leave. Emilia these days was rigidly minding her own business. (She had most kindly though at Alessandro's request postponed her holiday this year until the autumn.) Once or twice my mother had just gone to and blithely returned from Toulon (on the Desmirails' bus pass) with her arms full of presents for me, more trousers from the Bazar, books. Sometimes I suspected, and she denied, that she had been to the bank. Another day she walked all the way to the Villa Uley dropping in to tea with the Huxleys. Maria brought her back in the Bugatti, implying a routine lift after a pleasant visit: Maria was the soul of tact. I was aware of what she must have seen – the staggery walk, the glitter in the eyes, the erratic make-up.

Was it, or was it not, all right for me to go for outside advice? Whom *could* I tell? was one of the questions revolving in my mind. Maria? Aldous and Maria were my mother's friends. Oriane – unthinkable.

Philippe? A rock of strength. Yet there was that unassailable rectitude: what steps might he not take (had I not been told that there were laws . . .)? Moreover he had no real love for my mother. Renée? She would have been the warmest, the most absolving to turn to, but then she like Philippe had no rapport with my mother. How could I bring our tale to any of them? A sense of disloyalty, betrayal, blocked the way.

I tried – more than once – to talk to my mother herself.
  'It isn't good for you. It can't be.'
  'Yes it is. Very good.'
  'The way you are feeling in the mornings and whenever it wears off?'
  'That's why I have to take it. It's then that it does me good.'
  'You wouldn't have to take it, if you hadn't begun to take it.'
  'You know why I did,' she said sharply.
  'Please, please, think of your health.'
  'I have other things to think about.'

The Panigons (minus Frédéric who was still away doing his military service) asked us to one of their dinner parties. My mother accepted. Recklessly primed, she sailed through the evening without disaster: nothing worse than a high degree of animation, poor appetite, flagging towards the end. She touched on Alessandro's absence with exactly the right tone and length: he was travelling in Spain on his art-dealing concerns. When we got home she started to cry; it was the first time and she cried bitterly and long. She told me how frightful it was, what had happened between her and Alessandro, how unbearable his absence and what he was doing during the absence. Up till now she had hardly mentioned him, more concerned, I felt, with what she called her magic spells, her snatches of euphoria. Helplessly I tried to comfort her.
  Presently she asked me to give her another hypodermic. I protested. We won't be able to get through the week as it is, I told her. 'Oh just go down to Joyeu, tell him my attacks are getting more frequent.' She was so unhappy that I had to give in.

*

I did not think much about Oriane these days. If love can cast out fear, the opposite happens as well. Looking at her could give me a pang; when she wished she could still cast a spell; the intensity though was gone. Did this mean that my feelings had been any the less – any the less what? True? Glorious? Devastating? Real? Or did it show them up as immature, mistaken, presumptuous, an irrelevant luxury? *They had existed.* Here were questions I would learn to work out. Some time, *not now.*

The Desmirails had moved into their new, their ultra-new, house, all cubic, spacious, cool and white with huge shutterless windows – Venetian blinds keeping out the sunlight – and scarcely any furniture except bookshelves, large dinner table, Philippe's large desk, some not uncomfortable chairs. It had unique amenities (unique for Sanary) such as oil-fired central heating, bathrooms en suite, an electric cook-stove, built-in cupboards, twin beds, a refrigerator and a telephone. (The Villa Uley also possessed the two latter which when I happened to mention it distinctly annoyed Oriane.) They had named the house La Pacifique (with reference to the ocean?). Like all our houses including the Villa Uley it was not exempt from the endemic summer water shortage.

Oriane was going through a phase of conventional chic. Cousins with distinguished-looking husbands were staying at the Grand Hôtel at Bandol, the women spectacularly turned out. Oriane herself had given up the Desmirail twin look and the sublime simplicities of designer's workmen's clothes and chalk-white espadrilles for the more orthodox trappings of couturier elegance. Philippe showed no sartorial changes, Louis occasionally was made to appear wearing long trousers and a shirt. Oriane had become bored with buses: she was seldom seen at the headquarters of the CTL where Philippe with the help of the donkey-man and the over-paid (according to Oriane) staff was beavering on. Oriane and cousins would be off for days at Antibes or Juan; she'd stop me on the port to talk about the fabulous things she'd been engaged in. Nevertheless she appeared restless and put out.

I was introduced to the cousins, patronisingly shown off as one might a clever and devoted stray dog who followed one about. In point of fact I could no longer follow her about, even if I'd wished to or been invited to join the fabulous engagements, because it was getting more and more unsafe for me to leave the house. I went for very brief swims and turned over the little marketing there was to Emilia. My mother finding settled meals irksome, preferred to eat, if at all, off trays at odd hours. La Signora is not very well, I had to mutter in explanation to Emilia who replied, '*Se vede.*' It is seen. My mother had grown thin lately, unbecomingly thin. Her quiet or benevolently animated hours were getting shorter and this meant more frequent demands for a hypodermic which I tried to resist or rather stave off for an extra hour or half-hour that would be filled with threats to me and abuse of Alessandro. She had begun to turn against him, speaking of him, calling him names, in a way I had not thought her capable of before. Asperity, home truths, temper, these I was used to and able to accept. What she uttered now, during bad hours, was violent spiteful malediction that would have shamed a Madame Panigon. When, horrified, I tried to stop her, exclaiming at injustice and sheer lack of truth, I was shouted down. Ungrateful brat, you're on his side! Sooner or later, more often sooner, I gave her the screamed-for hypodermic.

Once I tried to stall with the excuse that the syringe had not yet been sterilised. (The spirit-lamp *was* slow in getting water to the boil.) You are lying, she said. I was.

After the deed was done – how I hated it – when new peace had settled on her, she would give me a sweet smile. Have I been very horrid? You have. Do forgive me. I melted.

'I told you,' she said, 'I am condemned to have two sides now.'

What frightened me was the increasing dosage. Five in any twenty-four hours by now was not unusual. There was the perpetual worry of getting the stuff in time; far too often we were near running out. It seemed I was always en route to Joyeu or trying to find a complacent chemist. The routine at Joyeu's consisted of my stammering out something about *ma mère* and another attack in the night, his looking at me bleakly from his opaque and shadowed eyes, heaving a sigh and after a pause, a long pause, slowly writing out a prescription. Once in a while he would say, '*Dites-lui de faire attention*', mostly he would say nothing. I would utter the customary formula (French patients pay on the nail at the door), *Combien je vous dois, Docteur?* He would name the unvarying modest sum. I had it ready. '*Merci.*' '*Bonsoir, Docteur.*' '*Bonsoir, Mademoiselle.*'

I was losing my nerve about going to the pharmacies and so exercised perhaps unnecessary care, hesitating, saying a prayer on the doorstep, asking for toothpaste and aspirin along with the prescription. I was never turned down (intense relief each time) nor was I ever asked to produce the rigmarole about heart asthma.

There was one brutish occasion at home when I dropped the syringe, a glass syringe already primed with the precious contents of an ampoule, on the tiled floor. It shattered. My mother crouched down trying to retrieve fragments with her fingers. Then she flew at me, pulling my hair. I did the most sensible thing I could, ran out of the house, started the car and drove down to the chemist, our friendly chemist. Fortunately it was neither siesta hours nor night. From then on we kept two syringes in the house.

Every five or six days or so, I received a telegram from Alessandro with a new address. Valencia . . . Toledo . . . Madrid . . . A very old bent woman acted as telegraph boy in Sanary then; I had become adept at intercepting her. My mother developed a second sense: a few hours later on those days she would ask, Where is he? I had to tell her. Make him come back, she would say.

Renée Kisling's car overtook me as I was driving back from a Toulon chemist. We both stopped, 'One doesn't see you, mon coco,' she said. 'You didn't come out dancing with us on the *quatorze*.' When I looked stupid, '*le quatorze juillet.*'

'When is it?' I said.

'Last week.' She gave her big laugh. 'You didn't hear the fireworks? You must be in love.' She looked me over. 'Not going well.' I hadn't been out to sea for weeks, would I come with her? I didn't think I could, I said sadly. She asked no questions. I wished she had. We resumed our cars and drove our ways.

They had been building a casino on the port at Bandol for the last year, a proper gambling casino authorised, if not for roulette, for its mini-cousin, boules (nine holes for the little ball to trickle into instead of thirty-six) and a *salle privée* for baccarat. This establishment was about to be opened by the Prefect of the Var with a gala dinner and a cabaret of *grandes vedettes* from Paris such as Maurice Chevalier and the aged, perennially fascinating *diseur* Mayol. Not only Oriane and her entourage had been talking of this event for weeks. Admission to *L'Ouverture du Casino* was by invitation only. We received one, the Huxleys received one (the net was cast fairly wide). It said *tenue de soir* which for the men was understood to be anything from the *Préfet's* white tie and the *Maire's* frock-coat down to a dark suit. Aldous, one might be surprised to hear, elected to go, so did my mother. In both cases it was mainly to hear and see Mayol once more weave with his extraordinary hands in the famous performance of the chanson 'Les Mains des femmes'. Aldous also went because he was at that time amused by local goings-on; my mother because the Huxleys had asked us to join their table.

For me (among other problems) there was the vexing question of clothes. I was *not* going once more into pale blue chiffon yet I had nothing else that could be called *tenue de soir*. Maria – having meanwhile had some second looks at me and realised that I was not nine years old and that any friendship with their Matthew, a very nice little boy indeed, would have to wait – Maria, prompted by some process of divination, offered an old mess-jacket of Aldous's that he had needed when they went round the world a few years before. We tried it on: it reminded me of my father's coats I had been given to wear in church when I *was* Matthew's age; my father had been a tall man, Aldous was taller. Maria, not abashed, undid seams: there was nothing beyond the wit of a little back-street tailor to take in. So it was. After a couple of sessions of pinning and adjustments, the mess-jacket was transformed into a nice fit. With it – again guided by Maria – I was going to wear a plain long black linen skirt (run up by a back-street seamstress).

My memories of the great night are mixed and full of holes. I cannot recall, for example, who else was at the Huxleys' table. Which of their likely friends? Raymond Mortimer? Chronology says probably not. The ravishing young Yvonne Franchetti as she was then (later married to James Hamish Hamilton, the publisher)? Possibly. The Charles de Noailles? Again possibly, though I think not. Clive Bell over from Cassis? Drieu la Rochelle and (another beauty) his wife Olésia? Quite possibly. What is certain is that, when we got there, we found women who looked good and men who talked well. Maria herself will have looked enchanting, with her face of a young El Greco saint, corals on her ears and in her hair a single brilliantly white flower from her garden.

When we got there. We, my mother and I, were late. Even at her best she had not much regard for time. First she had not wanted to get changed at all – for a little rustic do: where had I got such bourgeois notions? Then she threw herself into it all too much: orange lace, deep décolletage, a Spanish comb with a wisp of veil. I fancied myself in my *tenue de soir* and was anxious to be off and with the Huxleys and the fun. I urged her on; she resisted. At one point we both howled at each other in great wrath. (I discovered that I had, or was developing, a temper.) Then, simultaneously, we laughed. Don't take after me, she said. In the car at last, I found it difficult to drive in the long narrow skirt, my mother kindly helped me roll it up. That, too, took time. You see? she said. We felt reconciled.

Our entrance – well after Monsieur le Préfet, which was not *bien vu* given my mother's appearance, make-up and somnambulistic walk, cannot have been inconspicuous. However, we reached the right table, the men whose identities I cannot remember stood up, Maria said the right word, and there we were. A few minutes after, I saw the Desmirails glide in – two slight silhouettes, he in a dinner-jacket, she in a white sheath – later even than we were, odd considering Philippe's manners. They were followed by the splendid cousins; Louis, Oriane's attendant demi-god was missing. With hindsight *this* was the most memorable event of the evening – the disappearance of Louis from the Desmirails', from Europe and this story. At the actual moment it was a mere ripple. The dinner, pretentious though not bad, got served with some hitches and was eaten; the official speeches, pompous, deferential, spiced with predictable gallic wit, were sat through; the cabaret got under way and was enchanting. Maurice Chevalier *en chair et en os*, in flesh-and-bone as the French call a live performance, set the audience alight; Mayol entranced it, a fat old man miming a sentimental song. Those who ever saw his act recall what it was like; for the rest it is as though it had never been (unless, improbably, a scrappy film exists): Aldous and my mother, lured from their separate inner worlds, gave themselves to its small magic.

Later, anticlimactically, the lights went up and there was dancing. (Not taken on by the men at our table.) I got a few turns from Oriane's cousins' husbands. Passing me, she looked over my get-up and threw me an ungrudging *Très chic*. Next time we were in speaking distance, she said, *Louis m'a plaquée. Plaquer, transitif*, can mean anything from 'stood me up' to 'walked out on me'. She made it sound a great joke.

My mother held up well; our party was one of the earliest to leave – after a brief tour of the salles de jeu, and much head-shaking from Aldous – he simply could not understand anyone wanting to do anything as uninteresting as gambling: too *extraordinary*. My mother helped me rolling up my skirt again and we got safely home.

Next morning the first version of the Louis story was trickling around Sanary: the Desmirails had been late last night because Louis had turned up at their house in a rebellious mood dressed in a reach-me-down suit and an open shirt. Oriane, at her disdainful best, told him, 'You might at least have put on a tie.' Whereupon Louis lost his temper, shouted '*Zut pour la cravate!*', slammed the well-fitting doors of La Pacifique and rushed into the night.

Oriane, furious in her turn, was soothed down and persuaded to proceed without her *amant en titre*.

The first amendment came from herself; she told everyone who lent ear that what Louis had hurled at her was not the harmless childish *zut*. His parting shot had been, '*Merde pour la cravate!*'

What was not known until some days after, was that Louis in thunderous black mood had run into his brother on the port. Louis had poured it forth. The brother, an elder brother, married, who happened to be staying at the Hôtel de la Plage for a holiday, listened. Louis was fed up with fetching and carrying and being bossed about by Oriane. He had had enough. He wanted out. The brother saw his chance. One should remember that the family – solid, respectable, highly regarded in the Parisian art world – was *against* on every count: a married woman, indiscreet, keeping a young son from the family, keeping him from painting. The brother took Louis back to the hotel, settled him in his own room, fanned the flames; then left him and went to work. Quick work. He telephoned to their father in Paris, the father telephoned to an uncle in Marseille, the uncle chased up a sea captain of his acquaintance, a *capitaine au long cours*, whose ship – a tramp steamer – was lying in port ready to weigh anchor that very dawn on the way to the South Pacific. Louis meanwhile had been nourishing his wrath (helped by brandies and sodas). He would show the bitch, he would. The brother lost no time getting him into his car in the clothes (sans cravate) he stood in. A little after midnight he was on board, under the wing of the complacent captain and delighted with his destination. (Louis liked thinking of himself as a noble savage.) The ship, the brother was assured, would not call at any port for at least five weeks. The plot was a triumph of initiative, family solidarity and cunning, as well as will over matter when one considers the state of the French telephone system (now the pride of Europe) in those days.

Before sailing, Louis had found the time to scribble a postcard addressed to Madame Philippe Desmirail. It said in shaky block letters (I saw it: Oriane showed it to me): '*En Route pour Tahiti! Au revoir!*'

At first Oriane took it for a prank. The brother soon circulated the truth. Then Louis' father wrote her a restrained letter informing her of his decision – at the cost of great personal loss to Louis' mother and himself – to send his son to the other side of the world for a couple of years. (They must have considered her *very* dangerous.) Oriane appeared to take the loss well, making a story of it – and all that for *une cravate*. Later I learnt that it had shaken her badly, a bad blow, as bad in its way as the literal collapse of her tennis future on that court at Biarritz. Each time a Bovaristic dream shattered, a corner of a world she had created to revolve round herself ceased to exist. On a daily level the disappearance added to her serious under-occupation, running Louis the Satellite had used up some of her abilities and time (he *was* a malleable fellow). Now she began to suffer from a series of *crises de nerfs* – as they were always referred to – which from then on beset her at intervals in later life. At the time she suffered these in private, Philippe, also in private, bore the brunt.

What Louis felt the morning after his abduction is not known. He did not return to France until some fifteen years after the war, that is after an absence of over thirty years, as a middle-aged man (with a young Tahitian wife in his baggage) who had not become a latter-day Gauguin but a moderately unsuccessful export-import man. What had been a humiliation for Oriane caused much grief to his parents who did not live to see their son's return. Then, Louis sought out Oriane, who had long lived separated from Philippe, told her she was the love of his life and proposed marriage, averring that he could easily get rid of the young native wife. Neither took it very seriously, though Oriane was flattered enough to tell me (the physical change in him was much greater than the change in her). Together they enjoyed a few jokes about *la cravate*, then drifted apart for good. He is said to have returned to the tropics.

The story of his original departure on the night of the casino opening was relayed to Aldous by way of Maria. She was his eyes and ears for what was going on in the human world; for his books, she would explain, any odds and ends came in useful. So I was egged on to provide tales. Now the Huxleys, the born, the authentic Huxleys, not the wives they married, were dreadfully addicted to puns and verbal jokes, though Aldous less relentlessly so than his brother Julian. Louis's quarrel at the Desmirails' house *La* Pacifique, the Peaceful, and his subsequent destination, *Le* Pacifique, the Ocean gave him the opportunity for a very poor *jeu de mots*.

*

From Toni I had had listless notes. About her, I had heard rather more. She was not adjusting herself to the new life, she was beginning to realise. She missed Jamie. Was her sense of injury still intact? Rosie wrote, Toni would want one to think so, yet there might be a slight chance, a minute chance, that it could crumble. *If* the right thing occurred. Word had got to Toni that Jamie was moping badly and that it was showing even in his work. That shook her a little. Could she be brought to think, Rosie was asking herself, that the man had been punished enough?

Rosie was working on it – it wouldn't be the first time ever that a divorce had been stopped. She wrote a word to Surbiton telling Jamie she would like to talk to him. When he replied, he apologised about the delay: he had left his mother's – from where the note had been forwarded – and moved into London again. The address heading his letter was in Bloomsbury: he did not say so, but Rosie gathered that it was Cynthia's. Jamie had not asked what Rosie wanted to talk about, nor had he suggested a meeting. So that glimmer of hope was extinguished.

Now Rosie was beginning to feel that she really could not leave Toni and go off with Jack to the South of France. *He* was able to go this year, wanted to go, insisted on going, she herself longed to go . . . But when she thought of Toni – who had no one to go away with – stuck on her own in London, she felt that *she* ought to take her somewhere, a fortnight in Brittany, say. Oh, she did not want to. To be able to travel once more with Jack! She was torn. What was she to do – what did I think?

What *did* I think? My heart was with the lovers – they had already missed Sanary last year because of the Judge's troubles – one should take joy when one can, if one can, but can one? If Rosie felt so guilty about abandoning her sister? For whom things *were* pretty grim. Was it never possible for everybody to be happy? Did anything good have to be at somebody else's expense? I wanted Rosie to have her time with Jack, I wanted them to come. Did I really? Did I want to face – or evade – Rosie's questions at this point? Was I in the mood for burgundy lunches with a distinguished ever so nicely patronising judge? (That had been two years ago – it felt an age.) Would I not watch the swing-doors of the Hôtel de la Plage dining-room for my mother wandering in?

I wrote a shilly-shallying letter. It would be wonderful if they could come, though I understood her concern about leaving Toni (in the first summer of what must be a kind of widowhood), it was a hard decision to make.

That's how I wrote. What I should have said was, Do come, you're not being selfish, you're not being callow, you are doing enough for Toni as it is; she's brought it on herself after all. Don't miss your time with the Judge – she'll get over it: just two weeks in August, and she's arranged a lifetime of misery for herself. Hold on to all the healthy joie de vivre you can get – what else *is* there?

That's how I ought to have written. And did not. (Self-interest apart, my trust in joie de vivre was at a low ebb.) Might it have tipped the scales? Possibly. There was from early on a curious kind of confidence in each other's judgement between Rosie and myself, regardless of our difference in age. As it turned out, she decided not to go to Sanary that summer. It was the first time she had ever said No about anything to Jack.

Having survived the casino evening, my mother craved new distractions. By noon most days she would be ready with a plan for an outing. Let's go to Aix . . . (Too far, mummy, eighty kilometres each way.) To Cannes . . . (Twice as far.) We could stay overnight at some agreeable hotel . . . (They'll be full up, it's the summer season.) One always gets in with the right word to the concierge . . . (Agreeable hotels on that part of the coast are expensive.)

'How dare you talk to me about money – what do you think *he* is spending, gallivanting about the Iberian peninsula? He's spending *my* money.'

We were down to that kind of talk.

'With respect,' I actually said with respect as they do in the law courts, hoping to lighten the tone, 'it's his money, he earned it.'

'*At last.*' It had not lightened the tone. 'And *who* got him the jobs?

Who taught him? Who does he think he is now? He was *nothing*. I made him.'

I tried to stop my ears. Presently, when the spirit-lamp had brought the water in the little saucepan to the boil at last, she would become the other person again. When she did, she would say, 'Was I frightful? Was I unjust? Poor boy, he's got so much talent – who knows? he might have done rather better without me. How can I be so nasty about him? – but I am so unhappy. That's what it is – I'm nasty because I'm unhappy. And *he* made me.'

Another time round, she would accuse Alessandro of living off Doris. I couldn't counter with Doris being a penniless girl because she was and she wasn't. My mother soon caught up. 'He's travelling with Paul's money . . . in the car Paul bought . . . What does that make him? A double pimp – ? a kept man at two removes?'

Better, far better, to steer her back to the outings, however perilous. The trouble with these was twofold, the danger of not reaching home in time for the next hypodermic, which could make her suffer badly, needlessly, and me lose my head with anxiety. She airily suggested that I might give her the treatment en route – We could take the box of tricks with us, just like a picnic.

'And *where* am I supposed to be doing this?'

'Oh the roadside or in a lavatory, a lavatory *would* be more private.'

I was so horrified – and expressed this so vociferously – that for the time being she desisted. It was not a wise attitude on my part.

The other trouble with these excursions was that, however I tried to circumvent, we were spending too much money. She would leave my side and slip into a shop, buy several silk scarves at tourist prices or a piece of Provençal pottery, then a set of Provençal pottery, saying that they would sell at a good profit; she ought to be building up stock against Alessandro's next commission. By then she would already have stopped at a pâtisserie to order a vacherin or some other large cake to take home, where Emilia might eat two slices or three, and my mother and I as little as makes no difference.

From the frugal days in my father's château, through the years of fine careless impecuniousness with the Robbinses, I had learned to handle money, particularly the money one hadn't got. I knew that my mother's own quarterly income had dwindled to a very modest sum indeed. Whatever she had done for him and his family in the past – and she had done a good deal – it was what Alessandro earned now that was keeping her comfortably off. Comfortably, not extravagantly. I knew how relatively small inroads can destroy financial tranquillity – for people of slender means it is not a very long step between comfortably off and swamped by debt: I was being haunted by Mr Micawber's sixpence.

As foreseen, Alessandro's masons' and carpenters' bills were coming in. They called them their *petites factures* whatever the size of the sum and proposed to come by the house next Tuesday, say, and be paid, as was customary, in cash. You offered and shared a glass of red wine, *un coup de rouge*, counted out the notes, shook hands, smiles all round and that was that. The snag was that my mother had to write a cheque in the first place beforehand and tried to hang on to some of the money.

If it was I who snatched the cheque and went down to the Crédit Lyonnais to cash it, she would waylay me demanding some for herself; if it was she who managed to go to the little branch bank on her own, it was worse as it was I who had to get as much as I could out of her. We didn't have an easy time of it.

And how often she succeeded in cashing a cheque I knew nothing about, I could not be sure. I never saw a bank statement; she who used to leave everything about now took care to conceal them from me. When my own money came in – by international postal order – we reversed roles: I trying to conceal, she trying to get me to fork out. I resisted because I had to have something to fall back on for Emilia's wages and our daily food. I, too, had to get good at concealing.

Alessandro had been away now for a long number of weeks and she was on the alert for some sign or date. Secretly feeling the same I tried to keep her mind off as much as I could. One afternoon she proposed a drive into the back country – so peaceful, so beautiful; she was tired of beaches and people and shops. I jumped at it, concurring about the shops. From Bandol we drove to Le Beausset, from there up the pass over Le Brulat on one of those narrow white D roads on the Michelin maps, up further to Ste-Anne-du-Castellet and on. It was still and very, very hot – burnt bare country of noble contours where one feels free and enclosed in lucent space. When we came down to Le Camp where the D26 crosses the N8, the main road from Marseille (by which we were meaning to return), my mother said let's go on.

Let's go on further into the empty country, towards the Massif de la Ste Baume, see if we can find Signes, a village with an auberge by a river which she had crossed on her way to Haute-Provence with Alessandro. Indeed, we saw another D, a Departmental road and the kilometre stone said *Signes 20 Kms*, that seemed achievable. The evening – it was beginning to be that – was so serene, so was my mother's mood; I suppressed misgivings, we drove on. The last time she'd passed through Signes, they had been roasting a string of small birds at the auberge – yes, little song birds, so cruel, so awful of the peasants, but admit they taste good. We got there. The village and the auberge, by a gorge, dry now, looked deserted and remote. No little birds a-roasting – just as well. We sat by a mellow parapet and were served cool *vin blanc-cassis* by a woman, the shadows were getting longer and my mother restless. Time, high time, to think of getting home. We must have a *casse-croûte* first (my mother's insistence), before that long drive. But it wouldn't be a long drive, would it? We didn't have to go back the way we came? Surely, there was a short cut?

They brought the *casse-croûte* – it took a little while – anchovies, olives, oven-grilled bread. Sure, there was a short cut: if we didn't mind it not being a real road, we could take a left turn some five kilometres out of the village that would take us down eventually to the N8. I found a thread like a snail's trail on the map – the light was going fast – a thread classified *chemin d'exploitation*, a track for peasants' carts? It cut right down towards the coast, it would save miles and miles – if I could find it, if it led where it appeared to lead to.

My mother still dawdled. She lacked a sense of self-preservation. *At last* . . . I found the left turn, or what looked the likely left turn. We took it.

It was narrow, it was bumpy, it began to wind; I could see no guiding sign or stone. Quite soon I would gladly have turned tail – there was no place a car could turn. I pressed on, praying we were in the right direction, praying we would meet no other vehicle to pass. There was not; the track was getting to feel very lonely and at times uncomfortably steep. From time to time it seemed to me that we were climbing – on a descent towards the coast? I prayed some more, casting sideway glances at my mother trying to assess her state of mind, feeling that she was beginning to scent danger. I drove as fast as allowable in the conditions and tried to calm myself by counting blessings: we had plenty of petrol, I'd seen to oil, water and the tyres. All roads must ultimately lead somewhere – or must they? If they were tracks – *chemins d'exploitation* – might they not end at some uninhabited agricultural plantation? And how far was ultimately? It had been getting dark, now it was dark. The Ford's headlamps were good but I had not had much experience of serious night driving; after all I had only passed my driving test a little over a year ago and, notwithstanding Philippe Desmirail's training in double de-clutching, I was not an experienced driver. Still, all would be well *if* this track led somewhere. Somewhere *near* home.

Now my mother's questions were beginning. Are you sure this is the right road? We've been going an awfully long time, it seems to me? Oughtn't we to be down at the main road by now?

How much longer is this going to take?

From her tone, she was strained, impatient; she had not yet come to the excruciating stage of nervous craving and physical pain I had lived through with her once or twice before when a hypodermic had been too long delayed.

Damp was rising after the heat of the day and for stretches visibility was blurred by swirling mists. It was difficult driving.

Could we go a little faster? my mother said.

On and on we went. We seemed to be descending now. Still no signposts. Night noises had begun, tree-frog and cicada, nothing else; once I hoped I heard a dog bark. Two of the worst moments were when we came to crossroads. Don't you dare stop, my mother shouted. Her acute time had begun. I just drove: nothing could save us now but luck.

I knew what she was suffering. (One of La Rochefoucauld's most repeated maxims is to the effect that nothing is easier to bear than the suffering of others, *les souffrances d'autrui.* In some situations this is not so.) Another mist patch, another sharp downhill bend, my mother beating her own legs with her fists. Faster, she cried, faster. *Please.*

Nothing for it but keeping steady, keeping on. Quite suddenly the track debouched into a back street of a hill village, dead asleep, which I recognised as Evenos. Within minutes we were on the N8: we were less than fifteen kilometres from home.

The last stretch was the worst for my mother. Once on the main road she urged me to drive as if I were driving in a race. I felt as a horse might in a finish with nothing left to give, she was beating the steering wheel, she was beating my hands and arms; feebly, that made it all the more pitiful. Faster, *faster*, FASTER . . .

When we reached Sanary, I dared look at my watch for the first time: it was two o'clock in the morning. We drove straight to Docteur Joyeu's house under the dank trees – an unspoken decision, I was in no state to handle a syringe. Joyeu received us wordlessly – he appeared not to have been to bed – my mother, equally speechless, looked ghastly, she might well just have had some appalling attack. He put her on a chaise-longue and administered what was necessary. I believe she fell asleep for a while. I was gasping for breath: Joyeu handed me a glass half filled with a cloudy liquid with a vaguely pharmaceutical smell. I did not really want to, but I drank it. Eventually he aroused her quite gently. She opened her eyes. 'I will go home with my daughter,' she said, 'if she will kindly take me.' It was then that I had to try not to burst into tears.

I forgot; *she* asked, 'What do I owe you, Docteur?' He named twice the usual sum, speaking his first words that night, *'puisque c'était une visite nocturne, Madame.'*

*   *   *

We were both so unnerved that for some time after we could neither of us speak of that night-ride. Nor was there any question of undertaking further outings together. By the end of the week she told me she could go on no longer: *He must come back.* I would have to telegraph. Today. I begged her to leave him be – she had been so good to let him go: don't spoil it now. Let him come back of his own accord. It's not even the middle of August yet, leave it to him, it'll feel better for *you* if it is his decision.

She would not hear and ordered me to send the telegram. Say I am ill. 'It's nothing like appendicitis,' I said stupidly. 'Then *say* it's appendicitis.'

I held out. She demanded to be given his address.

When I held out again, she said, 'Let me remind you that you are under age, I can denounce you to your German guardians for not obeying your mother. You are out of control, they will take you over.'

I felt rigid with shock. Not that it worked any longer; it triggered off residual apprehensions, not real fears. In less than six months I would be twenty years old, a number of disagreeable things might still ensue, legally I was not out of such clutches, but I no longer led the life of, I no longer *felt*, a ward in chancery. I was shocked by my mother, and very angry. In this matter she and I had always been on the same side; she knew it had been my bugbear; I could not take the malice of her betrayal.

Coldly I told her that I had promised Alessandro not to recall him except in a real emergency.

'A real emergency! He made you promise *that*? The cad.'

'Of course he did not. We didn't speak about it. It was understood, some things are.'

'Stupid girl. Where did you get those gentlemanly scruples from? Not from me, nor from your father as I knew him.'

Next Sunday morning they were to launch a ship from the small naval yard at La Ciotat where it had been built, something pleasant to watch. The Huxleys were going with some of their friends, Maria proposed that we join them and eat a picnic afterwards in a rock bay on the far side of the harbour. I tried to tell my mother that it would be all right to go – I wanted to make amends for something I had felt guilty about in my mind: my squeamish refusal to give her an injection outside our own walls, putting her into the position of the other night. I would find a way of transporting a sterilised syringe, we would find a discreet place en route . . . 'If it will make you feel more free, I will give you the treatment wherever you like.'

She gave me a curious look. 'Too late, my dear. I've learned that lesson too. I've been giving it to myself – quite easy really – as you say, it makes me feel more free.'

I realised then that when I had been puzzled about the number of ampoules in the box, it was not I who had miscalculated. From that day on I never gave her, nor did she ask me to, another hypodermic. I continued seeing Joyeu and touring pharmacies for her supplies.

In the event we did go to La Ciotat. The launch of the ship, a small coaster, the slow glide under a noon sky into natural harbour was beautiful; and memorable.

A couple of days later when I came home to Les Cyprès after an errand, I found the sitting-room floor covered with splintered wood and glass. My mother, standing among the débris, said smugly, 'Isn't this what they call "breaking up the place"?' Indeed it looked like something seen in the movies.

'For God's sake, where's Emilia?' I said.

'I gave her the afternoon off.'

The weapons, I saw, had been a flat-iron and a stick. What sent a shiver down my spine was the crack across the looking-glass over the chimney-piece. That brought bad luck. She was ingrainedly super-stitious about a broken looking-glass, so was I. She couldn't have done this too on purpose?

She said, 'I've only just begun. Unless you think that this *is* an emergency?'

Linked into an inescapable chain of wickedness and betrayals, I walked down to Sanary, to the post office, asked for a form, wrote out the brief message in dictionary Spanish and addressed it Correo Restante Granada.

5

For the best part of a week we heard nothing, then one mid-morning Alessandro burst into the house. He looked unslept, red-eyed, streaked with dust and sweat. 'How is she? Is she ill?' He brushed past me, 'I must see her!' I wanted to prevent him, he went straight to her room.

When he came out again only minutes later, he still looked dreadful though in another way – stricken, bewildered, dazed. He fell into a chair. 'What has been happening? What have they done to her?'

I knew what she was like in the morning, the colour of her skin, the state of her hair, of her nightdress, the state of the room: I had seen the changes, I had seen them gradually. To him they were new shocks.

'What is that awful smell?' *Ether*. For some reason she had been using ether rather than neutral spirits as a disinfectant for her needles. I had ceased to notice it. Alessandro stayed slumped in that chair for some time. Emilia, unasked, brought him coffee and a jug of fresh lemonade. My mother came in, dressed now, said haughtily, 'You ought to have a bath.' Wandered out again. We seem to have spent the rest of the morning and the day and the time that followed sorting ourselves out at a slow pace with no aim.

At one point I said, 'Where is *Doris*?' He had left her in the car, had driven straight to the house, driven straight from the border, straight through the night. They had not been at Granada when the telegram must have arrived, they were touring the south of Andalucia, they were at Ronda in fact when it caught up with them, the telegram. They started off at once, driving north through central Spain, two thirds up to Madrid, eastward to Zaragoza, Barcelona and on, straight on. It was hot – August in Spain, a hot August, the height of the holiday season, crowded roads. How many days? They had practically no sleep: twice only they stopped at a roadside inn for a few siesta hours.

We found Doris sitting upright and awake in the Chrysler, she looked frightened, sad, and utterly exhausted. Her face and dress were covered with dust; the car and windscreen were filthy and sticky with dead insects.

My mother, nine-tenths in control of herself, made her come in, You must be dead, my poor child. While they slept – Doris in the spare room, Alessandro on my bed – I drove about Sanary trying to find an hotel room. Not a hole to be had; finally the Plage, where we were in good standing, relented and promised a maid's room after the weekend. So Doris stayed at Les Cyprès, urged to by my mother who went on treating her in a friendly detached way. Alessandro she mostly ignored, making conversation over his head. Suddenly Doris said,

'Where's Waldemar?'

'Good God,' said Alessandro, 'where's Waldemar? Gone, I suppose.'

'No, no,' Doris said, 'he wouldn't, not without saying goodbye to us.'

'Who is Waldemar?' I asked.

Oh well, a young German, a student, a Communist – he was keen on letting one know that – they had picked him up, rather he had picked them up, at the Spanish side of the border. The guards were refusing to let him in, something to do with his travelling on foot or not liking the look of his papers (it was the year before Spain became a Republic, six years before the outbreak of the Civil War), he was afraid the French might not let him back in again – so perhaps if he could cross with them in their car? Alessandro had other things on his mind but Doris was firm that people in trouble must always help other people in trouble. Once in France with Waldemar crammed in the back with the luggage, they had gone on giving him a lift. He was a Berliner – with nice manners – who wanted to see a bit of the world during the holidays.

Presently Waldemar drifted in, he'd been asleep under a cypress tree, now he wanted to say thank you and goodbye. As well as travel-stained, he looked under-nourished: a skinny hare. His French was atrocious in accent but grammatically correct; when he broke into German, he talked in Doris's educated Berlin voice. You must tell us all about the state of the Weimar Republic, my mother said and asked him to stay. We had no second spare-room; Waldemar said he would be happy sleeping on our terrace, he carried all he needed in his rucksack. In due course some water was doled out for *his* bath.

This domestic situation persisted for some days, my mother alternately withdrawing for long periods and reappearing with renewed animation; Doris heroically concealing what went on inside her while we were all too aware of how much there was to conceal; Alessandro taking gradual cognisance of the damage wrought during his absence, lounging about the house adrift in indecision. There was too much to speak about. Mostly we said nothing.

When he learned about it, Alessandro wanted to stop me from scrounging round the pharmacies. That really appalled him. I told him, If you or I won't do it, she will on her own; in a taxi, I suppose, with God knows what results.

Waldemar came and went, folding up his bedroll or whatever he slept on, rigidly uninvolved, exploring the countryside, puritanical about accepting meals; even the sticks of bread and salami for his walks had to be pressed on him. One afternoon we were all sitting round a table with my mother, Doris and he arguing about dialectical materialism. Waldemar and my mother stuck to Marxist points – he hair-and-hide in favour, she coolly against – with Doris declaring that most *good* people nowadays had to become Communists. Alessandro and I sat there rubbing our eyes.

'Yes: taking the red veil,' my mother said. 'Don't let yourself be tempted into doing that, darling. Don't believe you have a vocation.'

She was addressing Doris, not me.

Next thing, the nice-mannered young German was talking metaphysics.

When at last there was a room and Doris moved down to the Plage, things at home took a turn for the worse: my mother reverted to open scenes – accusations, taunts, cries for help disguised as cries of abuse. Alessandro would repeat that Doris was leaving, was ready to leave. And he to stay.

With me?

With you.

Why?

Wearily after a pause, he said, I told you I would.

Do you want to?

He did not have the courage to answer, she had the courage to ask, Stay with me as I am now?

After another pause, still from the other side of the room he said, You will not always be like this. You *cannot.*

There were the logistics of getting Doris back to Berlin. He still would not let her drive on her own. To put her on a train to return by herself after their time in Spain was a trifle unchivalrous. In the end Waldemar was persuaded to escort her. Then it turned out that he had never done such a capitalistic thing as learning to drive a car. He didn't have the train fare and he wouldn't take it from us. Doris, whom he accepted as a near-comrade, thought up a compromise: she would pay for their both going third class which was the price of one second-class ticket. (I suppose Waldemar agreed because he believed it was good for her to travel third.)

Doris left. Alessandro had to take her and the political young man to Toulon station. No chance to say a private goodbye. Just a straight return to Les Cyprès. I prayed that my mother would leave him some peace that day. She did.

Doris was gone. Nothing was changed.

We watched each other, not knowing what moves to make. Did you expect me to lay aside my syringe? my mother asked. Perhaps we had. Perhaps *she* had? Impasse.

It was broken by Maria. This is what happened. Her red Bugatti stopped in the curve outside our house. Maria was taking Aldous to the English dentist at Hyères, would I come with them? The Bugatti had a token seat in the back; as the passenger seat had to be pushed backward to its limits to accommodate Aldous's immensely long legs, the third traveller had to perch sideways, knees up like a jockey. Outside the dentist's Maria stayed in the car. She always did. In all those years and years of driving him – which he could not do himself because of his poor sight – to doctors, to meetings, to gurus and quacks, she always waited for his return by the very front door to save him a wait or a walk, however short, when he came out. She had a great regard for his time, which was to be used for his work and his thoughts, not for hanging about while she might have nipped into a café or a shop. (Yet with all her care – her life-long care – for Aldous, there was always time, money, strength – she was physically frail – to give to, to help, others, her family, her friends, the person at the door.) So there we were outside the dentist's in a tree-lined street. *'Viens t'asseoir près de moi.'* Maria and Aldous usually spoke French to each other at home. I climbed into the seat beside her. She turned her head – she had a sharp-cut profile – and gave me an intense quick look, like a bird facing one (it was a way she had), from those luminous green-blue eyes. *'Tu sais, ta mère est bien malade.'*

There was no contradicting.

Another darting look, *'Cela se guérit.'* This can be cured.

How?

It was Maria who found the specialist in Nice; it was Maria who made the appointment for a consultation. It was not as plain-sailing as that: the appointment was broken, and had to be re-made. It was Maria who had gone to see my mother, had walked into the house, into her room, had sat by her bed: called her by her name, spoke to her. We knew not what. My mother had a surrendering confidence in all that came from the Huxleys.

Alessandro and I took my mother to Nice. We went by train as the drive might be too tiring; we were beginning to realise how much this thing was weakening her physically. It was not an easy ride as she played at changing her mind, threatened to get off at stops. In the end we got there. My mother was ushered into the consultant's room at once. It was Alessandro and I who waited, not speaking, inwardly biting our nails. Once a nurse looked in, gave us a contemptuous look, we jumped up, she withdrew. When after an hour or more the door opened again, it was the great man himself. He gave a glance at Alessandro and said curtly, *'Vous êtes son fils?'*

'Son mari.' Her husband.

'Very well. You may come in.'

I stood up. 'I am her daughter.'

'You can wait here.'

'I looked after my mother on my own, I had better be present at this consultation.'

'As you wish,' he said coldly, and walked through the door. Alessandro waited for me to follow and went in after me.

My mother was sitting in a comfortable chair, I could not make out whether she looked more scared or defiant; anyway the light of battle had not entirely gone out.

The consultant said, 'I am informed that this addiction has developed in only a little over half a year. Is this a fact? I can hardly credit it, given the patient's overall condition.'

My mother looked as if she were about to interrupt.

'Yes,' Alessandro said, 'it began last February.'

If that was so – a relatively short period of intake combined with a very high degree of addiction and deterioration – it was the most remarkable and serious aspect of the case. He explained. The taking of a drug, an opiate, inevitably leads to addiction to the drug, that is, the mind and body of the taker can no longer function normally without the drug. Parallel to that addiction, that increasing need for the drug, goes an increasing tolerance of it: larger and larger doses are required – running in order to stand still, and these doses in turn increase the subject's deterioration.

That was the *inevitable* spiral. No one regularly resorting to drugs escaped having to increase the drug *sooner or later*. The time scale was a crucial point. Acquiring addiction could be a slow process. At one extreme end of the scale, subjects were known to continue on opiates for year after year before the changes and increases became marked; at the other they could be as rapid as they were in the present case. Galloping addiction. On an average it would take anything from fifteen months to three years to reach that stage. The determining factors? Constitution . . . History . . . Vulnerability in persons of low intellect was generally assumed, yet here the subject appeared to be of good intelligence . . .

'I wish,' my mother interrupted in clear tones, 'that you would cease to refer to me in this disagreeable manner. You are referring to me I take it? I am here, I am sitting here . . . *Professeur.*' She did not address him as *Monsieur le Professeur.*

'Madame.' He turned to her with a small bow, his cool tone only very slightly tinged with irony. If his *amour propre* was touched at all, it did not show. 'Let us then discuss your future . . . '

There he had the whip-hand. A course of detoxification in a specialised establishment. Imperative. Soonest. Delay would be at the expense of further damage to health and increased future suffering. No need to go to Switzerland or Paris: he would advise a clinic run by a top man a few miles above Nice. For her, he would not advise a cure in a public institution. The clinic in question was *not* a mental home: indeed they would not and could not undertake a cure without her consent. My mother gave in. Verbally, for the present. She had put and answered questions with dignity and self-possession. Now she appeared tired. A nurse came and gently led her into another room. The consultant signed us to remain.

'I have arranged for her to be given what she needs for a tranquil journey home. I shall also write out the prescriptions that will carry her through the coming days.'

Both of us nearly spoke.

'I am not asking you,' he went on, 'what your wife's previous sources of supplies have been. I practise here, in the Département des Alpes Maritimes. I have no responsibilities towards the authorities of the Département du Var. At the same time I must alert you to the fact that it may soon become extremely difficult to obtain the doses she has become accustomed to from any legitimate source so-called. Examination showed that so far she has been injected with the article in its pure state; that would no longer be the case once she is forced to obtain some form of it in the black market . . . ' He looked at Alessandro, 'Back-streets and bars . . . The stuff they offer can be dangerous.'

Alessandro said, 'This cure? What will it do to her? Will it hurt her? Is it very bad?'

Alessandro looked bowed by heavy sadness. When I first knew him, I saw him as the young man in Quattrocento paintings standing on the piazza near the scaffold, hand on sword or horse, witnessing grief; now he looked a figure of grief himself.

'Very bad,' the consultant said. 'These cures always are. However they do them . . . This will be in my colleague's hands. I do not consider your wife's an easy case.'

'What if she decides not to do it? If we put it off? What will happen then?'

The consultant threw up his hands. 'What will happen? Haven't you seen enough? Death. In some form or another . . . Of too much of the stuff or too little. Suicide . . . Not probable in her case, though possible; accidental suicide. *Entre-temps il se peut bien qu'elle aille assassiner quelqu'un.* I refuse responsibility.' Furiously, mocking me, he broke into English, 'She may well murder one of you, Miss, some fine day.'

We hastened to say we would do all we could to make her do as told.

'The decision rests with her, she will have to sign a paper. Unless you choose to have recourse to the judiciary, who might constrain her by an order, though as you are not French – as I assume – they might prefer to avoid that hornets' nest by deporting her. Well, I see that you are not contemplating this; so my children, what I advise you is to use your influence.'

'And she *will* be cured at that clinic?'

'Of course she will.' The consultant shrugged. 'They all get cured. The question always is how long will the cure last.'

Aghast, we said, 'You mean, she may . . . she could . . . ?'

'Become a recidivist.' He was not so angry this time. 'Yes, that is the great problem. Having experienced *Les Paradis artificiels* – ' he gave me another mocking look, 'I am sure Mademoiselle has read her Baudelaire – they go on striving to return. At whatever the cost. You must hope that she is not one of them.'

He saw us out; my mother was in the hall. He took her hand and said with some cordiality and strength, '*Allez, Madame, bon courage.*' He shook hands with Alessandro and me perfunctorily, already turning away. The nurse saw us into the taxi.

*   *   *

Those were ambiguous weeks, the ones that followed. Weeks, not days as hoped by the cool consultant. My mother's position, on any count, was an agonising one. What lay before her was unknown territory, a cruel ordeal, a move from one trap into another. The inevitability of either course made it more unbearable. Thus indecision alternating with terror, optimism, defiance was natural and human, and under-stood so by Alessandro and myself.

Alessandro was crushed by her suffering and his own sense of guilt. I did not feel guilt – not yet – only pity, tension and an overwhelming desire to be free, for this thing to be over, for my mother to be out of the house and off to that nebulous destination I, too, dreaded for her.

Alessandro, I felt sure, was possessed by this same desire and this increased his guilt. Use your influence, the consultant had said, and we did. When she asked, Must I? What will it be like? we gave the right answers – right from the medical point of view, right from the common-sense point of view – yes, yes, but our motives were not pure: we felt in our bones what the absence of her present self would be for us, and we longed for it with chafing, burning impatience. We might each still have given our life for her, yet when she contrived another delay, we felt murderous.

Maria came and exercised her benign wiles. 'Aldous says' was her opening when she wished to give weight to some opinion or advice. I was quite aware that Aldous more than probably had not said. He might have *concurred* with the opinion or advice, but he would not have initiated it himself. Maria seldom troubled him with problems, her own or friends', unless they happened to be helpful to the book he was engrossed in. Now my mother was bombarded with the 'Aldous says', Maria talked to her as though she were a child about to be packed off to boarding-school: Think how wonderful it will be when you are back again, when it's over and we shall all be there wearing our very best clothes to welcome you home. *I* would not have got away with such Sunday school twaddle; Maria commanded the magic of the pure in heart and my mother's sharp, sophisticated mind was soothed and charmed.

I will do it, she said. Maria tied her to a date (changed more than once).

*   *   *

Alessandro and I became aware of other realities. The charges of the clinic, which bore the name of a female saint, were high. A solid deposit was required upon entry. We didn't have enough money, Alessandro told me. She spent a hell of a lot while he was away in Spain. Rather more, it turned out, than I had feared. What can we do?

Last year's Wall Street crash was now – late summer of 1930 – reverberating in Europe. Even if we had been willing, which we were not, to inform on my mother, it was doubtful whether her trustees could help much. It was no time to sell stocks and shares. My own capital, such as it was, a minor's capital, was locked up. Alessandro thought of approaching one or two of his patrons, or patronesses, with a view to an advance on future work. He still could get work, he believed, in spite of the state of the market, but to *do* the work he had to be free, able to move. *What were we to do?*

Many years later I came across a letter of Maria's written during the Second World War to her niece, Claire Nicolas White. It was a long long letter – such as Maria used to type, rapidly and with eccentric spelling, late at night when Aldous was asleep – the occasion was either a twenty-first birthday or an engagement, and it contained good counsel on many things from washing one's brush and comb to helping with the housework without letting one's family notice it, and not insisting on being right even if one was. One item particularly impressed me. 'Always give to people *before* they have to ask.' This was what Maria did for us now. She sought me out. Your stepfather must be having a great many expenses, she said. (They called each other Alessandro and Maria face to face, but in absence referred to 'your stepfather' and 'Madame Huxley'.) Then she offered the money for the clinic. She had it on her. It was an act of generosity all the more remarkable as she was painfully aware of how hard Aldous had to work and over-work to earn their living. Each of her acts of generosity, and they were endless, was a

297

laceration for herself. One must add that in this realm her 'Aldous says' was unequivocally and perennially 'We *must* help' from his own mouth.

Alessandro was impressed. We must repay Madame Huxley, he said to me. (I am glad to say that eventually we did. Which, and I don't like to think of it, was not always the case with money Maria lent or gave me in my later life.)

Emilia went off on her postponed holiday. Before she did so, she gave Alessandro notice: she would not come back. No reason was sought or given. She owed us no loyalty, she was not a family retainer, though she had served us like one. It was decent of her to have told us, it would have been easier to leave with nothing said, then not return. We gave her an extra month's wages, drove her to the station and saw her on to the slow train that would eventually carry her to Livorno.

Alessandro engaged a *femme de ménage*. This, given the disorder my mother was strewing about the house, was a necessity if we were to stay on the right side of squalor. The best ones were in work; we were taken on by La Grosse Hélène, as she was known, a young local woman of vast bulk; her manner was jovial, if familiar, and she was known to be a gossip. That was now of little moment; there were too many subtle and less subtle indications that Sanary knew what was going on at Les Cyprès. Only Madame Panigon had been able to maintain a façade of pristine ignorance. She was too practised in knowing more about her neighbours than she ought to, to let on that there was anything she knew.

Eventually Aldous took off to Berlin with his learned friend J. H. W. Sullivan, learned in physics, mathematics, astronomy, literature and music; they were going to interview eminent scientists. We were in September. Maria was about to leave Sanary to stay with her family in Belgium. After moves and countermoves, on the last practicable day, Maria on her own drove my mother to the clinic at Nice. As they left, my mother kissed us both, then, looking at our stricken faces, said with a sweet and mocking smile, 'I *know* you couldn't wait for the gates of the prison house . . . '

6

A few days later I found myself translated into the serenity and order of a French household. In the morning, when the breakfast tray was brought and I pulled the Venetian blinds that shaded the wide windows, my large bare room became as one with the olive grove outside. The rest of the house was quiet; no demands were heard. I drank my café au lait slowly, book in hand, breathing, looking out. Presently I washed and dressed in a gleaming bathroom, at my own pace. Later: the knock at the door:

Bien dormi, Billi?

The message from Nice had been that it would be a long process, a month if not more; for the present the *chef de clinique* forbade any visit, especially from the husband. The clinic would tell us when the ban was lifted; meanwhile I would be allowed to telephone the head nurse once a week.

Alessandro went off, using the time for earning – he hoped – a little money. He was still the go-between of collectors and a few artists who liked to by-pass their regular dealers once in a while. (There Kisling had been of much help.) He was travelling in the Ford and had taken one of the dogs, Chumi, who was most used to his ways. He meant to go to Paris and Amsterdam, whether he had the intention of going to Berlin I had no idea and did not ask.

The Desmirails came and told me that I must stay with them at La Pacifique for the duration, as it were. (As I said before, everyone knew about our troubles.) *Pour le moment tu es ma fille*, Philippe had said; Oriane was soft and serious. I was as touched as I was surprised by such kindness and affection, and found it difficult not to cry. Les Cyprès was shut, La Grosse Hélène coming in twice a week to air and dust; the remaining two dogs – on the under-trained side – were put en pension with the wife of one of Philippe's drivers.

September storms, those waterfalls that drench the Midi at inconvenient moments, had broken the summer heat early. So far it had been a long bathing summer – mild swimming well before May – one could have gone on after the storm; we called it a day and changed into a more autumnal routine. To my astonishment I found myself writing; not merely keeping regular hours (like Aldous!), but actually *writing*. A novel. No more contorted essays. A story, a plot, *people*. It was painful, hard work and a great joy. The breakthrough had come about in this way: Oriane even at her nicest could not lay off play-acting for long. Perhaps it was not play-acting, to assume a role was nature. With no Louis any more nor anyone or anything in particular to glamorise her (the worldly cousins had returned to their native Paris), she tried to make something out of me. She had exhausted the, always limited, exhibitionism of what she now alluded to as our sentimental past; for the present I had been treated like a younger sister who needed looking after, very nice for me but hardly enough feather in cap for her before the world. So she became a literary patroness. She convinced herself that I was a writer of much promise, overnight I was turned into her *jeune écrivain. Mon jeune écrivain* is staying with me, *mon jeune écrivain est en train de faire un bouquin formidable*, she would inform the busmen, Madame Panigon, the company at Chez Schwob, who all knew better. Nevertheless by the force of her expectations, by instructing Suzanne, the *bonne à tout faire*, to tiptoe to my needs, by putting the right table and ruled paper in my calm and spacious room, she transformed the myth into reality. Some kind of reality; I eventually did finish that first novel. It was about a young man in the South of France and his adventures; the title was *An Expense of Spirit* (an unkind friend added, *In a waste of time*). Not unpredictably it was diluted Aldous Huxley – Aldous Huxley and plain water. It went the publishers' round, turned down first by Chatto and Windus – rightly so but to my desolation at the time – then by several others.

While I laboured – ill-served by a handwriting so bad that I could not read it unless I put the words together in block letters – Philippe spent his mornings looking after his paperwork and his buses (which continued to devour money); Oriane went into Sanary to market and in general kept house. It was not something she was much interested in, yet like nearly all French women she was brought up to do it efficiently and smoothly. An impeccable house, fine linen, a punctual sequence of meals, well-cooked, well-presented, without ever invoking a husband's help, were a fundamental part of *bien-séance*, the peace and seemliness of domestic life. Both Oriane and Philippe were congenitally tidy; their cupboards, drawers, tool-shelves were an aesthetic pleasure to behold. Of all the orderly French households I have known, the Desmirails' was the most exquisite one.

Released at noon, lunching with them was the reward. I already mentioned their perfect manners to each other – no nagging or snapping in that ménage – manners that included listening to what the other had to say. Their morning's forays into Sanary yielded amusing gleanings. Like many intelligent people, like Aldous, like my mother, Philippe enjoyed gossip of which he was both a source and a conveyor. Intelligent gossip, as opposed to gossip *tout court*, makes for good conversation. Philippe, though far from being a local man, knew – or invented – a good deal about the secret histories of Sanary inhabitants; two of his favourite butts were a retired military gentleman called Rose, referred to as *le Général Rose allongé*, and a moustachioed spinster of uncertain sex whose actual name was Mademoiselle Casanova.

Over coffee, Philippe, like Alessandro, laid out his patience cards while Oriane sewed. Philippe had a special patience board that rested on his knees while he sat in a deep chair smoking one of his small clay pipes. Idle hands stood out in this house – another of Philippe's recreations was tinkering with chronometers or the smaller parts of their many aged cars – so I, too, played patience and found that indeed it soothed the nerves and mind. Then it was back to the grindstone, Philippe to his Compagnie des Transports, alleviated by a little tennis; I to piece together the next paragraph. Oriane retired with a book.

Presently final release – how I waited for that knock on the door – from my *métier de jeune écrivain*: Oriane and I had tea together. Companionably. Then we picked up the two dogs at the driver's wife's, set out by car to a good starting point and went for a long walk. By the time we were back, Philippe had returned; we changed into indoor clothes and spent the hour before dinner reading on the terrace. Separate books, shared comments. Bernard Grasset and other Parisian publishing houses still sent their new novels to Philippe; parcels of pristine books were arriving at La Pacifique every few days. Their pages uncut as was the way with French books then. There were paper-knives of all shapes to hand: Philippe cut all the pages of a book meticulously before reading a word; Oriane and I liked stages, we cut the first eight, read, were brought to a halt, cut again.

Dinner at eight. The food at the Desmirails' was curiously neutral. What we ate was as unsensual as good food – it was good food – can be. I once heard Oriane describe a dish as 'correct'. We might have been a thousand leagues from Provence: no aromatic herbs, no colour, no spices, no garlic; above all no garlic. *Une question d'éducation*, Philippe would tell me, a well-brought-up person does not eat garlic, it may cause offence to someone else who has not. That the dilemma does not arise in the Midi as *everyone* eats garlic did not deter him from this precept. A deeper reason for his gastronomic reticence was, I thought, his post-war recoil from some forms of Frenchness, a protest against his compatriots' pantagruelism. The protest included wine. The Desmirails drank water at their table, Evian or Vittel. That mineral water phase is something I suspect Philippe has well forgotten and would not like to be reminded of today when, among other things, he has become quite a distinguished viticulturist with whom his friends have shared innumerable good bottles. The asceticism of his past, during what I now see as his dormant years, was part of the recuperation from the trauma of the 1914 War – his tenuous survival after three brothers killed, for all his poise and air of balance, he was then a being still retarded in some aspects of a man's life.

Even then he had remained French enough to have found it incon-ceivable not to provide wine at his table for a guest. A carafe of decent red was placed by my glass at every meal and it was regarded as natural that I should freely help myself to it.

After dinner, Philippe might try to teach me something, rudiments of physics, the development of motor car construction; on these occasions Oriane, already well-instructed, knitted. Or we played a game, mah-jong, three-handed *belote*; often we quietly sat, each reading a book. At bedtime, around eleven, Oriane made and Philippe drank some cocoa.

Once a week the telephone call to Nice had to be made. It was always a Thursday, and the news was never good. My mother had not reacted well to any treatment. They had difficulties with her as a patient. She had got hold of something she should not and they were loath to accept the blame. There was trouble with a nurse she had taken against. Once she tried to leave without authorisation – escape I should have called it – something you are not allowed to do once you have signed a paper of commitment, and the surveillance had been able to prevent it. The worst was that when complete withdrawal of the drug had finally been achieved, my mother's physical condition was very low. Various secondary complaints were emerging. My mother, once so healthy, was now a very ill woman. They foresaw, spoke of, a drawn-out and difficult convalescence.

When might I see her?

Possibly soon. Though so far she had not asked for any member of her family. There was now one nurse she had got fond of, and who was able to do something for her.

I got into a state well before those calls. It began by Wednesday evening. The Desmirails were very good to me on these days.

The best of the week for me was Sunday, because on Saturday night Philippe brought the office typewriter, a great clumsy thing used by Josée, the 'overpaid' secretary, on working days. Philippe unfailingly carted it up to La Pacifique every Saturday and took it back on Monday morning. On Sunday I typed out what Oriane and I, keeping an ironic tone, called *mes oeuvres*. I transferred six days' harvest of block letters on to stiff white paper. Was it all right? Was it wonderful? Was it drivel? I hoped, I feared, I exulted: seeing it in type was almost as good as print.

One of the rituals established by Oriane for her young writer was her impressing on the maid Suzanne never to intrude on me with such things as cleaning. (Any writer, old or young, genuine or aspiring, would jump at such protection.) Kind Suzanne only took broom and duster to my room in my absence, a quick dip after luncheon. For a time all looked well. I love order, excessively so according to some of my Anglo-Saxon friends, but well below Desmirail standards. One day Oriane decided that my room needed a proper tidying up, which was done by Suzanne during one of our walks. Fretting that 'my papers' might have been disturbed or, God forbid, discarded, I did a thorough check afterwards. Everything was in place except for an aspirin tube that was missing from the dressing-table. That tube had been given me by my mother during those last days of vacillating before the clinic. Would I keep it for her *without* opening it and trying to look what was inside? Would I give my word? She did not hold with this much herself but trusted that I would. Naturally I promised. It was a very minor Bluebeard's chamber, an almost weightless aluminium tube that made no sound when you handled it. I gave it small importance – so many bizarre things were going on at the time. When I left Les Cyprès I packed it with my brushes and things, and left it on the dressing-table. Now it was missing; Suzanne must have thrown it away; I didn't like to ask about it – it had probably contained some nefarious substance we were better off without. I did not regard it as a sacred trust (safe for not opening and looking) and dismissed it from my thought.

It was a good, a healing, a peaceful life that I was leading at La Pacifique – even without the bonus of being made to write – and I am for ever grateful to the Desmirails, for their generosity and affection – they were angelic.

Perhaps not consistently angelic as Oriane went, that was not in her nature, something drove her – it got worse in later life – to show claws from time to time. One evening at dinner – we were alone, some crisis with a theatre bus was holding Philippe at the garage – as I was helping myself again from the carafe of wine (a third glass? a fourth? I drank a good deal for my age), Oriane said in a velvet voice, 'You know, *ma chérie*, I should be *careful* in your place – after all, *ta mère est une morphiniste.*'

Instantly she was appalled (far more than I was) and cried forgiveness. 'How could I? *Je suis méchante.*' I understood or thought I did; we calmed each other, being certain that not a word of this would be breathed from either to Philippe.

Oriane talked a good deal on our walks. Some of them led to or passed by hide-outs – an abandoned hut, a sheltered clearing – she had discovered (used?). I thought of Louis. She was talking of other men. Future men. A banker in Paris, very clever, an *ambitieux* who would go far, who was waiting only for a sign from her . . . but he was middle-aged. The driver of bus number one was giving her smiles, but would need encouragement, a very well-set-up young fellow, one's husband's chauffeur – would it be amusing to be the French Lady Chatterley? (I'd like to have heard my mother's comment on *that*.) Her younger cousin's husband was mad about her too – I'd seen him: wasn't he handsome? – it would serve Adrienne right, she's been cuckolding him enough *and* she tried throwing herself at Philippe, on the other hand an affair en famille wasn't what one really wanted, was it?

What, I thought, shocked and puzzled, did Oriane want? Excitement? Amusement? Vanity appeased? There were elements of these in many love affairs . . . To *that* degree? *And what of Philippe?* Yes – one knew about Philippe's version of the post-war code of marital laisser-faire, his was based on tolerance (with a pinch of lassitude, indifference?), this was not unmatched by Oriane: her springboard was triviality and one-upmanship; her permissiveness, in thought if not in deed, lacked dignity (let alone the spontaneity of the Kisling milieu). Oriane talked a good deal about Philippe, how she loved and admired him. And in fact she did. They were inseparable, she believed (and would do her best, her worst, to keep them so), and they were alike: two of the same mould. Their tragedy was that he, too, believed this, at least for a long time. They were *not* alike, not in their characters (his had strength, hers self-will), not in their values. The twin-act of their youth was trompe-l'oeil; their affinity – so marked in their looks – a product of education, milieu, manners, a few shared tastes and distastes, and the great illusion of their marriage. They were just alike enough not to strike fire in each other as lovers; they were too unlike for her to go on subscribing to the fundamental tenets of his nature, his exceptional gentleness, probity, moderation; too unlike for him – once he awoke to it – to go on forbearing the lack of them in her.

There was a hunger in Oriane to be effective, to make a great splash, a longing for fulfilment, love, vocation; she had courage, dare-devilry and a taste for outrage, and if fate, as was likely, would fail to deal her the great hand, she would go hunting for it like a thwarted feline beast.

(Did all women carry the seeds of their own destruction? Toni . . . my mother . . . Doris . . . Cécile . . . Yet there was also Renée; and Rosie, dear sweet ugly Rosie; they were sound.)

While I was living under the Desmirails' roof, these misgivings about their mutual future were intimations, thoughts crystallising below the surface of my mind; what occupied it then, and is forgotten now, was the character of the young man in my novel, of whom I remember nothing except that he was likely to have spouted Mallarmé and Catullus, and that he had a mistress, a teasing, ravishing woman in her thirties whose name was Marie-Laure de Sainte-Trinide.

In the meantime, when I did not think of the clinic at Nice – which I did not as often as I could manage – I was happy.

7

When my mother was at last allowed to come home, we prepared for her, and ourselves, as well or as badly as we knew how. A young nurse, who had travelled with her, helped her out of the hired car. My mother held on to her arm – slowly they walked up the drive. The woman Alessandro and I saw approaching was gaunt and moved awkwardly. She returned our greetings with a vague compliance. We saw her face: it was lined, there were grey streaks in the chestnut hair; the eyes were dull.

When I had seen her at the clinic (lately I had been allowed to do so a few times), she was someone ill in a hospital bed, made ready for a visit, pronounced too tired to talk much – she was afflicted with acute pain and stiffness in her joints – I had not expected her to be herself. Here, upright, dressed and 'cured', the change struck home.

We went indoors. It was around three o'clock in the afternoon, seldom the best of times for an arrival. She sat down. I sat down. The nurse said it was time for her to be going. She kissed my mother who as if panic-stricken held on to her hand, then wordlessly let it go. Alessandro conducted the young woman to the car.

I had moved back into Les Cyprès two days before. Alessandro was already there. He had re-painted our hole of a bathroom to make it look brighter, and constructed a special table for the books and papers my mother liked to have about her bed. Maria (the Huxleys were back in Sanary) had filled the house with flowers, the room was scented with them and the late autumn fruit I had brought and arranged in a leaf-lined basket; La Grosse Hélène had put her energies into a cleaning; the dogs were there. My mother was as indifferent to their greeting as she had been to ours and all the rest.

Alessandro returned. (He had had a word with the nurse who told him that 'adjustment' was a difficult thing. The first days could be the worst; someone discharged had to be looked after with great care. Alessandro had looked after my mother always, no one better than he, *as a man looks after a woman.* Not a son, not a sick-nurse. Moreover – like myself, like many people who have known little of it – he feared and distrusted illness.)

'Would you like to go to bed now?' he asked. 'I suppose so.' She looked about her despondently. 'There isn't anything much else to do.'

I took her into their bedroom. 'How primitive the plumbing arrangements are in this house – is this all the running water you can manage here?' It was said with resigned surprise rather than reproachfully. 'You were comfortable at the clinic then?' I said, recalling my glimpses of it – a cross between a luxurious hotel and a discreet madhouse; I was also thinking of the bills.

'Comfortable?' she said, '*comfortable?* Oh, I suppose in a sense it was, one never lifted a finger.'

She looked at the large bed. The expression on her face was half fearful, half sullen. 'I think,' she said very slowly, 'that I shall require nocturnal solitude. Will you tell him that?' It would not be the last time that she was conveying a message to Alessandro indirectly.

That evening he moved his things into the spare room. I did not intrude on, nor wish to know about, his relief.

My mother's physical condition improved. She was able to move quite easily again, but her spirits were very low, and they infected us and everything we did. All her responses were grey. Nothing pleased her; few things markedly displeased her: she had become acquiescent. She talked little. Her zest for analysis had gone and so, except for a touch of hauteur shown now and again to Alessandro, apparently had her temper. In place of the alternating personalities of last summer, we were finding a new third.

I tried to break through by asking, 'Mummy, you are still very unhappy?' 'Happy . . . Unhappy . . . ' she said in the new slow way, 'I can't imagine happiness, I can't imagine anything. *Is* there anything?' She was afflicted by what they talk of in the carefree Midi, where it is said to strike in the afternoons, as *le cafard*, that heavy unmovable black thing that sits upon man's spirit and turns the finest day, the brightest prospect, into dust and ashes.

The man at Nice had given my mother a letter to a GP at Bandol. We were afraid now of all doctors. That one, a well-disposed, common-sensible, *homme-moyen-sensuel* sort of chap, was reassuring. Yes, he told us, she was going through a phase of depression. *Pauvre femme.* Not much to be done about it medically (not at that time, not at Bandol). He advised some mild sedative, Sedobrol or her ineffectual old friend, Paciflorine, and warned us to keep her from heavy sleeping pills. Distractions? rest? – they would not signify. Just patience . . . Time . . .

We tried to make her eat – she was far too thin – and get up and dress at least once a day. Alessandro and I cooked the things she liked, Madame Panigon (always kind to our faces) sent round some exquisite soup she had made herself. My mother would sit up wearily, drumming her fingers on the table, listlessly eating just enough to forestall comment and cajoling, waiting for Alessandro to re-fill her glass, then greedily gulp her wine. We used to tease her about how little she would drink, often no more than half a glass of claret with her dinner. Now, we did not resist her demand, 'Come on,' she said, 'amuse me, *if* you can.' I tried to talk about life at the Desmirails'. 'Oh dear,' she said, 'not exactly amusing, I'd call it a eulogy: first it was Oriane, now it is Philippe – my poor child, all your geese are swans.' She reached across Alessandro for the bottle. 'Are you asleep?' she said to him. The wine was bringing back something of herself. It was a relief.

The Huxleys gave my mother a kitten, an offspring of Matelot and Pussy, their Siamese couple. It was a beautiful small animal with creamy pale fur and all the right black tips. My mother took it into her arms and on to her bed where it made its home. Siamese are eclectic devils, this one allowed himself to be taken to by her. She called him Uley, which was the way the Huxleys' name was pronounced by the locals, Hs and Xs not trundling readily off their tongues. She played with Uley, with the papers on her bed for toys; she fed him on the best bits off her plate; when she got up she carried him in her arms. The dogs, whom she was still indifferent to, got up to trouble, she quelling them. It was the first breaking out of her deadly negativity.

As my mother was picking up, she became chummy with La Grosse Hélène, sending her off in mid-housework to do errands. (Could it be cashing cheques for her at the bank?) La Grosse Hélène, knowing and bonhomous, treated all of us with a mixture of the maternal and the insolent.

My mother became brighter, spurts of optimism with intervals of sullenness; she took to talking again. Some of our dinners were animated once more. At last she began speaking about the clinic, not about horrors – about people, staff, fellow patients. Now we learned that she had struck up a friendship with a Russian, a White Russian émigré, not in his first youth, who was undergoing his sixteenth detoxification cure. '*Sixteenth*. I'm not going through a *second*. Ever. That I promise you.'

Alessandro and I sat with folded hands and prayers in our hearts.

The Russian, his name was Ivan, 'Not very original of him, or rather of his father; but then that wretched man was stuck with Ivan as well: my Russian is Ivan Ivanovich.' Well, he had gone through the gamut, cocaine, hashish, opium, heroin. Opium was the best, he told her, if one learned one's way about it, one could make it last the longest. The Russian, a man of infinite finesse and cultivation, said that she would never get the full perfection of Turgenev unless she learned to read him in the original; she needn't trouble to learn Russian for Tolstoy whose style at times was clumsy, *he* read better in translations. She missed Ivan Ivanovich . . . She implied he had admired her. They had promised they would meet some day, when he came out, whenever that was; he did not trust himself for long in the outside world.

'I think I shall learn Russian. He's already taught me the Cyrillic alphabet.' She fished for paper and pencil and fluently produced 4 Cyrillics. Then cried out, 'Oh don't look at me as though I'd performed a circus trick – you are treating me as if I were a dangerous animal. I still am . . . Oh do I know what I am?'

Alessandro got up and uncertainly patted her arm. 'You see?' she said with a sneer.

On other evenings she would lament for the young nurse. '*There* was someone who knew what one needs when one's not well. She read one's thought.'

'That's because she is a nurse,' Alessandro said, unwisely perhaps.

For these evenings would end either in sudden flatness or in the now renewed tirades against Alessandro. To his face, behind his back.

'*He* brought me to this,' she would cry in sudden fury.

I tried to imply that *this* was over, must be put behind, she burst out, 'After what has happened to *me*! My ruined . . . health.' (She was unable yet to speak of the ruin of her looks.)

She slept heavily and long, sometimes into the afternoon. One day I came across the gin bottle in her bed. It fell out, it was empty, a bottle of Gordon's gin. She first pretended that I was dreaming, then that the bottle got there by accident.

The second time this happened – I had not waited for the bottle to fall and it was not empty – she was furious.

'And if you dare tell anyone, least of all the medical Cerberus at Bandol . . .'

So it was not just to cash cheques that La Grosse Hélène had been sent into Sanary.

'I believe that woman steals,' my mother said to me, 'are you missing anything?' No, of course not. 'Are you *quite* sure?'

'Quite sure,' I said. 'With all her faults, that's the last thing Hélène would do. She's honest. I dare say she steals our good name.'

'We haven't got a good name. With the loose life my husband leads.'

It had been predictable, the common-sensical Bandol GP said. And you can't stop her. They always find ways of getting at it. Try to make her take less, try to make it look natural, convivial, drink *with* her.

So we got in vermouth, orange juice, angostura, ice, and suggested wouldn't it be jolly if we had gin slings, Tom Collinses together or whatever. Goodness how false it rang. My mother wasn't taken in, that didn't suit her at all. She wanted her secret – to retire from time to time, return to bed with Uley and a bottle.

For a time she managed this rather well. It enabled her to be almost normal and up and about at most times. She went out by herself, shopping, to the hairdresser. The grey streaks in her hair disappeared, a good sign. Her taste for social life revived. She called on people, sometimes at odd hours, was invited on her own and went – almost on time – to lunch with the Panigons, the Kislings, the Huxleys. She even called on Oriane. (Philippe she avoided; she had an instinct about the granite below the graceful comportment.) And the best of it was that she was no longer immersed in depression, no longer desperate. What was bad, very bad, was her continuing hostility to

Alessandro. She treated him with mockery and scorn, making him feel a criminal, a worm. He bore the assaults with great courage.

'Don't you *want* to go and see your concubine?' she asked him in my presence.

He controlled himself with difficulty; in a sudden flash I realised that his anguish was about my mother's behaviour and not about poor Doris. Admiration as well as love for my mother had filled almost all of his adult life; for on to a year now she had been destroying her beloved self before his eyes. He could not bear it.

When I sought him out later, a possible time had come to ask, '*Do you want to see Doris?*' Oh no, he said. That could not be renewed. It had been paid for too dearly.

Soiled and spoilt, I thought. 'What is happening to her?'

He groaned. Poor little Doris. She would not go back to Paul. She no longer accepted his money. She was working for some political association, immersing herself in active German politics, ultra left-wing. Paul was heart-broken. 'I wish I were dead,' Alessandro said.

My mother received letters from her Russian, Ivan Ivanovich. She would snatch them, take them to her bed, hide them under a pillow. Perhaps they were love letters; perhaps she liked us to believe they were.

She had acquired a Russian grammar. Time she did something to improve her mind, and Uley liked to be called by Russian endearments. She might also take up soon her essay on Stendhal and Flaubert. She was talking to me as she used to, often very sweetly. So I told her about the novel I had started at the Desmirails' and not touched since.

She was serious about that. Did I realise how difficult it was to write a *good* novel? Perhaps the most difficult, and rewarding, of literary forms. She herself would have given everything – no, not everything, as her life would appear to have proved, but a great deal – to have written something: to have achieved that translation from experience into art. Might she have had the necessary talent? One could never tell unless one tried – and trying was work. 'I've never learned to work.' Writing was something one had to give oneself to like a vocation. If it hadn't been for all those love stories . . . Lived, alas not written.

As for me, her daughter, I might bring it off or I might not. *If* I had the talent, if I accepted that writing had to be served. 'Never look over your shoulder, don't think of a public, or reputation, or money – follow your inspiration, if you have it, then do your damnedest to pin it down, prune it, lick it into shape.' And it would be best for me not to marry, not to burden myself with a house and child. She grinned. 'Oh I know they all think I haven't burdened myself enough with you. But then I have *not* become a writer, here's a nice non sequitur. And now you must leave me. I need a little rest.' She smiled engagingly again, 'I will have a little nip and Uley may have a drop of it in his milk. I don't particularly want him to grow into a huge cat.'

On Christmas Eve my mother and I – Alessandro had some work that entailed his spending a few days at Aix – had dinner at the Huxleys in Maria's basement kitchen dining-room (Maria's entertaining was unconventional long before it became willy-nilly so for most of us). My mother brought Uley who was entirely ignored by his parents; Aldous was fascinated by this parental detachment and compared it favourably with human family patterns. He was himself much attached to the cool father, Matelot, who liked being in his, Aldous's, work-room, perching on his shoulder as he typed. So we sat at Maria's large oilcloth-covered table, talking Siamese cats, eating rose-leaf jam and salted almonds shunted to and fro on a miniature railway young Matthew had constructed for the occasion; my mother was in a good mood. It seemed possible again that life was tolerable.

We jogged along. For weeks on end my mother was quiet and aloof, Alessandro came and went, a peace was kept. I was writing again. A little and not easily. One winter afternoon I came back from a walk with Oriane, I had found her edgy, seething with discontent. She couldn't stand the silly buses, the dull life at Sanary any more, nor Philippe's stance that it did not matter what kind of work one was doing as long as one did one's best. (One's best! When money was going down the drain, drivers' wives were being treated in private clinics for ridiculous complaints at the Company's expense, and a rival line had started a service from Bandol!) *She* was going to Paris to see theatres and some civilised people, or she might well go to Switzerland and take a rest-cure in a sanatorium, where they were able to do wonders for one's nerves. '*Comment, idiote, tu ne savais pas que je souffre des nerfs?*' I managed to soothe her, said that I would find Paris better for *my* nerves than Lausanne, and went home. In the hall I was met by a faint smell of ether. Quicker than thought, my limbs began to shake, arms and legs doing an independent little dance. It was an odd experience; only after seconds, did my mind make the connection – this is what she cleans the needles of her syringe with. It had begun again.

When I first attacked her, she denied it. Ridiculous suspicions; we were degrading her with our surveillance. When it became more obvious – there were other signs besides the smell of ether, once we were alerted – she made the admission with a kind of triumph: what fools we had been.

'How long has this been going on?'

'None of your business any more.'

And so it turned out to be. One thing, both Alessandro and I made clear, we would have no hand in it this time. No assistance with the spirit-lamp, the whole witch's set-up, no touting in pharmacies. My mother said she did not need or want our help.

'You can do nothing to prevent me,' she said lucidly, 'short of extremes you would not envisage such as reporting me to the French authorities who might deport me or get me locked up – or very likely wash their hands of the whole thing. Equally it would be impracticable for you to deprive me entirely of money. You could keep me short of course, but we have credit . . . '

She was right. We had no weapons we could use.

Aldous and Maria had gone to London in January and would not be back for some time.

We did not ask when and how she got the stuff. The probable, simple answer was Joyeu. She had resumed resorting to the impenetrable Joyeu.

Once she saw that our sense of impotence had sunk in, she spoke more softly. 'Don't be so upset, don't be so afraid . . . It will not be like the other time. I can assure you of that. I shall be the master – my Russian friend taught me a good deal – I shall not let myself become a slave again. I shall control this two-edged offering of the devil and the gods, treat it as my escape, my treasure; I must ration the hours in my artificial paradise. Yes – it is that; and now I am cast out of any other. Though believe me – as you can't, poor mortals, because you have not tried it – the artificial one may well be the best, and one *can* return to it at will. I shall return as an acolyte, a visitor, *not* an addict.' She believed herself and there was pride in her voice.

I could have cried, 'You already are an addict or you would not have dared return.'

Indeed for a time – months – things were not terrible. My mother did ration herself: three or four times a week perhaps (we did not enquire too closely). In the interims, gin, wine, veronal at night. She kept herself quiet, hoarding states of mind; to me she could talk intimately at times, this always melted me; with Alessandro she kept a wary reserve. Once or twice she called him the poor boy. He applied himself to such work as was at hand.

*   *   *

Drugged or not, my mother did not like to be alone in the house of an evening; if one of us went out, the other had to stay in. We had been trying to keep up the ritual of family dinner, too often it fell apart. I was doing no work, and got away from home as much as I could. The Kislings and their friends were welcoming, I was seeing them regularly again; I also took to spending evenings at Bandol, meeting new people. It was spring, and hotels and bars were filling up. Those I met there knew nothing about me and our history, and this gave me the freedom to appear as what I chose to be. I was attracted by some of them and found that they were attracted to me. I began having affairs. They were not very serious or lasting, but they were with people I liked, often admired, and liked being with. It was friendly and sensual and open, the Kisling doctrine, as interpreted by me, in action; I was joyfully carried away. Not so much by any single lover – although these affairs were beside much else affectionate – as by the climate of love-making, the adventurousness of it, and the direct new way of entering into the lives of adults at ease with themselves. I was fortunate, or I chose well, for most of these were charming people, good people, some even remarkable ones. With many of them I remained friends a long time after, often for life. Only one or two were mistakes I don't like to think about. (Some of this began in that spring; it did *not* happen all at once.)

My mother called me to her room one morning, she was up and dressed and putting franc-notes into a bag. The two young dogs – who had been taken on again and were making reasonably good ménage with Uley – were watching her from the bed. 'I'm going to take the bus into Toulon,' she said in an off-hand way, 'I need that thing I gave you to keep for me.' What thing? 'The little aspirin tube, in September before . . . I went away.'

Oh that. 'I do remember now. I'm afraid it's gone.'

'*Gone*? Impossible!'

I explained how it had disappeared, got thrown away while I was at the Desmirails'. 'But didn't you know what was in it?'

'I didn't look. You told me not to, I had to give you my word.'

'Good God! What a fool you are, schoolboy's honour again. What *have* I brought into the world?'

'Mummy, what *was* in it?' I asked, really curious now.

There she hung fire. 'A scrap of paper,' she said at last.

. . . ?

'A receipt.'

'Oh that's why the tube was so light and made no noise. A receipt for what?'

'From the Mont-de-Piété at Toulon.' The pawn shop.

I thought I saw light. 'Did you pawn something, Mummy? The family silver? There isn't any.'

'It *was* family in a way – it was your father's . . . it was your gold cigarette case. Didn't you miss it?'

. . .

'I did it last summer, you see,' she said hurriedly, 'I needed some money, I don't remember what for, but I needed it. And you never used it. Well, I took it to the Mont-de-Piété and a miserable sum they gave me for it, those French misers, I forget how much, but it was miserable, such good solid gold too. I was going to redeem it of course before you found out. But then I had to leave, so I hid the receipt in the tube and entrusted it to you. See what that led to!'

My father's cigarette case. I had put it away carefully in a drawer with some sweaters I hadn't worn for some time.

'What would you have done if I *had* missed it?'

'We'd all have thought that La Grosse Hélène or someone . . . '

'La Grosse Hélène wasn't with us then,' I said furiously, 'we still had Emilia. No such hideous thought about her would have occurred to any of us.'

'No recriminations, please. You say it wouldn't occur to you that Emilia stole your gold case, but it can occur to you that your mother did?'

'My mother did steal my case,' I said. And then we didn't know whether to laugh or cry. 'You are the most impossible woman in the world.'

'Maybe so. Darling girl, I see you really mind.'

'It has been pawned before,' I said.

'*Has* it?' She brightened. '*You* did?'

'Well, not exactly.'

'Tell me.'

So I told her how in the age of innocence it used to be pawned by Susan Robbins to help make ends meet at the end of the month.

'Strike me pink,' said my mother, 'that isn't at all what I imagined your life with the Robbinses to be.'

'You imagined what I let you imagine,' I said.

'You mean you deceived me?'

'I did not strive to enlighten you. And you made it easy.'

She laughed. 'Not all schoolboy's honour – perhaps a chip off the old block after all? But why? Why didn't you let me have the full picture?'

Yes, why? 'Fear of change. I was all right with them. I used to be afraid of being with you at times, life with you could be incalculable.'

'Wasn't it that with the Robbinses, dashing from pillar to post to escape creditors?'

'Calculably incalculable. I wasn't involved with them; I felt free.'

'Curious truths seem to be coming out this morning,' my mother said. 'Perhaps we had better address ourselves to the task of getting your cigarette case back, now that you lost the receipt.'

That proved a sleeveless errand. My mother didn't remember the expiry date, six months? a year after taking it in? and she didn't remember that date either. She wanted me to engage Philippe – or the Kislings or somebody – to pull strings. I finally told Oriane, as the least shockable. She tried to get some bureaucratic process going; the ramifications were endless, we had no proof of any kind, none of us including myself tried very hard: it was just one of those things one has to learn to let go.

It was soon after that disclosure – connected with it or not – that my mother's upper hand was evidently slipping. The rationing had become slacker, she was resorting to her secret every day now, possibly more than once.

She loved talking about it – as she must have with her Russian – describing it as one might poetic dreams (these were the days before LSD). She told me that the effect was different now from the first time when she took it to overcome jealousy and rage; now she was taking it for itself, a purer aim. She wanted me to try. Just once so that I would know the nature of the experience.

One afternoon she handed me an ampoule; when I shrank from it she told me that there was no need for a hypodermic, not for a first time; I would probably reach something if I just drank it and stayed quiet. (Once I had seen her let Uley lick a drop from the syringe off her finger; Uley gave a little sneeze, then spat.) I took the ampoule to my room and lay down on my bed. (Alessandro was out of the house.) I held this tiny glass thing in my hand. Yes or No? There could not be the remotest chance of my getting caught by it, not by one small dose, but there was a revulsion. Yet I was curious. I would get to know what it was like, what it was like for her. What *was* it like? At the same time I felt a strong resistance, and a voice saying it was wicked to play with such a thing. For a long time I lay undecided, with the sun coming in through the half-closed shutters. In the end it was No.

When I returned the ampoule to her, she said, 'Not enough courage?'

My mother's action that afternoon brought me a plausible insight into the enigma of Docteur Joyeu. Proselytism.

My mother became convinced that La Grosse Hélène was spying on her – there was no *need* for spying – and took to locking her door whenever she went out. Hers was the only room in the house that had lock and key. Of course that key got lost soon. One day we came in together. 'Where is it? My key?' Nowhere. What to do – a locksmith? My mother with quick resource fetched a flat-iron and smashed one of the lower panels of the door. It gave easily – 'Flimsy,' she said – leaving an opening roughly the size and shape of that of an average dog-kennel. My mother got down on the floor and wriggled through this aperture with astonishing agility and invited me to follow her. I declined to be a snake woman.

'It's easy,' she cried from within, 'do come.' I remained obstinate. Her head appeared near floor-level. 'Then we must talk from where we are. Bring a cushion, I've got one.'

I fetched a cushion and we soon began talking quite normally, each crouching by one side of the hole. She reminded me how, when we were living in that villa on the hill, she used to eat her dinner on a stool by the fire off a tray while I insisted on having mine upright at a proper table. 'You're still pompous and bourgeois.'

When Alessandro came in and saw us, he swore – most rare – and slammed the passage door on what to him must have appeared the ultimate in disorder.

For some reason this situation continued for several days, my mother wriggling in and out of her room (quite inaccessible now to La Grosse Hélène) utterly, as it were, in her stride. Maria, too, caught us talking from our respective positions by the kennel, and must have reported it to Aldous. Years later I found the incident related in *Eyeless in Gaza*. Here also, it is the daughter (bearing not the slightest resemblance to me) who converses through the dog-hole with Mrs Amberley, the narrator's ex-mistress who has fallen into deplorable ways. There are embroideries and inaccuracies (to *my* mind) – novelist's licence – and of course Mary Amberley is no more, or less, my mother than she is the other one or two women Aldous was supposed by critics, friends and gossips to have used as a model for her character and conduct. There remains, however, a good deal of analogy. Huxley makes that mother and daughter scene – much play with a hypodermic – very distressing, including sordid detail. Invented? Observed by Maria and erased by me from memory? I would not like to tell. Rereading that chapter – buried in that overlong, chronologically jumbled novel – I am struck how *much* Aldous and Maria must have seen and interpreted at the time.

When the book first came out (in 1937), I was horror-struck – unmentionables disclosed (and distorted). When I remonstrated, Maria told me that he would put anything he got hold of into a book; sooner or later and in his own way. So if I had a story I didn't want to see in print, 'Don't tell Aldous.' (Perhaps I *had* told him a good deal.)

*   *   *

I received a communication from England advising me that the date for sitting that interpreter's exam had come. I'd forgotten nearly all about it, but jumped at the opportunity. It could be stretched into a week, ten days, in London; I had not been back for over a year.

My mother said, Oh yes, your education – You'll pass it with flying colours no doubt. I was less certain of that. (With reason.) Alessandro conceived a different hope – looking after her on his own, might it not, just possibly, soften her view of him? Help to mend? My own fear was that this could no longer happen – the springs of his present love were anxiety and guilt while the one thing that might still bring her about would be his desiring her as a woman. This, I knew instinctively, he did not, and when that is so the opposite will take its place. (I had learned a few things lately.) She had, irretrievably it would seem, impaired her looks; there was the disorder, the lack of care for her own person . . .

All *I* had in mind was to turn my back on it all for a space of time.

I said I did not know where I would be. I didn't want to stay cooped up at the flat on Parliament Hill. Toni found me a cheap room near the British Museum in what turned out to be a temperance hotel. I went to see the sisters at once and had a cheerful welcome from Toni. I found her coping, coping well; she had made her bed, she had chosen her future life, she had *done right* – she was going to get on with it. No complaining. The divorce was through and, although the decree had not yet been made absolute, Toni regarded this as sufficient to enable her to do what she had been looking forward to: seeing Jamie occasionally. He would come of an afternoon, they would walk the dog – who needed male company – come back to the flat for tea, with or without Rosie. The sisters would ask his advice about this and that; he was anxious that they should install a telephone, offering to pay the initial cost.

Toni refused. 'A telephone for what? For Rosie to call that man (the Judge) in comfort?'

About the fact that Jamie had incontestably moved in with Cynthia, she was unexpectedly tolerant. 'It's his business now, isn't it?'

Her present aim was finding a job to supplement her alimony, and Jamie was about to get her one; she was concentrating on saving enough money to go to Italy – she knew exactly where and when, La Scala, San Carlo, Rome – to hear a certain (very great) opera singer. Wayward or not, I was delighted by this recovery of her spirit; she asked what had been happening to *me*. I found it wrong to leave her and Rosie any longer in the dark. (I reflected that my mother knew *their* stories.) I tried to understate ours and to make it sound as undistressing as I could. They were distressed, and found it difficult to take in. One of Toni's reactions was to deplore what she called my environment; her duty was to write to my German guardians to inform them. The old threat from a new quarter.

I could not resist teasing her by telling her something of my own goings-on. 'Now you can think of me as badly as you liked to think of the Finchingfield women.'

'I refuse to think badly of you. I always treated you as an exception.'

'To what? To your rules?'

'They are *my* rules,' she said stiffly. I felt moved and a little flattered. Toni added sternly, 'I don't know why I do.'

Rosie was not buoyant; tense instead and unlike herself, when I was finally able to see her alone – not easy, but on my second afternoon Toni went off to a singing lesson – she told me point-blank that the Judge was in terrible trouble. Worse trouble than ever before. Not *gambling*? A form of gambling, the most perilous there was. I probably hadn't even heard of it.

Hadn't he given his word?

It wasn't horses or cards, this was not covered by his promise. He was speculating on the Stock Exchange, real hard speculation, taking risks on purpose – that was the essence of it, that was the thrill. Buying on margin, staking large sums one has not got on long odds of a stock falling or rising. It had gone well for him several times and he loved, he craved the excitement. Now it was not going well at all. He was in desperate danger.

'I didn't know anything about it for a long time. He didn't tell me what the trouble was two summers ago when we couldn't get to Sanary. Then some shares turned and did what he had staked them to do and he was saved. Just in time.'

And now, a few weeks ago, he *had* told her. He was in so deep that his friends – whom he had not told – would not or even could not bail him out. He sold the few pictures he had inherited, had a huge overdraft at his bank, owed more, much more, to his broker. Nothing very short of a miracle could save him.

'*Is* there a chance of a miracle?'

'He says there is.'

'And if not . . . ?'

'He will have to go bankrupt,' Rosie said. 'Resign from the Bench. And *that* is his life. The gambling is a kind of fantasy, perhaps because all the rest came to him so easy.'

It sank in – the uproar, the scandal. Poor man! But then I saw that he was not a man of whom one should say 'poor man'.

We sat silent for a while, in stony despair. Life is not tolerable, I thought; it is not what one feels when one sits in the shade, wine in one's glass, friends by one's side, looking at leaves and a sun-drenched column.

Presently, when I heard her key in the door, I asked, 'Does Toni know about this?'

'She does not. Nobody knows. It will come soon enough. Don't look so worried. It will be a bad time. Jack will rise above it. He says we'll live abroad. Perhaps we'll go to Australia or somewhere.'

I'll pull him through, was Rosie's meaning.

From the minute I began sitting my exam, I knew I was in the wrong place. I looked at the other people, the clothes they'd put on – a serious undertaking and I had come entirely unprepared. I carried an old fountain pen and a parcel with a bottle of Fino sherry I had picked up at a wine merchant's nearby to take back afterwards. I was called in for a viva and that was easy enough; I felt – or perhaps imagined – that I was surprising them favourably. Back with the papers before me, the questions, the task, I knew that it was hopeless and I had been a fool. My handwriting alone would be my undoing. The results, I was told, would be out in three months; they would be forwarded to my address abroad. I was wondering how I could best manage to keep them secret until my majority which was now just under a year off. Was I acting like a crook? Perhaps I was a crook.

*   *   *

Rosie told me that Jamie and Cynthia were going to get married in the autumn. It had not been a design on Cynthia's part – she'd had no particular desire to marry anyone again – Jamie had been so lost, she

323

was doing it out of a sense of obligation. Whatever the original motive may have been, I like to say here – though it goes beyond the time-span of this story – that they were happy together: Jamie's second marriage turned out well, and it brought him the children he had wanted and Toni would not or could not have. He remained a friend to Toni. And to Rosie. When the Second World War came with the threat of a Nazi invasion, he assisted his Jewish ex-sister-in-law to change her name from Falkenheim to his Scottish one. Rosie became Miss Nairn, and the sisters once more shared a name.

A few days after the shameful exam, I went first to the National Gallery then to Parliament Hill to pick up Toni. I was going to treat her to luncheon. Not at Schmidt's; at Bertorelli's. At least they were both in Charlotte Street. Toni was getting ready, the front door bell rang. Jamie stood in the passage at twelve o'clock in the morning unannounced. He didn't see me at first. 'Is Billi here? Her mother is in London. She telephoned me at the shop. She's not well, she wants Billi at once.'

I opened my mouth and screamed. I could hear it, it didn't stop. I knew I could stop it – it was voluntarily involuntary – it went on. I was amazed by the sound. So were Toni and Jamie. He said, 'What's wrong?'

I shall not go into all the details of my mother's escapade. I found her, as she had advised Jamie, at the Tavistock Hotel in Bloomsbury. She was worn out by the journey, and a touch apprehensive about what she had let herself in for. 'Oh, I wanted to surprise you, I thought it might be fun if I shared your little holiday. I want to go to some exhibitions, look up one or two people . . . '

She had already done so. Straight from Victoria to the house of a Bloomsbury writer, a one-time admirer (possibly). I gathered it had not been a success: he had called another taxi, taken her to the Tavistock Hotel and booked her in; there had been no mention of any further engagement. That was last night. This morning she remembered the name of the booksellers where Jamie worked, got the number out of the book, and here I was.

'Does Alessandro know where you are?' I asked.

'Of course not. He hasn't the slightest idea. Probably scouring the opium dens of Toulon for me. I wanted to play him a trick – *he* ran off to Spain, didn't he?'

. . .

'It seemed such a good idea yesterday, or was it the day before yesterday?' Alessandro was out, she found some money and her passport, packed a small bag, took the bus into Toulon and caught an express to Paris. She tipped the guard and he found her a wagon-lit. Well, then the Calais train, the boat, the boat-train. 'You know the route . . . tedious.' She added lamely, 'Now once I'm here we ought to be enjoying ourselves.' It transpired that she was getting short of money *and* short of her ampoules.

'I find I need more with all these exertions, it isn't at all the same as being peaceful at Les Cyprès with Uley.'

I went downstairs to get a telegram off to Alessandro.

We got to one or two galleries, even a theatre, a shop in the Burlington Arcade where she tried to buy me a scarf – nothing came off; all, like the traffic, the press of people on pavements, was to her both intrusive and remote. Once, seeing her walk into a restaurant: imperious, commanding a decent table, I saw her as others would see her – an apparition, emaciated, with a macabre elegance about her; the lined, intense face still beautiful – not a Giorgione any longer, a Rembrandt woman, an ageing Jewess howling by a wall.

I knew that she was scared, wanted it all undone, get wafted home. *How?*

Jamie arranged the appointment with a GP. He was pompous, distant, shocked. He prescribed what was necessary to see her through on condition that she left the country in twenty-four hours. It was no empty threat.

With her new supply, she became more relaxed. The English stuff was beautiful, far superior to what she could get in France . . . She urged me to get Jamie to set up a second visit, with another GP of course . . . Then there was the journey money, the lack of it. I had mine, but she had no return ticket; she would have to travel in comfort. I had to ask Rosie. She became flustered, embarrassed, unhappy – she was unable . . . she didn't have . . . 'Please don't explain,' I told her, having become all these things too. She did explain. She wanted to.

She had given what she had to the Judge, her savings and what she got for the bits of jewellery kept from Berlin. 'I mean I *lent* it to Jack; persuading him to take it wasn't at all easy.'

'Was it the Stock Exchange? Bait for the miracle?'

'No, no. *That* needs other amounts, I had very little. It's for him – to live. He's come to the limit of his overdraft, he doesn't dare cash a cheque at his clubs. With what I could give him, he was able to pay the quarter's rent, and give money to his clerk to go out for a newspaper or cigars. We have sandwiches sent in now in the evening.'

Jamie again. He paid for my mother's ticket, helped to get us on the train. The journey back was chaotic. My mother fainted on the boat and had to be carried ashore by a pair of British sailors. In Paris, she refused to go straight on to the Gare de Lyon, we had to make a stopover that lasted more than twenty-four hours, with my patience beyond breaking-point at all times. When we ultimately reached Les Cyprès, she was gratified if exhausted. To Alessandro she said, 'I hope you are feeling the better for my little absence.' In fact he looked almost as ill as she did.

*   *   *

After London, I strove to go out every night. Often it was not possible before my mother had gone to sleep. I would sit and watch for every yawn. 'Isn't it time for your Paciflorine?' 'Oh, time. Very well, you may get it for me now.' I would mix it – it was a sticky sugary brown liquid – with some lemon juice, a generous, an over-generous dose. It was pretty harmless stuff, supposed to make one drowsy; when it was slow or failed in that effect, I sometimes got away with 'Wouldn't you like some Paciflorine?' 'Haven't I just had some?' 'I don't think so.'

Appalled by my ruthlessness? Yes, I was; at the same time straining in every nerve to be out of the house; into night-life.

There was the hazard of my mother waking again and strolling into my room. When she found it empty and the hour was very late as it usually was, there would be trouble and a jumble of lies. If I was in, I would often be jumped out of sound sleep and kept from getting back into it for as long as she sat on my bed. How I willed her to go, how I had to fight to give a semblance of being awake. I liked staying up into the night myself yet once asleep nothing could entice me not to stay under – as though it were *I* who'd taken the Paciflorine – for the next nine hours. These nocturnal invasions were agony; I was not gracious about them.

One of my new friends fixed a small bolt on to the inside of my door. Now I was able to lock myself off from the rest of the house, and leave it by the window, less than five feet from the ground. On my returns, at first light or later, it was easy to climb in.

One depth of night though, *I* visited my mother in her room. I had eaten something – an unsound mussel very likely – that was upsetting me badly. I woke her, she saw me shivering, got up, put me back to bed, heated water for a bottle, made a tisane, held my hand, while I lay whimpering and grateful. She sat with me as long as needed. I felt much ashamed and told her so. 'Ah, people who are not used to feeling ill . . . ' she said. 'The sick have learned to look after themselves.'

When I had no engagement, or missed one by being too late, I would make my way to Bandol on my own to find company at an establishment called Chez Suzie, after the raucous, genial, greedy beetle of a patronne (beetle in appearance: she did not sing) who ran it. It aspired to be a *boîte* or a *bar américain* and was really a café where one could dance. One sat and drank outside in the balmy air not many yards from the sea; when the gramophone struck up and one was so inclined, one went inside to dance on a small floor that lit up sultry pink for a tango. It was frequented by people from the hotels and villas, off yachts in harbour, strollers-in when the casino closed. Suzie kept open till four a.m. or even five, quite legitimately. I became an habituée; meeting diverse and curious characters, who stood me drinks, most of them English or American (the ones still able to come in spite of the slump), they might be anything from an expatriate poet, or a Chelsea antique dealer to the spinster daughters of fathers who owned chains of Midland stores.

I drank *fine à l'eau* – not as watery as it sounds: brandy and soda – danced, went for strolls *à deux* under the night sky, heard some life stories. These appealed to Aldous and Maria. Aldous was fascinated by every aspect of my night-life and wanted full descriptions. He disapproved of what he called the night-club part of it, and would not take Suzie's as the harmless French café that it was. 'Have you been to your circle of hell again?' he would ask; then insist on hearing about it.

Alessandro did not have these outlets; his life had become lonely. When he left the house it was to walk the dogs or get some cigarettes. Liked by all, liking most, he had not come close to anyone at Sanary. Men he did business with were apt to treat him as a kind of younger brother; he did not himself enjoy the company of men; he liked to be with women. Now he shunned them.

I did not know how far my mother was aware of the destruction that was going on around her. The pitilessness she could show Alessandro repelled me. I did little to oppose it. What would become of us if I, too, became an object of hate in her eyes?

Meeting Toni (oh yes, they met in London – an unpropitious encounter) had turned my mother's thoughts on divorce. She remembered that her own marriage – Italian – was indissoluble, and used it as a new taunt. 'You *are* aware that you are irrevocably bound to me,' she would hurl at Alessandro, 'by religion, law and duty, or were you thinking of an *annulment*? Who would accord you one? The College of Cardinals? The Pope? Who would pay for it? What grounds do you have? They would laugh at you.'

To me he said, 'I never thought of divorce, I don't want to marry anyone else, I never thought of not staying married to her.'

'You must not hate so,' I said when we were alone.

My mother said, 'Look at me. He has destroyed me by doing what he did.'

'He did not mean . . . '

'The oldest excuse – not really mean to eat the apple – and the lamest.'

On other days, on other subjects, she would talk gently, reflectively. Then I could love her again.

Evelyn Waugh. She had saluted his stature in the days when I, guided by Rosie Falkenheim, had sent her his first novels. Now she had *Vile Bodies* by her side, one of the books Uley lay on. Did I realise how much despair there was in that novel? 'He must feel the despair I do. Someone who writes like that must either take to drink or to what I took to, or religion. I think it will be religion – he'll become a Catholic.' (I think Waugh already had at the time or was thinking of it; neither of us knew this.)

Out of the blue she asked me, 'What is that novel of yours about?'

I blushed. Then admitted to the young man in the South of France.

'Ah yes. Nearly everyone starts writing about their own experiences. Although these can't be quite yours. At least you are not writing about your school.'

I agreed that I did not have the most original of subjects.

'You have me. I'm a much more interesting subject than your dreamt-up young man.'

'God forbid, mummy.'

'One day. When you remember all this.'

'No,' I said, 'No, I don't think I ever could.'

She gave me a cynical smile.

Madame Panigon imparted that Oriane had had a nervous break-down, *une dépression nerveuse*, she called it, and had to be sent away to Switzerland. To a sanatorium, so-called . . . 'I always thought she was unbalanced.'

To divert Madame Panigon, I asked what news of Cécile? 'She's living in Paris with a man old enough to be her father, a *peintre-artiste*, no money to speak of. She's disgracing her family, they are getting married.'

*

I met Philippe on the port. The Desmirails were not part of my dissolute life. '*Oriane est en Suisse*, she's taking a cure.'

'Nothing serious, I hope?'

'I don't think so,' he said gently, uncomprehendingly, '*elle fait un peu de neurasthénie.*'

My mother looked at me wonderingly. 'I find it stranger and stranger to have a child. It was easy when you were little, but now there is a whole, grown-up, separate person . . . You stand here: and I think is this what *I* have produced? Giving birth is one thing . . . When you've given birth to something that goes on becoming someone else, then it turns so odd.

'It's not because you are like or unlike me – I think you are both – that's not the point. It's that you are supposed to be a part of me which – in the usual course of events – will be there when I'm gone. So I look at you and feel . . . I don't know what.'

'If you'd had the choice would you have had a child?' I said.

'You certainly came at an inconvenient moment – as I often told you before – it tied me to your father when I was already thinking of ways to leave him.'

'Was it the same with the other child?'

'*What?* What *are* you talking about?'

'There was a second child, wasn't there? I used to call him my baby brother in my mind.'

'Good God! Your knowing that!'

'Oh I knew. I also knew that it was a secret.'

My mother looked as completely thrown as I'd ever seen her.

'I kept the secret. Not that I thought of it a great deal. I was a very small child then, it was all so far away.'

'But *how*? How did you know? How did you find out? Who could have told you? Nobody was to know at the time. Certainly your father didn't know.'

'It was the pram,' I said. 'You gave it away, mummy, by sending for the pram.'

'What pram?'

'Don't you remember? It was *my* old pram – it was kept in the loft at Feldkirch. You wrote to the lawyers who were doing papa's side of the divorce asking for it to be sent to you.'

'Heavens, so I did.'

'Papa was puzzled at first and then he got upset, and then I wasn't supposed to know about it any more. The packers came and it was all hush-hush. He and Lina talked – you won't remember Lina, she came after you left us – I don't think I overheard much, only, "*How could she?*" and once, "That's *evidence.*" '

'Now I see how your father was able to make me the guilty party of our divorce. My folly. Not that it made so much difference.'

'They all guessed. *I* was quite certain that my pram was for your new child.'

My mother looked at me with a kind of awe. 'What did you feel about it?'

'Hoped that you'd be pleased with him – I don't know why, but I always thought of him as a boy – and that some day we would meet.'

'And then,' my mother said, 'when you did *not* meet him?'

'Yes, that made me feel most embarrassed. You see, when you sent for me to come to Italy – when you were about to marry again and we were going to live in Florence – I was expecting to find the baby boy. I nearly asked for him. Then I felt what a ghastly mistake that would have been. Either I had been wrong, or you had sent him away, to foster parents or someone, and didn't want it mentioned. Or . . . that he was . . . dead.'

'He was dead,' my mother said. 'It *was* a boy and he died after a few weeks.'

When we spoke again, I said, 'It must have been sad.'

'It was. I *had* wanted him. And I very much loved the man who was his father; we were going to marry, in fact as soon as my divorce got through. No, it wasn't O – O came years later, it was the man who gave me the Klee.'

'What happened?'

'After the child died, I didn't want the man any more. A curious reversal of feeling, but there it was. I broke it all off and left him.'

331

'Did he mind?'

'Very much.'

We both took a breath. Presently I said, 'Mummy, why on earth did you do it?'

'Do what?'

'Send for the pram. It's so absurd. I know you let my father keep the château and the park land and all the rest – you just gave it to him, just like that, privately, because you knew how miserable he'd be to leave it. I always admired you for that. And then you go and ask for one second-hand pram? You weren't hard up then?'

'It was a particularly *good* pram, made in England; I didn't see why I should be put to buying another one when there it was, resting on its wheels in the back-country of the Grand-Duchy of Baden, and your father had got everything else. I didn't think of the consequences.'

Something else occurred to me. 'Mummy, was it the Copenhagen pram?'

'Now what do you mean by that?'

'The pram you took me in one afternoon to that *garçonnière* . . . ?'

'Peter's. Your reminiscences! Peter . . . I loved him too, perhaps more than most – what a good writer we then thought he was – they called him the Danish Maupassant – now he's in limbo, almost completely forgotten. I didn't see him again after that summer. There was the War, and he died in 1917. Barely fifty, of a hundred cigarettes a day and other things.'

I said, 'Suddenly there was his photograph on your dressing-table: I remember his long hand with the cigarette-holder.'

'Your father saw it too. He came into my room and shied like a horse. I said to him, "I just heard – he died last week." Your father made a little bow and said, "I am so sorry." That was very like him.'

'Was it?' I said.

'Yes, it must have been the same pram. Can you see now how strange it is to have you? The things you remember, the things you know . . . And there I was, having no idea. Do I know you? Do you think you know *me*?'

'You are not easy to know, mummy.'

'Why did you never speak to me about the other child?'

'As *you* never did – when you talked of so much else – I felt it wasn't up to me, anyway I'd half forgotten. It was only a fact I picked up as a child, and looked on as a child.'

'And today? Does it look different?'

'Perhaps.'

8

The donkey-man came to the house with a message. I was to go to La Pacifique at once, there a person-to-person call from London was waiting for me, from – he held out a scrap of paper – Mister Nairn. I went with misgivings. Jamie was not the man to make international trunk calls lightly.

Philippe was there, he told the operator that I was available now, and after some waiting I was through. I heard Jamie say, 'The Judge . . . He shot himself . . . he is dead, he was found by Rosie yesterday afternoon.'

Before I could ask anything rash, he went on, 'Nobody knows why . . . It's all over the papers. It appears he's had one or two difficult cases lately.'

My mother said, 'You must go to her.' I borrowed the travel money from Maria. This time I had to ask. I told her something frightful had happened to a great friend. 'I shan't be of any use.' 'You will have tried,' she said. I took the train the same evening.

I saw Jamie first. He told me the bare facts. Rosie had gone to the flat in St James's and had found the Judge in his sitting-room in a chair, shotgun by his side. She left – unseen – and telephoned the police from a public box. She said she was a typist who had come by appointment to deliver some papers. She did not give her name; she said she did not wish for the publicity that might ensue, and the police accepted this. The press (miraculously?) were making no great play of The Unknown Woman who found him. They were casting about for a reason for the Judge's death – and so, Jamie said, must be Rosie –

the consensus seemed to be over-work combined with the public controversy over his conduct of some recent cases. A verdict of suicide while of unsound mind was foreseen, the papers already losing interest in the case.

'With luck nobody will find out about her having known him.'

'How . . . is Rosie?' I asked at last.

'Quiet,' Jamie said. 'Practical.' I thought that a curious expression.

I found the sisters frozen, Toni visibly the most: white, shocked, gauchely addressing Rosie like an invalid, repressing God knows what. Rosie looked much like herself, except for a certain rigidity of movement; she spoke little. Of what had happened not a word was said. They were no Latins – no physical expression of sympathy seemed allowable, no embrace, no taking of hands; likewise they were remote from their own warmer tradition, the Jewish sharing of grief, the sitting close and lamenting. All was dryness; chill.

Toni produced a tea. Rosie ate normally.

Some time later she suggested a walk with me on the Heath. As soon as the dog was off the leash, she talked. Everything she said was measured, spoken in a level, slow voice. She had had a wonderful life, perfect years. They were over.

'There will be nothing more for me. I shall not go Jack's way, I cannot do it to Toni. Think how scandalised she would be.'

I was glad to find in that last remark a hint of her old self. Perhaps whatever life does to people, there is left a spark of individuality that will out like an edge of handkerchief from a pocket.

'Besides suicide' – she was able to say the word – 'may not be in my temperament. In Jack's position I should have chosen otherwise. But then for him his reputation was his mainstay. As he was mine.' She straightened herself like a soldier, a very tired soldier after a very long march, like a soldier all the same. 'Isn't it splendid that it looks as though nothing will come out about debts or bankruptcy. It would seem that his people have paid up – as they would not when he was alive. The truth will never become public.' Her voice grew stronger. 'As Jack couldn't face the music, his survivors are making sure that nobody knows that there was music to face. He would have wanted that most. That's one thing I, too, can still do for him: nobody will hear the true story from me.'

I acknowledged how well she had kept it from her sister and Jamie, and I assured her of my own silence. (Which I kept. Well, for some fifty years.)

Would she like a change for a time? Travel? Could she bear coming back with me (I wondering what our house had to offer)? I supposed not Sanary now?

Not Sanary now.

Would she continue living with Toni?

Inevitably. Unless Toni ran off with some singer one day. Highly improbable.

How could one help her through the next few weeks? That was easy. 'I need a job. At once. Unless I start living off Toni.' In fact she'd already got a job; she was stepping into the one Jamie had found for Toni, an excellent job with a gallery. Toni was retreating quite gracefully.

'Waiting for another one to turn up?'

'Which Jamie is trying to find for her. Jamie has been very good.'

'And he doesn't even know why you really need a job.'

'Jamie doesn't ask questions.'

'What can *I* do for you?'

Nothing. It had been good of me to come. Jack would have appreciated it. 'He approved of you as a friend for me. The one friend he's ever met.'

One thing, yes: would I get her some books. She was taking sleeping pills – of course – all the same she got through a book a night. When I eagerly complied and made suggestions, she said, 'Oh, no real books. I couldn't look at those. Detective stories only, lots of them.'

I thought of guns – and worse – found in country-house studies and libraries: could she want to be faced with such? It must be true then what people said, that death in detective stories was quite unreal.

As Rosie had made clear, there was nothing I could do; so after just under forty-eight hours in London I was on my way back to France.

*   *   *

Entering Les Cyprès suitcase in hand, I found Waldemar sitting on the terrace reading a newspaper. I sought out Alessandro, 'What on earth?'

'He came back to pay us a visit. He wanted to say thank you for last summer. It seems he's passed his exams and is in some kind of job now. He brought his bound thesis as a present for your mother.'

'What are you doing with him?' I asked her presently.

'We've got a bed, haven't we? He's in Emilia's old room. A decent young man, though goodness how serious; and so prim and proper in spite of beavering away for the Revolution.'

I would not have wanted to go out that night; as it was, family dinner with Waldemar was in order. Alessandro cooked it. It was quite a pleasant evening; the main topic was politics with my mother teasing and at times bewildering the young German. (Of London, I would talk to my mother by and by; it could wait.) She retired, and we all went to bed early.

I was woken in the night by great noise in the house: I heard my mother's voice. I opened my door, there was a light on in the passage and I could see her standing in the entrance of Emilia's small room. She was in a nightgown and she was raving. Waldemar, I presumed, was in bed. 'I want you to realise,' she shouted, 'that you are sleeping under the roof of an adulterer . . . An *adulterer* . . .'

Now Alessandro appeared, the shouting increased; I slunk away. Used though I was to these nocturnal uproars, they pierced the marrow. I went back to bed, put some plugs I sometimes used for diving in my ears, pulled a sheet over my head. After a time the sounds subsided. I fell back into sleep.

I woke again when Alessandro stood in the door. He was fully dressed holding Chumi on a lead; on his head was the little white cap with a peak, such as golfers sport, that he wore on motor journeys. He signed me to be quiet; I took the plugs out of my ears, got up and followed him out of the house. We stood facing each other by the balustrade above the cypress terrace. It was just beginning to get light. He said, 'I cannot go on any longer. I must go.'

I was struck by lucid certitude. I looked at him with sudden immense affection. 'Yes – go.'

'Look after her. Be kind to her.'

. . .

'Philippe and Oriane, Aldous and Maria, and Renée will help you.'

. . .

'I shall send money, as soon as I can. Regularly.'

'And what will you do?'

'I don't know.'

'Oh Alessandro.' Then, irrelevance. 'Waldemar? What are we supposed to do with him?'

'He's already in the car; he's taken my bags. We'll go in Doris's Chrysler – it's got to be brought back – I'm leaving the Ford here.'

'So you'll be going to Berlin.'

'Not for long. Paul may find me a job – he's building somewhere in Germany. He can use a decorator. An *amateur* decorator.'

'You wanted to be a real architect, didn't you?'

'A real architect. A little late now.'

I recalled another time when I had stood with him when he was ready to leave at Sorrento and I, seeking reassurance for her, had asked, 'You will come back?' I did not ask this now. I was filled by a surge of love, impersonal love, as though he and I had become a link in the chain of the brotherhood of man. I put my arms round him, elated with his need for release; absolution. Such absolution as one human creature can give to another. We stood together for some moments. I had never felt so close to anyone.

The words came out, 'Go in peace.'

When he had left, I stood for a time by the balustrade. It was the break of another relentlessly beautiful morning in the Midi. There were steps. Alessandro had come back, he was carrying his Remington portable. 'You had better have that. Use it.' He was gone again.

I went into my room. The house was silent. I was about to shoot the bolt inside my door then realised that I could no longer allow myself to do this. I put the typewriter by the table I used for a desk, symmetrically, and went back to bed. It must have been about five o'clock. With luck I could count on a few hours' sleep.

Afterword

Jigsaw is my fourth novel and, I very much fear, my last. I finished it over ten years ago – a long time that went quickly, in idleness, in pleasures, in much private grief. The decade before, a good chunk of it, went into gathering the strength of mind to shape, reshape and finally write this novel with two sub-titles and an author's note trying to elucidate Who is Who, Who is Half-Who and Who is Not.

That note must be a clue as to why I went through so many hesitations, detours and delays before getting something down on paper that felt *right*. At the time this baffled and dismayed me: it was unexpected. I was no longer the innocent with the passionate aspirations to the literary life who, a quarter of a century before, had thrown herself with such a compound of conviction and self-doubt into her first (published) novel. I *was* a writer – a professional. I had just come out – we are in the mid-seventies – of a long discipline of servitude to factual truth (as far as *that* can be nailed down) – 'a biographer is an artist under oath' – six years of single-minded hard work on a biography of Aldous Huxley, and was looking forward to regaining my inventive liberty. As friends and editors were beginning to ask, 'And what are you going to do now?' 'What are you going to write *next*?' I would trundle out something to the effect that I was planning to return to the freedom of fiction. Well, *fiction*? Alone, at my desk, on my walks – now mainly in London streets or the back country of a more and more built-up South of France – I began to see pitfalls. What I had in mind – or wherever such directives originate – was to build a novel out of the events and people who had made up, and marked, my early youth: in fact the *Unsentimental Education* of my main sub-title. It had to be a novel in which the events had actually happened and happened largely as described; to invent, such was my instinct, would have been pointless: it mattered that these things *had* occurred. Truth here was an artistic, not a moral, requirement – truth to be presented in the terms of the novelist, not the biographer, terms that meant timing, selection, avoiding repetition . . . It involved using myself as a character in the centre of the narrative; in plain words, writing about myself, my feelings, my actions. There I felt resistance and avoided recognising its cause, deluding myself that it could be . . . what? Left out? Circumnavigated perhaps. (Did one *have* to have a parent?)

For the moment I put it all aside. London held many attractions, distractions, now that I was beginning to live there practically for the first time as an adult. I became active in PEN, joined committees, canvassed in elections, was asked to act as assistant consultant on an encyclopaedic volume on wine. I jumped into that: it required more acquisition of knowledge than fine-tuned writing; it devoured a full six months. Above all there were friends; friends in walking or short driving distance, old friends, very new friends, a few brothers in wine as I called them, droves of writers everywhere: dinners, dinner parties, cooking for dinner parties . . . An existence unlike any of my previous ones – unlike the euphoric years in Rome, the years rusticating in southern France: steady work, companionship, the sea, dawn markets of fruit and fish, rough gardening with scant water on hard ground. Unlike, also, the intervals of travel journalism that fed my desire to see and to learn and helped to finance my slow books; unlike the often months-long reporting of controversial or political trials in courts of law here and there from the Old Bailey to Frankfurt, to Paris, to Texas. Then all this had come to an end with the absences in pursuit of Huxleyana, live witnesses rather than papers, since most of these had been destroyed in a Hollywood hill fire. The base was still France, writing in my austere, whitewashed room, though I had to be away for stretches of time: in provincial England, in Italy, Paris, Holland, a year almost in America, coast to coast. And now urban England, a deliberate move, deciding on another kind of life; a very great wrench. I never stopped missing France. (France, one of the three countries I can feel almost belonging to – England: attachment to language and some institutions; Italy: romantic first love, visual, sensual; France: for everything else.) The new life now, London, if beset with real anxieties – how to acquire a place to live – was an interesting life of (guilty) leisure. As the right structure for my novel continued to elude me, they increased: the leisure and the guilt. Where was the proud professional? The writer who doesn't get down to the next book – I had faced this before – is once more nothing. (Do I sound like Cyril Connolly carrying on? Well, I know how he felt. At least I did not lie in bed crying 'poor Sybille'.)

The one thing I was in happy certainty about was my locale, my playground. A place I knew – none better – a fishing port on the French Mediterranean. Sanary. Sanary-sur-Mer. I had loved it. I still do. As it was then: small, unfashionable, modest – a French village, a back country of classical landscapes: hills, olives, vines. I had described it, briefly and under due constraint, in the part of the Huxley biography called 'The Apparent Stability' – Aldous and his incomparable wife, Maria, had lived, been at home there, for a good number of years. For them, as for myself, Sanary, their Sanary house (Villa Uley) had remained a *point de repère*, a compass point, throughout their lives. It was there that I spent a part of my adolescence and the best of my youth; there that I met the diversity of men and women who became mentors, examples, seducers, friends – loved friends, life-long friends . . . (Few of them at the time of my attempting this novel, alive.) Their origins were as varied as their codes of behaviour; most had come by choice, instinctive or rational. They were able to work and play in this place of benevolent climate and natural beauty remote from the centres of government and commerce, and dictate their private stories. *That* was in the brief span of time between recovery and new fear, the middle years between two wars. We are in the 1920s with the wish, the illusion that history *can* have a stop, moving into the thirties with our heads still in the sand.

So I had the time, the place, the people. Where was *I*? How plausibly could I insert myself, full-fledged, into a somewhat complex milieu in meridional France at the age of about sixteen? Who was I, where had

I come from? I needed *provenance*, an identity. Which must mean trotting out my short and recent past. I had little desire to go into what passes as my childhood. I had never been much interested in myself as a child *per se*, moreover I had already used tales that had come my way in a previous novel in which I had also tried to construct and interpret my own father's nature and life to the best not of my knowledge but of my imagination perhaps, plus guesswork. He had died when I was so very young; was there anything more to learn? Could I or should I invoke him again? (I often dream about him – sad, puzzled, remorseful dreams, where he is a lonely, hurt, forgiving man whose existence I, long grown-up myself, have ignored throughout the years, as callous as the unfeeling child I had been.) Then, quite suddenly, wide awake, I realised that I had thought and written only about what he may have been as a boy, as a young man, both scarred and spoiled, as the man in his marriages, in his role of a prisoner, the kept son-in-law, of the innocent tied to public scandal; what I had *not* done was recall *our* life, the actual, utterly isolated life of his last years that he and I led together in rather eccentric circumstances of *un*genteel poverty in quite grand surroundings in the depth of the county. I was about seven when it began, he must have turned sixty, I believe (children did not ask their parents' age in those days), still *very* handsome, still well turned out – those pre-1914 suits and shirts last for ever – and as I have said; isolated, cut off, alone. He saw no friends, no women. The house, in those parts called a château (twenty bedrooms, a considerable collection of Renaissance furniture and *objets d'art*, one bath), contained three inhabitants: a stranded man of the world; a bewildered, later acquiescent, somewhat know-all child; an elderly, good-hearted, deeply religious, *hard-working* village woman. The reason for all this was simple – no money. That had gone, radically so, when my mother left. It *was* her money and *she* had bought the château for her husband, my father, and let him keep it. That was a generous deed. It created a somewhat paradoxical situation – candles instead of electricity bills, masculine cast-offs (children's clothes do *not* last), claret in the cellar and at table but no cash for butcher's meat. (Hence decades into my adult life I would choose sirloin steak rather than Elizabeth David's gratin of courgettes.) The complete true tableau of my almost pre-historic origins appeared to me quite suddenly one evening in a public place, at dinner, with friends, noise, conversation, flooding over me, wine making thought glide on . . . 'This could be told, this is how one could make a book begin; "Antecedent: Germany".' Next morning I did begin. The substance was flowing as though it was already on film; as ever, alas, I had to look after the words.

In due course that screen went blank; the rural phase had reached its sudden end. My mother claimed me (her legal right; not exercised for long because of the complexities, one surmised, of her own life). Within days of that claim, travel arrangements were made and I was whisked into Italy. That was then, now I had to go on tending my book – there still were years to cover before my entry into that French fishing port – memories in another key had to be tapped to bring sense and movement into my chronological past. Overcoming reservations, refusing to face that these were bound to become more serious as the tale went on, I set to work on that next stage necessary for balance and cohesion. Italy. My *mother*. The one character I wished to keep minor and knew all along that it could not be done. I remembered her as intellectually rigorous. This I approved of and admired (and am for ever grateful for); I had also been aware of her lack of interest in children and took it for natural – which indeed it might be for more women than we are nowadays taught to believe. I am not sure how she came out in my version of our Italian encounter. I can hope that she would have done what she nearly always could: laugh at herself.

After I was hustled out of Italy – Sicily to the Midlands, direct – I had to manage another kind of literary hurdle: the banality of my first experience of England and the English. Middle class and middle-class bohemia was my initial lot, so novel, so strange to me, so flatly familiar to a potential reader. Not that I think of them – readers, that is – as a rule, my precept being that a writer should not look beyond his page, his work. Hope of approval by a handful of elders and betters: yes; aiming at sales, fashion, success: no. However, I do not *wish* to bore. I was hampered by this likelihood when I began describing my early English past. Parlour maids, icy bedrooms, sodden vegetables, Australian Burgundy, pony traps, Boots' lending library, the butcher calling, the crystal set . . . At the time of writing, not all of this had definitely vanished, and a butcher's van could still occasionally be seen, whereas by now, *our now*, the turning of the century, so much of English social and domestic life of the 1920s has receded into an historical past. Not certain of this yet, I had decided to lighten my trite circumstances by introducing an alien element into the Anglo-Saxon scene, the Sisters' Story – *not* from Moscow, from Berlin – a story I had often wanted to write: adult lives displayed to my barely adolescent self, their story true to a high degree, and originally conceived as a novella. As I got into it, I saw that it would fit well into this novel, a kind of counterweight, a link between the English and the French action of my jigsaw.

Did I say French? I did. We've got there at last. I have arrived in France, we shall get to the core of the action. I began, meandered into topographical descriptions . . . It was at *this* juncture that I got seriously stuck.

One day there came a nasty letter from my American publisher. (I had accepted – and used for living – an advance; how many years ago?) The letter gave me a jolt. It was not enough.

The dilemma remained: blocking future progress. This was not an articulate decision; I did not discuss the impediment with anyone. I didn't discuss it with myself I did not *think* 'conscience', 'betrayal', 'bad taste', I just had the feeling of being up to a wall like a horse refusing a jump while avoiding to give it even a glance.

Now that I *have* – given it a glance, and more than that – the obstacle can be defined in simple terms: it could not be right for *me* to tell what caused my mother's undoing; my *mother* could not be left out of the book; my mother could not be *in the book* if one left out the sequence of factors/events that had led to that undoing. (Caused as usual, as I see it, like most misfortunes by a concatenation and logic of character, circumstances and – a big item – chance.) *La ronde*, the circle. If one stayed caught in that circle, there could be no book.

It resolved itself. Without any discernible push. Overnight, as it were, the writer had won over whatever we might call it: filial duty, decency . . . I wanted to write this book, in this way, and I did.

I already owed my mother a very great deal, not in conventional 'maternal' terms, but for the articulate private education with which she imprinted on me her unshakeable rejection of war, nationalism, social injustice (the latter theoretically), her passion for literature and art, good literature, great art. Due to her I was able to clutch a book earlier than I might have reached for a doll. Such talent as I may possess must have been directly inherited from her, writer *manqué* herself. I shall always be grateful, although, sadly, I was not often able to love her; and now I owe her for *Jigsaw* as well. How would she have taken it? my exposure of the tragic – at times comical – misfortunes that overtook her? As I said, she was able to laugh at herself. How far could it hold, her belief that the written word carried its own absolution?

Enough. Right or wrong, the book got done. Expeditiously. One fine bright cold January day, my (later) friend, then future English publisher, Christopher Sinclair-Stevenson, gave me luncheon – something he does with supreme elegance and lightness of touch. We were at his window table at Chez Hilaire. Well then, your novel? (Elaine Greene, my agent, had paved the way some time ago.)

'I think I got beyond page 84 . . . '

'I see . . . '

He didn't; but he couldn't know. With Christopher one begins, at lunch time, with a Bloody Mary or with Krug. One drinks (and eats) well and wisely. One is at ease, elated, and one is still so when one leaves: ready to take on the day. Never a ruined afternoon. We parted on the pavement of the Old Brompton Road, we shook hands, then we embraced, an accolade *à la française*. I had just said, 'You'll have your novel by the beginning of June.' He did.

Aftermaths. Within weeks of eventual publication, a very unexpected light was cast on a prominent player in the sub-plot, the Sisters' Story. He was a judge, a real live High Court Judge, well-known in his time as brilliant, eloquent, somewhat controversial: great fodder for the Press.

What was heard off the bench on a morning could often be read in the evening papers. In fact, the Press knew nothing, but nothing, about his private life. Today it would have bloated the headlines. A few people must have known something; each would have come across one or another fragment of the truth. I, by the oddness of his circumstances, got to know a part of what seemed the core of it, the 'Judge's Story', such as I told it in the present novel. There, I strictly stuck to what I knew at first hand; which was little enough, if enormous in terms of the Judge's position and career. These I saw as safe – he had died in the early 1930s, and indeed for the next fifty years nothing of my end of the story appeared to have surfaced. Not so after Jigsaw. A friend, a very sharp-minded QC, confronted me with a straight inquiry. I was summoned – dinner at the Reform – cross-examined: the judge in the novel must have been, could not have been other than, unadulterated Judge X. He, my QC friend, put a few data together; I conceded. He was right. (And not going to proclaim it from the roof tops. One may feel smug enough knowing something others don't.) We sat on, speculating on the wonders of the cover-up. However, this was far from being that was that. Within days I was approached by a young woman who baldly declared herself, name and all, to be our judge's great-niece, professing affectionate memories of her uncle and no knowledge whatsoever of my facts about his life. She proposed to come and see me. We settled for a day and time. She would bring a surprise, she said, a big surprise. I would be unprepared – she would not prepare me.

When the bell rang, there were two strangers on the doorstep, a young woman and a man, a pleasant, quiet man, he turned out to be, a retired civil servant, of nearer seventy, one guessed, than sixty. She introduced him as the Judge's natural son. And here we had the pivot of another hidden story – one judge, two stories, parallel much of the time, two halves each ignorant of the other. No whiff of the son's existence ever reached the sisters, none of theirs ever reached the son. Now *he* had read *Jigsaw* and I, the sisters' surviving witness, soon read the typescript of the son's autobiography which tells, and tells it well, his half of the tale of what must have been quite a feat of double deception by an attractive and well-liked public man.

I got to like the son – he shares his father's first name (which will not be found in the book) – I talked to his wife. Sadly, he died early. I still hope that his autobiography, which contains a good deal more than his parents' story, will be published. All of this has left me with a puzzled sense about the relativity of given truth.

Books are apt to engender correspondence. I do not mean mere letters and their polite acknowledgement, but a good continuing exchange about some minor matter (and the more absurd the subject the better). The prize that time went to an elderly English gentleman established in France who wrote to me accusingly that the tramway line serving Sanary–Ollioules–La Seyne which I had mentioned (*very briefly*) had *never* existed. I wrote back to say that although the line had been defunct at the period described, I had seen, admittedly, no tram, but the actual tracks. He wrote back citing his authority; a vast tome entitled *L'Annuaire des Tramways de France depuis 1898.* I replied that I had actually stumbled, nearly turned an ankle, on one of those tracks, unmistakably *trams'*. He wrote back; I replied; it went on: never acrimonious, just obstinate and sure of our facts – *Les Tramways de France* v. my own feet . . . Who says that writing even an unaccommodating novel does not yield its pleasures.

SYBILLE BEDFORD, 1999

About the Author

Sybille Bedford was born in Charlottenburg, Germany, in 1911, and was privately educated in Italy, England and France. She published her first book, *The Sudden View: A Mexican Journey*, in 1953. By the time it was reissued, seven years later, as *A Visit to Don Otavio*, it had won a reputation as a classic of travel writing. *A Legacy* appeared in 1956, and three other novels have followed: *A Favourite of the Gods* (1963), *A Compass Error* (1968) and *Jigsaw* (1989), which was shortlisted for the Booker Prize.

The Best We Can Do (1958), an account of the murder trial of Dr John Bodkin Adams, was the first of Sybille's writings on the law at work. She reported on some of the most important criminal trials of her times, including those of Jack Ruby and the former staff at Auschwitz. *The Faces of Justice* (1961) collected her observations on the courts in England, Germany, Austria, Switzerland and France. *As It Was* (1990) brought together further essays on justice as well as her celebrated writings on food, wine and European travel. In 1973 Sybille published a two-volume, authorised life of her friend and mentor Aldous Huxley. Stephen Spender called the book 'one of the masterpieces of biography'.

For the last twenty-five years of her life, until her death in 2006, Sybille lived in London, where she was a vice president of English PEN. In 1981 she was made an officer of the Order of the British Empire, and in 1994 was elected a Companion of Literature by the Royal Society of Literature. Dogged by difficulties with her sight, she nevertheless continued to write and in June 2005, less than a year before she died, Sybille published a memoir, *Quicksands*. Bruce Chatwin saw her as 'one of the most dazzling practitioners of modern English prose'.

ELAND

61 Exmouth Market, London EC1R 4QL
Email: info@travelbooks.co.uk

Eland was started in 1982 to revive great travel books
that had fallen out of print. Although the list has diversified
into biography and fiction, it is united by a quest to define the
spirit of place. These are books for travellers, and for readers who aspire
to explore the world but who are content to travel in their own
minds. Eland books open out our understanding of other cultures,
interpret the unknown and reveal different environments as well as
celebrating the humour and occasional horrors of travel. We take
immense trouble to select only the most readable books and therefore
many readers collect the entire series.

All our books are printed on fine, pliable, cream-coloured paper.
Most are still gathered in sections by our printer and sewn as well
as glued, almost unheard of for a paperback book these days.
This gives larger margins in the gutter, as well as
making the books stronger.

You will find a very brief description of our books on the
following pages. Extracts from each and every one of them can be
read on our website, at www.travelbooks.co.uk. If you would
like a free copy of our catalogue, please email
or write to us (details above).

ELAND

'One of the very best travel lists' WILLIAM DALRYMPLE

Memoirs of a Bengal Civilian
JOHN BEAMES
*Sketches of nineteenth-century India
painted with the richness of Dickens*

Jigsaw
SYBILLE BEDFORD
*An intensely remembered autobiographical
novel about an inter-war childhood*

A Visit to Don Otavio
SYBILLE BEDFORD
*The hell of travel and the Eden of arrival
in post-war Mexico*

Journey into the Mind's Eye
LESLEY BLANCH
*An obsessive love affair with Russia and
one particular Russian*

The Way of the World
NICOLAS BOUVIER
Two men in a car from Serbia to Afghanistan

The Devil Drives
FAWN BRODIE
*Biography of Sir Richard Burton,
explorer, linguist and pornographer*

Turkish Letters
OGIER DE BUSBECQ
*Eyewitness history at its best:
Istanbul during the reign of Suleyman
the Magnificent*

My Early Life
WINSTON CHURCHILL
*From North-West Frontier to Boer War
by the age of twenty-five*

Sicily: through writers' eyes
ED. HORATIO CLARE
*Guidebooks for the mind: a selection
of the best travel writing on Sicily*

A Square of Sky
JANINA DAVID
*A Jewish childhood in the Warsaw
ghetto and hiding from the Nazis*

Chantemesle
ROBIN FEDDEN
*A lyrical evocation of childhood
in Normandy*

Croatia: through writers' eyes
ED. FRANKOPAN, GOODING & LAVINGTON
*Guidebooks for the mind: a selection
of the best travel writing on Croatia*

Travels with Myself and Another
MARTHA GELLHORN
*Five journeys from hell by a great
war correspondent*

The Weather in Africa
MARTHA GELLHORN
*Three novellas set amongst the
white settlers of East Africa*

The Last Leopard
DAVID GILMOUR
*The biography of Giuseppe di Lampedusa,
author of* The Leopard

Walled Gardens
ANNABEL GOFF
An Anglo-Irish childhood

Africa Dances
GEOFFREY GORER
*The magic of indigenous culture
and the banality of colonisation*

Cinema Eden
JUAN GOYTISOLO
*Essays from the Muslim
Mediterranean*

A State of Fear
ANDREW GRAHAM-YOOLL
*A journalist witnesses Argentina's
nightmare in the 1970s*

Warriors
GERALD HANLEY
Life and death among the Somalis

Morocco That Was
WALTER HARRIS
*All the cruelty, fascination and
humour of a pre-modern kingdom*